PRAISE FOR *SAVAGE*

"A great book . . . It's f***ing riveting!"

—Joe Rogan

"A rare gut-punch writer, full of grit and insight, who we will be happily reading for years to come."
—Gregg Hurwitz, *New York Times* bestselling author of the Orphan X series

"Absolutely fantastic! *Savage Son* is savagely good, and puts Jack Carr at the very top of the thriller genre."
—Marc Cameron, *New York Times* bestselling author

"A badass, high-velocity round of reading! The three parts of this masterfully crafted experience say it all—the trap, the stalk, the kill."
—Clint Emerson, former Navy SEAL and *New York Times* bestselling author of *100 Deadly Skills* and *The Right Kind of Crazy*

"With his third book in the James Reece series, *Savage Son*, Jack Carr HALO jumps the reader into that most dangerous game: man hunting man. With technical ferocity and devastating action sequences, Carr writes both from the gut and a seemingly infinite reservoir of knowledge in the methods of human combat. Loved it!"
—Chris Hauty, *Los Angeles Times* bestselling author of the *New York Times* Editors' Choice *Deep State*

"Jack Carr triples down with *Savage Son*. From the book's gut-wrenching opening to its sleep-stealing conclusion, Jack's homage to *The Most Dangerous Game* delivers the goods and then some."
—Don Bentley, author of *Without Sanction*

"Jack Carr is the real deal! He employs his years of combat experience as a U.S. Navy SEAL to make *Savage Son* a masterfully told, heart-thumping tale of modern conflict. Before you open the cover and start to read, get comfortable. You won't want to move until you finish."
—LtCol Oliver North, USMC (Ret.), *New York Times* bestselling author of *The Rifleman* and *Under Fire*

"If you like a fresh approach to action with authentic details and a believable main character, these books are for you. I'm a fan."
—David Morrell, *New York Times* bestselling author of *First Blood*, *The Brotherhood of the Rose*, and *Murder as a Fine Art*

"Jack Carr is back and at the top of his game in *Savage Son*, a heart-pounding, sleep-robbing, edge-of-your-seat thriller."
—Joshua Hood, 82nd Airborne veteran and author of Robert Ludlum's *The Treadstone Resurrection*

ALSO BY JACK CARR

The Devil's Hand

Savage Son

True Believer

The Terminal List

SAVAGE SON

A THRILLER

JACK CARR

EMILY BESTLER BOOKS

ATRIA

NEW YORK   LONDON   TORONTO   SYDNEY   NEW DELHI

EMILY
BESTLER
BOOKS

ATRIA

An Imprint of Simon & Schuster, Inc.
1230 Avenue of the Americas
New York, NY 10020

First Emily Bestler Books/Atria Paperback edition February 2022

EMILY BESTLER BOOKS/ATRIA PAPERBACK and colophon are trademarks of Simon & Schuster, Inc.

For information about special discounts for bulk purchases, please contact Simon & Schuster Special Sales at 1-866-506-1949 or business@simonandschuster.com.

The Simon & Schuster Speakers Bureau can bring authors to your live event. For more information, or to book an event, contact the Simon & Schuster Speakers Bureau at 1-866-248-3049 or visit our website at www.simonspeakers.com.

Interior design by Wendy Blum

1   3   5   7   9   10   8   6   4   2

Library of Congress Cataloging-in-Publication Data has been applied for.

ISBN 978-1-9821-2370-3
ISBN 978-1-9821-8461-2 (pbk)
ISBN 978-1-9821-2372-7 (ebook)

For Brad Thor, without whom this post-military chapter
of my life would not be possible
and,
to those who run to the sound of the guns.

Fortuna Favet Fortibus

"There is no hunting like the hunting of man, and those who have hunted armed men long enough and liked it, never care for anything else thereafter."

—Ernest Hemingway

PREFACE

I WAS, AND REMAIN, a student of war and of the hunt. Experiences in combat and in the backcountry helped shape me into the citizen, husband, father, and writer I am today. The one has made me better at the other. I suspect it has always been this way. It is the feelings and emotions from those most primal of endeavors that form the foundation of *Savage Son*.

I was first introduced to Richard Connell's masterpiece, "The Most Dangerous Game," in junior high school. Connell, a veteran of World War I, published his most celebrated short story in *Collier's Weekly* in 1924. Upon that initial reading, I was determined to one day write a modern thriller that paid tribute to this classic tale, exploring the dynamic between hunter and hunted.

Providing for and defending my family and country are hardwired into my DNA. Perhaps that is why "The Most Dangerous Game" resonated with me at such an early age, or maybe those primal impulses are in all of us, which is why Richard Connell's narrative continues to endure almost a century after it was first published.

Fast-forward thirty years. As I prepared to leave the SEAL Teams, I laid out all my ideas for what was to become my first novel, *The Terminal List*. The plot for *Savage Son* was among several of the story lines I was contemplating as I decided how to introduce the world to James Reece. For that first outing, I knew my protagonist was not yet ready for what I had in store. I needed to develop him through a journey, first of revenge and then of redemption, before I could explore the dark side of man through the medium of the modern political thriller. Is James Reece a warrior, a hunter, a killer? Perhaps all three?

Hunting and war are inexorably mixed. They share a common father. Death begets life, and in defense of oneself, one's family, one's tribe, or one's country, killing is often a part of the equation. Throughout most of human history, defeating an enemy in battle led to the survival of the tribe and the continuation of the bloodline. The same tools developed to defeat rivals in combat are analogous to those used in the quest for sustenance. Similar tactics are used to hunt both man and beast. Those who picked up a spear to defend the tribe were the same ones who used that spear to provide food for their families. The reason each and every one of us is alive today is the martial prowess and hunting abilities of our ancestors.

Much as the hunter, deep in the backcountry, often thinks of his family by the hearth, so too the warrior on the distant battlefield longs for a homecoming. Similarly, when they return home, the hunter dreams of going back to the woods, just as the warrior yearns for battle. Is it the guilt of no longer being in the fight? Not standing shoulder to shoulder with brothers in arms? Or is it missing the sense of belonging that only comes from being part of a team that has spilt blood in war? Or is it something darker? Is it *because* of the kill? Is it because that is the only place one can truly feel alive? Martin Sheen's line from *Apocalypse Now*, the movie my BUD/S class watched before going into Hell Week, rings true for those who have answered the call: "When I was here, I wanted to be there. When I was there, all I could think of was getting back into the jungle." Warriors can relate.

On the battlefield, I witnessed the best and worst of humanity. I have been the hunter, building target packages and developing patterns of life on our targeted individuals, using disassociated human intelligence networks corroborated by technical means to ensure we were taking the right player off the board before launching on a mission to capture or kill them. And

I have been the hunted, caught in an ambush in the Al-Rashid District of Baghdad at the height of the war.

The Global War on Terror has ensured us ample practice, sharpening our skills in the hunting and killing of man. Direct action, special reconnaissance, counterinsurgency, unconventional warfare, foreign internal defense, hostage rescue, counterterrorism, and counterproliferation of weapons of mass destruction are all crucial special operations mission sets, but it is manhunting that has become a primary focus of our operators and intelligence agencies over the past thirty years: Manuel Noriega, Mohamed Farrah Aidid, Ramzi Yousef, Khalid Sheikh Mohammed, Saddam Hussein, Osama bin Laden, Abu Musab al-Zarqawi, Ayman al-Zawahiri, Mullah Omar, to say nothing of the less well known HVIs targeted and killed or captured over the years. At the time of this writing, Ayman al-Zawahiri remains at large but rest assured there are teams of men and women actively hunting him down. It is a specialty in which we have become quite proficient.

My time in combat was but one chapter in my life. I am now an author. Though I've passed the torch to the next generation, my time in uniform will always be a part of me; those memories, lessons, and reflections are now finding their way into the pages of my novels.

One of the most intriguing passages in "The Most Dangerous Game" is this exchange between the protagonist, Sanger Rainsford, and the antagonist, General Zaroff, where the central theme of the narrative is revealed:

"I wanted the ideal animal to hunt," explained the general. "So I said, 'What are the attributes of an ideal quarry?' And the answer was, of course, 'It must have courage, cunning, and, above all, it must be able to reason.' "

"But no animal can reason," objected Rainsford.

"My dear fellow," said the general, "there is one that can."

Savage Son explores the darkest impulses of the human psyche. Do they live in all of us, repressed by the comforts and technology of the day? Have we advanced beyond those more primal instincts and if so, who will provide for and defend the tribe? *Civilized* society tends to keep warriors at arm's length, only turning to them in times of national emergency. *Break glass in case of war.*

We've been hunters and warriors for the majority of our existence. Only recently have we evolved, or possibly regressed, into beings with no connection to the land or the wild animals that inhabit it, while also outsourcing our duty to defend our families and our country. Whether this is a "progression" for our species remains to be seen.

Will there come a day when our survival depends on those primordial abilities? I suspect so. It might not be tomorrow or the day after, but then again, it might.

In either case, we would be wise to be ready, but right now, it's time to turn the page and hunt.

Jack Carr
August 22, 2019
Kamchatka Peninsula, Russia

A NOTE ON DEPARTMENT OF DEFENSE REDACTIONS

IN CERTAIN SECTIONS OF *Savage Son*, you will notice words and sentences blacked out. Just as with *The Terminal List* and *True Believer*, I submitted the manuscript to the Department of Defense Office of Pre-Publication and Security Review. What the government censors have redacted in my novels is surprising in that almost every word and sentence can be found in publicly available government documents and is part of the national discourse.

Select information should remain classified, yet the current review process is inefficient and ineffective, wasting time and resources to redact information that is in no way harmful to national security. At issue is freedom. The First Amendment is at the core of our Bill of Rights. It is "The First" for a reason. It is a natural right. It is not a right "given" by government and therefore it cannot be "taken" away. The review process is all about control. As I wrote in the preface to *The Terminal List*: "The consolidation of power at the federal level in the guise of public safety is a national trend and should be guarded against at all costs. This erosion of rights, however incremental, is the slow death of freedom."

Enjoy your time in the pages of *Savage Son*. Try to ignore the blacked-out sections, or better yet, try to decipher what the government deems so secret. If you read closely, I bet you can figure it out.

Jack Carr
February 10, 2020
Park City, Utah

PROLOGUE

Medny Island, Bering Sea, Russia

SHE WAS A STRONG one. Most humans would have given up by now, the deep snow quickly exhausting even the fittest among them. His snowshoes weren't exactly sporting, but no one said this was supposed to be fair. His heart rate increased, and he had to take a break to catch his breath due to the steep incline. She had taken the toughest route on the island, directly toward the highest peak. This was a first. *A feisty one.*

Still, the tracking was painfully easy in the waist-deep snow. He didn't speed after her; instead he relished the chase the way one would slowly enjoy a magnificent meal. No, that wasn't the correct comparison. This was more than that; this was carnal.

The winds howled as he crested the first of a spine of ridges that ran toward the summit. His quarry's trail had crossed to the windward side where the gale had already begun to erase her tracks with blowing snow.

Feisty and crafty.

The winds had shifted and cold, moist air was now blowing down from the Bering Sea. He looked toward the rapidly disappearing trail and watched the white wall of fog envelop the high ground before him, feeling the elation of finally matching wits with a worthy adversary.

Her jeans were soaked from the snow and her feet were numb inside her boots. She was post-holing through the deep white drifts, each and every step a physical challenge. She knew that to stop would mean death: death from hypothermia, death from those who hunted her. The pursuit had to be their game. Why else would they have let her go?

She was on an island or at least a peninsula; she could see water on both sides of the treeless landscape. Down to the shore would be the easy route, but that's what they would expect. The coastline was a death trap. She pushed herself up as her leg muscles screamed from the exertion of high-stepping through the powder. An accomplished endurance athlete, she was used to pain. She was comfortable being uncomfortable. A native of Montana, she was also used to being cold and wet.

God, I wish my brother were here. He'd know what to do, she thought, remembering their epic trail runs and how they'd cheer one another on at the jiu-jitsu academy.

The desolate tundra landscape meant she was somewhere in the far north; Scandinavia or Alaska maybe. More likely, somewhere in Russia. The men who took her rarely spoke, but they stank of Turkish tobacco. Her father's carpenter was an immigrant from Belarus; the odor of burnt leaf and sweat was one she remembered. If that was true, they'd flown her east. Whatever drugs they'd given her had worn off, and she had been fed surprisingly well. They must have wanted her strong. She looked to the sky and saw that weather was blowing in; fresh snow would cover her tracks and the dense fog would give her camouflage. She scrambled across the ridgeline toward the wind; she would make herself disappear.

. . .

The whiteout lasted nearly two hours. The hunter made his way back to the base camp to wait it out by the crackling fireplace with a leather-bound copy of *Meditations,* by the great Roman emperor and Stoic philosopher Marcus Aurelius. Sergei offered him a brandy but he passed, opting instead for hot tea. There would be plenty of time for celebration later; he wanted nothing in his veins that would dull the pleasure of what was to come. He savored the flavor of a tea smuggled in from China. He had acquired a taste for it on one of his postings, intrigued by the ritual, history, and a classification system to rival French wines in complexity.

Leaning back in the comfortable leather chair, he took in his surroundings. Above the fireplace hung an impressive Anatolian stag he'd taken in Turkey, a testament to both luck and perseverance. Next to it, a Tin Shan Argali sheep stared at him with lifeless eyes, a hard-won ram taken in the extreme altitudes of Tajikistan. The stone hearth was framed by a thick pair of Botswanan elephant tusks, each of which weighed in just under the mythical hundred-pound mark; he'd walked at least that many miles in pursuit of them. Though he looked upon these trophies fondly, he saw them as relics of a past life similar to the medallions he'd won in sports as a child. He had since moved on to more challenging and satisfying pursuits.

He pulled a Dunhill from the pocket of his wool shirt and lit it with the gold S. T. Dupont lighter that had been a gift from his father. He slid his thumb across the engraved double-headed imperial eagle emblem of the SVR, Russia's Foreign Intelligence Service; some vestiges of the czar had survived even communism. What to do about his father? *Not now. Later.*

He sipped his tea and visualized his stalk. He had several hours of daylight left, and it was imperative that he find her before dark. She would never survive the night in these conditions. Steam rose from his boots as the wet snow evaporated from the heat of the fire. The weather would soon turn. This snow would have wiped clean her trail, especially since she was clever enough to have used the wind to her advantage. He called to Sergei to ready the dogs. He was about to teach her a lesson in fear.

• • •

She had run out of elevation and was quickly running out of island. Her path had led beyond the exposed rolling tundra and into a set of jagged cliffs above the icy sea. The cold was all-consuming now and was beginning to sap her will to run, to survive. She was soaked from head to toe in a mixture of snow and sweat and was numb from the waist down. The agony in her feet had subsided, indicating that frostbite had set in. She rubbed her frozen hands together under her fleece jacket in a vain attempt to warm them. The biting wind was killing her so she moved to the lee side of the island and began to pick her way slowly down onto the sheer cliffs. She lost her footing once and slid fifty feet before she was able to arrest her fall on a small boulder. Part of her wanted to keep falling, to end it and deprive her pursuers the satisfaction of taking her life, but that was not in her constitution. That was not how she was raised.

As she hung desperately from the gray cliff, her eyes found it, a small space under a rocky outcropping that would conceal her from prying eyes and protect her from the deadly wind. She slid the toe of her boot until it found a hold, her hand searching for anything that would give her purchase. Her fingers slipped into a rocky crease, and she began working her way across the cliff face toward her destination. Inch by inch, step by precarious step, she made it. The spot was scarcely large enough to hold her but it was better than being exposed. She pulled her knees to her chest and pulled her arms inside her jacket, working her head down inside the fleece. She was suddenly aware of her thirst, her exhaustion, her fear. For the first time in ages, she allowed herself to weep, her tears and sobbing transitioning into an animalistic roar as she recognized her crying for what it was; she was mourning her own death.

* * * *

The cloud ceiling rose, and the snow slowed to a light dust in the breeze. The man drove the snowmobile to the spot where he'd left her tracks and signaled to Sergei to unload the hounds from the back of the six-wheel drive KAMAZ troop transport. Sergei looked longingly at the traditional bow of his people before leaving it in place and obeying his employer. Though the Koryak blood in his veins had been diluted over centuries by Cossack intervention, forced migration, and war, he still felt the pull of his native lands to the north.

The two bearlike Caucasian shepherds leapt down from the vehicle's cargo hold and began to test the air for the scent of their prey. Sergei had let them fill their nostrils with the scent from the woman's scarf; there were almost no foreign scents here to confuse them. Each animal weighed over 150 pounds and stood almost thirty inches at the shoulder. These particular animals, both of the mountain breed variety, had been born of a fierce military bloodline that went back to the early days of the Soviet Union. They had been chosen for their determination, ferocity, and their taste for human flesh.

He nodded to Sergei, who gave the dogs a whispered command. Their pissing, sniffing, and meandering ceased, and they took off up the grade with both men following on snowshoes. The beasts picked up the woman's scent quickly and charged up the snowy incline, nearly pulling the hulking figure of Sergei along behind them. The animals led them near the summit of the island's highest peak before turning downhill and out of the wind. He admired her desire to survive. This was his prescription for the ennui that had plagued him as long as he could remember. His hand moved subconsciously to the crossbow strapped across his back to confirm that it was still there; they were getting close.

Protected from the wind, it occurred to her how quiet it was. Her tears had lasted only a few minutes; it had felt good to get them out. *Keep your nerve, little one*, she remembered her father saying, his accent thick with the echoes of Rhodesia. That, she would. It was time to fight.

She grabbed handfuls of the spongy dark soil and rubbed her clothing until it was the color of her surroundings. Digging into the tundra, her hand found something hard and smooth. She scraped furiously, and she ran her fingers across its length to find the edge. Then, using a small rock as a spade, she unearthed what turned out to be a bone, likely a piece of seal rib brought to this perch by a scavenging bird. It was ten inches long, curved, and had a jagged sharp edge where it had split from the rest of its length. She turned it in her hand; now she was armed.

The silence was broken by the sound of barking dogs. This time the shiver that went up her spine was not from the cold. It didn't matter if the dogs could reach her, they would sniff her hiding place out; she was trapped. She peered over the ledge in front of her boots and saw the waves hitting the rocks several hundred feet below. The barking was suddenly very close; she could see and hear small pebbles roll past her as her pursuers made their way down the steep incline. She took a deep breath, held it, and exhaled as she adjusted her grip on the makeshift dagger.

• • •

For a minute the man thought that his prey had fallen to her death, but the dogs' interest in the rocky face suggested otherwise. He slipped the sling over his head and readied his weapon. The long carbon fiber shaft of the arrow was resting perfectly in its rail, the thin braided cable holding the limbs' kinetic energy at bay. He flipped up the caps on the scope and shouldered the modern rendition of the ancient tool to ensure that the lenses weren't fogged from the cold. His quarry was at bay; now he just had to wait for her to flush.

Sergei unclasped the brass hooks from the dogs' thick collars, releasing them from the yoke of the leather lead. They lurched toward the cliff, then slowed their pace to tiny steps as they tested the ledge. Their deep-throated barks were nearly deafening. The lead animal looked to his master, wary of the terrain before him. Sergei gave a command and all doubt evaporated; the dogs began a controlled slide downward. An ordinary canine would have plummeted into the sea but these were sure-footed mountain animals, bred for this very task.

• • •

She couldn't see them but the roar of their barks told her that they must be just outside her field of view, obscured by the wall of her stone prison. She pulled her left hand back into the sleeve of her jacket so that the material below the elbow hung empty. *Terror;* a snarling muzzle bearing wolflike teeth materialized before her. She flung her sleeve in its direction and the shepherd snatched it instinctively into his jaws. She pulled her hand from under her fleece and grabbed the beast by the collar as she plunged the seal bone into its neck. She screamed as she stabbed it over and over in unbridled rage, feeling the animal's hot blood spray onto her hands and face. Switching her attention to the dog's lungs, she used all of her strength to pierce its armor of thick fur. Her first blow glanced off a rib but the second and third stabs found their way into the chest cavity. The dog jerked out of her grasp and stumbled in his retreat. His footing lost, he tumbled out of sight.

. . .

Sergei shrieked as his finest hound plummeted into the Bering Sea, howling in agony. "*Ataka*," he commanded to the younger male, his voice devoid of its usual strength, hesitant for the first time to send his dog to do its work. Whatever uncertainty the animal felt was put aside, obedience taking over. Growling, he charged into the fray.

. . .

She scarcely had time to compose herself before the second dog came, all fur and fury. What this animal lacked in experience, he made up for in aggression. He ignored the matador sweep of the jacket sleeve and lunged for her throat. She pushed herself back as far as the mountain would let her, the dog's breath and musky coat heavy in the confined space. Saliva spurted across her face as the thunderous barking reverberated in her soul. She tucked her chin to her chest to protect her exposed neck and put her left arm across her face. Powerful jaws snapped onto her elbow, the canine's teeth piercing her flesh down to the bone.

She stabbed for the dog's flank and felt its hide give way as the seal bone found its home. This dog recognized the threat, shifting its attack to the arm that held the instrument of pain, tearing flesh and crushing through skin, bones, and tendons. The makeshift seal bone dagger dropped to the ground. Grasping a small rock with her free hand, she hit him again and again but he did not relent. Instead, he dragged her toward the opening, toward his waiting master. The dog outweighed her by thirty pounds, and her bloodied and beaten body was no match for her vicious antagonist. Her spirit, however, was anything but beaten.

Keep your nerve.

Knowing that she would be exposed in seconds, she whispered a quick prayer and grabbed the dog's collar with her right hand. The dog's actions were based on pure instinct, but she had the element of reason. Pulling him off balance, she bent at the knees and thrust forward with her feet toward the opening.

Freedom.

. . .

He had the scope to his eye now, ready to send his first arrow into her as soon as Sergei's hound pulled her clear. He would wound her first; no sense rushing to the climax. He disengaged the safety and put his gloved finger on the curved metal trigger of the Ravin. The scope's reticle danced, the inevitable result of blood, breathing, and adrenaline, but at this range, he would not miss. He would take her in the thigh, careful not to hit the femoral artery and give her a quick end.

The animal had her. He could see its rear legs moving backward; the anticipation made him feel uniquely alive. He saw a glimpse of her filthy jacket before the dog changed position and stumbled. Then he gasped. The woman's body flung headlong into the air, the animal's jaws still locked on to her. The pair seemed to hang for a moment before crashing downward onto the jagged rocks four hundred feet below.

The selfish bitch had robbed him of his kill. He dropped the crossbow in the snow and reached for a cigarette as he turned toward the lodge, commanding Sergei to retrieve the body as he stomped away.

No matter. The woman was just bait. He was after bigger game; she would still serve her purpose.

PART ONE

THE TRAP

"One does not hunt in order to kill; on the contrary,
one kills in order to have hunted."

—José Ortega y Gasset, *Meditations on Hunting*

CHAPTER 1

Kumba Ranch, Flathead Valley, Montana
Three months earlier

JAMES REECE RODE IN the passenger seat of the 1997 Land Rover Defender 110 in silence, taking in the serene beauty of the landscape. The road cut through a thick stand of ponderosa pines that towered in every direction. His college friend and former Navy SEAL teammate Raife Hastings was driving the British SUV and wouldn't tell Reece the exact nature of their destination. Raife's family had owned the sprawling ranch since they'd emigrated from southern Africa in the 1980s, when he was in his early teens. What had begun as a small and humble cattle operation had grown into tens of thousands of acres of prime grazing land and pristine wilderness. The family's successes in the cattle and real estate businesses had allowed them to expand their operations and they now owned properties throughout the state. Despite their hard-won wealth, Raife's father had ensured that the family never forgot their humble beginnings or took the opportunities afforded by their adopted homeland for granted.

As a former Navy SEAL, Reece had recently proven himself particularly skillful at adapting; he'd outwitted a national security apparatus set on killing him and then unraveled a plot that put the president of United States in the crosshairs. A man named Vic Rodriguez led the paramilitary branch of the Central Intelligence Agency as the director of the Special Activities Division. He'd then recruited Reece for the mission that had saved the president's life and

spared Ukraine from a chemical weapons attack. Vic recognized Reece's aptitude for aggressive problem solving and wanted to bring the frogman further
into the fold. As a result, Reece was technically now a temporary contract employee of the CIA's paramilitary Ground Branch, though currently his only job
was to recover from his recent surgery someplace where he could take a breath
and reset. Unbeknownst to his new masters at Langley, he had a more personal
reason for joining their ranks; two men needed to die.

Reece lifted his ball cap and ran his fingers over his closely cropped hair. He
hadn't had a haircut this short since BUD/S. They had shaved his head at Walter
Reed and, though it was beginning to grow back, he still hadn't accustomed himself to the feeling. He gingerly touched the scar on his scalp with his fingertips,
still amazed at how small it was. The procedure to remove his benign brain tumor
had been a complete success. He was relieved that he wouldn't be required to
undergo radiation or chemotherapy and was happy to be alive after all that he'd
been through over the past two years; there had been too much death.

The 4x4 crunched over gravel as Raife accelerated up a set of dirt switchbacks that led over a ridge.

"These things were always underpowered," Reece commented with a
straight face. The Land Rover/Land Cruiser debate was a near-constant source
of entertainment for the two friends, neither of whom ever passed up an opportunity to criticize the other's favorite vehicle.

"I should let you walk," was Raife's response.

Raife stopped the old Defender as it leveled off at the top of the trail. The
vista of the endless green trees leading to the massive alpine lake below was
breathtaking, even for someone who'd spent decades living on this land.

"It's beautiful."

"I thought you might like it."

"The view?"

"No, your new home."

"What are you talking about?"

"See that cabin down there by the lake?"

"Yeah."

"Lucky for you, my dad and father-in-law are James Reece supporters. They had it fixed up for you. They thought you might want a quiet spot away from everything to recover. It's yours."

"Are you serious?"

Raife nodded, pleased. It's not every day one gets to surprise their best friend with a new house.

"I don't know what to say."

" 'Thanks' would do it."

"Well . . . thanks."

"You always wanted to live in Robin's guest house." Raife smiled, referring to his father's middle name and knowing his friend would get it. "I'm sure he'll put you to work sooner or later and make you earn your keep so, if I were you, I'd play sick for as long as possible."

"Good tip."

"Reach under the seat."

Reece reached down and pulled out a SIG P320 X-Compact in a Black Point Tactical mini-wing holster.

"Mato thought that might come in handy," Raife said, referring to their former command master chief who now ran the training academy for SIG Sauer.

"Does everyone know I'm back?" Reece asked.

"You know this community, brother," Raife said with a smile. "We're worse than old ladies in a sewing circle."

Raife put the vehicle into low gear and let the engine rev as it slowly descended the grade that led toward the cabin. A circular crushed-stone driveway curved toward the home from the dirt road that ran past it. The wooden framed house had begun as a small pioneer cabin and that façade had been preserved and incorporated into the newer, larger structure. The building suited its surroundings and was large without being ostentatious. Raife stopped in front of the home's broad front porch and the two former commandos stepped out of the vehicle.

They wore jeans and faded T-shirts with holstered handguns that rode inside their waistbands. Reece wore his usual Salomon trail running shoes while Raife's Courtney boots were of a more traditional design, made from Cape buffalo hide and imported from his native Zimbabwe. In many ways, their choice of footwear typified their personalities. Though he'd moved around a lot, Reece was a native Californian, always looking for the latest and greatest piece of gear that might give him an edge in terms of performance. Raife was the opposite, a traditionalist who preferred the feel and soul of an earlier time. If Reece was Kydex, nylon, and Kevlar, Raife was leather, brass, and walnut.

The men's athletic physiques were obvious to the most casual observer, with broad, thick chests and powerful arms built by decades of intense physical training. Though their wardrobes were nearly identical and their builds similar, no one would mistake them for brothers. Reece's hair was dark with flecks of gray in his stubble. Raife was two inches taller than his friend's six feet and his build was leaner, with broader shoulders and a narrower waist. His longish hair was a sun-streaked blond that hung from the back of his cap and nearly touched his collar. His eyes were an almost iridescent green that stood in contrast to his tanned face. A discolored scar swept the length of his cheek. Raife stopped short of stepping up onto the planked wooden porch and made a sweeping gesture for Reece to take the lead.

The door was made of local Douglas fir and bore the scars of more than a century's exposure to the elements. Reece pressed the refurbished iron latch and the solid door swung open easily on new hinges. The two-story open space was bathed in natural light thanks to the large windows on the wall opposite the front door. The floor was Montana slate, a mosaic of grays and browns that contrasted with the blond planks that paneled the walls. A stone fireplace rose toward the open fir rafters. Reece's throat went tight when he saw what hung above the hearth.

"Is that my dad's bull?"

"Indeed, it is. He passed away before we could ship him the mount. We thought this would be a good spot for his elk."

The families had become close when Reece and Raife's friendship blossomed at the University of Montana. Reece's father, Tom, had visited the ranch in the fall of 2000 when both Reece and Raife had already graduated from BUD/S and been assigned to SEAL Teams on opposite coasts. Tom Reece, himself a frogman veteran of Vietnam, had elk-hunted during the visit and had taken the

six-by-six bull that hung in his son's new home. It had been the last time they'd
hunted together. The 9/11 attacks struck the following year and Reece had spent
the next decade and a half chasing Al Qaeda, ISIS, and their ilk to the far corners
of the globe. Tom Reece had passed away suddenly and tragically while Reece
was deployed to Iraq in 2003, killed in an apparent mugging in Buenos Aires,
Argentina, while working for the CIA.

A comfortable-looking nail-head leather sofa faced the fireplace and a
tawny hair-on cow rug covered the stone floor, framing a sitting area. Reece
noticed it bore the raised keloid scar of the Hastings family brand. Raife hung
back a step as his friend toured his new home, humbled by the generosity shown
to him by the Hastings family. There was a large kitchen with what looked to
be the original cast iron stove, surrounded by modern appliances, a comfortable bedroom with a rustic pine-framed king-sized bed, a guest bedroom, bath-
rooms, and a loft area that was set up as an office. Nearly every room in the
home had a view of the lake.

"I have one other thing to show you." Raife broke the silence and motioned
toward the door that led outside from the kitchen. He descended the steps and
strode toward a small barnlike structure. He pulled open the two large doors
and stood aside wearing a rare grin. Inside the detached garage sat a perfectly
restored 1988 FJ62 Toyota Land Cruiser, its bluish gunmetal gloss clear-coat
paint gleaming under the room's overhead LED lights. The vintage paint scheme
contrasted tastefully with the flat black aluminum wheels, off-road bumpers,
and roof rack.

Reece's eyes widened at the sight of the custom off-road vehicle. He'd been
forced to abandon his beloved Land Cruiser more than a year earlier as part of
a one-man mission of vengeance that had left a trail of bodies that stretched
from coast to coast. Since then, he'd driven Land Cruisers while working antipoaching patrols for Raife's uncle in Mozambique, but he hadn't had a vehicle
to call his own.

"It comes with the house. You know I'd never drive it so you may as well."

"Now I really don't know what to say."

"All of a sudden you're the quiet one?" Raife joked, referring to *Utilivu*, a

Shona nickname given to him by the trackers in Africa. "Don't just stand there like a *bloody* idiot, hop in."

Reece walked forward, as if he were approaching an extraterrestrial object. The door handle unlatched with a tactile and positive click; whoever had done the restoration work had done it exceptionally well. The dark interior combined utilitarian finishes and materials with style and comfort. The keys were in the ignition. The 376-cubic-inch, 430-horsepower General Motors LS3 V-8 roared to life instantly, its throaty growl tamed by an effective ceramic-coated exhaust system that allowed the vehicle to maintain a reasonable amount of stealth given its power.

"Not bad for a Japanese import, eh?" Political correctness was not one of Raife's strengths.

"I love it."

"This one's from Thorn," Raife confessed, using the nickname for his father-in-law. "He's taken pity on you in your weakened state."

"Where did he find it?"

"Don't you recognize her?"

Reece looked in the seats behind him and then back to his friend.

"It's yours. Ol' Clint couldn't bring himself to destroy her when you left California. He held on to it just in case. When he found out you were alive, he reached out to Thorn through the Special Operations Association. Their Vietnam network is strong. Thorn had it shipped out here, but not before having it fixed up for you."

"This is a bit more than 'fixed up'. This is a work of art!"

"Glad you like it. ICON 4X4 did the restoration so it should actually make it to town unlike your stock original. I almost forgot, look behind the seat."

Reece switched off the motor and looked over his shoulder. Hanging in a purpose-built Greyman tactical rack behind the seat was a Daniel Defense MK12 with a SilencerCo Omega suppressor and a Nightforce 1-8x24mm ATACR optic mounted on the receiver's top rail.

"Trouble seems to find you. I figured it would be wise to have more than that nine-mil pea shooter in your holster."

"You were not wrong, my friend," Reece said with genuine sincerity.

"Make yourself at home and relax. The family is flying in tomorrow and Dad is throwing a big dinner party in your honor."

"It will be great to see everyone."

"*Almost* everyone. You remember my younger sister Hanna. She's currently in Romania saving the world, but I think she's planning to come home for Christmas."

"It will be great to see her. And it gives me a few months to get into shape. As I remember, she was always doing those ultra-marathons."

"She won the Grand Traverse a couple years ago, so you have a lot of work to do."

"That's no joke. I've always wanted to do that. Crested Butte to Aspen, right?"

"That's right. Forty miles of ski-mountaineering over the Elk Mountain range."

"You have to have a partner for that one. Who'd she race with?"

"Me," Raife smiled. "And, if they didn't remove your liver along with your brain tumor you might want to bring it, along with a spare. You know how my family is."

"If I find an extra, I'll be sure to bring it."

"I'll be at the shop if you need anything."

"Hey Raife," Reece called out as his friend walked toward his Land Rover.

"Yeah?"

"You might want to check the oil in that Defender. It's been sitting there for a few minutes so it probably all leaked out."

Raife turned and smiled to himself as he saluted his friend with his middle finger.

CHAPTER 2

Bangui, Central African Republic

ROMAN DOBRYNIN WAS NOT a man accustomed to waiting. Usually, just the opposite. People waited on him: subordinates, security personnel, even foreign dignitaries. He was the Russian president's man in Africa, or at least in the Central African Republic. In his mid-fifties, he was a seasoned diplomat, having earned his stripes in the chaos that was Chechnya. He had proven himself to be an aggressive negotiator unafraid to threaten and then employ the darker arts of manipulation to achieve his, and Mother Russia's, strategic goals. Technically a senior policy advisor in Russia's Ministry of Foreign Affairs, he was their de facto senior man in the CAR. His official title was National Security Advisor to the President of the Central African Republic.

Russia was a power on the rise in Africa, and Dobrynin had counterparts in the Congo, Ethiopia, Guinea, Eritrea, and Mozambique. With France all but abandoning its former colony, Russia and China were quick to fill the void; arms deals, security training assistance, regional negotiations, lumber, diamonds, oil, gold, cobalt, and most important for Russia, uranium. Russia had vaguely disguised its intentions on the international stage, citing its involvement in the region beginning in 1964. Strategically located in the heart of the Dark Continent, the Central African Republic was the ideal hub from which Russia could move troops into neighboring countries while exploiting and exporting their natural resources. Dobrynin was there to ensure it was Russia, not China, that would control both the natural resources of this landlocked nation and, more important, their votes at the United Nations.

Though rich in raw materials, CAR was one of the ten poorest countries in the world. Its record of human rights violations including extrajudicial executions, torture, female genital mutilation, slavery, human trafficking, the sex trade, child labor, rape, and genocide made the country the perfect home for an outside power seeking to take advantage. It was a disenfranchised country ripe for exploitation.

The call had come from the chief staff officer of the general director himself, which meant it was one of the few calls Dobrynin had to take. It was made clear that his guest was to be granted every professional courtesy and that he was coming in at the behest of the president. In Russia the lines between official, unofficial, and private blurred to the point of virtual invisibility. This visit had all the trappings of the latter. Dobrynin knew that as deputy director of Directorate S in the Russian Foreign Intelligence Service, Aleksandr Zharkov could be coming to CAR for a variety of reasons. He also knew the Zharkov name and, much more than the call he'd received from his own high command, that was reason alone to accommodate the intelligence officer. Dobrynin wanted to keep his head attached to his body. One did not offend a *Pakhan* in the Russian *Bratva* and expect to stay aboveground for long.

Dobrynin watched the monstrous Antonov AN-225 circle the airfield and begin its final approach. He remained in his vehicle until the aircraft had touched down and taxied to the Russian-controlled side of the airport before disembarking the armored and air-conditioned Toyota Hilux. Straightening the tie on his Armani suit, he walked forward to meet his guest.

• • •

Deputy Director Zharkov waited patiently as the aircraft hinged just behind the cockpit, pulling the entire nose of the massive plane skyward. It stopped when it reached ninety degrees, leaving the fuselage open to the elements. Most planes have cargo ramps in the aft but the AN-225 has just the opposite. The nose gear slowly lowered the open beast to the ground, a unique design feature that allowed the largest aircraft in the world to load a staggering amount of cargo. A blast of heat off the tarmac nearly took his breath away, a clear indicator that he was no longer in Moscow; its intensity carried the distinctive smell of conflict. His mind raced with possibilities.

Scanning the tarmac, he saw a four-vehicle convoy of trucks surrounded by a perimeter of armed security. *Spetsnaz.* They had once been feared the world over as the premier special operations force of the former Soviet Union, based on what was touted as the toughest training ever devised by a modern military and because of their actions, the West would say atrocities, in Afghanistan in the 1980s. They had now been relegated to protection duties for those who wanted to be surrounded by the myth that was *spetsnaz.*

A man in a crisp black suit walked toward him flanked by two men from his security detail carrying AKM rifles.

"Director Zharkov, I am . . ."

"Roman Dobrynin," the deputy director completed the sentence for him. "It is a pleasure to make your acquaintance. Thank you for taking the time to meet me. I am sure you have pressing matters that require your attention. I have heard glowing reports of your progress here as national security advisor, advancing Russia's interest in the region."

"It is an honor to be of assistance," Dobrynin countered, his eyes moving up to the large airframe and then back to his visitor. "Are you alone, Director Zharkov?"

"*Da,*" Zharkov confirmed with a wave of his hand, as if there were nothing odd about him being the single passenger on the heaviest airplane ever built. With a quarter-million kilograms of payload capacity, the plane had completed its fourteen-hour flight from Moscow to the middle of the African continent and successfully inserted the senior intelligence official into the *heart of darkness.*

"No security detail?" Dobrynin asked, looking back to the plane.

"I prefer to travel light and without the trappings of my position that could draw undue attention."

Zharkov was dressed comfortably in brown pants and a beige safari shirt with the sleeves rolled up, a canvas pack slung over his shoulder.

"Besides, with your clout and control in the area I knew you would have security arrangements taken care of."

"Of course, Director. Shall we?" Dobrynin motioned toward the waiting vehicles, struggling to decipher if the director's words were a compliment, a warning, or simply condescending.

Zharkov nodded. "I understand you were briefed on my requests?"

"*Da*, we will take you to the hotel now and tomorrow we will go to the mines."

• • •

Zharkov took in the sights of the bustling city, politely listening to Dobrynin drone on about his most recent diplomatic victories. A five-thousand-man force of Russian military and contracted advisors were in the country training the CAR special operations forces on the finer points of counterinsurgency. Zharkov correctly assumed that meant a systematic campaign of terror aimed at keeping the dissidents in check and ensuring the current president remained in power and friendly to Russian interests in the country.

At each stoplight, the cars were swarmed by children, arms outstretched, their faces hopeful for a coin or a piece of candy. Traffic was at its usual stop-and-go, broken-down vehicles impeding their progress as scooters buzzed past like the swarms of insects that infested the nearby jungle. It was a country on its last breaths.

Just outside the hotel, a small convoy of taxis lingered, each flying a small Russian flag on the front bumper, waiting eagerly for the opportunity to ferry guests to and from the airport. At the approach of the convoy, the Hotel Ledger's guarded gates opened, and the depravity of the streets was left in the dust. The driveway curved up to the entrance, and the outside world was forgotten. Old-world opulence, no doubt a vestige of the French colonial days, permeated every aspect of Bangui's finest hotel; abundant marble and ornate tapestry were accented by rich African wood polished to perfection, its gold inlay reflecting the late afternoon light.

"My men will show you to your room. I trust you will find your accommodations acceptable. Will dinner in two hours be convenient?"

"That will be fine, thank you," Zharkov nodded politely and proceeded to the elevator to the penthouse suite, two *spetsnaz* and one bellhop in tow. As they arrived at the double suite doors, his new security halted him on the outside.

"Just a moment, sir."

"Open it," one commanded the bellhop.

They entered the six-thousand-square-foot suite guns raised, then performed a sweep of every corner before pronouncing it safe to enter.

Zharkov walked in and was not surprised to see two young girls who couldn't have been more than fifteen in thin white linen dresses standing obediently by the king-size bed. This was Africa. He eyeballed their lean, underfed bodies, dark skin a sensual contrast to their scant dresses. A bottle of vintage 1987 Dom Pérignon and fresh strawberries covered with chocolate were set at the table. He set his pack down and poured a glass of the cold sparkling wine, savoring the taste, and glanced at the agenda sitting on the table.

He looked back to the girls and was tempted, watching them shift nervously, fear radiating from their not-yet-vacant eyes. They still held a glimmer of hope.

He shook his head toward the door, "*Ukhady*," he said. "*Von*," the Russian said again, more firmly when they remained motionless.

Not knowing a word of Russian, the girls stood there unsure of what to do. Zharkov pointed to the door.

"*Out!*" he said, this time in English, pointing at the door.

Understanding the international language of tone and gesture, the two girls made their way slowly past him, still unsure of what they should do and beginning to worry they had somehow upset the man they had been told to obey and pleasure. Opening the door for them, he told his new security detail he did not want to be interrupted until dinner.

He'd been through enough prostitutes in this part of the world in his younger days and he needed to stay healthy; his mind was on his mission.

CHAPTER 3

Akyan Hotel, Saint Petersburg, Russia

TO IVAN ZHARKOV, INFORMATION was everything. It had been information, and his willingness to exploit it at all costs, that had led to his position of power in the Bratva, the Brotherhood, known to the rest of the world as the Russian mafia. His consolidation of St. Petersburg's Tambov Gang was the result of well-timed intelligence, brought to him by his eldest son, Aleksandr. Some even thought that, through Aleksandr, Ivan may have organized the arrests in Spain that took out the powerful gang's former leadership, though no one dared whisper such a thing. Ivan was the *Vor v Zakone*. No one, not even the government in Moscow, would cross him.

It was Ivan's lust for information that persuaded him to send an emissary to Argentina, where a CIA officer was offering him valuable intelligence. That job fell to Dimitry Mashkov, a trusted *bratok* who had interrogated enough Chechens during his days as a paratrooper in the 104th Guards Airborne Regiment to know when a man was lying. If he could break a fanatical Muslim, stay alive in Kresty Prison, and take out members of the rival Solntsevskaya Gang, he was confident he could discern if some American desk officer was the genuine article.

Dimitry spent three days interrogating the American in a Cordoba farmhouse and was convinced he was being truthful. Such an asset would be invaluable to Zharkov's operations. The trick was getting him from Argentina to

Russia, which meant airports and customs officials. Via his son, Aleksandr, the elder Zharkov had the appropriate influence to provide the man with a clean passport, but he would still have to traverse a series of international airports. These days, ever-present surveillance cameras using facial recognition technology made clandestine travel problematic.

Luckily, Zharkov's friends in the South American drug trade were the best in the world when it came to moving contraband; they ultimately provided the solution. The former spy was moved overland from his Argentine hideout to Caracas, where the failing government was ripe with corruption. For a staggeringly low sum, he was shepherded through the airport's already lax security and loaded onto a Havana flight without incident. From José Martí in Cuba, it was a direct flight to Moscow on an Aeroflot SU-151, an unremarkable event for a man carrying a legitimate passport of the Russian Federation. Aleksandr was able to smooth things over at Sheremetyevo, one of Moscow's four international airports, and the man had been delivered to Ivan just a few hours and a quick domestic flight later.

The CIA man was now parked in a hotel suite, waiting impatiently for what was, effectively, a job interview.

• • •

Oliver Grey looked at his watch, the iconic dive instrument that had influenced a thousand knockoffs. The stainless steel case and bracelet were worn and scored by a hard lifetime's worth of use, though they had accrued before Grey took possession. The acrylic crystal was burnished by time and the bezel and face were faded from months in the sun, a standing testament to the original owner's vocation. Behind the battered exterior, though, the hands of the precision Swiss instrument swept on unscathed.

He knew that the watch was a Rolex Submariner, and that its former owner was the late Thomas Reece. What he did not know was that Tom Reece purchased it on R&R in Saigon during his first tour in Vietnam with SEAL Team Two. He'd worn it on hundreds of ops both as a frogman and an intelligence officer, and had planned on passing it to his son, James, when the time was right.

He never got the chance. Grey had planned his demise, outwitting the legendary CIA case officer who was far past his prime, sticking his nose where it didn't belong when he should have been fishing or playing golf or whatever it is that retired spooks do with their free time. Grey had used the watch's absence to make the murder appear to be the result of a simple mugging in a South American city well acquainted with that brand of violence. Grey hadn't killed him with his own hands. He'd instead used his Cajun pit bull Jules Landry, who had brought him the watch as a trophy, eager to please his new boss. That was fifteen years ago. Now Landry was dead, castrated and left to bleed out on a dirty floor in northern Iraq. Grey had no illusions as to where his future was headed. He knew he was firmly in James Reece's sights and, if he hoped to survive, he was going to have to strike soon, before the frogman had a chance to track him down.

He will come for me and that Syrian sniper, Nizar, who put a round through his SEAL friend.

Grey had read all about it in the papers, how two Americans had thwarted the assassination of the U.S. president in Ukraine and saved Odessa from a chemical weapon attack at the last moment. The coup orchestrated by the late Vasili Andrenov, Grey's Russian handler, had ended in failure. Reece had been unsuccessful in saving the Russian president, and Senior Chief Freddy Strain had been killed in the attempt.

He needed to outthink James Reece before the SEAL could track him down and put a bullet in his head, or worse. Grey had no illusions about the true reason James Reece was currently in the employ of the CIA; he needed their resources to find his friend's killer. Since his former employer and the closest thing to a father Grey had ever known had been sent to a fiery grave, killed by one of the countless weapons with which he'd sown the seeds of revolution around the globe, Grey was now a *rōnin*. He needed a new master. Grey was sure that Tom Reece's son had been involved in Vasili Andrenov's assassination and he knew he was next on Reece's list.

Grey had endured the brutal questioning from the criminal called Dimitry as well as the excruciating overland trip taking him nearly the length of the South American continent, both only made bearable by the sweet tobacco he packed into his old billiard pipe. Add in the international flights on aging aircraft serving cheap booze, and Grey was in rough shape. They hadn't even offered him a coffee. An accountant by trade, he sought order in life, and that order was severely lacking at present. The watch was the only thing that had kept him sane, its hands moving steadily and predictably as his world became anything but. The irony was that the time wasn't even correct. He hadn't changed it since he'd left Buenos Aires.

Grey was not an imposing figure, and the travel had done nothing to improve his bearing. His beard needed trimming and had turned nearly snow white over the past few months. He wore a sweat-stained wool fedora over his cap of thinning hair, and his tweed coat was badly in need of washing. He hadn't been able to bathe since he'd left Venezuela and looked like a disheveled university professor, wearing a bitter halo of stale sweat and metabolized vodka. His appearance was in stark contrast to the spacious and orderly hotel suite. It was known as the White Suite, thanks to the snowy fabric that covered its luxurious furniture. A large freestanding bathtub sat just feet from the rounded bed on a waxed parquet floor. What he would give for a warm bath and some sleep!

His escort hadn't said a word, but had motioned for him to sit in a chair padded in white leather that faced a comfortable-looking love seat against the suite's wall. He was near the balcony and had a marvelous view of the Tsentralny District. Though mentally exhausted, he took comfort from being in the land of his ancestry. His plan had been to rise alongside his mentor, Colonel Vasili Andrenov, the right hand of the returning leader. Instead, because of James Reece, he was here to beg for a job from a criminal.

Grey expected the security men would look like club bouncers in leather jackets, but the *vory* bodyguards who protected the mob boss were clad in finely tailored business suits. The neatly groomed men could have passed for agents of the FSO or Federal Protective Service and, in fact, some of them had history in that organization. Four of them moved into the room and joined the stoic figure already watching over him. Grey was frisked for the third time, thoroughly and professionally. A few seconds later the door opened, and two more bodyguards entered, stepping aside to flank the opening.

Though Grey was familiar with the details of the man who walked through the door, thanks to his former duties as a senior analyst on the Russian Desk at the CIA, he was not at all prepared for who entered the room. Written reports and long-lens photographs from surveillance footage only told you so much, which is why Grey had always envied the men and women on the ground who gathered human intelligence; the people who looked their subjects in the eye. Instead of an imposing figure who instilled fear, he beheld a man of slight build and of medium height; this was no track-suit-wearing thug. Ivan Zharkov was also older than Grey expected, with a handsome face and thoughtful blue eyes.

A wolf in sheep's clothing?

Grey expected false bravado and swagger, but instead Zharkov walked with grace and poise. He wore a suit of thick charcoal cashmere with a burgundy silk tie knotted neatly at his throat. His beard was trimmed, his mustache purposefully bushier and more prominent. His hair had gone almost white. It was combed and parted neatly above his right eye. Grey couldn't help but think that Zharkov looked much the way Czar Nicholas II might have looked in his sixties had he not been shot by Bolsheviks in a basement alongside his wife and children.

His handshake was firm and his expression was warm as he invited Grey to take a seat. It seemed somewhat odd to Grey that he wasn't offered coffee or tea, though after his journey across the globe, he wasn't quite sure if it was time for breakfast or cocktails.

"Thank you so much for meeting me, *Pakhan*." Grey spoke first using the Russian term for "boss" and showing off his command of the Russian language that he'd spoken exclusively in his childhood home in Pennsylvania.

"It is I who should be thanking you, Mr. Grey. You have come such a long way."

"It was nothing," Grey lied.

"I was very sorry to hear about Colonel Andrenov's death. He was a friend of my business, and I know that he was like a father to you. You have my condolences."

"Thank you, *Pakhan*, that means a great deal to me. The colonel spoke highly of you."

"He exaggerated, I am sure. He did the country a great service by removing our president. He was a weak man who was selling us out to the Americans. I know you played a significant role in the operation. Blaming it on the Muslim savages was a touch of genius."

Grey nodded, taking credit for what had not been his idea.

"What has brought you from such a warm and pleasant climate to such a cold one? You have risked a great deal by making this journey."

Oliver had practiced his pitch many times during the past weeks. "I have, *Pakhan*, but it will be worth it, for us both. I know the capabilities of the U.S. intelligence community. I spent my entire career using all of their tools to track and analyze Russian people of interest. I'm offering that expertise to you. The Americans trained me well, *Pakhan*. I know everything there is to know about your rivals, about your critics in Moscow, and about the weaknesses of the Western nations' law enforcement efforts."

"You have my ear," the mafia leader acknowledged.

"I know where your rival organization, the Solntsevskaya Gang, is exposed and I know which members of your organization are working with the FBI and CIA."

Zharkov spoke without shifting his eyes from Grey. "Order some breakfast for our friend here."

One of his men nodded in response and swiftly left the room.

"Go on, Oliver."

The shift to his given name was not lost on the wayward spy.

A hearty breakfast was rolled into the room by one of Zharkov's bodyguards within minutes, the waiter having been stopped and searched by the security men in the hallway. Zharkov took only coffee for himself but an impressive spread of vegetables, cold meats, eggs, and pastries was presented to the famished CIA man. Grey ate quickly and drained the Bloody Mary as soon as he realized that it contained more than tomato juice. Zharkov ordered his bodyguards to keep the drinks flowing. When Grey put down his fork and took a breath, Zharkov continued the conversation.

"You've promised much, Oliver, and I'm willing to pay a fair price for the kind of information you claim to have. My father was a grain buyer when the communists were in power. He could have rubber-stamped the purchases, but he took pride in his work and only bought the best crops. He demanded a sample from every bushel that he could inspect. I need a morsel, Oliver, a sample of your wares."

Grey was prepared for the challenge. "I understand, *Pakhan*. I have information on Melor Sokolov of the Solntsevskaya Gang. Despite appearances, he is a homosexual."

"Interesting."

"He's a *suka*, too, a bitch."

"As much as that kind of behavior disgusts me, Oliver, men who have been in prison do such things. This is not shocking."

"I agree, *Pakhan*, but the man who puts him on his belly is a flight attendant for Air France. He is also an asset of DGSE. He's French intelligence. They know every move that the Solntsevskaya Gang makes and report much of it to the U.S."

"Now *that*, Oliver, is fascinating," Zharkov confirmed.

"I believe in long-term relationships, *Pakhan*."

"As do I, Oliver."

"I would like to become a permanent asset to you, to your organization."

Zharkov's bushy gray eyebrows arched upward before his eyes followed them to the ceiling, considering the proposal.

"I must ask you, Oliver, and I hope that you will forgive me for being direct, how can I be assured that you will not betray me the way you betrayed the Americans? How can I know that this is not an elaborate ruse to put a mole inside my business?"

Oliver was prepared for this as well. "I will not betray you because I am Russian. My mother was Russian. My grandparents who raised me were Russian. My *soul* is Russian. No, I will not betray you, *Pakhan*. Besides, where else would I go?"

Zharkov stared at Grey for a long moment, his eyes studying him for any hint of deception. There was no blink, no darting of the eyes, no twitch of the tiny facial muscles, nothing.

"What do you propose?"

"Just a fair stipend and an apartment with a view."

Zharkov considered the proposition.

"Twenty million rubles a year and a comfortable flat in one of my buildings where you will be safe."

Grey would have taken less but didn't want to seem overly eager. Twenty million rubles was roughly $300,000 U.S. Not bad for a wanted man.

"That is very generous of you, *Pakhan*, but there is one other thing."

"Which is?"

"I want a man dead."

CHAPTER 4

Kumba Ranch, Flathead Valley, Montana

REECE SETTLED INTO THE cabin and put what few possessions he had into the bedroom's dresser drawers and closet. He was struck by how quiet it was. He liked it. There was no television, Wi-Fi, or cell service. The Hastings family used two-way radios to communicate on the ranch, as they were the only reliable means of staying in touch. Repeater stations placed upon various peaks and ridges ensured that one was usually in range.

He opened the French doors that led toward the lake and walked toward the shoreline in the crisp, clean air. There were a pair of Adirondack chairs near a stone fire ring just feet from the water's edge. Reece took a seat and admired the view. Who would occupy the other? His pregnant wife, Lauren, and their daughter, Lucy, had been gone for almost two years now, murdered in their home as part of the cover-up of a deep-state medical experiment gone wrong. Avenging their deaths had brought him closure. *Or, had it?* His mission accomplished; what he hadn't expected was to live. He'd thought he was dying, a tumor slowly killing him from within. He had counted on joining his wife and daughter in the afterlife.

Africa had taught Reece to live again, but the Agency had tracked him down in Mozambique, sending his old sniper school partner Freddy Strain to recruit him. The carrot was that he could have his life back; the stick was that those who had helped him would go down. Reece chose the carrot. He had done what was asked of him; he'd killed the terrorist leader whose attacks had put the continent of Europe under siege, as well as the former GRU colonel who had masterminded the campaign of terror in an attempt to pave the way for his triumphant return to lead Russia back from the brink. Freddy had died saving the life of the president of the United States, taken by a sniper's bullet, a sniper who still walked free. A sniper Reece planned to kill. Reece would find him and the CIA mole who had provided the intelligence for the operation. In time, both would die.

His debt to America having been paid following the events in Odessa, Reece's new boss at the CIA, Vic Rodriguez, provided a safe house in Annapolis that Reece could use while he prepared for, and recovered from, surgery. Vic was slowly turning up the pressure, continuing his personal recruitment efforts on the former SEAL, who remained noncommittal.

Reece's friend Katie Buranek was like a guardian angel; she'd been by his side as he was wheeled into surgery and stood vigil while he recovered. She lived nearby in Old Town Alexandria. There she could work the D.C. Fox News desk and commute to their New York headquarters. It also allowed them to pick up where their friendship had left off. She had helped him unravel the conspiracy that launched him on his mission of vengeance, and she had paid the price, almost losing her life in the process. Unbeknownst to the former frogman, the tough young journalist had questions she needed answered; in matters of the heart, trust was paramount.

• • • •

Snow was falling on a morning when Katie came to see Reece after one of his physical therapy sessions. He was only a week out from surgery and would soon be leaving for Montana. Katie knew that Reece had a continued affiliation with the darkest side of the U.S. intelligence apparatus, though she hadn't probed. She'd seen a man she recognized as the head of the CIA's Special Activities Division with Reece's doctor at Walter Reed. As a journalist, and with her family's history with the Agency during the Cold War, she was not a believer in coincidence.

She also knew there was a place Reece needed to visit before he left for the mountains. Reece accepted their destination in silent resignation. It was time to say good-bye to someone.

Katie drove south, crossing the Potomac River, and traversed from Interstate 495 onto George Washington Memorial Parkway. The road wound through leafless oaks, the tall modern skyline of Rosslyn, Virginia, visible through the frosted passenger side window, Pierre L'Enfant's iconic neoclassical tribute to the republic across the river to the left. Reece never tired of seeing America's symbols of freedom: the Capitol dome, the Washington Monument, and the Lincoln Memorial.

Planes on final approach to Reagan National Airport roared overhead as Katie exited GW Parkway and steered her 4Runner through a plowed asphalt path that would have, at one point, been in Robert E. Lee's front yard.

Reece had been a casket bearer for too many funerals at Arlington National Cemetery over the years; consequences of a life at war. Katie pulled her SUV curbside on Pershing Drive and shut off the motor. Reece let her lead the way. Neither spoke. He knew where they were going. The sound of their footsteps in the freshly fallen snow was a haunting reminder that beneath this hallowed ground rested generations of America's bravest warriors.

Reece paused among the granite headstones in silent recognition at the grave of Johnny "Mike" Spann, the CIA officer killed by Al Qaeda at Qala-i-Jangi in Afghanistan. The Alabama native had been the first American to die in combat during the War on Terror. In the nearly two decades since, he had been joined by a legion of heroes who had given their last full measure for the nation.

Reece turned and looked toward Katie. She stood to the side of two headstones on the oak-shaded hillside. Reece approached and bowed his head at his father's final resting place.

THOMAS

REECE

JR.

MASTER CHIEF PETTY OFFICER

US NAVY

SEAL TEAM TWO

MAY 12 1946

JULY 9 2003

VIETNAM

COLD WAR

NAVY CROSS

Reece had visited his father's grave only once since the funeral in 2003. He could hardly believe it had been that long since he'd lost the old warrior. He pushed the mystery surrounding his father's death to the side and slowly turned his head to read the marker just beside it, a newer slab of granite stabbed into the cold ground.

JUDITH

FRANCES

REECE

MARCH 2 1951

APRIL 24 2018

DEVOTED WIFE

MOTHER

Despite the cold, Reece's entire body flushed with warmth. He fought back tears as he knelt in front of the stone tribute, a lifetime summed up by a few simple lines. His mother had suffered from dementia for several years and had lived her life in an Arizona nursing home after his father's death. Reece had, in many ways, mourned her since the cruel disease had robbed her memory. He had secretly held out hope that some miracle treatment could bring her back to him; now she was gone forever, back at his father's side. He treasured his last visit with her, when, in a moment of lucidity, she'd recognized her only son, reminding him of Gideon's mission in Judges. *"You've always been one of the few, James. Keep watching the horizon."*

Reece closed his eyes and whispered a silent prayer, asking his late mother and father to take care of his wife and daughter until he got there to take the watch.

I love you.

He wiped his eyes on his sleeve as he rose to his feet and felt Katie's gloved hand slip inside the crook of his elbow.

"I'm sorry, James," was all she said before turning to walk toward her waiting vehicle.

CHAPTER 5

Central African Republic

THE TRIP TO THE Ukrainian mines in the Christian-controlled district of Bakouma involved a two-hour flight east in the King Air turboprop. Two matching planes carried the envoy at 265 miles per hour toward their destination. Aleksandr had never hunted in CAR. Poaching and years of civil strife had decimated the game population, though he had hunted the jungles of neighboring Cameroon for bongo, sitatunga, duikers, and the elusive dwarf forest buffalo. He briefly entertained the thought of going after a giant forest hog while he was in the area, but the prospect of another rare game animal for his trophy room didn't excite him as it had in his youth. Now he required something more.

Aleksandr admired the rugged beauty of the African landscape. From the air it was easy to dismiss the reality on the ground, a place where the people had yet to progress past the foundation of Maslow's hierarchy of needs. A thousand feet below, malaria remained the leading cause of death, sanitary drinking water was scarce, accusations of witchcraft resulted in mob justice, HIV/AIDS affected at least 5 percent of the population, and women not only suffered the highest percentage of genital mutilation in the world but also endured one of the highest maternal mortality rates. The Central African Republic was not kind to its people.

Outside the few cities, the country remained embroiled in civil war, with fourteen separate factions of Muslim Séléka and Christian Anti-Balaka militias still vying for contested areas and set on wiping the others from existence. Ethnic cleansing in Africa was the default setting of strife, one that tended to turn on the swing of the machete.

The two turboprops touched down on a small dirt strip and taxied to the mine administration building. Under the watchful eye of no fewer than fifty armed Russian soldiers, groups of men labored in the sun extending the runway and constructing additional infrastructure to accommodate the ongoing rape of natural resources. Aleksandr noted the handful of local militia who were clearly outmanned and outgunned by their Russian advisors.

"We will see two mines today, Director Zharkov. We will start with the uranium mines and then move to the diamond mines as you requested."

"*Da.*" Aleksandr nodded, his mind working through the possibilities.

The Toyota Land Cruisers they were being shuttled in were a far cry from the newer armored Hiluxes they'd used in the capital, but their low torque and unmatched reliability made them the vehicle of choice this far from civilization. Even with the windows down Dobrynin's suit was soaked with sweat and Aleksandr wondered why the diplomat insisted on clinging to the formal trappings of Mother Russia. No matter; Aleksandr just needed to tour the operations, make his decision, then issue his directive.

Their three-vehicle convoy was led by a camouflage Peugeot P4 manned by two of the Russian advisors and one of the local militia leaders. Based on the venerable Mercedes G wagon, the P4 was the French version of a "jeep." Aleksandr smiled knowing Peugeot did not have an export agreement with Mercedes. *Never trust the French.* Trailing the convoy was an olive-drab Renault troop carrier with eight local militia members and four additional Russian troops. As they maneuvered the rutted roads toward the mines, Aleksandr noticed young men and boys turn away, ducking behind corners as the envoy passed. The counterinsurgency tactics of the *spetsnaz* were working; fear reigned supreme.

They sped through local villages as quickly as the low-torqued machines allowed, the front and rear vehicles bristling with overt weapons. The message was clear: do not fuck with this convoy. The poverty was not shocking to Alek-

sandr: thatched roofs, the occasional malnourished cow, dirty ditches ooz-
ing with excrement, and old men and women hovering near death in the dirty
streets. As in developing countries the world over, the only smiles belonged to
the children playing in the grime.

. . .

The uranium mine radiated destitution. The workers that Aleksandr observed
lining up to enter the shafts looked like zombies. Even children had been con-
signed as forced labor, the cost of a village overrun by HIV and AIDS. As the
raw ore was raised by hand in wooden buckets or pushed on a crude railway in
rickety carts, it was heaped outside the entrance in large piles. Aleksandr was
cautioned to stay on the observation platform, as the radiation level was toxic
closer to the piles of ore.

"What's their life expectancy?" Aleksandr asked his host, observing the
workers covered in boils and blisters.

"Less than a year," Dobrynin confirmed. "Luckily, conscript labor is not a
rare commodity in this part of Africa."

It reminded Aleksandr of the corrective labor camps, what the West insisted on calling *gulags* after Solzhenitsyn received the Nobel Prize in literature
for his *The Gulag Archipelago*. Solzhenitsyn was right about one thing: the prisoners were given the opportunity to work to death.

"I've seen enough. Take me to the diamond mines."

. . .

The convoy continued another two hours, as they pushed deeper into the hills,
the vehicles making slower progress. Aleksandr wondered if the reporters who
had "disappeared" a few months earlier were killed because they ran into the
wrong militia or were targeted by *spetsnaz* for asking too many questions about
the mines. No matter. What did they expect, poking around in what amounted
to a war zone in Central Africa?

A large white man who Aleksandr deduced to be from the Ural Mountains greeted them at the vehicles, shaking hands and introducing himself as Krysov Petrovich.

"Comrade Petrovich runs the mining operation. In the past seven months he has turned this into the most efficient and profitable diamond mining operation in the country," Dobrynin declared.

Petrovich wiped his sweaty forehead with a dirty rag and stuffed it back in his pocket. Aleksandr noticed Dobrynin fish a bottle of hand sanitizer out of his suit pocked and squeeze a liberal amount into his palm.

"The workers are paid a generous sum for their labor, generous for this part of the world, anyway," he continued.

"And theft? Is that a problem or are the wages enough to counter the temptation?" Aleksandr asked.

"Theft will always be a problem, Mister Zharkov," Petrovich said. "We have the unfortunate task of using unorthodox methods to deal with thieves. Come."

Petrovich led the way to what Aleksandr assumed to be roughly the center of the aboveground operation.

"These ungrateful savages still swallow raw diamonds to smuggle them out to sell on the black market. Every few months we need to remind the rest what happens to those who steal."

Aleksandr watched as thirty workers exited the mine, filthy and thin, their eyes darting about like cornered animals. *Desperate.* Russian troops lined them up and shackled them to a rail obviously put there for this very reason. Each of the chained men was given a liter of a magnesium sulfate solution to drink, the equivalent of a medical bowel prep. Within twenty minutes, violent cramps preceded an eruption of watery human excrement. Three were found to have expelled the raw stones after the local guards sifted through the malodorous mess.

"What will happen to them?" Aleksandr asked as the three offenders were led away.

"It's best if we show you," Petrovich replied. "In the meantime, follow me."

Aleksandr took the guided tour. Though he listened respectfully to the briefing on diamond mine production and expected output for the coming year, his mind was on the three men who had been removed for stealing; they looked fit enough, and living in this area meant they should have tracking and hunting skills.

Ideal candidates.

At the end of the shift, the entire workforce was assembled a few hundred yards away from the mine entrance, at the edge of a pit. They were addressed in their native dialect by the local militia leader under direct supervision of a Russian advisor. Aleksandr noted the quiet gloom that fell over the crowd. Death was in the air.

"What did he say?" Aleksandr asked.

"He said, 'This is what happens to thieves.'"

"Who are they?" Aleksandr asked, pointing to three people lined up across the pit from the gathered crowd: a woman who appeared to be in her thirties, an old man, and a boy who could not have been much more than ten. Their hands and feet were bound, and one leg was secured via chain to rusting chunks of metal. They were naked.

"Those are relatives of the three pilferers. The militia pulled them from the villages. This is the only language these barbarians understand."

The crowd started to protest and were silenced by a burst of automatic fire from a Russian advisor's AK fired skyward.

Aleksandr watched as a beat-up pickup truck was backed through the crowd, the three diamond thieves shackled naked to its bed. When they saw their relatives at the edge of the pit their primal screams pierced the air, arms tugging in a futile attempt to break free.

"Quite the deterrent," Dobrynin stated.

"*Da*, unpleasant but necessary," responded Petrovich.

Aleksandr remained unfazed, even as three guards climbed into the truck, grabbing the heads of the shackled prisoners and forcing them to watch their relatives across the pit be beaten with clubs until they could no longer resist. The woman was the strongest; it took several clubs to the head before her will to fight subsided enough for the men to pick up the heavy metal objects to which they were shacked and throw them into the pit.

The Dorylus, better known as safari ants, are found primarily in Central and

East Africa. Living in twenty-million-strong colonies they typically move from food source to food source throughout the year. These particular ants were fed well by design. They had no need to move. Their sting is incredibly painful, but the ants seldom use it; their jaws are strong enough to tear through the flesh of their prey. Indigenous people use them to close cuts that would require stitches in the developed world. Here, in the African bush, they would force the ant to bite on either side of a wound, breaking off the body and leaving the powerful mandibles in place to create a makeshift suture that could close the cut for days at a time.

The three thieves were forced to watch their loved ones thrash help-lessly about on the floor of the pit, the ravenous safari ants quickly covering their bodies. With no way to swat them off and anchored to the pit with what amounted to a ball and shackle, they endured the torture of being eaten alive. The old man's heart gave out well before the ants found their way into his brain through his eye sockets. The woman was lucky; she was all but brain dead from her clubbing before she hit the bottom of the pit. The boy, though, the boy's screams would haunt the crowd for the remainder of their lives, his high-pitched cries lasting over twenty minutes as he was slowly eaten by the insatiable in-sects. When his screams turned to a whimper and finally ended, the three thieves were shackled to iron balls that were then thrown into the pit, where they endured the same slow deaths as their relatives. Within minutes the three workers were covered with ants. Vain attempts to pull the shackles off amid primal screams and groans filled the evening air. Death took twenty minutes. Within an hour, bones were all that remained.

"That should keep them in line for another month," Petrovich stated.

"Do you have any other questions?" Dobrynin asked his guest.

Aleksandr shook his head.

Yes, the diamond mines would be perfect. Of those scheduled for execu-tion for smuggling the precious stones, Petrovich could keep one every now and then to feed to the ants as a warning. Those of sound mind and body would be airlifted to Aleksandr in Kamchatka, and then on to Medny Island.

There they would at least have a sporting chance.

CHAPTER 6

Old Town Alexandria, Virginia

KATIE BURANEK LEANED AGAINST the wall of her Old Town condo lost in thought, watching the raindrops hit the window and slide down to pool on the ledge. She cradled a glass of white wine in one hand while rubbing the cross around her neck with the other. She should have been contemplating her next move at the network. Did she want her own show or was she content to investigate the stories that interested her; ones she believed were of importance to the American people? Instead she was thinking of Reece, recovering in Montana and coming to terms with a future he thought didn't exist. Was she a part of that equation? Would he forever be haunted by visions of his wife and daughter, taken from him by a consortium of politicians, military officers, and private sector financiers? Or was Reece learning to live with their memory, his life a positive testament to their legacy?

Katie's eyes focused on a drop of rain as it hit the glass and trickled down the pane, weaving its way among its relatives, all born of the same gray clouds.

Thinking back to Reece's surgery, she felt a tinge of guilt for what she'd done afterwards, but before she could surrender to her feelings, she had needed to know the truth.

• • • •

"Can I see him now?" Katie asked the doctor.

It had not been lost on the reporter that establishing a relationship with Reece's female surgeon might allow her access not normally granted to non-family members. She had made sure the doctor had seen her with Reece on each of his visits for updated MRIs, CT Scans, X-rays, and pre-op procedures. Looking the part of the devoted girlfriend was intentional. She needed answers.

"He's just coming back out from under anesthesia. He'll be a bit groggy, but I know he can have visitors now."

It didn't hurt that Dr. Rosen was a big fan of Katie's book. The surgeon had seen enough soldiers, sailors, airmen, and marines come through Bethesda over the years to feel a kinship with them and know how they felt about Benghazi. Katie Buranek's debut nonfiction account, aptly titled *The Benghazi Betrayal*, pulled back the curtain on what had happened in the lead-up to the thirteen hours when a small group of CIA contractors fought for their lives while politicians half a world away, in no danger of being overrun, could hardly be bothered to respond to requests for reinforcements. The surgeon would not forget one of the SEALs who was killed that day. He was a corpsman she'd had the pleasure of getting to know in this very hospital when he was recovering from wounds sustained in Afghanistan before joining the Agency. Katie would get special treatment.

"How did it go," the young reporter asked.

"All things considered, I am extremely optimistic. Brain surgery of this type has evolved exponentially in recent years. We had an option to actually do this with a local anesthesia, though we usually do those for tumors situated close to the section of the brain that controls speech. In this case, due to the size and location we opted for general anesthesia, so he's been out for close to four hours now."

"Any side effects we need to worry about?" Katie asked, deliberately using "we."

"Well, he might not like his new haircut. We had to shave his head to remove a flap of bone to give us access to the brain to remove the meningioma. Everything is back in place. We'll keep him here tonight, maybe tomorrow depending on how he does, but he can start light exercise in about three weeks and ramp it up to his normal regimen in about six."

"Thank you for taking such good care of him."

"It's our pleasure, Katie."

"I'd love to be there for him when he wakes up."

"He's just down the hall. I'll be in to check on him shortly."

Katie slipped her laptop back into a bag and made her way down to the recovery room.

She shot a smile at the anesthesiologist as she entered.

"Hey, Dr. Port. How's our SEAL doing?"

"Just bringing him back now, Katie."

Dr. Port was a Katie fan as well. In his off time, he volunteered with the Maryland State Police SWAT team as a medic, so he was well acquainted with the community of law enforcement tactical response units often made up of military veterans. He was there to ensure nothing went wrong with his newest patient, who had become something of a legend in the small fraternity of special operations.

"He'll be dazed for a few minutes as the anesthesia wears off but will be back to his old self in no time. You're welcome to hang out here as long as you'd like. A nurse will be checking periodically, and Dr. Rosen will be in soon to evaluate. I'm sure they told you we will be keeping him overnight for observation but from what I understand, the surgery was extremely successful."

"Thank you, Doctor," Katie said, touching her hand to her heart.

"This is what we do, Katie. Dr. Rosen is one of the best in the world. Reece here was in good hands. I'll be back in a few."

Alone in the room, Katie looked down at the man who had saved her life more than a year ago. Bound and gagged, she remembered being forced to kneel on the floor of the Fishers Island mansion with strands of explosive det cord wrapped tightly around her neck. A CIA assassin in the employ of the federal government had pressed the button on a remote detonator connected to the explosive flexible cord. If his finger came off the button, she was dead. She was an insurance policy to ensure Reece did the right thing that night. She was in the room with him now to find out if he had.

Young for what she had accomplished thus far as a journalist, her series of stories on the Benghazi fiasco and the resulting bestseller opened doors and established her as an investigative journalist who would follow the truth, regardless of where it led. That is what she was after today: truth.

Who was James Reece? she wondered. Was he a domestic terrorist, as the government had proclaimed when they were desperately trying to find and kill him? A vigilante hell-bent on avenging his murdered wife, daughter, and unborn son? Was he a disgruntled veteran who brought the wars to the home front after the ambush of his SEAL Team in the mountains of Afghanistan? Was he her savior? Or would he have blown her head off to avenge his family? Was nothing sacred in that quest, including her?

Looking up and down the hall outside his room, she softly closed the door. Taking a seat next to his bed she took his hand in hers. Thumbs gently stroking either side of the IV imbedded in his vein, she thought back to that rainy night off the coast of Connecticut. She had been in a state of shock, her face bruised and bloodied, as Reece loaded her aboard a Pilatus aircraft that was to be their extract. She moved up the steps in a daze, her body exhausted as the adrenaline that had sustained her through the violence of the previous hours subsided. Her mind barely discerned the voices; they sounded muffled as if she were submerged in water with someone shouting at her from above. It had somehow registered that Reece was not coming with them.

As Reece stepped back to close the door, Katie had turned sharply in her seat and snapped out of her trance.

"Reece, how did you know Ben didn't have that detonator connected? How did you know he wouldn't blow my head off?"

Reece had paused, looked Katie in the eye, and over the sound of the wind, the propeller, and the rain, replied, "I didn't," before shutting the door and moving off at a run toward the marina.

I didn't. Those words had haunted Katie ever since.

She had masked her uncertainty since their reunion, waiting for the right time to conduct this interview. Her father had taught her that trust is the foundation of any relationship. He'd been a spy whose family was extracted from what was then Czechoslovakia by Reece's father. She knew Tom Reece had defied orders to bring them out and that if he hadn't, her father would have been executed and she would never have been born. Escaping to the United States in the 1980s, Katie's father had been, and still was, a big Ronald Reagan fan. *Trust but verify*, he had told his children.

Katie intended to verify.

Reece stirred, his eyes flittered, once, twice, and then opened to take in the vision that was Katie Buranek.

"Hey, sailor," she joked, knowing that even though Reece had spent his entire adult life in the navy, he would never consider himself a sailor. These days, the navy plowed through the world's oceans on computer chips powered by nuclear reactors; wind and sails were of a bygone era.

"Katie, you didn't have to wait." His voice was raspy from the breathing tubes that had kept him alive during the almost four-hour surgery. "But I'm glad you did," he added with a smile.

"Well, the anesthesiologist is kind of cute, so . . ."

Now was the moment of truth.

Having a father who had passed medical information to the Americans on top Czech party officials in the name of freedom meant she was well versed in the worlds of medicine and espionage. Katie had listened and learned.

Witnessing the Warsaw Pact's response to the Prague Spring in 1968, a young Dr. Buranek decided he did not want his family to live as he had under the iron fist of Soviet Bloc repression. The winds of change had started to blow. His position as a physician and surgeon for the party elite gave him access to medical records and sometimes put him in a position to ask certain questions after a surgery as his patients emerged from the fog of general anesthesia. The post-anesthesia phase, when they were uninhibited, was the time to elicit key pieces of information of interest to the CIA. Party officials were always guarded during medical procedures, but per human nature, the thugs in dark suits would occasionally slip up and turn away to flirt with a nurse, sneak a cigarette, or go to the bathroom. That was when Katie's father would work in a question passed to him by the Central Intelligence Agency. Reece was in that same phase of the post op drug sequence, though since the introduction of Versed fentanyl in 1990, the effects were even more dramatic. Sometimes called truth serum, Versed fentanyl was used for pain control and sedation in postop, a time when Reece would be most vulnerable and susceptible to questioning. Fentanyl was an opioid pain-killer while the Versed was an amnesic sedative that left a target ripe for an exploitation they would never remember; a controlled amnesia.

Of course, Katie could have just asked Reece over a dinner in Georgetown but then she remembered his eyes that night on Fishers Island as he fired four rounds into Ben Edwards's face. They were ice cold. No remorse. She needed to know with absolute certainty and the "truth serum" provided her the opportunity she needed. Katie knew the clock was ticking. With every second that went by the effects of the drugs would lessen. It was now or never.

"Reece," Katie inquired as naturally as possible, as if she were asking where he wanted to go for lunch, "when we were on Fishers Island, I asked you how you knew Ben didn't have the detonator connected to the explosives around my neck. Do you remember that?"

Reece's smile faded. He closed his eyes and nodded his head.

"Stay with me, Reece," she continued in her most soothing voice, continu-ing to stroke his hand. "Did you know it wasn't connected?"

Reece's eyes stayed closed and Katie was worried he had drifted off.

Damn it, this is my only chance.

"Reece, did you think it was connected?" Katie pressed.

"I knew," Reece said, opening his eyes to look into hers, before closing them again.

Shit, rookie move, which question was he answering? Did he know or not?

Katie's head snapped toward the door at the sound of approaching voices. *Shit.*

They'd be at the room any moment. She had to know.

She just needed a few more seconds.

Spinning in her chair, she looked for a way to lock the door. *Nothing. Are you kidding me?* Frantically she scanned the room. She had been with her father in enough hospitals to know that as high-occupancy facilities, the doors were all required to be auto closing. However, the fire code and the practical necessities of efficiently running a hospital were often at odds. In violation of the fire code, auto-closing doors had to be kept manually open so doctors and nurses could move up and down the halls checking on patients. Seeing a rubber door stop, she grabbed it and shoved it under the door, kicking it securely in place before once again taking up her position at Reece's bedside.

"You knew what, Reece?" she asked, switching back to a calm, inquisitive tone.

Reece murmured something almost inaudible.

"What?" she asked, leaning in closer.

"I knew it wasn't connected."

Katie's body visibly trembled. All the months of pent-up wonder and doubt were answered through the side effects of narcotically induced slumber.

She heard a hand shaking the doorknob followed by the concerned voice of the nurse, "Excuse me. Excuse me!" She heard from the hallway.

Just a few more questions. *Damn it.*

"Reece, how did you know?"

Nothing.

"How did you know, Reece?" Katie pressed on, now hearing another set of hands rapping urgently on the door frame and knowing she had only a scant few moments before Reece emerged from his haze.

In a whisper Reece answered through the drugs, "Ben was standing too close. The blasting cap. The PETN in the det cord. He was too close."

The knocks were now joined by another voice at the door.

She would not get another chance, so she pressed on ignoring what now must have been causing a scene in the hallway.

"Reece," Katie continued with a bit more urgency in her voice, "why did you say that night on Fishers that you didn't know? Why did you make me think that all these months?"

Still in the land between dreams and reality, the Versed fentanyl lowering inhibitions to a level where, no matter the answer, all would be right with the world, Reece responded truthfully, "I didn't want you waiting on me, Katie. I was going to die that night and I didn't want you to feel loss the way I had."

Katie gulped, her eyes misting over, suddenly aware of a tightening in her chest.

Suddenly aware again of the banging outside, she rose and gracefully crossed the room, opening the door to the concerned faces of Dr. Rosen, Dr. Port, the nurse, and a security guard.

"I am so sorry. We just needed some privacy."

"Ms. Buranek, you can't block the door to the room," a clearly agitated Dr. Rosen lectured, as she and Dr. Port moved to Reece's side to check the monitors attached via wires and tubes to his body.

Putting on her most demure and apologetic smile, Katie lowered her head. "I really do apologize. I just did not want a special moment interrupted."

"It's okay, Doc," Reece said groggily, struggling to push himself up to his elbows, "We had to discuss something here in the SCIF."

Dr. Rosen's demeanor softened. "Well, don't do that again, frogman, or I'll have you keel-hauled."

"Aye, aye, Doc." Reece smiled, attempting to raise his hand in salute but only managing to lift it a few inches off the bed.

"It's okay," Dr. Rosen assured the security guard who didn't know quite what to do in the presence of the cable news personality and the man whose face had been plastered on televisions and newspapers across the country just over a year ago. "I'll take it from here."

"Yes, ma'am," he replied, walking back into the hall.

"You just rest up, Commander," the doctor said, switching into military mode. "Katie, you can stay here with him if you'd like. Just promise me you will not bar the door again, no matter what powers of persuasion he attempts to exert."

"I'll be on my guard."

As Dr. Port injected a micro dose of narcotic into Reece's IV to assist with the transition out of his dream state, Dr. Rosen turned to Katie. "He'll be up and walking around in a few hours, if you can believe that. He's going to be fine."

"Thank you, Doctor."

Moving toward the hallway with Dr. Port, the surgeon stopped and turned back toward Katie, who had again taken up residence at Reece's side. "I hope you got the answer you were looking for, Ms. Buranek."

Not taking her eyes off the frogman who had appeared to drift back to sleep, Katie replied, "I did."

Alone again in the recovery room, Katie wondered if Reece remembered her questions. If so, she knew that memory would soon dissolve along with the remaining mixture of Versed fentanyl.

"Rest up, James. I'll be here when you wake up."

CHAPTER 7

ALEKSANDR ZHARKOV WASN'T SURE what his father was up to, but as the deputy director of Directorate S in the nation's Foreign Intelligence Service, his ability to assist him was substantial. That was the entire reason he held the post; to be the eyes and ears of the *bratva*. Directorate S was responsible for the illegal intelligence operations of the former KGB: deploying strategic long term deep-cover operatives into foreign countries. They were more commonly referred to as sleeper agents. He commanded the nation's most effective assassins.

Aleksandr knew that citizens of the West were getting soft. Most of them believed the red threat had ended with the collapse of the Soviet Union and that Russian spies were now only found in eighties movies. The truth was that the SVR had more sleeper agents imbedded throughout the United States and Europe than they ever had during the Cold War. The open borders of the European Union and America's current obsession with terrorism left them vulnerable for penetration. They remained blind even when sleeper cells were activated to kill Ukrainian military intelligence officers in 2017, a former employee of the current Russian president on the streets of Washington, D.C., in 2015, and almost one person a year in Great Britain since the beginning of the decade.

Unlike traditional intelligence officers, illegals lived a complete lie. Instead of operating under a semilegitimate "cover for status" position, usually a job at the embassy or consulate, illegals had to enter a nation with little aid from their own government and blend into their new country. Aleksandr knew he would have been a brilliant illegal because he had mastered the lie; he could do it without the slightest hint of remorse. As was his father's wish, he had run illegals at postings across the world, and his success had driven him rapidly up the ranks of Directorate S, eventually landing him back in Russia in a position to pass intelligence to the family business. Aleksandr could create virtually bulletproof false identities as well as produce legitimate Russian Federation passports to match them. For someone trying to smuggle a person across international borders, Aleksandr Zharkov could work magic.

A posting in the intelligence world might seem like a strange place for the son of a mafia boss, but in Russia, as Aleksandr knew, there was a long history of associations between the government and organized crime that predated their Sicilian counterparts by almost a century. From the czars to Stalinist Russia through the waning days of the Soviet Union and into the heyday after the fall, the Red Mafia was imbedded in almost all facets of state affairs. The *bratva* was not an outside criminal threat, but rather part of the government itself. When Stalin betrayed his criminal ties during the Great Purge, he inadvertently created an even stronger organization that had survived and thrived to this day. What might raise eyebrows in other parts of the world was business as usual for the Russian Federation. Aleksandr was simply continuing the tradition.

The director had what he described as a "functional" relationship with his mob boss father, but there was an underlying rift between them that went beyond the traditional father-son power struggle, a chasm that developed when Aleksandr was still a boy.

Ivan had insisted that his eldest son pursue a career in the nation's intelligence services, a career that would surely pay dividends for his father's business interests. Aleksandr had sacrificed his entire adult life climbing the ladder of the SVR, a ladder that had led him through countless third-world hellholes, places where not too many questions were asked when a man went missing.

Meanwhile, his two younger brothers lived the good life, chasing women, driving fast cars, and putting coke up their noses in Paris, London, New York, and Miami. His father promised him that, in the long run, he would be the *Pakhan* and his brothers would be his lieutenants. Yet, year after year, his brothers rose in influence, building their own networks. Aleksandr knew that he was too valuable to his father in his current position to leave and that his younger siblings at this point would not let him simply walk in and take what they now considered theirs. Aleksandr felt the pull born of a primal instinct from a time when people lacked the ability to reason, when they were no different from every other animal roaming the earth. Civilization was a more recent introduction to the evolution of the species. Despite that thin veneer, instinct still requires the young bull to exert his dominance over the herd. That time was approaching for the Zharkov line, and Aleksandr would soon make his move.

CHAPTER 8

Saint Petersburg, Russia

SEVEN HUNDRED KILOMETERS TO the northwest, Ivan Zharkov had left Oliver Grey in the suite, giving him a chance to bathe, rest, and recover from his travels. Prostitution was one of the *Bratva*'s primary rackets, and the mafia boss had offered Grey a woman for the night. Upon Grey's refusal, Ivan had offered him a man. Grey graciously declined both, which caused some confusion on the part of his host. The embarrassment of Grey's one sexual encounter with a female was an experience that he did not wish to repeat.

The vodka left Grey buzzing, but after a long bath in the room's extravagant tub, he felt almost human again. He was beginning to doze when a knock on the door sent a surge of adrenaline through his body. Wrapped in a bathrobe, he peered through the peephole and spied a small bearded man carrying an attaché case.

"Can I help you?"

"I am Lev, the tailor. *Pakhan* sent me."

Grey breathed a sigh of relief and opened the door. He had half-expected to see a tall American holding a suppressed pistol instead of the small, potbellied man impeccably dressed in a three-piece suit. The tailor walked into the room without shaking Grey's hand and began to unpack the tools of his trade. Lev insisted that Grey remove the robe and began taking measurements with a physician's disinterest in his stark nudity. Each measurement was entered into a small notebook with a small stub of a pencil. Grey was embarrassed and spoke nervously as the man worked, ignoring his attempts at conversation as though they didn't speak the same language.

"Put on your robe, we need to pick fabrics," Lev said as he snapped the small notebook shut and wrapped it with a thick rubber band. He spread books of swatches across the bed and motioned for Grey to examine them.

"Mr. Zharkov has generously paid for three suits and five shirts. I will make you more, if you choose, but they will come from your own pocket."

Grey spent close to an hour narrowing his choices, ultimately picking a brown tweed, a charcoal window pane, and a blue chalk line. He didn't want to look like another one of Zharkov's security men. He chose plain, solid shirts that would keep his life simple; he knew better than to tackle the daily challenge of matching his clothes.

"I do not make shoes or ties. For those items, you should go to the Passage on Nevsky Prospekt. It is not far." The man looked at the small gold watch on his wrist. "These items will be ready in two days." He quickly packed his bag, returned his black Homburg to his head, and walked swiftly out the door.

It was late afternoon when Grey stepped out of the hotel and began a lei-surely half-hour walk toward the city's upscale shopping district.

You are safe here, Oliver. There is no need to worry.

Though he had only been to Saint Petersburg a handful of times, always on CIA business, he felt strangely at home here.

He absorbed the splendor of Saint Petersburg as he wound his way through the streets, admiring the intricate Baroque and neoclassical architecture. His path took him onto the Nevsky Prospekt and across the narrow Fontanka River via the Anichov Bridge. He took a small detour to walk the grounds of the Alex-andrinsky Theatre, filled with mothers watching their bundled-up children play-ing in the park. Taking a seat on a bench at the edge of the Mikhailovsky Garden, he packed his pipe and tried to relax. The city was alive. It was hard to believe there was a time not that long ago when Russia's cultural capital was almost de-stroyed by the Axis powers in World War II, back when it went by the name Leningrad. Grey seemed to remember that snipers were somehow associated with the siege, or was that Stalingrad? The thought of snipers caused Grey to abruptly move from his bench and continue toward his destination. He looked up at the surrounding buildings, half-expecting to see James Reece behind a scope. The analyst in him attempted to banish the notion.

Reece could never find me here. I am now protected by the bratva.

Grey crossed the street and walked the remaining block to the Passage, an upscale shopping arcade that dated back to the 1840s. As he strolled through the long building, all marble and plaster, peering into the hand-painted plate glass windows of the various shops, Grey felt transported to a different era. The building was a striking example of Russian prominence with its intricate tile floor, detailed dentil interior trim, and vaulted glass ceiling. Most of the customers displayed noticeable signs of wealth: oversize ornate watches for the men and long furs, high-end handbags, and diamonds for the women. Everyone chatted on iPhones as they shopped. The proceeds of Russia's raw materials—oil, natural gas, gold, copper, and magnesium—extracted by tough, filthy men who drank hard and died young, were converted by the nation's elite into hard currency that flowed through luxury arteries such as this one. Grey's family had always been at the base of this class pyramid, but he was working his way up.

He took his time shopping, carefully selecting the ties, socks, underwear, and T-shirts that would comprise his new wardrobe. He completed the ensemble with a frightfully expensive pair of shoes that put a significant dent in his stack of euros. Each vendor made change in rubles, allowing him to accumulate local currency without having to deal with the formality of banks.

He found a barbershop and spent some of his new money on a haircut and a beard trim. The heavily tattooed staff were all young men who obviously spent a great deal of time and effort emulating the appearance of American hipsters; it seemed that one could not escape the West's cultural poison even in Mother Russia. Two men lounged on the black pleather couch in the corner, playing a soccer video game on a large LCD television monitor that hung on the exposed brick wall. Grey spoke little but listened intently, trying to gather as much practical knowledge as possible about his new home. He had done his best to enjoy the day, but a gnawing sensation that he couldn't seem to erase continually interrupted his contentment.

The vodkas he downed with dinner did nothing to shake his feelings of impending doom. He stumbled more than once in his haste to return to the safety of his hotel, his eyes darting from shadow to shadow and rooftop to rooftop, the specter of James Reece his constant companion.

CHAPTER 9

Kumba Ranch, Flathead Valley, Montana

REECE CRANKED THE POWERFUL motor on his new Cruiser and listened to it hum. He pulled out of the garage and gunned the motor as he turned up the steep grade, testing the vehicle's torque as it climbed. It responded instantly and flew up the gravel track, spitting rocks as it went. He crested the ridge and took it slowly down the switchbacks. No sense flipping his new ride on the first day.

He hit the ranch's main road and turned in the direction of the refurbished barn that Raife used as his workshop, a twenty-minute trip by vehicle.

The two friends had joined the navy a year apart, taking separate paths until finally serving together in Ramadi, Iraq, at the height of the war. When their task unit lost two SEALs to a roadside bomb, Raife went off the reservation, using their tactical HUMINT network to find the IED cell leader responsible, a man named Hakim Al-Maliki. He then used that same network to deliver a package to the terrorist after a sanctioned raid to capture him was called off by higher authority. Al-Maliki was a CIA asset and his value as a long-term penetration agent meant he was off-limits as a target. The device that sent Al-Maliki to the afterlife contained a fertilizer-based main charge with commercial detonators from Pakistan, an IED profile common to Ramadi at the time. The CIA was furious, accusing Raife of killing their prized asset and demanding he be prosecuted. The navy had not been sure what to do and immediately launched an investigation. Reece was the only person who could identify Raife as the bomber and he refused to cooperate with investigators, causing no shortage of consternation between the navy and the CIA and between Reece and Raife. Raife didn't want to see Reece's reputation tarnished by investigations, and Reece wasn't about to be a witness against his blood brother.

Due in no small part to his friend's refusal to provide any useful information to investigators and out of concern for the damage it could do if the facts of the case became public, Raife was eventually cleared of the accusation. The CIA protecting an insurgent responsible for blowing up members of the U.S. military, long-term penetration agent or not, would not play well in the court of public opinion. *Wasn't the job of SEALs to kill terrorists?*

Raife was removed from theater and assigned to the Naval Special Warfare Cold Weather Warfare Detachment on Kodiak Island in Alaska. There he put his ample outdoor skills to use training new SEALs to survive and thrive in the austere climate of the North. It was a perfect fit for the adopted son of Montana but, as an officer, he couldn't stay in the job indefinitely. He had grown tired of watching men and women come home from endless wars in Iraq and Afghanistan physically and emotionally broken; it was time to move on. When he received orders to move into a staff role down in Coronado, he dropped his papers and resigned his commission.

He first took a job in finance, throwing himself into it with the same zeal with which he had attacked all of life's challenges, but he felt suffocated by life in Manhattan. Raife was rushing to the office one day when he received a text message telling him that his old team chief at ███████ had shot himself in the heart. He'd left a suicide note apologizing to his wife and children and asking that his brain be used to study the effects of traumatic brain injury and PTSD. After two weeks in Virginia Beach assisting the family and attending the memorial and funeral, Raife decided it was time to go home.

As Raife made the long drive from New York to western Montana, his mind went to work. He needed to find a way to help transition his former teammates into life beyond the fight, a bridge to the next chapter in life. You couldn't just hand them a suit and help them write a resume; they needed to find purpose again.

Raife also examined his own life. A natural loner who thrived in the solitude of the outdoors, Raife still knew something was missing.

Annika Thornton had been his on-again, off-again girlfriend since high school. Their fathers were close friends and adjoining landowners in many of their real estate holdings. It had been Annika's father, Tim, who had encouraged Jonathan Hastings to diversify his cattle earnings into Montana real estate; that move had proven to be vastly more lucrative than ranching. While Raife chose to attend the University of Montana in Missoula, Annika was accepted to Yale, and they drifted apart. When Raife was based in Virginia Beach and she was in graduate school at Wharton in Philadelphia, their relationship rekindled, and Raife had nearly proposed.

When he received word that he'd earned a coveted slot at Green Team, his personal life was forced to the back burner. Annika took a job in San Francisco and, soon after that, 9/11 hit. Raife's life was focused on his endless overseas deployments, and hers was spent making her own way in the business world. They kept in touch and reunited whenever their geographic paths crossed.

When it came time for her father, Tim "Thorn" Thornton, to pull back on the reins of life and spend some time away from the business, he was finally able to convince Annika to return to Montana. She was serving as the chief operating officer of a Dallas-based energy firm and on a path to be the company's first female CEO. She had proven to herself and everyone else that she could be successful on her own. No one would doubt her ability to serve as president of the family's vast petroleum and real estate empire. The two childhood sweethearts were finally back in big-sky country.

The wedding of Tim Thornton's only daughter could have been a lavish affair, the formal joining of two families who were some of Montana's largest and wealthiest landowners. Instead they opted for more subdued nuptials at Raife's uncle's hunting operation in Niassa Game Reserve, Mozambique.

When the newlyweds returned from a three-week honeymoon that took them across South Africa from Cape Town to a private game reserve in the Sabi Sands, Raife went to work building the next chapter in his life. Both the Hastings and Thornton families had been leasing their land to hunting outfitters for years, and some had been more dedicated than others when it came to managing the natural resources. Raife built a plan that would sustainably manage the ranches' wildlife while providing a path forward for his fellow special operations veterans.

He consolidated all of the leases into a single outfitting business that handled everything from the booking of the clients to the processing and shipping of the meat. There were a surprising number of closet hunters among his associates in the world of New York finance and, thanks to his time spent on Wall Street, he rapidly built a steady stream of clients. Word spread quickly that Raife delivered a high-quality outdoor experience, and he soon had a waiting list.

A hunting operation is only as good as its guides and that was an area where Raife was able to differentiate himself from the rest of the industry. He hired the best outdoorsmen he had served with in the military, including several of the instructors from Kodiak. They were hardworking, competent, reliable, and fun to be around; the clients loved them, and they delivered. The guides received a steady stream of income while finding time to take a breath and evaluate their priorities outside the world of special operations. Raife's goal was to connect successful businessmen, entrepreneurs, and financiers with hardened operators. This created an informal network that became known as Warrior/Guardians. Those in the private sector connected to a community of talent that was unprecedented in modern society and that was often shrouded in secrecy. Both groups recognized the value in bridging the divide between those who did the fighting and those who paid for it, and more than a few internships, businesses, foundations, and fresh starts were born under the Montana skies. When the operation began hosting wounded veterans on hunts as part of a foundation funded by successful clients, the guides found even greater purpose. Bonding under the stars, these men and women, many of whom had been grievously injured by IEDs, began healing the emotional wounds of war.

The business was doing well and was financially viable, but Raife and his guide team quickly realized that they had a problem on their hands: many of their clients, successful individuals who led busy lives, couldn't shoot very well. Wounding animals was unacceptable so, in typical Hastings fashion, Raife made a plan. He hired retiring instructors from the SEAL sniper school in Indiana to design and implement a hunter training program on one of Thorn's properties outside Missoula. He made attendance a prerequisite for booking a hunt and client performance improved drastically. Once word got out, the school took on a life of its own and was soon making more money than the outfitting business. Ironically, government contracts with special operations units provided the school's most reliable clients.

The final piece fell into place when Raife was personally guiding a client who had drawn a once-in-a-lifetime Rocky Mountain bighorn sheep tag in the Missouri Breaks. After a tough stalk, the client's expensive custom rifle went "click" when it should have gone "bang," and the old ram that they'd been tracking for days gave them the slip. Working in the dark by headlamp back in camp that night, Raife diagnosed the problem. His discriminating eye noted several issues, all of which came as a shock to the client. The hunter asked Raife if he'd be willing to build him a dependable rifle and the former SEAL's career as a custom gun maker was born.

Reece pulled his Land Cruiser in front of the structure that served as the gun making shop and parked next to Raife's Defender. He opened the metal shop door quietly; Raife's eyes never lifted from his work as his friend entered his domain. The space was large but not excessively so and was filled with the various tools of the trade. Reece expected to see modern computer-controlled machinery but, instead, found himself among aging but well-maintained equipment with names like Bridgeport and Hardinge, relics of America's industrial age. The cast iron hulks were painted a glossy gray and looked like something that one would encounter in the machine shop of a navy ship. There were rifles on a rack in various stages of completion, numerous workbenches, and a hand-loading table stacked with the tools necessary for loading precision ammunition. A blue Dillon press for handgun rounds sat next to a heavy green single-stage used for rifle cartridges. Boxes of dies lined the cabinet above.

Raife was wearing a jeweler's magnified optivisor over the worn ball cap that he'd turned backward to accommodate the device. He stood over a waist-high bench vise, focused on the partially shaped blank of French walnut that was clamped inside its cork-covered jaws. He wore a heavy leather apron and his blackened hands held a small chisel.

"There's coffee," Raife said, nodding his head toward a desk against the wall without moving his eyes from his work. "Sorry, no honey."

Reece chuckled as he poured the steaming liquid into an enameled mug painted with the Black Rifle Coffee Company's logo. He took a seat on a stool a few feet away from Raife and watched as his friend coated a rifle's action and barrel with a thin black sludge using a small paintbrush. He then lowered the steel into the inletting of the walnut stock and tapped it with a rawhide mallet. He lifted the barreled action and examined the inletting, taking note of where the black oil had marked the raw wood. A dozen chisels, gouges, and scrapers were strewn on the bench in front of him and he selected one. He made a series of small cuts with the razor-sharp tool before retrieving the barrel and repeating the process all over again. Reece always appreciated watching true artisans at their craft and he sat silently as Raife focused, gently inletting the metal work into the wooden stock so that the two became seamlessly joined.

Finally satisfied, Raife turned off the lamp above his work and breathed a sigh of relief.

"How long does it take?" Reece asked.

"The inletting? A few hours."

"No, the whole rifle."

"I'll probably have two hundred fifty hours in this one by the time it's ready."

"That's like two months."

"Six weeks, but you never were a numbers guy. Yeah, it's a lot of work, which is why I don't sell them cheap."

"What will that rifle run?"

"About fifty grand."

"Rich kid shit." Reece smiled.

"That it is."

"Where'd you learn to build rifles?"

"Back in Africa you had to be self-reliant to survive, so I learned from doing.

I wanted to get the trade right, so I spent six months apprenticing with D'Arcy Echols in Utah."

"He built the .300 Win Mag my dad gave me."

"He's the one; best there is. Jerry Fisher down in Big Fork put me in touch with him. For two months all he let me do was sweep the floor and polish metal; my rite of passage, I guess. Then he took me under his wing."

"He sure can build a tack driver. I need to track down that rifle. Not sure what happened to it when I skipped town."

"It's in my vault."

"What? How'd you get it?"

"Liz gave it to me. You left it in her plane along with some other gear. I hid it until you got pardoned so they couldn't use it as evidence."

"That was nice of you."

"Don't mention it. Figured if you got killed or went to prison, I'd at least have a nice rifle."

Reece frowned. "By the way, I noticed an interesting article in a *Petersen's Hunting* magazine in the cabin."

"Did you?" Raife asked.

"Looked like one of the photos was taken right across my lake. Written by S. Rainsford. You wouldn't happen to know him, would you?"

Raife offered a rare half smile.

"Good catch. I do some outdoor writing under that pen name. Most don't get the reference today. Just trying to avoid the stigma of being another SEAL author. Let's go get you your rifle, eh?"

Reece briefly wondered if his urge to hold the rifle again was because it was one of the few tangible links left to his father or perhaps something darker. The last time he'd pressed its trigger he'd sent a bullet through the brain of one of the men who had masterminded the death of his wife and child. He'd made the killing look like a hunting accident in order to buy the time he needed to cross the remaining names off his terminal list.

Later that night, Reece sat alone by a fire at the water's edge, the Echols Legend across his lap. He alternated his gaze between the empty chair to his right and the mountains across the lake, a wilderness he'd never explore with his wife, daughter, or unborn son. He remained unmoving but for his finger slowly caressing the outside edge of the trigger guard, the fire dying to embers, glowing only when the wind picked up off the lake.

As the sun rose the following morning, Reece's finger continued to stroke the trigger guard, his only companions the memories of the dead.

CHAPTER 10

Saint Petersburg, Russia

IVAN ZHARKOV PUT DOWN the newspaper and took a sip of his tea. He sat in a leather armchair in his bedroom, unable to sleep. His late wife would have chastised him for taking caffeine this late, but it didn't make any difference. It wasn't the powerful stimulant, nor was it the demands of his position as one of Russia's most powerful figures in organized crime that robbed him of his rest: it was Aleksandr.

His eldest son's birth had been a difficult one for Katrina, and the depression that followed had been even worse. Ivan was too busy to notice but, in hindsight, she and the child never formed the crucial bond between mother and child. Katrina would stare out the window as the child cried, attending to his physical needs when necessary but never nurturing his emotional ones. She became cold, distant, unattached. When she took her life with a .25 ACP Korovin TK pistol, it was a young Aleksandr who found her, lying in bed after just having finished the last page of *Sofia Petrovna*. When Ivan entered the room and grabbed his young child to shield him from the grisly sight of his dead mother, he thought the boy was in shock. He didn't accept until years later that it wasn't shock; it was curiosity.

Aleksandr remained a mystery to the elder Zharkov. The boy was bright and handsome and, from the outside, was everything a father could want. Inside, though, there was a darkness. Aleksandr could be cruel to his younger brothers, even when they were quite young; their nannies had to protect them from him. His actions weren't out of anger or jealousy; rather, they were for amusement.

On their first hunt, north of Moscow in the ancient forests of the Yaroslavl District, Ivan's worst fears were confirmed. They had taken the train together and ten-year-old Aleksandr had watched the country pass by the large windows in silence. It was a beautiful October day when the father and son ventured out from their cabin. This was a traditional European driven hunt, meaning the hunters were assigned stands or positions and the animals were pushed in their direction using hounds. Ivan's peg was a hundred or so yards away from Aleksandr's, far enough away to give the boy some independence but close enough to keep an eye on him. To commemorate the hunt, Ivan had given his son a custom 8x57mm Mauser sporting rifle that Ivan's father had brought back from the Great Patriotic War, no doubt looted from a German officer. The rifle was deeply engraved in the Germanic style and had been fitted with set triggers and a Zeiss scope in claw mounts, a testament to the proud tradition of Teutonic gun making. Aleksandr had long admired the rifle in his father's cabinet and was delighted to now call it his own. Since so few things seemed to bring him joy, it warmed Ivan's heart to see his son's eyes brighten.

The distant bark of the hounds grew louder as the game was driven before them. A boar sped toward Ivan and pitched forward as he made a perfect running shot. The sound ringing in his ears in the stillness of the morning, Ivan saw a brown blur to his right. *Moose!* A second later, he heard the report of Aleksandr's rifle and the unmistakable sound of a bullet striking flesh. There was silence and then a crash, no doubt the sound of the moose collapsing. It was a break of protocol to leave one's stand before the drive was finished but Ivan wanted to be by his son's side. He jogged toward the sound of the crash, his eyes searching for a sign of either hunter or prey.

He saw the moose first, crippled with a spine shot and struggling in vain to drag itself away from its tormentor. The large mammal dwarfed young Aleksandr, and Ivan was afraid that the moose would stomp the youngster or bludgeon him with his palmated spread of antler. But, as he approached, his concern turned to disgust; Aleksandr stood without fear, watching the animal writhe in agony. He was smiling. Ivan ran to the front of the animal to give himself a safe shot and fired a round into the bull's chest, dropping him to the ground and putting an end to his suffering.

Turning to face his son, Ivan slowly took possession of the Mauser, chilled by the hatred he saw burning in his child's eyes. That hatred directed toward Ivan for ending the animal's agony prematurely would haunt the mafia boss for the remainder of his days.

CHAPTER 11

Petersburg Petroleum Company, Saint Petersburg, Russia

GREY HAD BEEN SURPRISED by the location of his office. He knew that Zharkov effectively controlled the regional oil firm, but he wouldn't have imagined that he would find himself working openly in the headquarters of a publicly traded company. His morning commute was a relatively easy one from his flat near the city's center. His office was only a few blocks from the Piskaryovka rail station, in an industrial section of town.

Zharkov expected immediate results and Grey delivered. The first order of business was to turn over the names of all the men and women in Zharkov's organization, many of them residing in the United States, who were known FBI and CIA informants. Each would then be analyzed and evaluated for possible blackmail or the most permanent of solutions as a warning to others.

As he settled into his routine, he found it was strangely similar to his time at Langley. Delivering some quick wins for Zharkov's organization provided him a little leniency in terms of how he spent his time and resources; his most important project was a personal one.

Feeling dapper in his custom suit, he strode with a newfound confidence that would have shocked his coworkers at the Agency. He used his access card to enter the building and took the elevator to the executive level. As he passed her cubicle outside his office, he bid good day to his administrative assistant,

Svetlana, a sturdy and attractive widow a few years his senior. She doted on him in a manner that he hadn't enjoyed since childhood, taking his coat as he walked by and fetching him tea or coffee without so much as an ask. She would straighten his tie and brush lint from the shoulders of his new suits, doing everything but licking her fingers before fixing his hair.

With no social life or family to distract him, Grey devoted every waking second to his new cause: finding James Reece. His analytical brain examined seemingly endless mountains of information. He scoured the media accounts of Reece's one-man war that had left a trail of bodies from California to Wyoming, from the southern tip of Florida to the stormy New England coast. From there Reece had vanished, only to reappear in Odessa, Ukraine, where Grey had seen him before the assassination of the former Russian president.

Other than a few media references to the presidential pardon that had been issued the previous fall, James Reece was a ghost. The White House had refused to provide justification for the act, citing "national security concerns," but the mere existence of that pardon all but proved Reece's involvement in thwarting the attack on the U.S. president. Save a powerful man's life and he'll forget about the few murders you committed along the way.

Having exhausted his media search, Grey shifted his focus to sifting through the dry minutiae that was his specialty. A detailed search of property records led to no surviving family members. Reece was an only child and Grey had arranged his father's death years earlier. According to an obituary run in the Flagstaff, Arizona, newspaper, his mother had died in a nursing home a few months ago. The only existing property record was for his home in Coronado, and Grey confirmed that Reece was not living there. If he'd purchased a home or a car, Grey would have found it. He'd never registered on any social media platforms and didn't appear to even own a traceable telephone or have an email address. The whiteboard of Grey's office was covered with every detail he could gather from Reece's past, an algorithm of names, places, and dates. So far, he couldn't find the X, but he knew it was only a matter of time.

CHAPTER 12

ALEKSANDR PULLED OPEN HIS desk drawer and drew out a small braided loop of hair, a memento of his first *real* hunt. He had been training at the Institute when he realized how much pleasure it gave him to inflict pain on his fellow human beings. As a young and attractive male recruit, he was chosen for the famed SVR program that trained students in the art of what they unofficially termed *sexpionage*. The course's goal was to position the illegal agents to manipulate assets of foreign governments or corporations using their bodies. Because fetishes made for excellent blackmail material, much of the course focused on spotting individuals with unusual or even bizarre sexual preferences.

According to the instructors, it was not uncommon for Western women in positions of influence to seek out men who would dominate and even humiliate them behind closed doors. Deep down, it seemed, these women wanted to play a subservient role to a man. Many of them liked to be choked during sex and students were taught to give them the sensation of actual asphyxiation without causing any permanent physical harm; it was a fine line. Aleksandr found himself wondering if any of what the instructors said about powerful women was true but quickly brushed the thought aside. In the SVR, one did not question authority.

Unlike in the movies, the practical applications of these lessons were not performed in front of the class but took place in a bedroom with an instructor or coach standing by. The entire sessions were filmed for later feedback. It began simply enough, with a fellow student playing the role of the female asset. Ordinary intercourse took a turn when the female began asking to be called filthy names, which Aleksandr complied with. She then requested that he tug on her hair and slap her, just as she had been instructed. Aleksandr struck the side of her head with an open hand above the hairline so as not to bruise her face and felt an immediate jolt of arousal. He struck her harder and harder, knocking her nearly unconscious before he finally wrapped his powerful hands around her throat.

His hands became a vise and he felt himself engorge with a fresh course of blood flow as an erotic switch was thrown somewhere in his brain. His female counterpart began to gasp for air and her face flushed bright red and then purple, the veins and arteries of her neck standing ropelike under her skin. She coughed out the safe word, indicating her desire to discontinue the exercise, but that only drove him to squeeze harder. The instructor stepped in and tried to pull Aleksandr's hands from her throat but he was in a frenzy of arousal that added to his already considerable physical strength. The instructor yelled for help as the female student began to lose consciousness and, within seconds, three men were prying him from his victim.

One of the men delivered a powerful blow to Aleksandr's kidney, just as he was reaching his climax, his knees buckling in a combination of ecstasy and pain. He was dragged from the room naked as the instructors attended to the female student's medical needs. Aleksandr was removed from the course pending an investigation, and only his father's significant political influence prevented him from being summarily dismissed. The emotional scars of that event caused the female student to voluntarily drop from the program and, after years of substance abuse to self-medicate the trauma of the event from her conscious mind, she eventually died of a heroin overdose.

For Aleksandr, his international postings became his hunting grounds, first for the region's game, and then for people. It began with the killing of a prostitute in Hungary. Law enforcement officials begrudgingly investigated the murder, a small-caliber bullet to the head, but, thanks to his advanced tradecraft, false identities, and frequent movement, the killing remained unsolved. The murder of women involved in the sex trade in the developing world was not an uncommon occurrence. This sad truth allowed Aleksandr to move among the unwanted, hunting and killing for sport in back alleys and motel rooms in countries difficult to find on a map. Though Aleksandr fancied himself a hunter, criminologists would have another term for him: serial killer.

When his early human prey lost their appeal, Aleksandr needed a new challenge, and it was during an assignment in Asia that he found it. A contact in Bangkok led him to an illegal hunting operation in Myanmar, long before a cease-fire agreement ended the nation's sixty-year civil war. Poaching was rampant in the vacuum left in the absence of a national government. He had been promised the freedom to pursue endangered animals, including the Asiatic black bear and leopard. The local guides were talented hunters, but the area was simply shot out in terms of game. The outfitter offered him a village girl as a consolation prize, which Aleksandr accepted. It wasn't until they brought her to the camp that he realized she was not just another female being forced to fulfill his sexual desires. She had been accused of cheating on her husband and her punishment was death. Aleksandr was being offered the thrill of hunting a human being.

She was released, barefoot and terrified, into a jungle clearing at midnight and allowed to run through the night to make her escape. The temperature was already soaring when they found her tracks at dawn, her tiny feet making deep impressions as she ran. Aleksandr had hunted his entire life but had never felt such adrenaline, even when killing whores. He knew he would never again feel any real passion for pursuing four-legged beasts. They had to bring in hounds when her tracks disappeared in a thickly canopied boulder field; the ancient monoliths offered no sign of her footsteps.

The dogs had her bayed in a tree by lunchtime, their deafening barks making the scene all the more chaotic. The guide offered Aleksandr a battered AK, but he refused it; the gun would be too quick an end.

He took a *dha,* a simple but effective swordlike machete, from one of the trackers and began to pelt his terrified and dehydrated prey with stones. She shouted out in agony as one of the rocks struck her knee. A well-placed stone to her temple knocked her unconscious and she fell limply from her lofty perch, striking the ground with a hollow thud. The baying barks of the dogs rose to a fever pitch, and Aleksandr yelled for their handlers to drag them back so that they could not attack his kill.

A painful slash of the *dha* across her naked thigh shocked the girl awake. Aleksandr paused and looked into her eyes; her enlarged pupils revealed nothing but terror. The pleasure receptors in Aleksandr's brain sparked and flushed his body with endorphins. Holding the blade downward in a two-handed grip, he pushed it slowly into her bony chest, feeling the last beats of her heart pulsing through the blade.

CHAPTER 13

Kumba Ranch, Flathead Valley, Montana

THE ENTIRE FAMILY WAS gathered, drinks in hand, on the expansive deck of the ranch's main house, with its commanding view of the largest lake on the property. All were dressed up for the occasion. For the men, that meant clean blue jeans, dress shirts, wool vests, and boots. Reece had gone into Whitefish to shop. It felt good to be wearing clothes that weren't borrowed. The ladies had taken the opportunity to class it up even further.

"You men clean up well for a bunch of glorified ranch hands," Annika teased. She was wearing an emerald green dress that clung tightly to her tall, slender frame. Her eyes were the color of her dress and, like her husband's, almost luminescent. She carried herself with a quiet confidence, and she showed an unmistakable affection for her husband; their subtle physical contact, a touch on the back here, a grip on the elbow there, was that of a couple deeply in love. Reece could not have been happier for the two of them but couldn't help but think of Lauren, briefly wondering where he would be today had she not been killed.

Jonathan and Caroline Hastings, both in their early sixties, made a handsome couple. A lifetime of honest hard work had kept their tall bodies lean. Caroline wore a broad-brimmed hat religiously to protect her face and neck from the sun's devastating rays, a habit passed to her by her mother as a child on the family's ranch outside of Bulawayo, Zimbabwe. The result was a face that made her appear far younger than her actual age, with only the finest of lines peeking from the corners of her eyes. Jonathan had not been so fastidious when it came to protecting himself from the African sun and his dark complexion resembled the battered cowhide boots on his feet. Though he did his best to refrain these days, he had been a smoker in his younger years, and the broken capillaries on his nose and cheeks bore evidence of his love for drink. Caroline suspected he still snuck a hand-rolled tobacco smoke every now and again but had yet to find his stash. He had the bright green eyes inherited by his son, but they were hidden behind a broad forehead and a perpetual squint that protected them from the sun. He still had the look of a predator.

The main room was tastefully adorned in dark woods and stone, with beautifully exposed beams running along the high ceiling, leaving room for the multiple shoulder mounts of animals primarily from Africa and North America. Reece stopped in front of a full-body grizzly bear mount that dominated the room from its position next to the stone fireplace. He was so entranced that he didn't even notice that Jonathan had joined him.

"That's really your dad's bear," Jonathan said, handing Reece a Tamarack Ale in a frosted mug. "To Tom."

The two men touched glasses and took long sips of their beers.

"I wounded that big guy in Kodiak. Not proud of it, but it happens."

Reece had heard the story many times but knew how much Jonathan reveled in its telling.

"In we go. Into thick brush after this wounded monster, me with my .375, our guide with his .45-70, and good ol' Thomas Reece with a twelve-gauge of all things. He'd used a shotgun in Vietnam as a point man."

"A Model 37," Reece confirmed.

"That's quite the scattergun, used number four shot if memory serves."

"That's right. They measured those engagements in feet, not yards in the delta."

"He was good in the woods, that one. I sure appreciated that steel nerve when this griz charged from not more than ten yards away. Tom Reece had his Ithaca to his shoulder, kneeled down for the most effective angle, and sent two slugs into the bear's chest before I even knew what was happening. This poor devil didn't take more than two steps. Heart-lung shots. Your dad was cool as a cucumber."

Reece smiled, thinking of the two older men out testing their mettle on Kodiak.

"I wanted to give him this mount, but he said Judy would kill him. Ha! I think he was more afraid of her than he was of the Viet Cong."

"You may be right about that."

"I miss your old man, lad. Bloody good chap."

"I do, too, Jonathan."

"That trip he took with you when you were thirteen, that was one of his fondest memories."

"Mine, too."

Reece thought back to that rite of passage. Driving up through British Columbia in their old Wagoneer to Alaska, his dad had taken a detour and pulled onto an unpaved road, before stopping in a dirt pullout. For the next three weeks they'd trekked through the wilderness with only small packs and a light survival kit. Tom had taught his son to navigate, set snares, build shelters, and fish on their journey through the rugged backcountry.

Reece took one last look at the grizzly and nodded in respect before joining the rest of the family on the deck.

"It won't be long now, boys and girls," Jonathan said, a hand over his eyes looking to the horizon, scanning the cloudless summer evening sky. They heard it before it came into view, the two powerful Wright radial engines humming across the water. Zulu, Jonathan's seventy-pound five-year-old Rhodesian ridgeback, barked and wagged his whiplike tail.

"There he is!" Jonathan said, pointing toward the opposite end of the lake. The setting sun reflected on the aircraft's silver fuselage, its bright red trim making it all the more visible to the onlookers. The pilot banked the aircraft and made a low pass over the water; all hands waved as he passed them at nearly eye level. He made a wide, sweeping turn to check the lake's condition and began to reduce power. The lake's calm surface made for a challenging landing since it robbed the pilot of much of his depth perception, but he knew the aircraft and the conditions well. The aircraft's keel broke the glassy surface of the water like a knife, and the pilot eased it gracefully from airplane to boat as it settled onto the lake. The plane was a 1955 Grumman Albatross, and the pilot was Tim Thornton, Annika's father.

The family made their way down to the lake as the classic aircraft taxied to the dock. Thorn cut the power and let the flying boat drift toward his welcoming committee, waiting with bumpers and lines to secure the amphibious plane. When the plane's door opened, Thorn's contagious smile won the crowd.

"Hey, Dad!" Annika shouted.

"Hello, my dear. Good evening, everyone."

Thorn hopped down onto the dock extension built to accommodate his flying yacht, whiskey bottle in hand; he hadn't lost his politician's flair for the dramatic. Annika ran to him, and he lifted her off her feet. She might be the president of his multibillion-dollar empire but, in his eyes, she'd always be his little girl.

He hugged his son-in-law warmly, and greeted each member of the entourage with the same genuine warmth. He said something in Caroline's ear that made her giggle before embracing her husband in a bear hug. He handed Jonathan the whiskey bottle and turned toward the former navy man. Reece had only met Thorn a handful of times and had not spent much time with him.

"Great to see you again, James. I'm glad to hear that your health is on the mend."

"Thank you, sir."

"Let's get that bottle open before Jonathan gets the shakes, shall we?"

"Lead the way," Jonathan retorted as the extended family walked together toward the house.

Tim Thornton was one of five children of Irish immigrant parents, born and raised in Butte, Montana, during the baby boom of the 1940s. Known as "Ireland's Fifth Province," Butte had boasted the highest percentage of Irish residents in America at one point, exceeding even that of Boston. Thorn's dad, like most of his former countrymen, was a miner who toiled long hours in the nearby copper mines in order to provide for his family. His father would come home from a shift looking like a stone statue, so covered in dirt and dust that his son could not even recognize him. Thorn would see the "copper sores" on his father's forearms after he'd scrubbed the grime from his body. His parents rode him and his siblings hard, determined that academics would lead them away from the mines and to a better life. If he stayed in Butte, he'd be lucky to land a job as a machinist or boilermaker. If he was unlucky, as most were, he would find himself a mile underground, digging out copper to feed the electronics market.

The hard work paid off when Thorn won an appointment to the United States Naval Academy at Annapolis. He struggled in the institution's tough regimen of engineering and mathematics but thrived on the boxing team, where he quickly earned the respect of the upper classmen. He graduated in 1967, when the Vietnam War was in full swing. The safer choice would have been to head to the navy's surface fleet, riding out the war on an aircraft carrier or destroyer with clean sheets and hot food. Instead, he volunteered for the Marine Corps. He served as an infantry platoon commander in the 3rd Battalion, 3rd Marines and was awarded the Silver Star and Purple Heart for his actions during Operation Kentucky.

Thorn left the Marine Corps in 1971 and entered law school at the University of Montana in Missoula. During his first year he lost his father to lung cancer, no doubt from a lifetime of exposure to the dust in the mines, but his grief was tempered by meeting the love of his life. Kathy Roberts was a graduate student in the university's geology department and, like Thorn, had family roots in Ireland. Their courtship was a brief one and they were married at Saint Anthony's in Missoula before Thorn had taken his final exams. The couple eventually moved back to Butte, Kathy doing fieldwork while Thorn studied for the bar exam. He passed the bar and found work in a local firm, doing everything from wills and real estate closings to defending local miners who'd been arrested for petty crimes.

Thorn found success in law, thanks to a strong work ethic and his ability to connect with clients. He began to see that Montana was being stripped of its natural resources on the backs of men like his father and that the lucrative proceeds were flowing toward corporations in New York and San Francisco. It was a complicated situation and, when he was approached by local civic leaders to run for the state's open U.S. Senate seat, he saw a way to do something about it. The native Montanan and decorated veteran with blue-collar roots won an easy victory, but Thorn quickly found that fighting an experienced guerrilla army in the jungles of Vietnam was a more honest battle than those he would wage in the halls of Congress.

Thorn had a front-row seat for some of the last days of true statesmanship in Washington. He was at the table when President Reagan and Speaker of the House Thomas "Tip" O'Neill threw partisanship aside for the benefit of the country, in contrast to the "us against them" politics popular on both sides of the aisle. His contemporaries were career politicians looking to stay in office above all else. Thorn didn't mind the fight and didn't mind sleeping in his office, but eventually the fundamental dishonesty of the entire process wore him down. When he became a father, the time away from family became too much to bear; it was time to go home.

His departure from D.C. came at a time of historic lows in terms of oil prices. Kathy saw that extraction technology was changing rapidly and realized that there was a real future in the state as a petroleum producer. In 1988 they gathered some outside capital through Thorn's contacts in Washington and poured much of their savings into buying a failing energy company with leases across the state's northern border. Thorn's desire to be home with his family was the impetus for him learning how to fly and he traveled between his oil fields and Butte in a Piper Cherokee that he piloted himself. The family of three lived a relatively humble existence as prices dipped even further during the early 1990s. Fortunately, they had diversified their assets, and their struggles in the oil and gas market were tempered by the state's expanding real estate and tourist economies. Thorn doubled down on land and stretched his credit to its absolute limit.

Oil found its bottom in 1998 but they kept their operating expenses low, stayed in the black, and even managed to buy up additional leases from struggling competitors. The price of oil doubled by 2000 and did so again by 2005.

The company increased its production to full capacity. When the financial crisis struck in 2008, the oil market hit an all-time high and Thorn sold most of his highly valued oil and gas holdings at the peak of those values.

Thorn's oil business made the family a fortune, but it was a company that almost put them under that ended up cementing their position as one of the wealthiest families on the planet. Thorn had founded Neversweat LNG Development LP, a liquid natural gas company, in 2005 at a time when a major increase in LNG imports was projected. He'd invested heavily in building a liquid natural gas importation and regasification facility in Freeport, Texas. In 2008 the shale gas revolution hit the United States, turning the industry on its head. With no further need to import LNG, the project looked like it would put the Thorntons into bankruptcy, but the scrappy miner's son wasn't out of the fight. He asked his engineers to reverse the regasification process. With the reserves discovered in the United States, Thorn knew the country could become a source for worldwide LNG exports. The only thing he needed to do was change a few laws. He worked with old friends at a law firm in Denver and applied pressure to the right politicians in the swamp; the Department of Energy approved the first U.S. LNG export license for Neversweat LNG in 2008, catapulting them from millionaires to billionaires. That was when Kathy found the lump.

Annika took a leave of absence from her career and they fought the dreaded disease as a united family. Kathy stood proudly at Annika and Raife's wedding, despite the devastating effects of the chemotherapy; her strength inspired them all. Still, the cancer was aggressive and had been discovered too late. She died on a Sunday morning, in the historic Butte home that she had lovingly restored, Thorn holding one hand and Annika the other.

Thorn's healing had taken place on horseback, hunting the mountains and fly-fishing the lakes and streams of Montana and Idaho with Jonathan as his trusted friend and confidant. Almost fifteen years later the wilds remained his mistress, with Thorn never remarrying or even dating. He preferred to live with his wife's memory.

The women drifted off toward the living room as the men congregated in the walnut-paneled bar. Jonathan pulled the top from the rectangular bottle of

Neversweat bourbon and poured two fingers for each of the men present. The Montana whiskey was named for the two-thousand-foot-deep Neversweat copper mine near Butte. The mine was called Neversweat due to its unusually cool temperatures, which made it a relatively comfortable work environment in an otherwise miserable profession. The men held their glasses out in a salute, each of them thinking of the fallen brothers they'd left behind in Vietnam, Rhodesia, Afghanistan, and Iraq. Warriors all four.

"To the lads!" Jonathan toasted.

"To the lads!" the others replied, before joining the women at the dinner table.

The meal had its intended effect of welcoming Reece into the fold. Each course had been prepared by either Jonathan or Caroline and was paired with a wine from the Franschhoek and Stellenbosch vineyards, in which the family maintained ownership interests. Reece feasted on duck, pronghorn, and elk but the main course was a grass-fed beef filet from the family's main cattle operation near the Missouri River Breaks. The conversation was kept light with no mention of politics, battles fought, or departed loved ones, and for the first time in ages, Reece felt that he was part of a family.

While the groups were chatting noisily over a dessert of homemade apple tart with cinnamon, Raife rose to his feet and tapped his silver fork on the petite crystal glass of Groot Constantia Grand Constance on the table before him.

"We have a little announcement to make. A very little one, actually." He turned and smiled at a blushing Annika. "Father, Mother, you are going to have another grandchild to spoil and, Senator, you will have your first."

The room burst into joyful applause. Everyone rose to their feet and there was round after round of hugs, back slaps, and celebration. Jonathan rushed out of the dining room and returned with a bottle of vintage Dom Pérignon champagne in each hand. Reece was overjoyed for his friend. A brief wave of sadness hit him as he thought of his own wife, pregnant at the time of her murder, but he pushed that darkness aside to share in the moment.

As the celebration wound down, Thorn motioned for Reece to join him on a corner of the deck.

"What are your plans, Reece?"

"I'm not sure, sir. I'm figuring that out now."

"First of all, stop it with this *sir* bullshit. It's *Thorn*. Second of all, I know you didn't ask for it, but let me give you some unsolicited advice."

Reece suspected the Hastings clan had asked Thorn to extend a bit of wisdom to the wayward frogman.

"When my wife died, I didn't have anyone to hold responsible," Thorn continued. "No list to work through. I know there is nothing anyone could have done. It was Kathy's time. The Lord needed her and so he called her home. I think about her every day. I haven't set foot inside our old home since the funeral."

"I'm sorry."

"My point, son, is don't let the bastards who took your family take your future from you, too. Don't let them win. It's too late for an old warhorse like me. It's not too late for you."

Reece swallowed hard and nodded, hoping it was too dark for Thorn to see his eyes.

"Jonathan told me you are thinking about joining up with the Agency."

"I've been giving it some thought," Reece admitted.

"You be careful with them, Reece. They can be tricky bastards. I still have connections in Washington, even more so than I did as a politician. Being in energy has meant significant donations to both parties. If there is ever anything you need, don't hesitate to ask."

"Thank you, sir, I mean, Thorn."

"Think nothing of it, son."

That night Reece slept in his bed, in the cabin, his chair by the lake unoccupied for the first night since his return to Montana.

CHAPTER 14

Saint Petersburg, Russia

DESPITE HIS BEST EFFORTS, Grey could find no trace of James Reece. He weighed his options.

It had not escaped Grey during his extensive research that investigative journalist Katie Buranek had been the sole voice to shed doubt on the prevailing story line that Reece was a SEAL-gone-rogue, right-wing nut job, and domestic terrorist after his family was murdered almost two year's ago. Grey knew her as one of those impossibly beautiful cable news blondes who were also quite brilliant. He googled her to find she had risen to prominence with a series of stories on Benghazi that became the basis for a bestselling book. Her exposé on the Reece affair was initially ridiculed by the media elites until she began releasing hard, irrefutable facts that backed up her seemingly implausible conspiracy theories: emails, voice recordings, financial records, and her personal involvement as a witness. What began as a corrupt attempt to monetize a drug that promised to block the effects of PTSD resulted in one of the deadliest events in U.S. special operations history. Buranek's award-winning coverage of the events destroyed the administration's version of them and ultimately took down a sitting president. She appeared to be the female version of Woodward and Bernstein. During an exclusive interview with Margaret Hoover on *Firing Line*, she gave a gripping account of being kidnapped and eventually rescued by the former navy commando.

Was she now the closest thing to a family Reece had left?

Grey considered having Katie killed and then hitting the funeral with a team of *bratva* killers on the assumption that Reece would be in attendance, but that was messy, and Reece might anticipate the move. And if he didn't show, he'd be alive to still use all of his ample skills and resources to hunt Grey to the ends of the earth. No, Grey needed to hit Reece on home soil, when he least expected it.

Grey was beginning to lose faith in his own analytical abilities when Svetlana shuffled into his office and slid his pay envelope across his desk. He stared at it for a long moment, then leapt to his feet in an uncharacteristic show of emotion.

"That's it! I know how to find him!"

"Of course, you do, my dear." She didn't have the faintest idea what he was talking about but, after watching him work obsessively for so many weeks, she was happy to see him so excited. "I'll go get you some tea so you can work."

Knowing Reece's employer was the key. Employees, even contractors, had to be paid. Getting paid meant bank accounts, direct deposits, wire transfers, Automated Clearing Houses. It meant a trail. Even if those payments were going to an alias, Grey could narrow it down to where Reece would be on the CIA pay scale. It was a start.

Luckily for Grey, Russia was the home base to an inordinate number of computer experts: hackers. He could pass along a simple request and, within minutes, have a dozen or more freelance hackers working on it. It was like having his own personal NSA. He never encountered any of these individuals firsthand, as they all worked remotely from who knows where; all of their anonymous interactions took place via the Dark Web. He used two computers as he worked, a network desktop for all of his internet searches and email and a sterile laptop with no modem for all of his sensitive work. With no link to the outside world, it would be nearly impossible for an intelligence agency or freelance hacker to access his computer without physically taking possession of it. Each night before he left the building, he locked it in a secure safe in his office.

As a former CIA employee, Grey had an important piece of the puzzle already in hand; he knew the bank routing and account numbers used by the Agency to pay their employees. His request was simple: the location of every bank account where CIA employees and contractors were receiving payment. While the Agency's firewalls were a significant barrier, those of most financial institutions were not. Stealing the info from the receiving end of these transactions was a relatively simple process for the team of hackers. Within days, Grey had a printed list of accounts, organized by geography.

He culled the vast majority of accounts dotted across the greater Washington, D.C., area. He'd studied his target and knew that Reece wouldn't live in a large metro area: D.C., New York, Miami, Atlanta, Los Angeles. His next assumption was that Reece would set up his bank account in the name of an LLC or corporation in order to hide his identity. He separated those from the list, narrowing it down to a few hundred individual accounts. Most of these were clustered around traditional hubs of special operations activity, places like Fayetteville, Pinehurst, Niceville, Columbus, San Diego, and Virginia Beach. The former locations would all be home to ex-army operators, with the latter two being popular spots for frogmen such as Reece. Still, he figured those cities would be too on-the-grid for a guy who had spent some time as "Public Enemy Number One."

He dug deeper on the more remote locations: Kettle Falls, Bear Valley, Tombstone, Hamilton, Boone, Sandpoint. Grey ran basic searches on each location, looking for something that would set it apart from the others. Nothing stood out. He stayed in his office until well after midnight, alone since Svetlana had finally left him just before eight. She brought him tea and cookies from the stash of goodies she kept in her filing cabinet. She picked up his suit coat from the back of a chair across from his desk, brushed it off with her hands, and hung it on the hook behind his office door.

"You work too hard, Oliver, you need to rest," she said as she walked around the desk and stood over his shoulder. Her strong hands smoothed the fabric of his dress shirt across the top of his back. Grey stopped and inhaled her perfume, a scent that triggered dark memories of his childhood. Her touch stirred a warmth inside him, and he felt a rush of blood to an area he thought was devoid of feeling. Embarrassed, he began to shuffle the papers on his desk, stumbling over his words like a schoolboy. Svetlana leaned in close and whispered him a loving "good night" before walking away. Staring at the empty doorway, Grey sat for a moment in shock, his lifelong impotence shattered by the matronly touch of his assistant. Without bothering to lock his computer, he bolted for the restroom.

CHAPTER 15

Kumba Ranch, Montana

THEY RAN FOR AN hour on the twisting backcountry game trails that wandered through the maze of towering pines. The carpet of pine needles that littered the landscape cushioned their footfalls and was far kinder to their knees than asphalt or concrete. Each day Raife chose a longer route with a steeper grade, always pushing his friend a bit harder as his body strengthened.

Both men carried handguns on their grueling backcountry trail runs. When you've hunted terrorists for a living and were responsible for killing a Russian intelligence colonel in line to be the next president of Russia, going anywhere unarmed was not a smart option. Reece carried a compact Glock 29 short-frame 10mm he'd borrowed from Jonathan in a modern Kydex Outback chest harness made by Blackpoint Tactical, while Raife's larger and far older handgun was stored in its leather holster inside a small pack.

"When are you going to trade in that BB gun for something more grown-up?" Raife chided between breaths.

"Maybe when you stop carrying antiques into the field. That thing probably needs to be field-stripped already. We've been running for almost a half hour; a speck of dust may cause a malfunction."

Raife's skills with a handgun met, or even exceeded, his prowess as an athlete. With phenomenal eyesight and exceptional hand-eye coordination, he fired his prized 1911, a pistol that had history in his family dating back to World War II, when his grandfather had carried it as a member of the Long Range Desert Group in North Africa, as if it were an extension of his body. Raife had always found shooting the Colt 1911 .45, customized by the talented South African gunsmith Dale Guthrie, to be a therapeutic escape from an otherwise chaotic world.

Cresting a hill to begin what he knew would turn into a sprint to the finish, Reece dodged a branch and between breaths asked, "Did I tell you I started shooting 1911s?"

"Really?" Raife asked, picking up the pace.

"Yeah, with my Glock."

Raife stifled a laugh at the old joke as his friend found a final reserve of energy and they crossed the finish line neck and neck.

After catching their breath and grabbing some water, they moved to the shooting range behind Raife's workshop for a timed course of fire with their chosen pistols.

"Ears," Raife said, tossing his friend a set of electronic hearing protection. After all the explosions and gunfire they'd experienced throughout their time in uniform, both were sticklers about preserving the hearing they had left.

They moved into what they called a "Prevail Drill," a twenty-round course of fire developed by one of their University of Montana professors who had been a Special Forces Project Delta sniper in Vietnam. The six stages varied from five to twelve yards and included standing, kneeling, single hand, and dual target engagements under a specified time tracked by a shot timer. Anything outside the "ten zone" meant failure and was intended to indicate they would have died in a real-world gunfight. Both operators put all twenty shots in the kill box.

As they topped off magazines, Raife caught Reece eyeing his recurve bow that hung on a stand on the shooting range.

"Let me know when you are ready to take off your training wheels and shoot something that takes some skill," Raife said, mocking the modern compound bow he knew Reece had been spending time with lately.

"You mean this old struggle stick?" Reece asked. "Mind if I give it a shot?"

"Be my guest. When you're ready we'll head down to Colorado and have

South Cox measure you for a Stalker and stop in to see Tom Clum for some lessons."

One of Reece's favorite things to do was surprise his old blood brother. Unbeknownst to Raife, his guest had been spending time in Glacier Archery working on his traditional bow technique.

Reece gripped the ancient weapon, pretending he was unfamiliar with how to properly hold it, registering Raife's folded arms and smug look.

Slowly picking up a beautiful wooden arrow from the stand, he took a breath and centered himself. His short routine had become subconscious: load, anchor, back perpendicular to target, bent slightly at the waist, elbow inside the string; arrow, target, string, archer as one being, one natural system.

Reece's fingers scraped along his face and past his ear into the follow-through and finish position, his arrow slicing through the mountain air before striking the kill zone of the 3-D mule deer target at thirty-five yards.

"Nothing to it," Reece said to his astonished friend with a smile. "Remember, *the arrow that is not aimed* . . . See you tomorrow."

. . .

Reece maneuvered through the trees toward his section of the ranch and thought through the rest of his day. He planned to head into Whitefish to run some errands while Raife scouted for deer and elk. The Hastingses' family attorney had set Reece up with a bank account and post office box in the name of one of the family's corporations to help conceal his location. His military pension and CIA paychecks were direct deposited into his account under the alias David Hilcot, courtesy of the CIA's director of Clandestine Services. There were no documents that placed his name on the cabin where he lived and the utilities were all billed to the Hastings family, making him virtually invisible in a modern world, where privacy was all but dead. Once a week, Reece would make the hour drive to Whitefish to check his mail and fuel up on caffeine at Montana Coffee Traders. He would sweeten it up to his heart's content, browse the local bookstore, and spend some time talking shop with the resident bow-hunting experts in Glacier

Archery. If anyone recognized him during his forays into civilization, they didn't let on. For Reece, the "keep to oneself" culture of northwest Montana certainly had its benefits.

Back at his cabin, Reece approached the line and took a breath. Though he loved the challenge and purity of traditional archery, he also couldn't separate himself from the adage he'd learned on the battlefield: *exploit all technical and tactical advantages*. His compound bow blended the past and present for him in a way that felt natural.

Archery had always been a pursuit that centered him, calmed him. A place where all worries and stresses were put aside, a meditative state where archer, bow, arrow, and target were connected. To the uninitiated, archery looked like a hobby. To those who lived the way of the bow, it was much more. Archery was discipline. Archery was freedom. Archery was Zen.

Stance, grip, shoulder, anchor, peep, pull, and finish, Reece thought, reviewing the basics. As with anything in life, the best do the basics exceptionally well.

The range was set up with multiple foam shapes of realistic-looking animals at distances from ten to one hundred yards. Reece had never taken a hundred-yard shot with his bow at an animal but being competent with his setup out to that distance certainly increased confidence when his prey was within forty.

Reece looked the forty yards to his target, a foam-shaped bull elk.

Build your foundation, Reece, he remembered his friend and one of the best archers on the planet telling him years earlier. *Winning starts from the ground up*. Reece had hit it off with John Dudley years earlier at the Total Archery Challenge, a 3-D archery shoot held at various locations around the country. Reece had been a solid archer, growing up with a bow in hand, but he was primarily self-taught. "Dud," whose life had been the pursuit of excellence in the science and art of archery, had passed along lessons that brought Reece's skills with the ancient weapon to new levels. They were lessons Reece would never forget.

Reece glanced at his feet and moved them into a perfect neutral stance, his back foot just slightly off centerline, then adjusted his grip.

The shot begins and ends in your hand.

Going through his shot routine focused his mind and emptied it of thoughts that would interrupt the process and therefore disrupt the flight of the arrow. Reece's time with the bow was not so much about hitting the target as it was about the discipline of the art. It was a meditative state where any outside influences and distractions ceased to exist. There was no murdered wife and child, no mission of vengeance, no brain tumor, no dead teammates; no past, no future, no betrayal. There was only the now; the flow of the process. The discipline. There was only the shot.

Reece raised his front shoulder, locking it forward and down for stability before slowly pulling the seventy-four pounds of PSE's EVO NTN to full draw. He then anchored his drawing hand lightly against his cheek, his eye moving to the round peep sight, aligning his front pin in its center, the tip of his nose just barely touching the string. His sight pin was in a slow, effortless float on the kill zone as he eased his thumb to the trigger of the Nock2It release. This was a moment of solitude. The focus was bliss.

As with the many rifle shots he'd taken in training and combat, at his natural respiratory pause he executed, the tension from his back and shoulder naturally flowing through his arm to his thumb on the release, transferring the bow's potential energy into kinetic energy and into the arrow as the cams returned the string to its neutral state.

Just before the shot broke, the elk target transformed into someone Reece had only seen in surveillance photos, a short man with a stainless steel watch. A man Reece was going to kill.

It was as if Reece's bow had fired itself. He followed through just as he would with a rifle, the arrow rotating flawlessly, finding its mark almost half a football field away. He was in the zone. It was effortless, perfection. He repeated the process five more times before moving downrange to collect his arrows. This ritual had become part of his morning routine. This was his meditation. Now, with a clear mind, he would move forward and continue to recover. The scars on his head were not the only ones healing. The emotional strain and trauma of the past two years needed to heal as well. Reece knew those kinds of wounds have the tendency to fester and tear, and would be felt long after the incisions on his scalp were a distant memory.

CHAPTER 16

Saint Petersburg, Russia

IT SEEMED AS THOUGH the CIA had half of the nation on the payroll. Contract employees were making big money working overseas gigs. When the military drew down their footprint in places like Iraq, Afghanistan, the Horn of Africa, and Colombia, they filled the void with experienced special operators. Men who could train, equip, and lead local "indig" units against America's enemies. Some did it for the money, some in the name of patriotism, and some because they simply couldn't let go of the action. Whatever their motivation, they were invaluable tools in the fight and the government paid them accordingly.

He had reached the last financial institution on his list: Flathead Bank & Trust. The monotony of these searches had nearly lulled his mind into complacency, but now was not the time for that. He was running out of patience when he needed it most. The checking account in question was owned by HDI, LLC, which appeared to be a holding company with numerous accounts, many of which held significant amounts of money. The account in question received two direct deposits every month: one from the Agency and a second from the Department of Defense that appeared to be the appropriate monthly sum of a retirement payment for a prior-enlisted O-4 with twenty years of service. He worked with renewed focus.

What, or who, was HDI, though?

Grey found scans of closing documents on the website of the Flathead County treasurer in the name of HDI, Hastings Diversified Investments, signed by its president, a man named Jonathan Hastings. A web search of that name brought up numerous results, most of them associated with Hastings's various landholdings. Jonathan Hastings was on the board of directors of the Montana Cattleman's Association, the Montana Outfitters and Guides Association, and the Selous Scouts Regimental Association. On the second page, Grey found an engagement announcement, dated June 2014, in the Montana Standard.

"The Honorable Timothy and Katherine Thornton of Butte are pleased to announce the engagement of their daughter, Annika Grace, to Raife J. Hastings, son of Jonathan and Caroline Hastings of Whitefish. Raife is a 1999 graduate of the University of Montana and is a rancher, having recently retired from the United States Navy, where he served as a Lieutenant Commander in the Navy. A September wedding is planned." There was a photo above the announcement: two young, beautiful people, posing candidly and looking very much in love. The woman looked like she could be a model with her perfect jaw, long, graceful neck, flawless skin, and delicate shoulders. Her suitor looked like a thirty-something version of the Marlboro Man: hard, gritty, and masculine yet undoubtedly attractive. Grey could just make out a scar that ran down the man's face, making him look even more intriguing.

Grey looked at the whiteboard; James Reece had attended the University of Montana and was the same age. They were both in the Navy and the Hastingses' family ranch, located in some of the most remote country in the lower forty-eight, would be an ideal place to hide from the world.

Had Raife Hastings been a SEAL?

Grey felt the rush of victory. He might not have the intimidating physical power of the men he hunted, but he had the intellectual advantage. He still needed on-the-ground confirmation, but if he had located his target, Reece would soon be reunited with his dead family.

CHAPTER 17

Brighton Beach, Brooklyn, New York

KOYCHEV LOOKED AT THE package delivered by courier the previous evening. Though there were various electronic means of communication thought to be secure from the prying eyes of the American law enforcement and intelligence agencies, an old-fashioned hard copy, hand-carried on a Moscow to New York flight, was still the best way to stay off their radar.

He used his pocketknife to unseal the padded manila envelope and dumped the contents onto his desk. There was a small stack of papers, a thumb drive, and what Koychev recognized as an Iridium GPS tracking device. There was a cover letter of sorts, typed in Russian and signed by a fellow *Avtoriet*, a brigadier in the organization. The letter was indirect, making references to events and people that only the reader would understand. It was an effective, if informal code; no computer or word sleuth could decipher it. The message was simple: locate the target, identify his vehicles, and develop a pattern of life. This was to be acted upon with the highest urgency as the request was coming from the Big Boss himself. It didn't take a man of Koychev's experience to determine that someone's days were numbered.

He pulled an inexpensive laptop from his desk, one that he never connected to the internet, and slid the thumb drive into the USB port. The first file was a series of photos of a man, both in and out of uniform. Koychev recognized him from the media coverage: a former SEAL who had gone on a rampage after the deaths of his wife and daughter, becoming the most wanted man in America. Other files contained satellite imagery, maps, bank account records, and other fragments of data that would help find and eliminate the target.

Koychev closed his eyes and thought about the problem at hand. His people were accustomed to operating in cities where they could hide among the masses of humanity. Putting men, particularly foreigners, into such a remote part of the United States would attract immediate attention. He had an idea. He typed "Whitefish Montana bartender jobs" into Google and found two current openings. One of those jobs would work perfectly.

He called his most reliable female employee into his back office, taking a moment to admire her before giving her his instructions.

"Tanya, you are moving to Montana."

CHAPTER 18

Whitefish, Montana

TANYA WAS NOT PLEASED when Sergey sent her on this assignment, but she'd quickly fallen for the natural beauty and easy pace of the small resort town. Ski towns across the American West were often staffed by Eastern Europeans during the summer months and Tanya befriended a group from Bulgaria and Serbia. Within two weeks of her arrival, she had moved into a crowded house where she shared a bedroom with Elitza from the city of Sofia in the Balkans. She mostly worked nights, pouring drinks at a local bar and flirting with the fly-fishing guides, their wealthy clients, and seasonal residents of this idyllic community.

Most mornings, she could be found sitting on a bench on Central Avenue, sipping from a to-go cup of coffee. Just another young girl in yoga pants, scrolling away on her iPhone or reading a magazine, taking in the warm sun and clean mountain air. Her bench just happened to give her a perfect view of anyone going into or coming out of Flathead Bank & Trust across the street.

Tanya was worried that she wouldn't be able to identify the man that she'd been asked to locate. From the photos, he looked similar to a decent percentage of the men in town: late thirties, tall, probably bearded. She began to typecast the men she observed, each of them falling into one of a few molds: mustached cowboy locals, scruffy fishing guides, pudgy summer tourists, or obviously wealthy Californians with property nearby. None of them had the hardened look of a combat veteran.

It was late morning, and she was about to give up for the day; she'd offered to work a double and needed to shower before opening for the lunch crowd. She started to walk up the sidewalk toward her home a few blocks away when she saw a Toyota Land Cruiser turn down Central. The off-road SUV looked to be of an older vintage but was in like-new condition and tricked out with an aggressive bumper, lights, and a roof rack.

Interesting.

She leaned against a light pole and pulled her phone back out of her pocket.

The driver was the correct height, about six feet tall, and had broad shoulders and thick arms. He wore jeans, a T-shirt, and hiking boots and looked like he might fit in with the guide crowd. A ball cap and sunglasses shielded much of his face and a dark beard masked what was left. The black glasses looked different from the typical fishing shades so popular in town, but it was his demeanor that gave him away. While nearly everyone else she saw walked with a carefree attitude or had their face buried in their phones, this man's vigilance set him apart. His head moved constantly, as he took in his surroundings before locking the door of his truck. He reminded her of a fitter version of some of Koychev's men who sometimes passed through Brighton Beach, hard and serious.

He disappeared into the bank, and she went back to her bench. She opened her camera app and prepared to frame a photograph while looking like she was mindlessly shopping or checking a social media platform. She sat with her knees to her chest to steady the shot and, when he emerged from the bank, she took a burst of photos followed by a video. He opened the back hatch of his SUV and retrieved what looked like a case for a musical instrument, which he carried two storefronts down into a place called Glacier Archery.

Tanya sent a text message with the video and photos to Koychev in New York, then rose from the bench to prepare for the lunch shift.

CHAPTER 19

REECE DIDN'T HAVE AN exact routine, but he would head to town at least once a week. He would hit the bank, the post office, the archery shop, and the bookstore. He had become a bit of a regular at Loula's and would often stop in for a late breakfast or lunch during his forays into civilization. One of the waitresses, with an accent he'd narrowed down to somewhere in the Balkans, had a crush on him. She always commented on how polite he was. Despite her best efforts, though, he hadn't asked her out.

When he walked through the door of the cafe, Tanya knew that she had about thirty minutes until he would be done eating, maybe longer if Elitza was extra chatty. She waited impatiently before making her move, just in case he'd left his wallet or phone in the truck and came out to retrieve it. After an agonizing few moments, she crossed the street with what to anyone but the closest observer appeared to be a black cell phone in her hand. She knelt next to his right rear tire as if to tie her shoe and reached as far under the vehicle as she could. Her view was blocked by the running boards, but they would also prevent anyone from spotting her handiwork without physically crawling under the SUV. She twisted her shoulder and knelt further to slide the device over the top of the frame rail and felt the tactile click of the powerful magnet as it took hold on the steel. Brushing the dried dust and dirt from her hand on her pants leg, she rose and continued her walk as casually as possible.

. . .

Halfway around the globe, Oliver Grey remotely activated the GPS tracking device on his desktop terminal and waited several seconds before the software triangulated the transponder's location. The image on his screen blurred and then settled on the northwestern United States, the pixelated image clarifying as it zoomed into the town of Whitefish, Montana. A blinking red indicator signaled the location of the Iridium GPS tracking device from James Reece's vehicle. The software program overlaid the vehicle's location on existing satellite imagery from Google Earth, providing real-time location data.

After what seemed like an eternity, the dot began to move, slowly at first and then more rapidly as the vehicle left the confines of the small town and reached the highway. The dot slowed several miles out of town and turned onto an unpaved road. After winding through timber and open meadows, gaining altitude as it progressed along its path, the dot stopped at the edge of a large lake and made no other movement for the remainder of the day. Grey scrutinized all of the available imagery of the location, and it was clear that there was a cabin or house there.

Grey reached into his desk drawer, removed a bottle of vodka and a glass, and poured himself a shot. Raising the drink to the dot on his screen, he smiled. He'd found the son of his first betrayal and current tormenter of his dreams. Montana is where they would strike.

CHAPTER 20

Kumba Ranch, Flathead Valley, Montana

"I DON'T SEE HIM," Reece said, scanning across the valley with his Swarovski range-finding binoculars.

Raife held his older Zeiss binos to his eyes, his hands cupped across the brim of his ball cap to stabilize the 10-power image. "See the rocky face to the left of the pines, giant pile of rocks?"

"Check."

"Come down one hundred meters and you'll see some smaller boulders with a clump of green brush in front of it. See it?"

"I see the brush."

"See his tines?"

"No . . . wait. I see him," Reece said, with excitement in his voice as his brain separated the deer's velvet-covered antlers from their nearly identical surroundings. "He's huge!"

"He's a good one. Let's put the scope on him." Raife let his binoculars fall to his side on their long leather strap and began unstrapping a tripod and spotting scope from the outside of his Stone Glacier internal frame pack. He and Reece had hiked up the ridge before dawn, hoping to catch the wise old buck out feeding before he snuck back into the safety of his bedding. The morning air was cool, and steam rose from both men's bodies after the tough vertical climb.

They knelt just below the ridgeline opposite the mule deer, glassing him from a safe distance across the canyon. Raife had been watching the buck all summer and, when the opening day of archery season came on the first of September, he would make this same journey with his primitive recurve bow. He efficiently set up the spotting scope, quickly locating the animal through the heavily magnified glass. The slightest touch of the spotter or tripod would knock the 60-power image from its target, so he carefully backed away from the scope without disturbing it, motioning for Reece to take a look.

Though the deer was more than eight hundred yards away, Reece could see every detail through the optic. The sun was just beginning to break over the tops of the tall pines, bathing the buck in shadowless light that a photographer would kill for. He probably weighed three hundred pounds, and his thick body was dwarfed only by the size of his headgear. The summer had been a wet one, even by local standards, and his antlers had grown to their full capacity thanks to the lush mountain grasses. He would rub off the velvet soon, exposing the hard, bonelike tangle beneath. The rack was as thick as a man's wrists at each base, and spanned out nearly three feet. Each side of the buck's antlers held four points plus a smaller brow tine, making it a "four point" in western parlance. Its forks were deep, its points long.

The deer was a living symbol of Raife's family's conservation efforts. He was old and healthy. He had evaded the bullet and arrow season after season, learning the habits of those who pursued him. Raife would hunt him alone, on foot, with a weapon that had existed for ten millennia. If one of a million little things didn't go wrong during the stalk, where the buck had nearly every advantage, Raife would put a handmade spruce arrow through his lungs. The meat would sustain the Hastings family during the brutal Montana winter and provide an all-natural source of nutrition for Annika and her baby. God willing, their child would one day hunt one of the many sons or grandsons that this buck had sired. The cycle would continue, just as it had since the first hunters roamed the earth.

"How old is he?" Reece asked, breaking the silence.

"Eight, maybe ten. He has the face of a really old buck, and I found his sheds from last season. They were a bit bigger than what he's wearing now, so he's a little past his prime. He's a smart one. Look at how open the country is around him. He can sit in that spot and see anyone or anything coming up from below. If anything tries to get him from above, he'll hear it on the rocks. He has the wind in his face most of the time and he only has to walk a few yards to feed, which he probably does at night."

"What's the plan?"

"I'm going to come in above him. I'll do it barefoot to avoid making noise coming over the rocks."

"What are the winds like around here?"

"I'll wait until the middle of the day, when the thermals will make my scent rise. I'll get as close as I possibly can and wait for him to stand."

They hiked back down the ridge to where their trucks were parked at a pace that allowed them to talk.

"The ranch has changed a lot since college," Reece said.

"Thanks. It's been a lot of work. My dad did most of it while we were deployed. The land was overgrazed and overlogged when we acquired it. There was so much fuel on the ground, a fire would have been catastrophic. There's no money in getting a bunch of dead trees out but we did it anyway. We did some careful burning and a lot of reforestation. The natural grasses are healthy, and we've thinned enough of the timber to let some vegetation grow. We are struggling a bit with the grizzlies and wolves, but that can't be helped. Overall, our elk herd is coming back from the winter kill a few years back and, as you can see, we have some beautiful deer."

"I got to experience revitalization similar to that in Africa. When we started really hammering the poachers, the game figured it out and moved back in. I wish I could have stayed longer to see how it all turned out."

"Uncle Rich has kept it up as much as he can. Dad and Thorn actually started a foundation stateside to help keep up the fight. They wouldn't be where they are now without you starting it up and showing them how effective antipoaching operations could be with the help of some modern targeting and intelligence practices."

"That's one of the ways the Agency found me."

"Well, that's what you get for showing off. When is your girlfriend coming out?"

"She's not my girlfriend . . . she's um . . ."

"It sure is funny to watch you get all flustered whenever her name comes up."

"If she can get away from work, she'll be here Labor Day weekend."

"If we're lucky, we'll have the backstrap from this buck for dinner during her visit."

"I'm sure she'll be impressed."

CHAPTER 21

Saint Petersburg, Russia

GREY STUDIED REECE'S HABITS like a chess player would a worthy opponent. He would only get one chance. Once the element of surprise was lost, the hunter would become the hunted. Grey had no intention of becoming Reece's prey. His strategy would be to lull Reece into the complacency of his tranquil surroundings and then strike fast and hard. He had built an initial plan, and it was time to present it to Zharkov. His boss had been patient with him, but there was very little in it for the organization; he wouldn't approve using his resources for a reckless venture. The elder Zharkov wanted Grey's attention back on running counterintelligence operations for the *bratva*.

Grey gathered his files and put everything into a manila folder. After shutting down his computer and locking it in the safe, he slipped on his custom jacket, the fit of the fabric giving him a physical confidence he'd lacked for most of his life. He opened the door of his office and stood in the doorway. Svetlana swiveled in her chair and faced him head-on.

"How do I look, Svetlana?"

"Oh, you look so wonderful, Oliver." She was immediately at arm's length, fretting over him. She straightened his already-straight tie, brushed a piece of lint from his lapel, and ran her hand across his bearded chin.

"You are ready, Oliver. You have worked so hard for this; go show the *Pakhan* how smart you are."

Oliver held his head high as he took the elevator to Zharkov's office. He was ready.

• • •

Zharkov looked over the written narrative of the plan for the second time. He had to admit that it was sound. Grey had done his homework; the CIA had taught him well. Zharkov had taken a gamble by hiring him, but that wager was already paying off. He set the target package down and looked at the figure before him. Grey's transformation since their first meeting was evident. The CIA analyst had been an alcoholic mess, a loner and a filthy genius teetering on the brink of disaster. Like a puppy from the street, Zharkov had cleaned him up, fed him, and given him a purpose. And, just like a dog, Grey had given Zharkov loyalty in return.

"This is a good plan, Oliver."

"Thank you, *Pakhan*. With the appropriate resources, we can eliminate the target."

"I agree. There is something missing, though."

Grey looked perplexed.

"It is a very thorough plan to kill Mr. Reece but it says nothing about his friend Raife Hastings."

"Why would we kill him?"

"Because I don't want him coming after us when we kill his friend."

"I see. That is going to require more resources, more people. It will complicate the plan significantly."

What Grey did not know was that Zharkov had done his own intelligence gathering. A jet belonging to Hastings's father-in-law had taken off from Nice, France, just hours after the rocket attack that killed Grey's mentor, Vasili Andrenov, in Basel, Switzerland. Andrenov had left behind a fortune. Zharkov had many associates in common with the late Russian expat and made some quiet inquiries as to whether there might be a reward for bringing to justice those responsible. Andrenov had surrounded himself with an extremely loyal group of advisors who now controlled the resources of his lucrative foundation.

In exchange for killing James Reece and Raife Hastings, Zharkov would quietly receive a ten-million-euro reward. The money would go into his own pocket and Grey, out for his own revenge, would repay Zharkov with a lifetime of gratitude.

"Add Raife Hastings to the target deck, and you will have my support," Ivan declared. "Kill them both."

CHAPTER 22

Yaak River Valley, Montana

DIMITRY HAD FLOWN THROUGH Moscow and New York and finally into Seattle. He'd driven the breadth of Washington State, picking up the weapons in Spokane. The Sinaloa Cartel's network throughout the United States was an extensive web of hubs and spokes, allowing for the efficient transportation of contraband throughout the country. Though designed to move narcotics, that same network could move anything from teenage girls to weapons, including the dozen AKM rifles that his team would use on this operation.

Personally, Dimitry preferred the AK-74 he'd used during his own military service, a weapon that fired the smaller, high-velocity 5.45mm round rather than the more venerable 7.62mm Russian cartridge, for which the AKM was chambered. He loved what the little 5.45mm did to flesh. It created wounds so devastating that the Afghan *muj* called it "the Devil's Round." The arsenal mark indicated its Russian origin, sent no doubt to feed some insurgency in Central or South America during the 1980s. A rifle was a tool, and these tools would work fine after a good cleaning.

He steered the panel van through the darkness, following the directions that had been provided to him by the local asset. Rumor had it that Tanya was a tasty thing. Maybe he'd get a chance with her at some point during this operation. She had rented a remote farm in the Yaak River Valley, an extremely distant corner of Montana known simply as "the Yaak." Situated only miles from the Canadian border, the Yaak was the kind of place where people minded their own business. A place where gunfire wouldn't raise many eyebrows. A place where men could gather and train.

He crossed over the East Fork of the Yaak River and saw a sign that said "Stabin' Cabin 100.'" Dimitry caught the landmark but his English missed the pun. The gravel road wound through the trees, his headlights catching the movement of small clusters of white-tail does who rose from their beds as he steered among the thick pine trunks. The landscape finally opened up to a lakefront clearing with a cluster of structures arranged near the waterfront. There was a sprawling main house, two smaller cabins, and a large barn, plenty of room to accommodate his team and their equipment. Best of all, the closest neighbor was miles away.

Dimitry backed the van up to the doors of the barn and shut off the engine. A tall man with a shaved head walked toward him, his eyes squinting in the headlights. He opened the door of the van and stepped out, just as the figure reached him.

"Dimitry?"

"*Da.*"

"I'm Vitya." The men shook hands, sizing one another up like a pair of male lions assessing dominance. Vitya was taller and thinner than the new arrival but looked to be close in age. Losevsky Vitaliy Vasilievich was a Saint Petersburg native who had served in the GRU, Russia's military intelligence agency, attached to a *spetsnaz* commando unit. He was trained in collecting intelligence in forward areas, helping some of Russia's fiercest warriors access and exploit their targets. He had served in South Ossetia in 2008 and, after returning to civilian life, found his skills were marketable to Ivan Zharkov and the Tambov Gang. He had been sent to Brighton Beach, but bounced around the United States, living primarily in Miami and Los Angeles. Unlike most of the Brotherhood, Vitya had no criminal record, so he was able to move freely on his own passport rather than one procured by Zharkov's son.

"Any trouble with the weapons?" he asked.

"No problems. Come help me unload them."

Dimitry opened the back doors of the van and dragged one of two long Rubbermaid tubs toward the bumper, nodding for Vitya to take hold of the other end. Each tub was loaded with a half dozen rifles that had been smuggled across the southern border. Ammunition was easier to acquire in the United States and Vitya had bought a sizable quantity in Nevada on his way up from LA. The men stacked the two weapons containers next to three wooden crates stenciled with a mixture of Cyrillic and English markings. Each crate held two 700-round sealed metal "spam cans" of 123gr. FMJ ammunition with lacquered steel cases. The ammunition was loaded in Russia by Barnaul and exported worldwide to feed the millions of AK-series rifles built during the Cold War. The guns and ammo, often carried by illiterate child soldiers, fed insurgencies, dictatorships, and drug wars, and helped keep women subjugated across the developing world; the Soviet Union's everlasting gift to humanity.

Dimitry pulled a tarp over the arsenal in the unlikely event that someone might wander into their secluded training site.

"There has been a slight modification to the plan," Vitya said.

"Oh?"

"We now have two targets."

Dimitry nodded. "We will have enough men to take out triple that."

"Let's have a vodka, friend." Vitya motioned toward the main house.

Dimitry didn't argue. It wasn't in his nature to turn down a drink.

CHAPTER 23

SVR Headquarters, Moscow

THE PHONE ON ALEKSANDR'S desk rang twice and then went silent. Thirty seconds later it rang once and then ceased. He looked at it and sighed. He was tempted to ignore it but knew that he was not yet at that stage.

He pushed himself back in his chair and marched from his private office. As deputy director of Directorate S, he didn't owe anyone an explanation of where he was going.

Aleksandr made his way toward Gorky Park, named for writer and activist Maxim Gorky. Stopping to gaze into shop windows from time to time, he used the glass to look for tails. He doubled back twice, but didn't notice any familiar faces, even ones hastily disguised with a different hat or sunglasses.

Aleksandr missed the old park. It was so much easier to conduct business back before the vacant buildings and crime-ridden paths were transformed into clean and Wi-Fi-enabled eco-friendly family zones.

The intelligence officer fished a phone from his pocket and dialed a number.

"What do you know about an American family named Hastings?" Aleksandr's father did not waste time with pleasantries. It was important for him to maintain his dominance.

"Context?" Aleksandr inquired curtly. It was also imperative for him to establish that this conversation was about business and not about being controlled by a domineering father, head of the *bratva* or not.

"Roots in Rhodesia before the unpleasantness. Son was an American Navy SEAL; first name, Raife. They may be connected to another SEAL who interfered in the assassination attempt of the U.S. president last year, the same event that was successful against President Zubarev."

"Commander James Reece. I know the name. I'll look into it. Anything else?"

"Yes, status update on the situation in Africa," he said, referring specifically to the Central African Republic.

"My directorate's assessment has been forwarded through the proper channels as requested. They will arrive on the desk you specified."

Aleksandr knew the desk in question was that of the foreign secretary and that the *bratva* had already exerted the proper encouragement to sign the papers. In this case it was half a million euros in a Swiss bank account and pictures of his grandchildren playing in this very park. The message was clear.

"Good."

The contract to extract uranium and diamonds from the CAR made the pittance paid to secure it well worth the small investment.

"Anything else?" Aleksandr asked.

Ivan paused. He wanted to ask about Medny Island. He wanted to ask about the rumors he'd since verified that his son was importing prisoners from Africa to hunt in the barrens of the Russian Far East. He wanted to ask his eldest son to join him at the family compound in the heart of Siberia. He wanted to know why his son had such hatred for him.

Instead he answered with a terse *nyet* before ending the call.

Aleksandr looked at what the American intelligence agencies called a burner phone in his hand. It was an unnecessary precaution. His connection to the *bratva* was an open secret. In fact, it was the very reason for his rapid ascension through the ranks. One did not cross or insult the son of *bratva* leadership and expect to be long for the world.

He'd use the phone for the remainder of the month and then drop it into the Moskva River.

His father was getting old. Old men make mistakes. Soon Aleksandr would leave government service with enough information to blackmail half the Kremlin. That intelligence, coupled with the power of the world's most feared criminal organization, would see the Zharkov family influence solidified over Russian politics and business for another generation.

It was his father's time to go.

CHAPTER 24

Yaak River Valley, Montana

THE TEAM HAD FILTERED in over the past few days, enforcers from Miami, Los Angeles, and Boston. Dimitry would have preferred that Ivan just hire a team of Wagner Group mercenaries to handle this, but he knew the CIA kept close tabs on those with Wagner affiliations trying to enter the United States.

They split into two teams of six, one led by Dimitry and one by Vitya. To build unit cohesion, each team slept together, ate together, and trained together. A few of the men had military experience but most did not. While Vitya performed his reconnaissance missions on the targets using the tools of his trade, Dimitry created a training schedule to turn these street thugs into something resembling soldiers.

In the mornings, they ran and hiked the trails that surrounded the lake, heading up the relatively gradual incline hills behind the cabin and then into the steeper mountains beyond. These daily journeys ensured that they were all fit to move overland in this terrain and helped them acclimate to the altitude. They were all young and adapted quickly to the physical training.

They would return to the barn each morning, shirtless and covered in sweat, their tattooed bodies on full display. Prison tattoos served like badges on a military uniform in the Brotherhood, with each crude ink design representing a significant crime or event. One could assess the experience of a gang member by their tattoos the way a white-collar employer could read a resume. Dimitry had only served as a senior sergeant in the Russian Army, but he wore the uniform of a World War II field marshal when it came to ink.

After breakfast, Dimitry led them through the process of field-stripping, inspecting, cleaning, and lubricating their rifles so that they would be intimately familiar with their operation. He built a makeshift firing range and personally guided each of the men through the process of zeroing their weapons. Each magazine was fully loaded and tested. Those that experienced stoppages made their way to the bottom of Okaga Lake.

During the afternoon, they practiced small unit tactics. The team learned the basics of fire and maneuver, bounding overwatch, and spent hour upon hour practicing the effective L-shaped ambush. Dimitry taught them everything except how to retreat. In order to keep the gunfire to a minimum, the men carried unloaded weapons and used the age-old "bang, bang!" method of simulating gunfire on the targets.

After dinner they were free to drink, smoke, and joke, bonding in the same manner that men have done under similar circumstances since the beginning of time. Many boasted about sexual conquests, either real or imagined. Tanya was a favorite topic. She was responsible for delivering groceries to the team on a semiregular basis, and the men all looked forward to ogling her tight body when she came to call. Cell phones were not permitted and, other than the satellite television that seemed to always land on adult entertainment channels, she was their only link to the outside world.

They trained six days per week and quickly began to act as a cohesive team. They would never stand a chance against a real military unit but, with the element of surprise on their side, they would get the job done. The key would be the target package, and Vitya was building a vivid intelligence picture on that front.

. . .

Vitya watched the screen of the iPad, steering the drone to track the vehicle's progress below. The custom SUV was easy to spot, making target identification a simple process. He could hear the whine of its powerful engine as it climbed the hill. The driver eased off the accelerator as the vehicle crested the rise, moving almost silently as it approached the tight turn ahead.

He was close enough to see the driver's bearded face as the Toyota rolled past, his attention diverted to something below, probably a phone or perhaps the stereo. The brakes engaged as the hairpin curve approached, and Vitya saw the red lights illuminated as the vehicle reached the corner. One couldn't take this blind turn at more than 30 miles per hour and the thick copse of evergreens provided the ideal concealment that his team would need. That turn was where James Reece would die.

CHAPTER 25

Kumba Ranch, Flathead Valley, Montana

REECE STOOD BAREFOOT, STARING out at the lake behind his cabin. The water was dead calm, without the slightest breeze to ripple its surface. He adjusted his feet on the soft carpet of short pine needles and squatted to grasp the thick handle of the seventy-pound kettlebell before him. Exhaling sharply, he thrust his hips forward, driving the cast iron weight to full extension, keeping his core muscles flexed as it floated briefly at the top of its arc. Gravity swung the bell downward, and he let it fall between his legs as he sucked a breath of air into his lungs. Up he came again, repeating the process until he'd done ten perfect swings and set the weight back onto the ground. He dropped to his chest and executed ten push-ups, then went back to the kettlebell, alternating reps until he'd performed a hundred of each.

His chest heaving and his shoulders searing with lactic acid, he picked up his bow and tried to get his breathing under control as he drew. His arms felt the let-off of tension as the cams engaged, and his eye found the green fiber optic sight pin through the rear peep entwined in the bow's taut string. The aperture of his vision blurred everything but the sight as his thumb found the cold aluminum of the release. He didn't fight the pin's movement, but increased tension using his upper back muscles, transitioning that pressure naturally to his thumb, the sight picture settling into an ever-decreasing orbit at the target's center. The snap of the bowstring echoed in his ears as the carbon fiber arrow sped from zero to 340 feet per second in an instant. His eyes did their best to track the arrow during its half-second flight and his ears registered the hollow "twock" of its impact on the target.

He drank water from a Nalgene bottle as he caught his breath and progressed to a series of Turkish get-ups, box jumps, shoulder presses, and goblet squats with kettlebells of various sizes. He alternated each section of his workout with a shot or two from his bow in preparation for a bugling elk at thirty yards. To prepare for just such a moment, Reece practiced shooting under the stress of a tough training regimen.

His combined workout and archery session had lasted the better part of an hour. After a quick shower, he slipped on a pair of semi-clean jeans, a T-shirt, and trail running shoes. The compact 10mm Glock stayed in the chest rig for his trail runs so he press-checked his SIG P320 X-Compact and placed it in the holster behind his right hip.

Be prepared.

Raife would be out watching his big muley buck at this time of day, so Reece skipped his shop visit and took the most direct route off the property. He was a few miles from the ranch's main gate on his way to town when his phone came alive. The hilltop was the first area with reliable cell service during his weekly trips to Whitefish and, inevitably, alerts would sound as text messages were received.

It was a clean cell phone, or as clean as one could get in the age of information. It was purchased through and registered to the Hastingses' land management company. The only people with the number were the Hastings clan, Vic Rodriguez at the CIA, and Katie Buranek. Most days he could expect a photo of her getting ready to go on a news segment or views from her workout running through the Washington Mall. It was their way of maintaining a long-distance friendship, or was it something more?

He glanced down at this morning's picture: Katie holding up a copy of John Avlon's book *Washington's Farewell*. She'd managed to add a graphic to the photo saying, "You've got to read this! It's fantastic!" Reece had no idea how to add graphics to a photo but couldn't help but smile at the image. He'd have to stop by Bookworks in town and pick it up or have it ordered. He briefly wondered if he was becoming too predictable. He dropped his phone back in the cup holder and brought his attention back on the road as he approached the turn ahead. His grin faded as his thoughts returned to the present; if he were planning an ambush, he'd do it right here. After a lifetime of war, it was hard to turn off the primal side of the brain. Old habits die hard.

CHAPTER 26

Yaak River Valley, Montana

THE HIT TEAM ROSE to their knees as the SUV rolled through the kill zone. Selector switches went to fully automatic and nervous fingers quivered over triggers. The vehicle's forward progress slowed to a mere crawl, providing the perfect opportunity.

Now!

Vitya initiated the ambush with the explosive device, filling the kill zone with flying debris and dust. A second later, the entire team raked the vehicle with 7.62mm rounds, splintering glass, puncturing steel, and ripping through plastic as the bullets chewed through the SUV's exterior. The deafening roar of the fully automatic gunfire was brief, followed by the metallic chatter of a half-dozen simultaneous magazine changes. A second volley of fire from the high ground raked the smoldering vehicle as the maneuver element moved down the embankment, opening up at close range as the support team's magazines ran dry.

Vitya pushed toward the vehicle, his men firing as they went to ensure their primary target had no chance of survival. As their weapons all went dry, Vitya saw the youngest member of the team change magazines and run forward to the driver's-side door. He stuck the muzzle of his AK through the shattered window and emptied all thirty rounds into a mannequin at knifing distance. That had not been part of the plan. Vitya would have to keep an eye on Oleg Guskov.

Dimitry blew the whistle, ending the exercise. Though the men had fired live ammunition, the target vehicle had been a derelict Isuzu Trooper towed on a long rope by the farm's John Deere tractor. The SUV was riddled with bullet holes and the ambush had been a complete success. After weeks of training, rehearsals, equipment checks, and more rehearsals, the assassins were ready.

CHAPTER 27

Glacier Park International Airport, Kalispell, Montana

REECE LOOKED UP AT the LCD monitor on the wall and back at his RESCO dive watch. The flight from Minneapolis was running a few minutes late. You could probably get away with parking curbside at such a small airport, but Reece had parked in the short-term lot, not wanting to get a ticket from a local cop looking to do his part in the Global War on Terror.

He was dressed in what passed for formal attire by local standards, clean Kuhl pants and a half zip. His beard was a bit shaggy, but all in all he thought he looked presentable. He felt self-conscious holding the bouquet of flowers and shifted them nervously from one hand to the other, finally dangling them down his right leg like a drawn saber.

Was he being too forward? Shit. He hadn't done this in a long time.

The CRJ 900 regional jet seemed to move in slow motion as it taxied toward the jetway, finally releasing its passengers into the newly renovated terminal. Reece waited as the plane's occupants passed out of the secure area of the terminal: a cowboy, a traveling salesman, an elderly couple. He finally saw her through the glass. Her blond hair was pulled back into a ponytail and she dragged her roll-aboard suitcase, a copy of Brad Thor's *Backlash* tucked under her arm. Wives shot dirty looks at husbands who'd turned to look as she passed.

Her face lit up when her eyes met Reece's, and he felt himself smile. It felt good. She laughed and stomped her feet as she drew near, letting go of her bag as she wrapped her arms around his neck. He kissed her cheek, and she took his face in both hands, turning his head for a quick peck on the lips, erasing any doubts about where their relationship was heading.

"The mountains certainly agree with you!" Katie said approvingly. "You look great."

"You do, too. You always do."

"Stop," she said, in mock embarrassment.

She turned his head and ran her finger over the pinkish scar on his scalp where the neurosurgeons had done their work. "Barely noticeable."

"Not too rough looking?"

"Not by a long shot, though I'm not sure what I think about this," she said, running her fingers across his beard. "Looking a little gray, Mr. Reece."

"It's the mileage," he acknowledged with a raised eyebrow.

"Expecting someone special?" Katie inquired, nodding her head toward the flowers.

Reece suddenly became aware of the bouquet he'd picked up on the drive in.

"Oh yeah, sorry. These are for you."

"They're beautiful," Katie said, bringing them to her nose. "Thank you, James. So thoughtful."

Reece picked up her suitcase as they moved through the airport, his eyes subconsciously sweeping the area ahead; first hands, then bodies, then faces. The sixth sense that had kept warriors alive since time immemorial was reminding him that his peace could never last.

• • •

"This is spectacular!" Katie said, taking in the majesty of Montana.

Reece drove as they talked, steering the Land Cruiser up the Flathead Valley toward Kumba Ranch. "I've always loved the mountains. I also need to keep a low profile for security reasons. I'm still processing the fallout from Odessa and from . . . well, you know . . ."

"I understand. So," Katie said, changing subjects, "what do we have in store for the weekend?"

"Nothing too crazy. I'd love to show you around the ranch and do some hiking. Raife and his family are dying to meet you."

"Sounds great. I'm up for anything!"

"Ever fly fished?"

"I may have dabbled a bit," she said coyly.

"What does that mean?"

"It's the one thing my dad enjoys almost as much as golf. He and his doctor buddies would do one big fly-fishing trip a year. He started taking me and my brother out on weekends when we were kids."

"I'm self-taught, so maybe you can give me some pointers."

"I'd be happy to. I even brought my Winston four-weight."

"What's a Winston?"

"Oh, James, I have so much to teach you."

"You'll lose cell service in a minute and probably won't have it again unless we come back to town. Do you need to make any calls?" Reece slowed the SUV and navigated the tight turn that wound through the timber.

"Nope. I'm all yours. No distractions."

She powered off her iPhone and dropped it into her purse, then feigned dusting off her hands to symbolize her release from the electronic leash.

They caught up throughout the drive, Katie admiring the view and Reece pointing out various landmarks as he drove through the property. He paused the Cruiser at the crest of the hill above his cabin to give them a commanding view of the lake, then steered down the track toward it.

"Is this it?" Katie asked.

"This is it."

"Wow! What a view!"

Reece pulled the truck sideways in front of the cabin and Katie was out before he could make it around to open the passenger door for her. She stood in the dirt driveway admiring the home.

"Incredible," she said as Reece led the way to the front door, holding it open and stepping aside with a welcoming wave across the threshold. Katie stepped inside, taking in every detail. She walked to the center of the living room and looked upward to the vaulted ceiling. Reece stood silently just inside the door, waiting for a sign of approval.

"Well, what do you think?"

She looked almost teary-eyed as she faced him, her flushed face illuminating with a bright smile. "It's beautiful, James. I love it."

"Can I get you something to drink? I have beer, wine, water. I can make coffee."

"I'd love a beer. It's past five on the East Coast."

"A woman after my own heart."

Reece pulled two bottles of Wheatfish, a local lager, from the refrigerator and popped the caps using a Bottle Breacher from the kitchen drawer. He handed one to Katie and raised his own in a toast. "Uh . . ."

"To new beginnings," she helped, tapping the neck of his bottle with her own before taking a long pull without breaking eye contact.

They walked through the French doors and out into the cabin's backyard, which essentially ran uninterrupted to Canada. Katie kicked off her boots and walked barefoot on the carpet of soft grass as Reece led her toward the water. The temperature was a perfect 71 degrees and a cool breeze blew across the gin-clear lake, causing tiny waves to ripple softly against its bank. The lake's opposite shore was framed by mountains covered in towering emerald pines.

High ground, an advantageous position, Reece found himself thinking.

"This place looks like a screen saver," Katie remarked.

"It really does, doesn't it?"

"I'm so happy to be here with you, James."

She turned to face him, looking up at him with a devilish grin. "Now would be a good time to kiss the girl."

Reece didn't hesitate, leaning forward and taking her face in his hands. She wrapped her arms around his neck, drawing him back toward her and kissing him deeply. They both lost themselves completely in the moment. Reece finally pulled back. "Welcome to Montana."

CHAPTER 28

Kumba Ranch, Flathead Valley, Montana

KATIE SHOWERED WHILE REECE began to prepare dinner. He would introduce her to the Hastings family soon but tonight it was just the two of them. The guest cabin had come with a Traeger grill and Reece had become very proficient in its use as he cooked his nightly meals lakeside, enjoying the age-old ritual of smoking wild game. With the smoker going out back, he worked diligently in the kitchen.

He rubbed an elk tenderloin with a mixture of freshly chopped herbs and sliced the makings of a fresh salad, enjoying a glass of Tuck Beckstoffer's finest pinot noir as he prepared their meal. A stack of logs crackled in the large open fireplace, bathing the room in a flickering golden light. He heard the door open and looked up as Katie emerged. She was barefoot and her hair was down. She looked right at home in jeans and a flannel.

"It feels so great to be out of D.C."

"I'll bet." Reece smiled. "Wine?"

"Absolutely!"

Holding the glass by its stem, she swirled it twice. She held it up to the last light of the Montana evening and took a moment to enjoy its aroma before taking a sip.

"Is this a French burgundy?" she asked, puzzled.

"Actually, it's a pinot noir from the Sonoma coast. It's called Semper."

"I've always wanted to try that! I love the name. It isn't like any pinot I've had before. It's tremendous."

"The winemaker hunts with Raife on the property. He always comes equipped with a few cases of his favorites. I liberated tonight's selections from Jonathan Hastings's wine cellar."

"I knew those SEAL skills would come in handy. And, what are you preparing to accompany such a splendid *vitis vinifera*?"

"The pinot goes with the chips and salsa." Reece smiled. "For the main course of elk tenderloin, we'll switch it up."

"Elk? Is that what this is?" Katie asked, pointing to the mounted bull on the wall.

"It is. My dad shot that bull years ago."

"Admittedly, I don't know much about hunting, though I did love the venison your dad would drop off as I was growing up."

"How's your dad doing?" Reece asked.

"For someone his age, he couldn't be better. He retired from his medical practice and plays a lot of golf. I think he's driving my mother crazy."

"Good for him."

"Can I help?" Katie asked.

"Nope, I've got it handled. You just relax and enjoy your wine."

"So, did you catch this thing?"

"Catch it?"

"Catch it, kill it, whatever you're supposed to say."

"Ha! Well, you can say kill or harvest. I typically like to use both, as *harvest* sounds too much like you are picking corn and *kill* doesn't convey to people that you are actually eating the meat. I was a little busy last fall, so this comes from Raife's freezer. The Hastings clan has enough venison in their combined freezers to feed a small army."

"It looks really lean."

"It is. It's also good for you. About as organic and free range as you can get. You hungry?"

"Starving."

"Good. Let's toss it on the grill."

Reece carried a platter outside and Katie shivered as she watched him put the meat and sliced vegetables onto the charred steel grating.

"Gets cold here when the sun goes down, even in the summer," he said.

"It's probably still eighty and humid in D.C."

"Let's fix that," Reece said, walking a few steps toward a stack of firewood and picking up a propane tank with a hose attached along with a Bic lighter. He opened the valve on the tank and the fuel began to flow from the tubular attachment at the end of the hose. He sparked the lighter and a foot-long flame erupted from the nozzle. He picked up the propane tank in one hand and held the nozzle in the other, walking toward the stone fire ring that sat between the Adirondack chairs. The nozzle bathed the stack of split logs in fire, starting them ablaze almost instantly. He worked the flame back and forth until he was satisfied before closing the tank's valve.

"What is that thing? A flamethrower?"

"Montana fire starter. Come get warm."

They sat together, sipping wine as their dinner cooked nearby, staring into the open flames as the last light of day slipped away.

Even with Katie by his side, Reece couldn't help but think that halfway around the world, teams of special operators were just returning to base after hitting a target. He knew the only time most would hear or think about them was if something went wrong and it was reported on the news. They'd be returning sweaty, dusty, possibly bloody. They'd turn over any enemy detainees to the proper authorities, top off magazines, replace batteries in IR lasers and flashlights, and get ready to do it all over again tomorrow. Those men and women on the front lines provided the blanket of freedom that allowed Reece and Katie to enjoy this evening by the lake. Reece would never forget that they were out there. Not long ago he had been one of them. He'd never witness another sunset without thinking of them and sending a silent prayer their way.

In response to Katie's questioning look, Reece glanced at his watch and jumped up to attend to the cooking. He flipped the tenderloin and took the vegetables off the fire to cool, standing vigil over the grill for the last few minutes that the elk needed to complete the outside sear.

He probed the meat with his knuckle and, satisfied, pulled it from the fire.

"Let's go inside. Almost ready."

As the meat rested, Katie found a candle in one of the kitchen drawers and placed it next to the bouquet that she'd put in a vase on the table. Reece added a light dressing to the salad and tossed it with two large forks, placing a portion on each of their plates. He flanked the salad with slices of grilled squash and zucchini and drizzled them with balsamic vinegar. Finally, he sliced the tenderloin into half-inch sections, inspecting the meat as he cut. The outside was charred, and the center was a warm, red medium-rare. *Perfect.*

"This looks amazing. I didn't know you could cook."

"I'll be out of recipes in two days. I didn't want to burden Raife's family with feeding me, and there's obviously no restaurant nearby, so I've been doing a lot of grilling. I don't think I've ever turned the oven on."

"Then grilling it is."

"Are you ready for the next pairing?" Reece asked as he set their plates on the rustic farm table.

"You know I am. What has Jonathan Hastings's wine cellar produced for us next this evening?"

Reece held up the bottle next to a glass decanter, "It's named for *To Kill a Mockingbird.*"

"One of my favorite novels of all time," Katie declared.

"Mine, too."

Katie opened cupboards until she found what she was looking for.

"For a wine as special as Mockingbird Blue, we need the right glass," she said, pulling two large Bordeaux glasses from the shelf.

Tuck Beckstoffer's famed cabernet had been breathing in a decanter since Reece started preparing dinner. He gave them both a healthy pour as they sat down to eat.

"Cheers," Reece said, as they clinked glasses.

Katie swirled the wine and held it to the candlelight, admiring its legs. She then closed her eyes and breathed in its aroma through her nose before taking her first sip.

"What an elegant red," she noted. "Great balance for such a full-bodied cab."

"How do you know so much about wines?"

"My little secret is that I didn't start out to be a journalist."

"Really?"

"I did two years in the viticulture and enology undergrad program at UC Davis."

"I'll have to look both those words up next time I get cell service."

"Let me help you. Viticulture refers to growing grapes. From the Latin word for 'vine.' And enology is the science of winemaking."

"What made you switch?"

"Honestly," Katie said, "the war. My dad. *Your* dad. I felt like this country had provided my family so much opportunity. Seeing those freedoms squandered and eroded by pandering career politicians while young men and women who stood up to volunteer to defend the nation kept coming home in caskets made me angry. When Ambassador Stevens, Sean Smith, and your friends Ty Woods and Glen Doherty were killed in Benghazi, I knew I had to do something. Politicians left them to die. Politicians who would never be held accountable. So I transferred to English at Berkeley and then went to Columbia School of Journalism for my master's. That's where I started work on *The Benghazi Betrayal.*" She paused. "Sorry to get so serious."

"*In vino veritas*," Reece said, bringing the red wine to his lips.

"'In wine lies the truth.' I knew I liked you, Mr. Reece."

"What do you think of the elk?"

"It's delicious. I could eat this every night."

"That's good because it's about all we really have available," the former frogman said with a wink.

"It's so peaceful, Reece. I can see why you came here."

"This feels like home. I felt this way in Mozambique until they found me."

"What did you think about when you were in Africa?" Katie wondered aloud.

"Ah, a lot of things, I guess. I went to Mozambique to die and ended up learning to live again. I found purpose out there, using my old skills to counter the poachers. I thought about my family. And, I thought a lot about the people who had helped me in the U.S. after Lauren and Lucy were killed. I wondered if I'd put them in danger or if the government was going to figure out who had assisted and take legal action against them."

Katie nodded and gazed into her glass.

"And," Reece continued, "I thought about you."

"You did?"

"That might have been the only thing that kept me alive. This sounds strange, but even though I thought I was dying, thinking of you gave me hope."

Katie swallowed, her eyes misting over as she thought of all he'd been through.

"I thought of you, too, James. It drove me crazy not knowing if you were dead or alive."

"I'd been living for so long thinking I was a dead man, I didn't know how to live believing I had a future."

"And now?"

"And now I'm figuring out that future."

Katie took a breath.

"Well, this is certainly a good place to do it," she said, looking around the spacious lakefront cabin.

"I think so," Reece confirmed.

"Now on to more important topics, like if there is any more Mockingbird Blue?" Katie asked, holding up her empty glass.

Katie moved to the living area as Reece refilled their glasses from the decanter in the kitchen. She sat on the couch, her legs pulled beneath her.

Reece carefully handed her the wine before taking a seat, her knee lightly touching his thigh. They were both aware of the contact and neither made an effort to move.

"Are you going to go back to work for them?" She didn't have to specify whom she meant by "them."

"Possibly. I'm connected as a contractor right now. There's something I need to do, and they might be the only ones who can help."

Reece didn't offer more, and Katie didn't push, instead asking, "When you got quiet out by the fire, what were you thinking about?"

Reece paused. "What I always think about when the sun sets: that somewhere the enemy is out there, planning, getting ready to hit us again, and that there are a select few getting ready to take the fight to them."

"Do you feel guilty that you are not with them?"

She was extremely perceptive, from a women's intuition or a journalist's savvy, Reece wasn't sure.

"Not really guilt. It's more like I feel a responsibility to keep fighting."

She put her hand on his. "You're safe here, James. Take some time. I'm here to help."

They each took long sips of wine and stared into the fireplace. Reece broke the silence first. "I don't know how safe it is. What happened in Odessa, it's not over."

"Let me face it with you, James."

She was brave. Reece felt choked up as he remembered her black-and-blue face, blood trickling from her nose, neck wrapped in explosives, looking up at him with pure terror in her eyes.

"Katie, I knew that det cord wouldn't blow."

Katie's blue eyes connected with his of piercing brown. "I know."

They kissed one another breathlessly, each of their hands caressing, exploring. Katie rose without another word. Taking Reece by the hand, she pulled him to his feet and led him to the bedroom.

CHAPTER 29

Saint Petersburg, Russia

GREY WAS LIVING IN his office, monitoring events in Montana as best he could without making direct contact with the team on the ground. Tanya, the female asset sent in from New York, was making her daily social media posts. These seemingly innocuous ramblings and photographs, mere cells in the entire biosphere of web traffic, were a direct signal to Grey that the ground team was on track. Since Reece's movements were never exact, especially given the holiday weekend, the team had moved into position and would remain in place until he appeared. As soon as the secondary team received word that Reece was down, they would move in on Raife Hastings and finish the job.

Accounting for Daylight Savings Time, there was a nine-hour time difference between local time in Russia and Montana. Eight a.m. local at the target was 5:00 p.m. for Grey, which meant that late nights were part of the program. It was approaching 10:00 p.m. now, and he had been in the office for more than fourteen hours. His freshly laundered dress shirt was wrinkled, his tie was loose, and his jacket was hanging in its usual spot on his office door. For Grey, the monotonous hours of waiting for a subject to move was nothing new, but, given his personal connection to this target, that experience didn't make this wait easier. He grabbed a pint of good local vodka from his desk drawer and took a long pull before pouring a splash into the tea that Svetlana had delivered to him before she left for the evening.

The target vehicle had moved on Thursday, making a stop at the airport in Kalispell, no doubt picking someone up for the weekend. *The reporter?* Maybe that explained why he hadn't left his cabin this morning, despite the late hour? Sooner or later he would have to go to town and, when he did, the hit team would be waiting.

CHAPTER 30

Flathead Valley, Montana

VITYA STARED AT THE screen of the tablet, trying to will the blinking light that represented the target vehicle to move, but there it sat, in front of the lakefront cabin. He and his team had hiked to the high ground above the ambush site the previous afternoon, setting up camp three hundred yards from the road in the dense forest. The GPS tracker would give him at least thirty minutes' notice that the target was on its way, which was plenty of time for them to set the trap. For now they rested in shifts, fiddled with their weapons, ate salty dehydrated meals out of plastic bags, and drank enough coffee to give them all atrial fibrillations.

Vitya's team was tasked with killing James Reece. He was the primary target and would be eliminated first. Then the second team would kill Raife Hastings.

He walked down to the ambush position for the twentieth time and surveyed the scene. The IED was positioned at just the right angle to rake the road with its 700 3.2mm steel ball bearings, which would shred everything in their path at 1,200 meters per second. The convex mine was concealed under a bed of pine straw at the base of a tree. Its wire was buried along the path. Vitya carried a green plastic firing device in his jacket pocket. He'd used the M40 test set included with the mine to confirm that it was working properly and would send the electric pulse necessary to power the blasting cap and fire the mine's plastic explosive. He couldn't risk a premature explosion so he would only connect the detonator when he had confirmation that the target was on his way. It would be a shame if the bait was caught in the powerful blast; he hadn't even had a chance to sample the goods, but that couldn't be helped; every battle had collateral damage.

He looked down at the AKM slung at his side. It was spray-painted in a green and brown camouflage pattern to eliminate the glossy shine that had burnished through the original finish by years of rough use. After spending the preceding weeks with the iconic weapon, he had become interested in its origin and often wondered about the stories it could tell. Its stamped steel receiver differentiated it from a true AK-47, though that name would forever be associated with Kalashnikov's deadly design. He saw the arrow-in-triangle proof mark of the Izhevsk Armory, the small-arms factory turned "machine building plant" that had armed Russia's fighting men and women with everything from muskets to machine guns since the early nineteenth century. Behind the arsenal mark was the year the rifle was built: 1975. Vitya was younger than his weapon.

The name "RICARDO" had been carved into the wooden buttstock by one of its previous users, trench art from the latter days of a Cold War battlefield now relegated to the pages of history. Ricardo was probably a Sandinista, given the weapon's Central American pedigree, but due to the widespread distribution of Russian weapons, Vitya couldn't be sure.

Was Ricardo waiting to ambush a group of CIA-backed Contras when boredom took over and he decided to carve his name into his weapon? Had Ricardo survived?

Vitya would never know.

CHAPTER 31

Kumba Ranch, Flathead Valley, Montana

REECE AWOKE EARLY, HIS body unaccustomed to the warmth of someone else in his bed. He didn't move, not wanting to disturb Katie's sleep as she lay on her side next to him. She looked peaceful, her face content, the rhythmic rising and falling of her bare shoulder the only movement. He watched her for an eternity in the semidarkness, taking in every detail. A tiny gold cross hung askew around her neck on a wire-thin chain. Reece felt a sense of harmony that he hadn't known since his family was taken from him.

As the sun shone through the crack in the bedroom's heavy curtain, she stirred, her hand sliding across the cotton sheet until it found the musculature of his bare chest. She opened her eyes and smiled at him, sliding her leg toward his own and pulling herself into his embrace.

"Good morning," she purred.

Afterward, they lay side by side, Katie running her fingers over Reece's lean chest and stomach, tracing the outline of each muscle with her fingers.

"How did you manage to spend almost twenty years in the military and walk away without a tattoo?"

"That was probably my greatest accomplishment." Reece smiled.

"Ha! Let's eat. I'm starving."

. . .

After bringing in split logs and stoking the coals in the stone fireplace to take off the morning chill, they ate a breakfast of scrambled eggs and fruit, before packing a lunch and heading for the mountain. Reece led the lakeside hike uphill to one of the small tributaries that fed the larger body of water. They fished each pool in the rocky creek from below, out of the trout's line of sight, working their way uphill as they went. Katie looked like she'd been born with a fly rod in her hand, the sunlight filtering through the trees and catching the long leader as it S-curved its way through the air before settling onto the water's surface.

They pushed off their waders and ate their lunch in a sunny meadow, taking in the midday warmth as they drank 75 Wine Co sauvignon blanc from enameled metal cups. They made love under the cloudless sky before dozing on the blanket Reece had spread out on the hillside. Katie caught the first trout of the day that afternoon, a beautiful rainbow that she held up for a photo before they put it on ice in the soft-sided Yeti cooler that had carried their lunch. She caught two more fish to Reece's one as the day progressed, which led to an amusing discussion of his angling abilities.

That evening, Reece drove her to one of his favorite spots on the ranch, a high vista where they sat on his tailgate drinking local microbrews as the elk herds grazed into the grassy valley below. Katie slipped on Reece's jacket as the sun fell beneath the next ridge. In the coming weeks, the bulls would begin to rut, filling the mountain air with the enchanting sound of their bugles. The young bulls were already acting the part, posturing and chasing one another halfheartedly as the mature males watched patiently from the timber.

Back at the cabin, Reece pan-fried the breaded trout filets while Katie stood at the stove beside him, preparing a dish of brussels sprouts mixed with bacon. They selected a Silver Oak cabernet from Napa Valley as Katie recounted how her skill with a fly rod had put their dinner on the table.

As what was one of her best days in memory came to a close, Katie's eyes once again took in the room and came to rest on her suitor's back right hip. It had not gone unnoticed that Reece was never out of arm's reach of a weapon.

CHAPTER 32

Flathead Valley, Montana

AFTER TWO COLD NIGHTS spent in the mountains, Dimitry's men were beginning to bitch. Despite their training, he had to remember that these men were street thugs, not soldiers, and were unfamiliar with prolonged physical suffering and hardship. He cursed Ivan for not figuring out a way to bring professionals in to handle the hit. They had camped in a patch of thick timber without even the luxury of a fire. Each morning he had led them to their overwatch position and waited for the call from Vitya that would initiate the second phase of the operation, the elimination of Raife Hastings.

They were four hundred yards from the Land Rover and its sole occupant, Raife Hastings. They watched him climb a ridge and stare through his telescope at some distant object. Dimitry studied the man through binoculars, careful not to risk any lens glare that would give away his position. He moved like one of the mountain lions that were known to inhabit the area, light on his feet yet powerful, covering rough ground swiftly and efficiently. Still, he only carried a handgun, a short-range weapon against a half-dozen men with rifles. Add in the element of surprise and their advantage of holding the high ground, and it wouldn't even be a contest. Even if their target got lucky and took out one or two of them, Dimitry's team would overwhelm him with sheer firepower. It was the Russian way.

Dimitry suppressed a smile, thinking of Stalin's adage, *Quantity has a quality all its own.* All they needed now was the signal to execute.

Dimitry checked the sat phone for the hundredth time that morning, ensuring it was powered up and had a strong signal. He resisted the temptation to call the other team and see what the holdup was, but the rules were clear: his team was not to engage until it was confirmed the first target had been terminated.

What had he heard in one of the American movies he was so fond of? *Terminate with extreme prejudice.* Dimitry liked that.

He watched the disappointment on his men's faces as their target collapsed the legs of his tripod, strapped the optic back onto his day pack, and moved toward his vehicle. It was the second day in a row that they'd had him in their sights, completely unaware of their presence, and were forced to let him slip away. *How long could their luck hold out?*

As the Rover's 2.5-liter turbo diesel engine grunted to life, Dimitry signaled the men to move back, pulling them to the concealment and relative security of the thick evergreen forest. If the signal came before tomorrow morning, they would move as quickly as possible overland and hit him at home. Doing so would give up many of their tactical advantages, but it would be their only option.

The order to kill would come soon enough.

CHAPTER 33

Kumba Ranch, Flathead Valley, Montana

IT WAS SUNDAY BEFORE Reece was finally willing to share Katie Buranek with the Hastings family. Raife's mother, Caroline, had arranged a lunch to welcome Reece's friend to the ranch and attendance was nonnegotiable. Reece and Katie went on a long hike that morning and Katie, who was raised to never show up at someone's home empty-handed, took the opportunity to gather wildflowers that she'd assembled into an impressive arrangement of glacier lily, clematis, and purple asters upon their return to the cabin.

"Awful quiet over there," Reece said as they made the short drive up to the main house.

"After all you've told me about this family, from the Rhodesian Bush Wars to the Selous Scouts and everything they've accomplished in this country, I'm more excited than anything else. And Raife's father-in-law is Senator Tim Thornton, of all people! I feel like we are going to meet royalty."

"They will be more intrigued by you and your family's story. Nothing to worry about. Besides, Jonathan is probably already drunk."

"Ha! Okay, my kind of people."

As they rounded the corner toward the homestead, the lake and dock came into view, the Grumman Albatross rocking gently at its mooring.

"Whose plane is that?" Katie asked in astonishment.

"That's Thorn's. He flies it in from one of his surrounding properties in Montana or Idaho. He's here for opening day tomorrow morning. He hasn't missed one since . . ." Reece paused. "Since his wife died."

They pulled up in front of the house and Katie let Reece open the door for her. She was pleasantly surprised when he took her arm in his as they walked toward the home's sprawling front porch, the simple gesture helping put her at ease.

Jonathan and Caroline greeted the couple with genuine joy, both hugging her before she could get through the door. True to his reputation, Jonathan held a green bottle of Namibian Windhoek Lager in his paw and handed another to Reece as he entered the foyer.

A man who reminded her a bit of an older Indiana Jones rose from a leather chair by the fireplace and extended his hand, "Ms. Buranek, Tim Thornton. I am very pleased to meet you."

"It's an honor to meet you, Senator."

"Please, call me Thorn. I much prefer that. 'Senator' conjures up too many memories of my time in the swamp," he said, referring to Washington's unofficial moniker. "And, thank you for your series of articles and the book on the Benghazi mess," he continued, shaking his head. "Those boys deserved better. Politicians in and out of uniform left them to die. But, enough unpleasantness. Let's get you a drink."

"What can I offer you, Katie?" Caroline Hastings asked.

"What are you having, Mrs. Hastings?"

"Please call me Caroline. I'm having champagne."

"That sounds wonderful."

Jonathan appeared with a crystal flute of France's finest and handed it to their guest.

"We have one other surprise for you both," he said. "Liz, would you be a dear and join us?"

Reece's eyebrows arched in amazement as all five feet, four inches of Elizabeth Riley appeared from a back guest room. The two had first met in Iraq during the height of the insurgency. Riley's OH-58 Kiowa had been shot down in Najaf, her capture and torture seemingly inevitable. A few blocks away Reece's sniper team was set up in an overwatch position of a heavily IED'd stretch of road. Hearing the situation on the radio, Reece defied orders and launched a hastily organized rescue, putting the aviator deeply in his debt. She recovered from her injuries but was medically retired from the army. She became like a sister to Reece and his late wife, Lauren, and a close aunt to their daughter Lucy. Riley was unflinchingly loyal to her friends and, when Reece needed help avenging the deaths of Lauren and Lucy, she was there on wings.

"Liz, what are you doing here?" Reece asked after a strong embrace.

"I work for Thorn now," she replied in her thick southern accent. "He has more planes than he can keep track of."

"Liz, you remember Katie."

"Of course, we've kept in touch. It's not every day you spirit a kidnapped reporter off Fishers Island in a Pilatus in the middle of the night."

The two women embraced like old friends.

"Come out and have a seat. Caroline has everything set up out back," Jonathan said, leading his guests through the home and onto the back deck via the open French doors. A long table flanked with wicker chairs had been set up on the back lawn overlooking the lake. The table was covered with a flawless white starched tablecloth of fine linen, and place settings of the family's best English silver and bone china were located at each seat. Brightly colored fresh flowers, now including the ones that Katie had brought, overflowed from a vase at the table's center.

Jonathan had just pulled out a chair for Katie when Raife and Annika came strolling across the lawn.

"Katie, I'd like you to meet my friends, Raife and Annika Hastings."

She rose, shaking hands with Raife. "So nice to meet both of you. I've heard so much about you."

Annika hugged her warmly.

"We're just glad that you are real, Katie. I was beginning to think that you were a figment of Reece's imagination," Raife said with a grin.

"We promise not to scare you off, Katie," Annika added, elbowing her husband in the ribs.

"Please, everyone, sit," Caroline said, before taking her seat at the far end of the rectangular table from Jonathan.

Both younger couples sat beside one another, arranged so the women could chat at one end of the table while the men gathered at the other.

Jonathan and Caroline brought the meal out in courses, each with an appropriate wine pairing. Raife drank sparingly. Opening day of archery season was the following morning, and he had work to do. Reece and Katie had no such obligations. They both joined in the festivities with Thorn, Liz, and the elder Hastingses, enjoying the fine South African vintages.

"Don't be afraid to try my famous hot sauce," Jonathan reminded the table. "Goes great with everything."

"Don't believe him," Raife warned. "He makes it with homegrown ghost peppers. If you value your taste buds, you'll shy away."

The conversation was light and jovial, much of it surrounding humorous stories from Reece's and Raife's younger days.

"Does Katie know about your crazy Alaskan adventure, Reece?" Jonathan prodded.

"Ah, I don't think I've mentioned it yet," Reece responded.

"Alaskan adventure?" Katie asked.

"Yeah, how long did that insane escapade take you?" Raife teased. "Three months, wasn't it?"

"Sixty-four days," Reece responded, shaking a finger at his friend.

"Oh, do tell," Katie pushed.

"I'll tell you," Jonathan jumped in, ever the storyteller. "Your man here, Katie, he decides he wants to spend some time in Alaska before he ships off for boot camp. His father, Tom, God rest his soul, had a trapper's cabin in the middle of nowhere up there so Reece had a bit of experience in austere conditions, but of course he wanted to take things to the next *bloody* level. He decides he wants to trek across, what was it, Reece, the Talkeetna glacier?"

"Close." Reece smiled, looking sideways at Katie.

"Doesn't matter," Jonathan continued. "This wild bloke decides he's going to head into the Alaskan wilderness, *alone*, trek across the Talkeetna glacier, to the, uh, what river was it? No matter, to some glacial river and then kayak to the ocean."

"Kayak?" Katie asked. "Where was he going to find a kayak in the middle of the backcountry?"

"Ha! That's the best part, Katie," Jonathan went on. "He pulled it behind him, over the snow."

"You did *what*?" Katie asked, turning her attention back to Reece.

"Well, I had it tied to me so if I fell in a crevasse the idea was that the kayak would slide over the top and I'd be suspended underneath. Then I'd just jumar up and continue on."

"Jumar?" Katie asked.

"Ascenders. They allow you to pull yourself up a rope. You can use a smaller piece of line and make your own as well."

"Best part is," Jonathan said, jumping back into the story, "this was before cell phones and sat phones and constant connectivity. He tells us and his parents that he'll be back in a month. Sixty-four days later he comes kayaking into Cook Inlet none the worse for wear, other than looking like a vagrant."

Reece shrugged. "It was a good pre-BUD/S workout."

"And that wasn't the end of it," Jonathan continued. "This mountain man then sells his whitewater boat and mountaineering gear, buys a sea kayak, and spends a month island-hopping his away around Prince William Sound."

"What did you eat?" Katie asked.

"I pulled a lot of the staples behind me in the kayak, potatoes and rice, and I hunted and fished my way across for protein. I had a little .22 in the kayak that I'd use for squirrels and beavers, and a fly rod for trout and arctic grayling. Once in the sound, I trolled off the kayak for salmon."

"I'm surprised you didn't starve to death. Remember, I've seen your fishing abilities," Katie joked.

Laughter was a near constant around the table, with Jonathan having an amusing tale to tell about everyone there.

As the early evening dinner wore to a close and the air temperature began to drop, the men moved to the fire pit while the women moved inside. Thorn packed a pipe, knowing his friend would like nothing more than to roll a fresh tobacco cigarette, yet with Caroline so close, he wouldn't dare. When the old warhorses started discussing their plan for the following day, Reece and Raife stepped a few feet away, Raife not wanting the scent of tobacco to negatively impact the next day's hunt.

"Good luck tomorrow," Reece said.

"Thanks, buddy. If you're around, I may need help packing the meat out."

"Well then, I changed my mind. I hope you don't get him." Reece chuckled. "I'm planning to take Katie into town in the morning, but we'll zip back if you need me."

"Reece," his friend began, "what were you looking at during dinner?"

"What do you mean?"

"You know what I mean. At times you were *here*, but you weren't really *here*."

Reece had forgotten how well his blood brother knew him.

"Nothing. Well, not nothing. Just a feeling. Something's not right."

"Something's always not right, brother," Raife offered, scanning the distant tree line. "Remember what your dad used to tell us?"

"Trust your instincts," Reece recalled.

"After everything you've been through, don't let the past ruin your today," Raife said wisely, nodding toward the main room, where Katie sat with the rest of the family.

"Remember what *your* dad used to tell us?" Reece responded in kind, nodding toward the weathered old Selous Scout.

"He's always full of what he thinks is good advice."

Reece's eyes narrowed and his head turned back toward the shadows.

"He said, 'It's not paranoia if they're really hunting you.'"

PART TWO

THE STALK

"Civilized men are more discourteous than savages because they
know they can be impolite without having their skulls split, as a
general thing."

—Robert E. Howard,
The Tower of the Elephant

CHAPTER 34

Saint Petersburg, Russia

THE STRAIN WAS BEGINNING to wear on Grey, who had scarcely left his desk in days. The plan was contingent upon Reece leaving the ranch yet he hadn't left the property in seventy-two hours. Changing the operation at this stage was a recipe for disaster and would require breaking his self-imposed ban on active electronic communications. Remembering what the duo had done to his mentor and handler with an RPG-32, Grey was beginning to worry.

Svetlana made her nightly visit before her departure, tea in hand. This time, however, she carried a cup for herself, which was a first. She set a cup down in front of Grey, who sat at his desk staring intently at both computer screens before him. He looked up at her with exhausted eyes and snapped his laptop shut. There was something different about her tonight.

"I brought you some tea, Oliver."

"Thank you. I see you have some for yourself. May I offer you a touch?" Grey lifted the vodka bottle from his drawer.

"That would be wonderful, Oliver."

He poured a finger of the clear liquid into her cup and filled his own to the brim, sipping tentatively to test the temperature.

"Why do you work so hard? What is it that can't wait until tomorrow?"

"Something very important, something that will make them fear me."

"Anyone who knows how smart you are should fear you."

"The Americans think that they are so powerful that they fear no one."

"Ah, you will show them, Oliver." She took a long pull from her own cup and set it down, rising from the chair and walking behind the small man. Her scent filled his nostrils as she began to massage his shoulders with her powerful hands, releasing the tension that had built up over the preceding days. Her hands worked their way up the back of his neck and onto his head, where her fingers made tiny circles on his temples. He let his head fall back with a sigh and closed his eyes. Svetlana leaned forward, pushing her ample bosom into contact with his head, and began rubbing his chest. She smiled as she saw the front of his trousers rise.

Grey opened his eyes when she swiveled the desk chair so that he was facing her, his body tensing as she ran her hand to his groin.

"Such a big, strong boy."

"No, Svetlana, I can't . . . I . . ."

"Shh, Svetlana will take care of everything. You be a good boy." She pulled open her blouse, exposing her breasts, which Grey immediately began to grope and kiss. She pulled her skirt up and sat on his lap, breathing heavily in his ear as she ground herself into him. He gasped audibly and his body quivered and lurched forward, nearly knocking Svetlana from the chair.

"I'm sorry, I . . ." He pushed her from his lap, a dark stain visible on the leg of his tailored slacks. Unable to look at her, Grey stood uncomfortably for a moment before hurrying from the room.

Svetlana did not hesitate. She pulled a USB drive from the pocket of her skirt and quickly inserted it into the port on his laptop. She walked to the office door and stole a look down the hallway.

A small LED on the drive flashed red as the device downloaded the contents of the computer's hard drive. Svetlana walked out to her own desk and shuffled around as she kept an eye toward the restrooms. Picking up her phone, she sent a text message before dropping it back into her purse. When she heard footsteps in the hallway, she returned to Grey's office and palmed the USB drive. She was straightening his chair when he returned, his eyes averted. She wrapped him in a warm hug, holding his face to her chest.

"Good night, my sweet Oliver."

She kissed the side of his head and walked from his office.

. . .

That evening, a young man rang the doorbell at her apartment. When she answered, he handed her a bag of carryout food. Inside a wad of paper money, Svetlana passed him the USB drive. Within an hour, the contents of the drive were being exploited by a trusted team of technicians from Directorate I of the SVR, the office of Russian intelligence that specialized in digital forensics and cyber exploitation.

CHAPTER 35

SVR Headquarters, Moscow

BY THE TIME ALEKSANDR Zharkov reached his desk at 8:00 a.m., the report from Saint Petersburg was already in his inbox. His attention was diverted by a mild crisis in Damascus that morning, so he didn't get a chance to open the document until the afternoon. The cover sheet summarized the raw intelligence and made reference to both the source of the information as well as some of the more relevant documents recovered from the subject's hard drive.

Svetlana had performed beautifully, just as he'd known she would. The Russian intelligence services were the best in the world when it came to manipulating subjects using sex, and the psychological analysis of Oliver Grey had been spot-on. Aleksandr had pulled in all information on Grey going back to the original paper files, when he was first spotted, assessed, and developed by the Soviet-era GRU before his recruitment by the late Vasili Andrenov. It was always amusing to Aleksandr when he saw state documents marked with stars, hammers, and scythes, the pseudo-religious emblems of communism.

Upon their reexamination of Grey's records, the SVR's psychoanalytical team had come up with a secondary diagnosis, one that went deeper than the obvious father issues. As a result of his father's absence and eventual abandonment, his mother had overcompensated and inadvertently created an unhealthy relationship with her son. He was unable to connect with women his own age or younger because, deep down, he still hungered for a mother. Svetlana had been successful in earning Grey's trust and bringing his repressed gerontophilia to the surface.

Aleksandr had placed Svetlana, one of his most experienced assets, into his father's business more than a decade ago and she had consistently provided him with accurate, timely, and relevant updates on the activities of his father and brothers ever since. He double-clicked on a PowerPoint file titled "Montana OPORD" and began scanning the pages. He quickly realized that the operation in question had already been put into motion.

He scrolled to the profile on the targets. He recognized the name of Lieutenant Commander James Reece, U.S.N. (Ret.), immediately, thanks to the widespread media coverage of his attack on a ring of conspirators responsible for the deaths of his family and SEALs under his command. The SVR had actually tried to locate Reece after his disappearance in an attempt to recruit him and offer him the chance to defect but had been unsuccessful in tracking him down. Aleksandr also knew that Reece was suspected in the death of former Russian intelligence official Vasili Andrenov, though nothing had been proven. It was obvious from the intelligence package that his father's new asset had organized a *bratva* hit team to kill James Reece either in retaliation for the Andrenov assassination or before Reece could mount an offensive of his own against Grey.

The second target was more of a mystery. Raife Hastings, also a retired SEAL officer, was a resident of western Montana. The African-born Hastings owned an outfitting business and had made a name for himself as a builder of fine custom hunting rifles. Hastings was apparently married to the daughter of a billionaire oil and gas man who'd previously served in the U.S. Congress.

Could it be him?

Aleksandr, ever the hunter, was an avid reader of outdoor magazines published around the globe. He had become mildly obsessed with a columnist who wrote occasionally under the pseudonym of "S. Rainsford," a nod to the protagonist of Richard Connell's 1924 short story, "The Most Dangerous Game." The columns were the author's firsthand accounts of his solo Montana backcountry hunts, told in brilliant detail. Unlike most of the glorified advertising that passed as outdoor journalism these days, whoever "Rainsford" was, he was a hunter.

Aleksandr pulled up the background check via Russian intelligence channels he'd requested a few months back. They had failed to identify an "S. Rainsford" but had compiled a list of twenty-four possibles. Rifle maker and hunting outfitter Raife Hastings was on that list.

Aleksandr leaned back in his chair and tilted his head toward the ceiling.

S. Rainsford, now he would be a formidable adversary. Adding his friend, James Reece, to the draw would be the hunt of a lifetime.

Aleksandr had once managed to attract a famous hunter from the States to hunt brown bear with him on the Kamchatka Peninsula. Despite the way he was portrayed in his articles and television series, the man was actually hopeless without a guide. When Aleksandr turned the tables and made him the prey, he wept and begged before becoming desperately lost. His ineptitude and lack of spirit took almost all of the pleasure out of the hunt; Aleksandr had seen better woodsmanship from Moscow prostitutes than he had from the overweight American.

Rainsford and Lieutenant Commander Reece would be fighters.

Finally, a challenge.

Aleksandr made his decision. He pulled an aging paper Rolodex from his desk drawer and searched for a number that he hadn't dialed in ages.

CHAPTER 36

Kumba Ranch, Flathead Valley, Montana

THE SUN WOULD RISE at 6:55 a.m. Raife had been awake since 4:00 a.m. He turned off his alarm so as not to disturb his pregnant wife and slipped out of bed. He sipped black coffee as he dressed in a light wool shirt and pants, pulled on a knit stocking cap, and laced his buffalo hide Courteney boots. Everything he wore was designed for maximum mobility and stealth.

With the prospect of running into a grizzly bear a real one, Raife slipped his inherited 1911 handgun into the leather holster behind his right hip. He remembered his dad's joke about .45-caliber pistols and giant predators. "Why do you file off the front sight of your 1911 when going into bear country?" his father had asked. "So it doesn't hurt as much when the grizzly shoves it up your ass."

Raife had never found it very funny.

It was only a ten-minute drive from his home. He made the trip with just his parking lights on so as not to spook game or ruin his night vision. He donned his pack, picked up his recurve bow and quiver, and stood silently in the darkness to acclimate himself to the sounds of the predawn morning and confirm the speed and direction of the light breeze. The morning was cool but there was no frost. Satisfied, he began the hike toward his glassing spot. He wanted to be in position to observe the buck well before the first rays of light illuminated the valley.

With practiced efficiency, he climbed the steep grade, the simple tire soles of his boots legendary for quiet stalking. At forty, Raife was in the best shape of his life and, given the field in which he'd spent the early part of adulthood, that was saying something. The sky was just starting to lighten to the east, the nighttime display of stars washed away by the first rays of sunlight. He set himself up for a long morning of glassing, arranging his tripod and spotting scope before pulling an apple from his pack. He took a bite as he swung the powerful scope toward the buck's lair, its coated German lenses gathering every bit of ambient light.

The buck should have been out feeding on the mountainside at this point in the relative safety of the darkness, but there was no sign of him. He pulled up his binoculars and began to scan, trading magnification for the wider field of view. Nothing.

The slight change in temperature would not be enough to move the animal from his summer range, so that wasn't it. It wouldn't be the first time that he'd watched an animal for weeks, only for it to disappear the moment that the hunting season opened. Prey species seemed to have a sixth sense when it came to the hunt. Raife thought about his conversation with Reece the previous evening and took an extra moment to survey the high ground behind him before turning his attention back to the scope. As the sky turned from gray to pink, it became increasingly obvious that the buck had left his hide. Something had spooked him. *Wolves, maybe?* It was conceivable. *A poacher?* Not out of the realm of possibility. Raife needed to adapt. The wind was still light but steady and the thermals wouldn't be much of a factor this early in the day. It was time to move. The son of Rhodesia packed his spotting scope and picked up his bow before setting out quietly down the draw.

Raife's tracking mentor had been a master. Melusi was a member of the Matabele tribe, a Bantu offshoot of the powerful Zulus. The Matabele people were defeated in battle by the Dutch Afrikaners and were effectively banished to what is now Zimbabwe. Like all great African trackers, Melusi spent his childhood tending the herd, responsible for protecting the family's cattle, sheep, and goats from neighboring tribes or predatory animals. With no fences to contain their herds, Melusi and his peers would spend their days tracking each wandering animal by its spoor. It was a tremendous responsibility to place upon a child but Melusi had a nearly supernatural gift for reading the ground and quickly took to his job.

Melusi had taught Raife to read sign from a young age, in much the same way he was taught by his own elders. One of Melusi's favorite tricks was to take Raife to a salt lick, where animals of various species would gather to consume the valuable mineral. Melusi would squat in silence, smoking a hand-rolled cigarette while Raife pointed out each individual animal's tracks. He would nod as Raife called out each name in English, Shona, and Ndebele. By age six, Raife could tell a waterbuck track from that of a kudu and, before he was eight, he could tell the age of a track to within a few hours. He was able to read animal spoor in the wilderness the way an urbanite used street signs. Raife's tracking skills had brought more than a few Taliban and Iraqi insurgents to an untimely end, and had earned him the respect of the hunting guides with whom he worked.

· · ·

The buck's sign was everywhere, thanks to the many weeks he'd spent sleeping, eating, urinating, and defecating in the immediate area. Raife made increasingly widening circles, searching for a track that led away from the site. He found it on the uphill side of the bedding spot, near the rockslide that made up the ridgeline. He saw the deep impressions of the buck's hooves as he hopped in the manner unique to an alarmed mule deer. Something had spooked him. Raife hadn't seen any wolf or grizzly sign in the area, nor had he heard any wolves howling recently. No one other than family or friends had permission to be on the property, so he shouldn't have been startled by another hunter. Raife took a seat and glassed the surrounding terrain, looking for any sign of what might have spooked the deer. After nearly thirty minutes of searching, he picked up his bow and began to follow the trail.

Even a good tracker would have lost him in the rocks but Raife's skills had long since progressed beyond simply "good." He went to his hands and knees and was able to make out the disturbed lichen on the rocks. Once over the knife edge of the ridgeline, the animal's path took it through the thick summer grasses, where his trail was more visible to the trained eye. It was difficult to tell how long the tracks had been there, but he estimated that they were at least a few hours old; the stems of grass were beginning to return to their natural position after being folded downward by the buck's passing.

Raife stood back up. He was on the stalk.

CHAPTER 37

Central Intelligence Agency, Langley, Virginia

VIC RODRIGUEZ DIALED REECE'S number for the fifth time and, as usual, it went straight to voice mail. He'd received an emergency call that morning from Craig Flynn, a retired CIA officer who had previously served as the Moscow station chief. Flynn had been contacted by a senior official in the Russian SVR named Aleksandr Zharkov, whom he had known from his Moscow posting but had not heard from in years. Director Zharkov claimed to have come across information on a Russian mafia operation under way in Montana to kill James Reece and Raife Hastings. Due to the time-sensitive nature of the intelligence, he said there was not time to go through official channels. Because of Flynn's history with Director Zharkov, he assessed the information to be credible.

Flynn had worked with Reece's father in an operation to extract a doctor from Czechoslovakia during the Cold War, so he instantly recognized the name James Reece. Though now retired, Flynn still had close connections at Langley, including the director of the Special Activities Division.

Changing tactics, Vic hit the intercom button on his phone, "Valerie, connect me to the Flathead County Sheriff's Department in Montana."

. . .

Reece showered and made the necessary preparations to keep his promise to take Katie into town. The plan was to have a late breakfast, walk around a bit, and decide whether to stay in town for lunch or get something for the road and head over to Glacier National Park. Clouds had moved in overnight. Fall seemed to be kicking at the door. They each carried a mug of Black Rifle's finest coffee as they left the cabin and climbed into Reece's Land Cruiser. Katie was even trying hers spruced up the way Reece took his, with local honey and a bit of cream. She found it endlessly amusing that the tough commando liked his coffee a bit on the sweet side. Making the turn onto the paved highway, Reece thought back to his conversation with Thorn a couple of weeks ago and with Raife the previous evening. It just might be time to start a new chapter, one that did not involve U.S. intelligence covert action programs. It might be time to start a new life with Katie.

. . .

For Dimitry and his team, watching Raife Hastings move into and out of his daily glassing spot had become routine. At any point, they could have initiated the ambush but, until word came from Vitya, all they could do was observe.

Today was different. He'd arrived far earlier than normal, the men watched as he readied his gear by the light of his headlamp before leaving the vehicle. Then, instead of looking through his scope for a few minutes and returning to his truck, Hastings packed his gear and moved into the valley that he'd so painstakingly observed under the team's watchful eye. Dimitry also noticed that he carried a different weapon today: an ancient-looking bow with a small quiver of arrows. One man with a bow against six with rifles. He had watched his share of American western films on television to know how those odds had worked out for the Indians.

Dimitry stared at the sat phone, willing it to ring. He didn't know where the target was going but, sooner or later, he would return to his Land Rover. When he did, they would be waiting. The sun rose, and the valley was soon bathed in an orange glow. He thought of the gray walls of his prison cell back home, the screaming, the blood. The phone vibrated.

He answered it and listened as Vitya informed him that they would be initiating their ambush in just a few minutes. He'd grown to like the man and was appreciative of the heads-up. There was a decision to make. Should he wait here for Hastings to return? What if the attack raised the alarm and the American military or police came with their helicopters? No, he needed to move in on the target and take him out. It was time.

Dimitry slipped the phone into his pack and pulled it on over his shoulders as he stood. His men didn't need to be told to do the same and soon they were all patrolling past Hastings's vehicle, six abreast. Hastings had a head start of several hours but was surely trekking slowly as he stalked whatever prey he was after. Dimitry only hunted men.

It felt good to be moving after so much waiting. His legs felt strong as he climbed the ridge, the rifle light in his hands. Dimitry watched his men with pride. Dressed in surplus American camouflage uniforms and moving with speed and discipline, they could almost pass for soldiers. He called a halt as they approached the first ridge and he crept carefully forward to reconnoiter the next valley. He could see the marks where the legs of Hastings's tripod had dug into the soil and he raised his binoculars to scan the space below him. Satisfied that the target had gone ahead, he waved his men forward.

• • •

Vitya saw the vehicle move on the screen and quickly dialed Tanya using the burner cell phone that he'd brought along for the occasion. The signal was good on the high ground, and she answered after three rings. They spoke in English.

"Hello?"

"Is Dan there?"

"I'm sorry, you have the wrong number."

"My apologies." He pressed the "end" button, terminating the call. He whistled, getting his men's attention quickly. Their chronic boredom quickly became excitement as they moved down into their prepared ambush positions near the road. Vitya and the rest of his four-man assault team were situated on the long side of the L, with the two-man support-by-fire element carefully crossing the road to a position perpendicular to the target vehicle's route. When he slowed the SUV to make the turn, Vitya would initiate the ambush with the IED. The vehicle would take fully automatic fire from the front and side, with 180 rounds in the first volley alone. No one in an unarmored vehicle would survive it.

Vitya watched the iPad impatiently as the target drove along the ranch roads. Just as it turned onto the highway, Tanya pulled up in her blue 2003 Jetta. She parked the vehicle on the road's narrow shoulder and, as she'd been instructed, popped the hood. She stood helplessly in front of the vehicle wearing yoga pants and a tight tank top, hands placed on her hips. Assuming that chivalry was not yet dead in this northwestern part of the country, they were counting on their target stopping to assist the attractive motorist in apparent distress.

Vitya watched the red dot accelerate on the asphalt highway and knew from experience that it would be in the kill zone in less than five minutes. He moved the selector switch on his AKM to the Cyrillic marking for "full-auto" and set it down on the bed of pine straw beside him. Pulling the M57 firing device from his pocket, he connected it to the trailing end of the wire that led to the claymore mine's blasting cap. Only the small wire safety bail stood between the device's handle and a catastrophic explosion. He looked at each of the men on the assault team and received nervous but ready nods from them. He couldn't see the camouflaged figures of his second element but was confident that they were in place. Everyone knew their jobs.

Vitya looked at his watch. He needed to give Dimitry a heads-up that the ambush was about to be initiated. Even in the unlikely event that their communications were being monitored, there wouldn't be enough time for anyone to stop them. He pulled the sat phone from his pouch and pressed the preset key that would place a call to Dimitry's identical unit. He held the device to his ear as he waited for it to connect to the satellite in orbit. Once the call went through, Dimitry answered almost instantly.

"Yeah."

"We will initiate in five minutes, be ready."

"Understood."

Looking back at the iPad, he saw that the target was two minutes out. He fiddled nervously with the mine's firing device, shifting it from one hand to the other. He heard the high-pitched whine of a diesel motor climbing the rise and a shot of panic gripped his chest. Reece didn't drive a diesel. The driver let off the accelerator as the vehicle crested the rise and a blue flatbed F-250 pickup rolled into view. Whoever was driving had seen Tanya and was rolling to a stop in the kill zone. The driver pulled onto the shoulder opposite her Volkswagen and left the truck idling as he stepped down onto the pavement.

A tall mustached man in his fifties and wearing jeans, boots, and a denim jacket approached Tanya, no doubt offering his assistance. They were too far away for Vitya to hear their conversation. Her body language told the story; she dismissed the man with a wave of her hand, no doubt telling him that help was on the way. The man lingered persistently. Whether it was out of a genuine desire to help or because of Tanya's tank top did not matter to Vitya; he needed this cowboy to get the hell out of the way. His eye moved back to the iPad, where the dot rounded the final bend before it would make its way up to the hill where they waited in ambush. This changed nothing; he would blow the mine and initiate the ambush no matter what.

Reece gripped the wheel with both hands as he steered up the steep grade ahead, driving slower than normal so as not to alarm his passenger. He let up on the gas pedal and let the Cruiser coast over the rise, spotting two vehicles pulled off the side of the road ahead of him. From a distance, it looked like a female with car trouble and a man who'd stopped to help. It was nice to be back in a place where people actually cared about their fellow citizens.

On cue, his iPhone came alive with the various indicators of the modern age as he entered the service area. Ordinarily he would sneak a look at his phone to see whether there were any messages from Katie but, with her by his side, there was no reason. She had a real job and was far more accustomed to living in a connected world and, despite enjoying a well-needed respite from life's distractions, she fished her phone from her purse when she heard it come alive. Reece was taken by surprise when the phone actually began to ring through the vehicle's hands-free Bluetooth system, "Private Number" showing up on the LCD screen on the dash. Reece pressed the screen to decline the call, not interested in talking to anyone who wasn't currently riding with him.

The phone rang again and that sixth sense he'd been trying to ignore all morning forced him to answer it. He pressed the green icon to answer the call.

"Hello."

"Reece, it's Vic, where are you?" Despite their history, receiving a personal call from the head of the CIA's Special Activities Division wasn't exactly routine. Reece leaned slightly forward in his seat.

"I'm in Montana, heading into town. What's happening?"

"No time to explain; there's a Russian mafia plan to hit you and Raife Hastings. It's happening *today!*"

Reece looked at the cars parked beside the road and considered the sharp curve ahead. He slammed on the brakes, sending Katie forward until her progress was arrested by the seat belt. The jolt slung her phone out of her hand and it crashed into the floorboard at her feet.

"Get down!" Reece yelled, pushing her head down below the dashboard. He put the Cruiser in reverse and the powerful engine revved as the tires spun, finally catching as the SUV lurched to the rear. Smoke billowed from the off-road tires as Reece executed a textbook J-turn, sliding the vehicle from reverse to forward in a fraction of the time it would take to make a three-point turn. The rear window of the Cruiser exploded in a shower of tempered glass as a burst of 7.62mm rounds from a member of the support element raked the back of the vehicle. Reece pushed his foot to the floor and took advantage of all 430 horses as he sped away from the kill zone.

"Are you okay?" he asked, looking at Katie for any sign of injury.

"What?"

"Are you hit?"

"No. I don't think so. What was that?"

"You just survived your first ambush."

"My first?" she asked, thinking back to the time that a taxi driver had opened fire on the two of them on a Los Angeles sidewalk.

"Good point. Your second."

"Reece, you okay?" It was Vic's voice coming through the speakers.

"Yes, sir."

"You with Raife?"

"No. I'm with Katie."

"Roger th . . ." The phone lost signal as they drove down the hill at almost 100 miles per hour.

"Katie, I need you to reach behind the seat. There's a rifle mounted to the back of it. Grab it and put it next to me."

Katie unbuckled and turned around, returning with the rifle that Raife had put in the truck for his friend, just in case. Reece knew it was loaded but took his right hand off the steering wheel to perform a quick press check. He slid it to where he could access it quickly and, without looking, turned the knob on the left side of the scope to illuminate the reticle.

He reached for the radio mic hanging on the dash and pressed the talk button.

"Reece for Raife, over." Static. "Raife, Raife come in, over." Nothing. "Reece to Kumba base, over. Reece to anyone on this channel, this is an emergency, over."

No response. Raife was too far from the main road to hear the gunfire and they were too far from the ranch to be in radio range. It would take them a few minutes until they were inside the repeater network that allowed the ranch staff to maintain contact while on the property. Reece pushed the Cruiser to the maximum speed that its low gear ratio would allow, the knobby tires propelling them back toward Kumba.

CHAPTER 38

Saint Petersburg, Russia

GREY STARED EXCITEDLY AT the screen of his desktop, watching the signal from the Iridium GPS indicator steer toward the ambush site. It wouldn't be long now. Svetlana had made an excuse not to stay late, which suited him just fine. He couldn't stomach the embarrassment of his recent performance and pushed his sexual attraction for her to the back of his mind.

He felt a tinge of jealousy for the men who would send Reece to his grave, men who had no grievance with the SEAL commander. To Grey it was personal, while to these men, who would get to see the action up close, it was a professional job.

The dot made its way to the highway, and Grey shifted nervously. He crossed and uncrossed his legs and wrung his sweaty palms. The dot finally began to climb the hill. He rose to his feet, pushed his chair backward, and leaned forward with his hands on the desk. The dot moved to the top of the terrain feature and began to slow; then it stopped. He willed the dot forward, first silently and now vocally.

"Go, go! Move forward! Keep going!" The dot began to move backward, first slowly and then more rapidly away from the well-laid ambush. "No, no!"

Grey snatched the phone from its cradle on his desk and dialed the number from the Post-it note on the side of his monitor. It took forever to connect and then rang several times before there was an exasperated answer in English, with a thick Russian accent.

"What?"

"What happened?" Grey shouted.

"I don't know! Some cowboy stopped to help right in the kill zone. Then the target stopped and took off."

"Did you fire?"

"Not until he drove away."

"*Shit!*"

"What do you want us to do?"

"Call the other team and tell them to execute. Move to the ranch house. Kill the primary target. Wait, just kill *everyone!*" he yelled into the receiver.

"We don't have a vehicle. The girl drove away and isn't answering her phone."

"*Shit!*" Grey slammed the phone, ending the call.

•   •   •   •

A few valleys away, Raife knelt at the track in the sand, its crisp outline indicating its extreme freshness. The droppings in front of it were still glistening with moisture. The deer's gait had changed to a relaxed meander as he'd increased the distance between himself and whatever had startled him from his lair. With a flick of his wrist, Raife shook a cotton infant sock, sending a small white puff of the talcum powder inside into the air. The light breeze blew the powder back and slightly to his left, indicating he still had the wind in his favor.

He moved into a prone position and slid his body forward so that he could see into the open valley below him. It was one of the largest meadows on Kumba, a grassy bowl hundreds of yards across that was intersected by small creeks and a few scattered trunks from ancient toppled pines that were bleached nearly white by their exposure to the sun's rays. Slowly he pulled the strap of his binoculars, bringing them within reach. He painstakingly searched the valley through the 10x lenses, systematically searching each quadrant of ground before moving his focus to the next. Ten minutes into the exercise, he saw it. The flick of an ear. The buck had bedded behind one of the fallen pines, its body concealed by the trunk and its massive antlers blending in perfectly with the single remaining branch that jutted skyward from the tree. But for that tiny movement, Raife never would have seen him.

Finding the deer was the first step; now he had to make a plan to work himself within range. He traced a muddy creek bed backward from near the buck's position and figured that it would give him just enough terrain to crawl beneath the deer's line of sight. If he could make his way to the creek without being spotted and could crawl the length of it without being heard, and if the wind didn't shift to blow his stalk, he might have a shot. He rolled to one side and shrugged off his pack, taking only his bow and quiver and what little was strapped to his body. He unclipped the Motorola two-way radio from his belt and laid it on top of the pack before backing over the ledge and out of sight of the valley below. He walked bent at the waist and to the left to put him in position to move down the ridge behind the buck; it gave him the wind's full advantage and made it less likely that the deer would spot his movement in its peripheral vision.

Melusi would be proud.

CHAPTER 39

REECE TOOK HIS FOOT off the accelerator as they approached the ranch entrance, and steered the Cruiser through the steel gate that was visible from the road. The truck rumbled over the welded pipes of the cattle gap, and he punched the gas. He picked up the radio mic and made his third attempt at contact.

"Reece for Raife, over." It would make sense that Raife would have his radio turned down, assuming that he was still hunting. "Reece to Kumba base, over." He waited a few seconds before repeating the call. "Reece to Kumba base, over."

"Kumba base here, go ahead, Reece." It was the voice of Caroline Hastings.

"Kumba base, we have an emergency. *Terrs* on Kumba, over. I repeat, *terrs* on Kumba." He used the old Rhodesian vernacular for "terrorist," which was a term that, as a veteran of the Bush War's home front, Caroline was more than familiar with.

"Roger, Reece. We will lock down here, over."

"Is *Utilivu* with you? Over." Reece asked, using the Shona nickname for Raife in case they were being monitored. There was a long pause.

"Negative, Reece, over."

"Roger that. I'm bringing my friend to you for safekeeping, over."

"Roger."

Reece drove at the absolute limits of his and the vehicle's abilities. As he skidded the Toyota to a stop next to the main house, he saw Jonathan, Liz, Thorn, Caroline, and Annika rush to meet him. Jonathan was carrying what looked like his old wartime FAL rifle at a high port, its crude green and brown "baby shit" camouflage paint job still evident after nearly three decades. He wore his daily work attire of boots, jeans, and a western shirt but with a faded nylon chest rig strapped across his chest. His face was alert, and his eyes were bright. He was in his element. Thorn had his bolt action deer rifle in hand.

Caroline carried a classic Brno model 602 in one hand, its muzzle pointed skyward with her elbow locked into her hip. She stood beside Annika protectively, a stoic look on her face indicating that this wasn't the first time that she'd protected the family's home from armed men with bad intentions. She rushed to open the door for Katie and wrapped her with her free arm as she climbed from the SUV.

"Reece, what's happened?" Jonathan asked.

"Not sure, sir. Katie and I received a call from the CIA on our way into town. They missed us, but not by much. The information we received says this is Russian mafia and they are here for me and for Raife. I am so sorry, I . . ."

"Never mind that now, son," Jonathan said, taking command. "It sounds like they're just after the boys, but you never know. Caroline, it's just like the old days. You know what to do. Thorn, Liz, you stay here. There are ARs in the gun safe and a stack of loaded magazines next to them. Grab them and keep 'em close in case those bastards get in the house. Annika, Katie, get in the vault and arm yourselves, but only lock yourselves in as a last resort in case these *terrs* try to burn you out. We'll be back, as soon as we get Raife."

All nodded in unison, and Caroline led the other women quickly toward the house.

"Hop in," Reece said. The older man nodded and opened the back door of the Cruiser. He put two fingers in his mouth and whistled loudly.

"Zulu, come!" On cue, the family hound came bounding around the corner of the house and jumped into the SUV without hesitation. Jonathan took a seat, the muzzle of his rifle resting between his feet. As soon as he slammed the passenger door, Reece hit the gas, spitting gravel as the Cruiser fishtailed down the driveway.

CHAPTER 40

RAIFE'S FEET WERE SOAKED and numb from stalking through the icy creek. It was the only way to stay below the buck's vision. He moved at a painfully slow pace to reduce the noise signature, the glacial stream freezing his calves. When he was within one hundred yards of the deer, he set down his bow and moved carefully onto the grassy bank. He unlaced his boots and set them aside on the dry land. Ordinarily he would have made his final stalk wearing just his wool socks, but, given their saturation, he was afraid that they might make a squishing sound, betraying his presence. He removed them as well and laid them out on the stalks of grass to air dry. He pulled the knit wool cap from his head and tore a handful of vegetation from the ground. Weaving the long strands into the fabric, he transformed the simple hat into a crown of local camouflage.

He was on all fours now, crawling in the long grass the way he'd watched lionesses hunt in Africa. He wondered for a moment how many men had crawled through this same valley, bow or atlatl in hand, in pursuit of deer, elk, or even mammoths. It wasn't uncommon to find the flint artifacts of hunters past when the soil on the ranch was turned over by spring rains.

He pulled the powder-filled sock from his hip pocket and gave it a shake to test the wind; it was light but holding. He slipped it away and continued his slow crawl, his bow in his right hand. He put his weight on his knuckles so as not to damage the bow as he moved. It was slow going but now was not the time to rush. Sneaking a peek, he saw that he was sixty yards from the branches of the fallen pine. A good shooter with a compound bow could take a shot on an animal of this size from where he knelt but, with a recurve, even an archer of his talents needed to cut that figure in half. Raife eased back into a crawl and began to close the final yards.

Forty yards. He slipped an arrow from the leather-covered quiver attached to the bow's frame and carefully nocked it onto the braided bowstring. He held the bow in his left hand, his pointer finger holding the arrow securely on its rest. In ten more yards, Raife would rise to both knees to keep his hips on a level plane and bring the bow to full draw. The buck would stand up and Raife would have a split second to release the shot before the animal bounded out of range. His breathing was rapid, and his mind was totally focused on the next move, the next soft spot to place his hands and knees. Despite the cool morning temperatures, rivulets of sweat ran down his face. To Raife, there was no feeling more natural, more human, than the stalk.

He wrapped two fingers of his right hand around the string and purposefully relaxed his left hand's grip on the bow. His body rose slowly but deliberately, his eyes focused on the spot where he knew the buck's shoulder would be. Raife's head was just clearing the crest of the grass stalks when he saw the buck lurch to his feet; it was always shocking how big these animals were at close range. Raife froze. Something had spooked the buck, but his focus was over Raife's head toward the ridge behind him. *The sixth sense.* Morphing from hunter to warrior in less than a second, he sprinted forward as the ground around him came alive, eruptions of dirt showering upward and the unmistakable crack of supersonic rifle rounds passing nearby.

Instincts, hardwired from nearly two decades of sustained combat, took over. His hands released the bow as he sprinted toward the tree that had been the buck's hiding spot, the Colt coming effortlessly from its leather holster as he ran. He could hear the incoming rounds chewing into the earth around him. Halfway to the tree, he dove the remaining yards, his body going fully horizontal as it flew for the only available cover.

He hit hard on his belly and knees and rolled back the way he'd come, pressing his body against the trunk of ponderosa pine. Rounds impacted the thick wood fibers but, thanks to the velocity they'd lost on their way to the target, none penetrated completely through.

There was no "why me?" or "why now?" clogging the former commando's consciousness. Instead, he was entirely focused on prevailing. He was lying on his side, body parallel to the trunk of the tree. He turned his head to ensure that no one was moving in on the ridge behind him.

Take a breath, look around, make a call.

Raife took a moment to take stock of the situation. Multiple bad guys with Kalashnikovs; he'd been shot at by them enough times to know exactly what they sounded like. No sign of a belt fed, which was good news. He hoped that they didn't have an RPG. If there was a sniper among them, he'd already be dead, which meant they probably didn't have anything more capable than AKs or AKMs.

He had a handgun that was designed when Taft was in the White House. It held seven rounds in the magazine and one in the chamber. Two more magazines were stowed in a leather pouch on his belt. The ridgeline where the fire was coming from was an honest 300 yards from his position and it was farther, almost 500, to the next ridge behind him. He was essentially in the bottom of a gigantic bowl, hiding behind one of the only available pieces of cover. It wasn't good, but it could have been worse; *it can always be worse.*

The creeks such as the one through which he had just waded all flowed into a swampy area to his left, which would be chest-high with water at the moment. That meant that, when these guys started trying to flank him, they would have to do so from his right. The volume of fire coming his way became more sporadic as his attackers began to change magazines. He could hear someone yelling in a language other than English, no doubt their leader taking command of the situation. He must have directed them to conserve ammunition because the full-auto bursts were replaced with a steady stream of semiautomatic fire designed to keep him in place so that they could maneuver to make the kill.

Raife low-crawled to the extreme left end of the log and slowly began to ease his way forward until he could see one of the shooters. The first figure was prone, the dust from his rifle's muzzle blast giving away his position. He continued to push himself forward with his toes as he brought his 1911 to bear, searching for a larger target at this extreme range. The third figure he spotted must have been the leader; he was up on one knee, directing the other members of the team with his left arm.

Raife was in what was known as the rollover prone position, an incredibly steady way to shoot a handgun. The distance would have been unfathomable to most shooters, but Raife's dedication to training with the 1911 at extreme handgun ranges was about to pay off. His thumb pushed down on the safety unconsciously as his hands brought the pistol to full extension. His eyes found the serrated front sight and held it at the midway point of the target's torso, the steel blade rising halfway above the rear notch to accommodate for the distance. He exhaled deeply and trusted the area wobble of his sights, all focus on the front post as his finger pressed evenly back against the trigger. The shot broke, and he completed his follow-through before shifting his eyes to the target in case a correction was needed. His ears registered the hollow sound of a large bullet slapping flesh, and he saw the distinctive Russian weapon drop to the ground.

• • •

Reece raced down the dirt roads with both hands on the wheel, Jonathan directing him at each turn. He was familiar with the ranch, but no one knew the land the way Jonathan did. Reece could see Raife's parked Land Rover as they came around a tight bend, and Jonathan motioned for him to stop. He rolled down the window to listen and Reece shut off the motor. They heard the unmistakable sound of rifle fire in the distance. Jonathan considered the terrain for a moment and pointed forward on the track.

"Drive up to this ridge and drop me off. You continue down this road and you'll likely come up on whoever is after Raife. I know you can handle yourself."

Reece cranked the motor and sped up the incline ahead. The road took them up a ridgeline that ran parallel to the direction of the gunfire. The ridge appeared to be the highest terrain feature in the area, so Reece would most likely come in above the action. Several hundred yards up the ridge, Jonathan motioned for Reece to slow down. He opened the passenger door while the Cruiser was still rolling and prepared to bail out. As soon as the vehicle stopped, his boots were on the ground. Zulu jumped between the seats and followed his master out the door.

Reece sped forward. He rolled all of the windows down and, thanks to the Cruiser's effective exhaust system, could hear the gunfire clearly over the engine. By the sound of it, he was getting close. He braked to a halt just below the military crest of the next hill. He grabbed his carbine and climbed out of the SUV. Running to the rear of the vehicle, he opened the back hatch to retrieve a small backpack before moving on foot toward the sound of the guns.

CHAPTER 41

THE TEMPO OF FIRE increased, indicating the flank had begun. This was small-unit tactics 101: one element provides a base of fire to fix the enemy in place while the second element moves to close the distance and gain an improved fighting position. The covering team then leapfrogs ahead and takes up the next advantageous position until everyone on the objective is dead.

Downrange, if found in such a scenario against a numerically superior force, Raife and his team would have used all of their firepower, as well as whatever fire support was available, to break contact with the enemy. This was different. He had no team, no real firepower, and certainly no fire support.

Oh, to have a radio and an AC-130 gunship circling overhead right now.

He turned his body around so that his head was facing the right side of the tree and eased his way forward, ever so slightly gaining an angle on the opposing ridge. The lead figure was running obliquely downhill toward Raife at somewhere past 150 yards, AKM swinging as he sprinted forward. Raife lay prone, his abdomen flat on the ground, and his body aligned with the moving figure. He waited for the attacker to stop, since even he couldn't hit a moving target at this distance. The man took cover behind a boulder that left only his head exposed and immediately began raining accurate fire on Raife's position. Raife fired quickly, rushing the shot just a bit, and saw dust fly in the man's face as his bullet impacted the rock. He fired another round and slid back behind his rapidly disappearing cover just as a burst of fire stitched the ground in front of him, sending clods of dirt and pine fragments into his face. Raife was about out of time.

Another assaulter got a little too confident as he bounded past his team member behind the boulder. Taking a knee in a spot high enough to allow him a direct line of fire into Raife's position, he was rewarded with a hardball to the lung that quickly took him out of the fight. These men were not fanatical Fedayeen hopped up on amphetamines; they were street thugs used to getting by on bravado and intimidation. Raife didn't know how many men he was up against, but it sounded like fewer than ten. He'd hit at least two of them. Still, the odds weren't good. Taking advantage of the moment, Raife pulled a fresh magazine from his pouch and performed a tactical reload. He stuck the partially loaded mag in the back pocket of his pants, where he could reach it if necessary.

The fire was intense, with multiple shooters putting rounds directly into Raife's position. Only his attackers' mediocre marksmanship skills and a slight dip in the ground were keeping him from getting hit. He made himself as small a target as possible, hugging every inch of the terrain as rounds hissed and cracked over his head and pounded the ground in front of him. There was a lull as one of the shooter's magazines ran dry and Raife snuck a peek; two men were bounding in to within one hundred yards at a dead sprint. He snapped off two rounds in their direction, which sent them diving for cover.

He didn't think about the fact that he'd survived multiple combat deployments targeting Al Qaeda and ISIS and was about to get killed on his own ranch in Montana. Nor did he think about his pregnant wife just a few miles away. Instead he thought about improving his fighting position and exploiting every technical and tactical advantage he could. If this was his last stand, he wasn't going to make it easy on them.

• • •

The Teams had a saying: "Don't rush to your death." There was hardly ever a good reason to go barging into a target at full speed without carefully assessing the situation. The one big exception was a hostage rescue mission, where safety was sacrificed for speed in the name of protecting the hostage. There was another exception: when your friends were in trouble. From the sound of it, Raife was in a really bad spot. Reece heard at least a half-dozen rifles firing from multiple positions, interrupted only by the occasional pop of what must have been Raife's .45.

He slowed his progress just for a second as he reached the top of the ridge, and crawled the final few yards so as not to silhouette himself at the peak. The noise from the rifle fire rose abruptly as he cleared the rise, the sound waves no longer absorbed by earth and trees. Reece saw a group of three men ahead, bounding toward the only piece of cover in the valley below. There was no time to make a more thorough assessment; they were moments away from overrunning Raife's position.

He had a pair of range-finding binoculars in his pack, but he wasn't going to waste precious seconds retrieving it. Reece estimated the camouflage-clad shooters to be about three hundred yards away so he dialed the scope's magnification to six-power and found a solid prone position. He held for two mils of elevation on the optic's Christmas-tree-shaped reticle and sent a 77-grain round into his first target, which toppled to the ground from a dead run. The suppressor mounted to his rifle didn't mask the supersonic crack of the bullet, but it did disguise the muzzle blast, making his location difficult to pinpoint. The shot caused immediate confusion among the members of the assault element, and the firing came to a precipitous halt. Reece heard Raife's pistol boom in response. *He was still in the fight.* Reece fired another round into the fallen man to keep him down for good, then shifted left to acquire a new shooting position.

Firing resumed from below, a long burst echoing across the valley. Reece spotted the source, a proned-out figure just uphill from the one he'd just put down. His first round fell short, sending a visible geyser of dirt skyward. He made a slight correction and fired three more times at a steady cadence. Reece watched the man writhe violently through the scope as his body fought against the unseen force that had shattered bones and severed organs.

The last man saw the fate of his teammates and took cover behind a boulder, sneaking single shots in Reece's direction before disappearing once again.

Reece cranked the scope up to its full magnification and shifted his body to a more stable position. He put his weight on the rifle's magazine, digging it into the ground like a monopod for stability. The shooter's exposures from cover were random, a bit like a game of Whac-A-Mole, but there were only so many options. Reece exhaled, put his finger on the trigger, and took up most of its weight as he waited for the target to appear. He saw the muzzle first and knew that the head would follow. The AR's sear broke from its tension just as the shooter's head was moving clear of the boulder. Reece saw chunks of brain matter take flight and heard the smack of the bullet's impact a moment later.

CHAPTER 42

DIMITRY'S ARM HURT LIKE hell but it bled very little. The bullet had hit his forearm just below the elbow, rendering the arm all but useless.

Who in the hell could shoot a pistol like that?

He held his weapon awkwardly in his left hand now, but his job was to command, not necessarily to shoot. He had kept one man back with him to make up the base element as the maneuver element pushed toward Raife Hastings.

Dimitry watched as the assault team bounded to within one hundred yards of the target. They had him flanked. It would all be over in a matter of minutes. Dimitry saw one man go down. He would have to be left behind, since they had no ability to carry his body out on foot. None of his men carried identification though the tattoos would give them away as *bratva* if killed or captured. By that time, the rest of the team would be across the Canadian border and possibly already in the air, bound for safe houses on the other side of the Atlantic.

Observing the final assault through binoculars, part of him wished he'd stayed in the army, but the officer bullshit outweighed the fighting by too heavy a margin.

There was no sign of movement behind the log where he'd last seen Hastings take cover.

Maybe he was already dead?

His eyes saw another man fall as a shot echoed across the canyon.

What in the hell?

Dimitry lowered his binoculars and scanned the ridges for a shooter.

A pistol reverberated in the canyon and another three rounds tore across the open bowl from the new rifle in the fight, the sonic report bouncing around the terrain like a pinball. Whoever was shooting had to be to Dimitry's left. He barked at the Russian next to him and told him to change magazines. He flipped his own weapon upside down and held it between his knees so that he could change its magazine left-handed. That painfully slow process complete, he motioned to his comrade to follow him.

They jogged forward, side-hilling just below the crest of the ridge that circled the valley. It was tough going and both men were quickly winded. Dimitry heard another shot, but this time he could hear the muffled muzzle blast. The hollow sound that echoed back from the valley below told him that another of his men had fallen. *Shit!*

Dimitry knew the shooter was close so he bent downward as he ran, using his muzzle to motion for his comrade to do the same. They cleared a small rise and his eyes quickly found the new source of gunfire. The man was prone behind his rifle and focused on the valley below. Dimitry stepped behind one of the large pines that dotted the landscape and braced his wounded right arm against the bark to steady his aim. The sniper was only fifty yards away.

Dimitry was right eye dominant and struggled to find a good sight picture from his left shoulder. He'd closed his right eye, and the blurred figure filled the crude open steel sights of the AKM. He began to press the rifle's heavy trigger when the last member of the team opened fire to his left, the sniper disappearing in a cloud of dust and debris.

CHAPTER 43

REECE SCANNED THE VALLEY but saw no sign of movement. He would skirt the ridgeline to his left until he had eyes on Raife and, assuming that he was ambulatory, would cover his movement out of the kill zone. His brain had made the conscious decision to rise but his body had yet to respond when the world around him exploded. A searing heat slashed across the back of his calf amid a deafening blast of sound. On instinct, he rolled away from the fire and found a slight depression that gave him momentary defilade. He spun to his right, searching for targets, and the image in his scope became a collage of greens and browns. *Shit.* His optic was still on full magnification. He fired three quick rounds before grasping the power ring and quickly dialing down to 1x to address the closer threat.

He was taking accurate fire from extremely close range, and his available cover could be measured in inches. If one of them had a frag to throw, it would be over in seconds. Reece's world was all muzzle blast and dust, with rounds landing all around him. He fired ten rounds, trying to push his enemies behind cover. His eye caught movement as one of the shooters moved laterally to achieve a better angle, one that would put Reece directly in his line of fire. Reece moved the rifle to engage but, before his finger found the trigger, he watched the man's head explode in a shower of bone and brain tissue. His body fell like a dropped sandbag as his brain discontinued its instructions to the muscles that held him upright. A rifle's report, audibly louder than that of the AKMs, boomed twice more.

Jonathan Hastings was charging through the pines, firing his battered FAL from the hip like he had done during countless ops as a young man. Reece had never seen him look so alive.

Reece rose to his knees and watched as Zulu pounced on a downed man, the canine's powerful jaws locking on his enemy's throat. Jonathan kicked the man's rifle clear and held the muzzle of his 7.62mm battle rifle to his chest. Reece safed his rifle and stood. As he did, he was reminded of the wound to his leg. It hurt, but he could run, and he sprinted forward to link up with the Selous Scout.

The attacker appeared to be gut shot and had also taken a hit to the upper leg. He held his bloody abdomen with his wounded hand as he fought with the other to break away from the hound's death grip.

"Zulu, release!" Jonathan snapped. The dog complied instantly, barking in the wounded man's face as he did so.

"Good boy, Zulu. Find Raife. Find Raife, Zulu."

The dog considered the command for a moment before putting his nose to the ground and making ever-widening circles in search of a scent trail. Within a minute, he was thundering down the valley toward the spot where Raife had entered the creek. He barked at his pack and boots. Reece took a knee and searched for additional threats as he heard the downed man mutter in a language that he could not decipher.

"It's Russian," Jonathan said, without being asked. He jabbed the man in the chest with the flash hider of his rifle. "How many others?"

The man shot back a look of confusion. Jonathan repeated the command in Afrikaans and received the same nonresponse.

Reece looked back into the valley and saw the hound trailing the creek toward the log that had been Raife's Alamo.

"I'll go check on Raife," Reece said.

"Right. I've got this bloke."

Reece didn't run directly into the valley. Instead he took the high ground that made a sweeping path to his left, following in the footsteps of the assault team. He held his weapon at the low ready as he ran, just in case any of the bad guys decided they were no longer dead, remembering more than a few soldiers had been killed that way. It took two minutes for Reece to cover the distance to where the bodies were scattered. As he arrived, he yelled out to announce his presence to Raife. No sense getting shot by your best friend.

"Raife, it's me!"

Reece checked each body as he approached, tossing weapons aside as he moved. The first stared skyward with lifeless eyes and the second hadn't stirred from his face plant since Reece had hit him with Black Hills' finest 77-grain projectile. He held his weapon at the ready and gave the boulder a wide berth as he approached the third figure, but his efforts were unnecessary; the head shot had been immediately and predictably fatal. The last downed man had been the one Raife shot before Reece had arrived and, despite what looked like a serious chest wound, he was still alive. Reece kicked the man's rifle away as he fought for breath. Reece would render aid only after he was sure that his friend was safe and the fight was won.

He watched as Raife rose to one knee and changed magazines, relieved beyond belief that his friend was uninjured. Reece strode down the hill toward him and felt a smile spread across his own face as Raife clambered to his feet. Raife walked to where he'd ditched his bow and held it up in two pieces, its limb split by gunfire. Zulu stood nearby, his tail wagging so hard that it swung his torso like a pendulum.

"I thought you were going to kill that buck today?"

"Guess I'm slipping."

"Maybe you should put some shoes on, in case there are any more bad guys to kill."

"A rifle might be a good idea, too."

"Good plan. We have two wounded," Reece said, changing subjects. "This guy here and one Jonathan has detained up on the ridge."

"Where's Annika?"

"She's okay. She's with Katie, Liz, Thorn, and your mom at the house."

"Good, Mom can take care of them, but we need to get back there, *now*."

Raife worked his way up the creek bank to retrieve his boots and pack and, within minutes, had linked back up with Reece. Reece had a basic aid kit in his pack and was working to assess the man's wounds. Saving this man's life was a simple matter of necessity; they needed information. Raife shook his head as the man expired from the shot that had taken out both his lungs.

The last living attacker was seated against a pine tree. Jonathan was standing over him doing his best not to pull the trigger as the two SEALs approached.

"Jonathan, can you bring the truck down? Let's throw this guy in and get to the house."

The attacker was pale and his BDU top was soaked with blood. Reece unbuttoned the surplus uniform and cut through the undershirt. Beyond the blood, the man's entire chest and abdomen were covered with crude ink: prison tattoos.

Reece did a primary assessment, noting the gut wound and an entry wound six inches above the knee. The leg was contorted, and Reece guessed his distal femur was shattered. He heard the sound of a vehicle approaching as Jonathan pulled the Cruiser into a nearby clearing and opened the tailgate. He carried a blanket from the SUV and spread it out next to their prisoner.

"Raife, can you grab a tourniquet from the driver's-side door?"

"Sure thing, mate."

Raife tossed the tourniquet to his friend, who quickly applied it six inches above the wound. Reece then stuffed some gauze into the hole in the man's stomach.

"Let's move him," Reece said, positioning him and rolling him onto the blanket.

Their detainee screamed in pain as his severed femur ground into the flesh and arteries of his leg when they loaded him into the cargo area of the Toyota. A swift rifle butt to the head from Jonathan knocked him back into unconsciousness.

"I'll drive," Jonathan said. "Raife, we'll stop at your truck so we can have a secondary if we need it and you can grab your rifle. Whoever these *terrs* are, it's time to kill them all."

• • •

Saint Petersburg, Russia

Helpless and alone, Grey thought that after all the failures that made up his life, he should be used to it by now. His adrenaline high had crashed and morphed into a state of depression as the transponder on Reece's vehicle raced away from the highway ambush site. Somehow, someway, he had escaped. No one was that vigilant, unless the team on the ground had made an unfathomable error or he had been warned.

Things went from bad to worse as he watched Reece's vehicle travel back to the main house and then directly to a remote area where the second team had conducted their ambush. He called Dimitry's phone; there was no answer. He then called Vitya, who couldn't explain how Reece had evaded the ambush; everything had gone perfectly until that cowboy had pulled over and the target vehicle had reversed course and drove away. His team had stolen the cowboy's truck and were now heading to the ranch to finish the job. Grey didn't need to ask what happened to the cowboy. Without a doubt he was dead.

Even though the first attempt had failed, the mission was far from over. There were still two hit teams on the ranch. Their targets were outmanned and outgunned. Barring some miracle, James Reece and Raife Hastings would soon be in the ground.

CHAPTER 44

Kumba Ranch, Flathead Valley, Montana

DEFENDING THE HOMESTEAD WAS something that was bred into Caroline Hastings's very being. As a child of Rhodesia, she'd watched her mother chase lions off the family farm while her father was away. Later, during the long and bloody Bush War, it was she who had defended the family's *lowveld* ranch while her husband was at war. On the Dark Continent, self-reliance meant survival, and as a woman of both the African frontier and American West, Caroline was no stranger to the way of the gun.

The home's spacious vault was built from thick concrete reinforced with yards of steel rebar and would withstand anything short of an air strike. Caroline marched her fire team directly to the gun room. With military precision born of practical necessity she handed Thorn an AR-15 with iron sights, knowing that he would be familiar with it from his days as a marine in Vietnam. It was essentially the same weapon as his old M16A1.

"Keep your deer rifle with you. We are going to high ground to keep them off. Once they get in close or into the interior, drop it and go with the AR. Here are your extra mags," she said, handing him an old LBE belt and harness filled with loaded 5.56 magazines.

"This brings back memories," he said. "Just like we had in Nam."

"Liz, take this," she said, handing her a scoped AR and three magazines.

With a proficiency instilled by her military training, Liz pulled back the charging handle and pressed the bolt catch. A quick glance confirmed it was unloaded so the former Army Aviator inserted a magazine and released the bolt catch, slamming a 5.56mm round into the breech.

"Annika," Caroline commanded. "You take downstairs. Hold on that front door. Use the hearth for cover. That thing will stop an artillery round. Stay down and only fire if they make it to the house." Annika was already pulling the Benelli M1 Super 90 from the rack and shouldering a bandoleer of shotgun rounds. "Take my body armor," her mother-in-law continued. "I know yours is in your house."

"You sure, Mom?" Annika asked.

"Protect that child," the Hastings matriarch ordered. "But if you die this day, die bravely."

Who is this family? Katie wondered as she watched the scene unfold. These people were prepared for war.

"Katie."

"Yes, ma'am," Katie answered quickly.

"Can you shoot, dear?"

"I've shot a Glock a few times at the range, but that's it."

"Then take this," Caroline said, pulling an AR with an Aimpoint optic off the wall and performing a press check. "It's loaded and this is the safety. Just flip it, like so, and pull the trigger. You have twenty-eight rounds in the magazine. Liz, take Katie to your guest room at the end of the hall. You are our rear security on the lower level. Tuck inside the bathroom. These walls are stone and thick wood. Use that to your advantage. If we hear you shooting, one of us will come to reinforce. Katie, just put the stock in your shoulder, aim this red dot at whoever tries to come across the back garden, and shoot them until they go down."

Katie stared wide-eyed at the woman who just a day ago had seemed like a western version of Martha Stewart; she had transformed into a warrior.

"Are we clear?" Caroline asked, looking each of her newly minted recruits in the eye. "Good. Remember. No one is coming. It's up to us. Take your positions."

Caroline opened the bolt on her Brno rifle and pulled it back far enough to confirm that there was a round in the chamber. The magazine held five rounds of the venerable .375 H&H. Another was in the chamber ready to go. Ten more rode in a leather belt around her waist and she'd stuffed another ten in her pockets. The rifle had served her well since she'd first picked it up in 1971.

The home was still and silent, many of the windows open to let in what might be the last warm air of the season. Caroline had positioned herself on the second floor, inside a dormer window that faced the most likely enemy avenue of approach. She didn't have to wait long to hear a diesel motor and tires gnawing at the dirt and gravel road.

A blue pickup came into view, its motor accelerating. She didn't hesitate, dropping into a seated position and resting the rifle's forend on the windowsill. Unlike the CZ 550 and most modern rifles, the Brno safety needed to be pulled back to fire. Caroline's thumb clicked the safety into position, her cheek dropping to the weathered Turkish walnut Lux pattern stock, and centered the front post with the 200-meter leaf of the express sight on the driver's-side window.

The Brno was made in Uhersky Brod, Czechoslovakia, when it was under Soviet occupation in the late 1960s. Now a rifle built in the ashes of the Prague Spring was about to be unleashed on a new Russian enemy. The heavy rifle barked, the recoil pushing into her shoulder as her round turned the windshield into spiderwebs. Though she couldn't see from her perch, the 270-grain bullet took the driver in the throat. She cycled the bolt quickly and sent a second round through the center of the glass, which gut-shot one of the men in the backseat. The driver's foot came off the gas pedal thanks to his severed spine and the big Ford began to slow.

With their leader in violent death throes, his severed artery splattering the truck's cabin with hot blood, the rest of the men panicked. When the fourth round shot away the rearview mirror, the four assaulters who were still able to move bailed out of the vehicle as it came to rest. They had trained for and expected to deliver a violent ambush, not be ambushed themselves. Taking cover, they fired wildly on full automatic, spraying the large home with 7.62mm rounds. With no leader, the men didn't communicate, they didn't maneuver, they didn't flank; they just hunkered down and burned through their ammunition as they continued shooting into what moments before had been a beautiful mountain home.

Caroline was single-minded in her purpose, firing a single round before moving to a different room and finding her next target through a new window. After the initial volley, she was careful to stay well back so that her rifle's protruding barrel would not give the enemy a target. Her objective was to keep them pinned down so that they couldn't approach the house. If they set it ablaze or moved inside, she would lose the tactical advantage.

It hadn't been a question of what to do when the attack came. It was all about executing a preplanned emergency response, habits instilled in a different time and place, habits born of necessity in the African bush. That plan and those skills now kept her family alive. She remembered her own mother tucking her into bed and explaining the reality of life in Rhodesia: *if someone with mal intent enters our property, they have declared war on our family.*

These *terrs* had declared war.

A shooter found the courage to roll out from behind the truck's rear wheel, firing as he rose to charge forward. Caroline's next shot took him in the chest. She topped off the rifle with six more rounds as she moved into an adjacent room, looking for her next target.

CHAPTER 45

OLEG GUSKOV WAS ITCHING for a fight. As the youngest member of the crew he had something to prove. The other five had military or police experience, albeit rudimentary, or had come of age in the 1990s, the heyday of Russian organized crime. He'd had to endure listening to their stories of what amounted to urban combat as the gangs fought for control of the new Russia, carving it up in a Darwinian contest for control of the underworld.

Oleg had looked over at his boss when the bullet took Vitya in the throat. He watched as the man who had helped train him for this mission went white, his eyes bulging, mouth struggling to bring in oxygen in an attempt to delay the inevitable.

Oleg felt another round as it passed between him and the dying driver and heard Pavel grunt from the backseat.

The truck veered left and ran up and onto a stump, arresting all forward progress. As Oleg watched his team leader die, the rearview mirror exploded just inches from his face.

What now?

Another round impacted the vehicle.

He heard and felt the rear passenger doors open as the gangsters bailed out to find cover. Oleg followed suit, trying to figure out how to open the huge vehicle's door, groping to find the handle and throwing it open just in time to avoid the .375 round that took out his headrest.

Falling to the dirt, he low-crawled to a rock by the side of the long driveway, propped himself up, and depressed the trigger. Nothing happened. He could hear his comrades return fire, spraying the front of the house with bullets. He looked around long enough to see Boris charge forward from behind the truck and take a round to the chest. Serov and Taro were behind cover, continuing to let loose with their AKs.

Ah, the safety. Oleg pushed the safety to "fire" and watched as his rounds hit fairly close to his intended target, the far right upstairs window. He was surprised at how quickly his magazine ran dry.

He had to move. He had to make a name for himself. If he could get to the house, he knew he could kill everyone inside. That would make the *Pakhan* proud. Maybe he would even rise in the ranks?

He remembered Vitya and Dimitry say that a moving target was harder to hit. When he heard his comrades send another long volley into the upper level of the house, Oleg got up and ran.

• • •

"Stay barricaded behind this doorjamb," Liz said. They could hear Caroline or Thorn engaging from upstairs. Single shots. And they could hear the return fire from outside.

"You are far enough back in the room where it will be hard for anyone approaching to see you. Cover this sector here," Liz said, indicating an area of the backyard beyond the guest room patio.

"Where will you be?" Katie asked.

"With only two of us, we won't be able to cover all the angles, so I'll be mobile. If you see anyone, take your shots. I'll come to support if I hear you fire," Liz responded before disappearing into an adjacent room.

Katie had survived two ambushes and a kidnapping since Reece had come into her life. And now she was fighting for her life. At least this time she had a vote. She had a rifle.

• • •

Oleg moved through the trees. Had they seen him? He hoped his comrades' full-auto barrage had distracted the upstairs shooter long enough for him to get out of the line of fire and approach the house from the back or side. He was going to get inside. He wouldn't be a *Shestyorka* for long.

. . .

It didn't happen the way she had thought. One second Katie was running through the possible scenarios in her head and the next second a skinny man in a black leather jacket holding what she recognized as an AK-47 was sprinting across the garden.

She tried to call for Liz, but her mouth was dry and wouldn't make a sound.

When he hit the patio, he came to a stop by a pillar that helped support a second-story back deck.

Katie watched him peer cautiously around the support, then creep to the glass door that led to the back guest room. He was less than thirty feet away.

"Liz," she tried again, not knowing if any sound escaped her lips. She was certain that even through the glass the thin man could hear the beating of her heart.

Take the weapon off safe, Katie, she told herself.

She was sure the man outside heard the almost inaudible click of the safety moving to the "fire" position.

Less than ten minutes had passed but she still struggled to remember what Caroline had told her: *put the stock in your shoulder, aim this red dot at whoever tries to come across the back garden, and shoot them until they go down.*

Katie pulled the stock into her shoulder. Her eye found the red dot of the optic.

Where did he go?

Her eyes traveled back to the pillar.

He was kneeling, part of his body concealed by the round support. The AK was pointed directly at her. Before she could press the trigger, the glass door exploded.

CHAPTER 46

CRESTING A RISE, THEY could hear shooting. Jonathan pinned the accelerator to the floor.

"We are coming in on the X," he called out. "No time for anything fancy. They could already be in the house."

Tactically, Reece wanted to take the high ground and flank, but this was an in-extremis situation. Katie and the others could already be dead or dying.

It was time to kill.

A blue F-250 sat at an awkward angle in front of the house, three of its four doors open. Two men here behind nearby trees, firing sporadically at the home. They were completely unaware of the approaching vehicles to their rear. Jonathan slammed Reece's Land Cruiser to a stop and bailed out, sprinting forward with his FAL at the ready. Knowing that vehicles quickly turned into bullet sponges in combat, Reece opened the passenger door and instinctively took up a solid position at the base of a large rock. Raife skidded his Defender to a stop behind them, and, armed with his truck rifle, a SIG SG 553 carbine, raced after his father.

Reece found a target, dropping him with a solid head shot. Jonathan fired as he moved, ten rounds from the FAL tearing through a man at the base of a tree. Raife had reached the truck within seconds, clearing it and putting rounds into a man in the backseat and another in the driver's seat.

The three sprinted toward the house. Reece's head swiveled up and around to take in the surrounding area, looking at positions on the high ground.

Stacking on the front door, the three prepared to make entry. Visions of Reece's wife and daughter riddled with bullets dying in a pool of blood on the floor of their home flashed through his thoughts. Jonathan's voice brought Reece back to the present.

"Caroline!" the former Selous Scout yelled. "Annika!"

"We're here, Dad!" his daughter called back.

"Three coming in!" Jonathan shouted.

Zulu charged through the breach and went straight for Annika, taking up a protective position at her left side.

"You okay, baby girl?" Jonathan asked, kneeling next to her.

"I'm fine, Dad. Mom is upstairs with Thorn. Katie and Liz are down the hall in the guest bedroom. I just heard shooting down there."

Reece sprinted down the hall without waiting for more.

"Katie? Katie?"

Nothing.

"*Katie!*"

"I'm here, James," Katie said.

She sat on the bed. Liz was next to her. Glass was strewn across the back entry where the door had once been.

"Are you okay? Stand up," he said, pulling her to her feet and looking her up and down for injuries. "You're not hit, are you?"

"No. I'm okay."

"Don't worry about me," Liz interjected sarcastically. "I'm just fine."

"Sorry, Liz. Is everyone else okay?"

"I think so. Well, not this guy," she said pointing her rifle toward a man on the patio.

There was no need for a security round as half his head was missing.

"Liz?"

"He almost got the drop on us. Katie here did a fabulous job."

"Did you . . . ?" Reece asked.

"No," Katie answered. "As I brought my rifle up, he fired and the whole room seemed to explode. I fell back into the bathroom. I guess he was a bad shot, or I was lucky. Maybe both. Next thing I know Liz is standing over me."

"It was just like Iraq, Reece. It's been a while but my self-preservation instincts are still strong."

"Thank you, Liz."

"James, I was so worried about you," Katie said. He could feel her body shake as they embraced.

"Come on. Let's go check on the others."

Annika was in a chair at the kitchen table, and Jonathan was coming down the stairs with his wife as Reece, Katie, and Liz entered the main room.

"Where's Thorn?" Reece asked immediately.

"He's upstairs keeping an eye on things, just in case. We're not sure that was all of them."

"Reece, you're hurt!" Katie exclaimed as they emerged into the lighter portion of the home and she spotted the bloody tear on the back of his jeans.

"It's just a scratch, I think."

"Let me look."

"Now?"

"Yes, now."

Reece took a seat and pulled up his right pant leg. He jumped as she touched the wound, which had been effectively cauterized by the heat of the bullet. The round had just grazed the back of his calf, leaving a half-diameter channel as it plowed its way across the flesh.

"See, I told you it was fine."

"I'll dress it anyway."

"Let me get you what you'll need, dear," Caroline said, exiting the room.

Reece laid his own carbine on the table next to Caroline's bolt gun and prepared to endure Katie's medical treatment.

"Who were they?" Katie asked, her journalistic mind already working to understand the events that had unfolded.

Reece looked at the others around the table.

"Not sure. We think Russian."

"Russian?"

Caroline returned and handed Katie a plastic tub loaded with first aid supplies.

She pulled her chair close to Reece's and propped his leg up on hers before dabbing the wound with a Betadine-soaked gauze pad.

"Do you know what you're doing?"

"My dad was a doctor, remember?"

"Does that mean 'yes'?"

"Don't worry, I also watched a couple of episodes of *Grey's Anatomy*."

She used her finger to coat the wound in ointment before covering it with a pad and wrapping the entire calf with several loops of gauze.

"There. Done."

"Not bad," Reece admitted.

Caroline nodded approvingly.

"All right, lads," Jonathan said. "The authorities will be here soon. We need to talk. Why are Russian mobsters attacking us in Montana?"

Reece looked at Raife and then back to Jonathan, and then to Katie, Caroline, and Annika.

"I'm sorry, sir. It's my fault. I think they were after me. I should have known better than to come here and put you all at risk. I should have known they'd find me."

"None of that, lad," the weathered old man snapped. "We are all still aboveground. That was nothing compared to what the *terrs* and Mugabe's thugs did in Rhodesia. I'm just getting warmed up. Will they be back?"

"If I stay, they might, but let's also not make any assumptions until I talk to the Agency. They might be able to shed some light on all this." He looked to Raife. "Remember, there were two hit teams. One was after Raife, so unless they didn't know which one of us was which, let's not count out Raife being a target as well. It could mean someone knows you were with me in Switzerland."

Raife looked at Annika, whose concern was more than apparent.

"Also," Reece continued, "please check in with your other daughters. Have them go someplace safe."

"It's safe here now," Jonathan remarked.

"Had they hit us at night with NODs, lasers, and a more capable force, stand-off weapons, we wouldn't have stood a chance. We got lucky and we were prepared for this type of an attack. A more professional unit could have taken us; all of us." Reece looked around the room as the severity of the situation sank in.

"I'll call the girls now," Caroline said, moving to a landline next to the couch.

Reece leaned across the table, his eyes intently moving between the father and son.

"There's only one person who can tell us what's going on and right now he's dying in the back of my truck."

"Give me ten minutes with him," Jonathan stated. "We'll see how tough he is once I wrap him in tires and start burning them."

"Unfortunately, we can't do that," Reece said. "LE has got to be inbound, so we are on the clock. If they get their hands on him and he lawyers up, we'll never get what we need."

"What do you suggest?" the elder man asked Reece.

"Liz, how far is it to Thorn's most remote cabin?"

"About an hour in the Albatross, why?"

"Okay. Liz and I will take Stalin out there to the cabin," Reece said, indicating the Russian bound in the Land Cruiser. "You two get ready to meet the sheriff. Even local LE is going to put together that there is more going on here than meets the eye. I'll call my contact at the CIA and see if he can throw up some veil of national security to stall things. In the meantime, I've got work to do."

"Reece, are you sure you want to do this?" Raife asked.

Reece looked around the room. Instead of seeing Katie, Annika, Liz, and Caroline, he saw the ghosts of his dead wife and daughter.

"I think I know who's behind this. He might be after us both for taking out Andrenov in Switzerland, but I think it's about something even more personal. I need to know where he is. Our one link may already be bleeding out in my truck, so we need to move. I'll be back when it's done. Oh, Jonathan," Reece said. "Do you have any more of those homegrown ghost peppers?"

CHAPTER 47

INFANTRY BATTLES ARE UNCOMMON in Flathead County, Montana, despite an extremely high rate of gun ownership. Because of this, the law enforcement response was predictably substantial. Every available deputy made their way either to the ranch or the scene of the attempted roadside ambush.

The entire family was seated at the kitchen table along with the Hastingses' attorney, Brad Cahill, when the authorities arrived at the house. Cahill was a former Army Ranger and U.S. attorney for the Montana District and was a close friend of both the Hastings and Thornton families. Cahill's trademark white Stetson sat on the table but, at his suggestion, the rifles were tastefully relocated. A regional SWAT team from the FBI field office in Salt Lake City arrived shortly after the deputies in a pair of Bureau helicopters, having been alerted by a call from Vic Rodriguez of a possible ambush in progress. Within hours, the ranch was crawling with armed agents, and a mobile command center was set up near the main house. With everyone they came to fight already dead, the SWAT team took on a force protection role while the Evidence Response Team went to work.

Vic had spoken to the on-scene supervisor while inbound, citing a slew of legislation passed in the wake of 9/11, so the investigators were sensitive to a national security angle. Having an attorney and a respected and wealthy family on scene didn't hurt, either. Vic's phone calls prompted the decision not to alert the media. The last thing that anyone wanted was a bunch of conspiracy theorists from either end of the political spectrum camped out in front of the ranch's gates.

One by one, each of the participants gave statements to the investigators, with Cahill ensuring that both the questions and responses were appropriate. One member of the ensemble was conspicuously missing: the quiet bearded man who had been staying on the ranch for the past month. Crime scene technicians were scattered across the ridges and valley floor, marking, photographing, and cataloging every piece of tangible physical evidence.

It was nearly six when a black Tahoe pulled up to the ridge. Jonathan and Raife Hastings watched as a man in tan cargo pants, hiking boots, and a dark fleece jacket emerged, shaking hands with the lead investigator, who pointed him toward the main house.

Vic Rodriguez was a Miami native and the son of Cuban exiles. After college, he had served as an Army Special Forces officer before being recruited by the Agency, where, in the midst of the War on Terror, he achieved a well-earned spot at the top of the CIA's paramilitary food chain. He was the rare Washington animal who was respected by those both above and below him in the chain of command. It was Vic who had seen the potential in Reece and arranged for him to be recruited into Ground Branch in exchange for a pardon of his past transgressions.

Vic was in his late forties with closely cropped graying hair and blue eyes that belied his Castilian heritage. He spoke in broadcast neutral English, yet he could flip to his parents' native tongue midsentence.

Jonathan and Raife met him at the door.

"Mr. Rodriguez, welcome to our home. It's not usually this shot up."

"Mr. Hastings," Vic said warmly. "And you must be Raife," the Agency man said, extending his hand.

Raife hesitated, then took the outstretched hand. After his experience with a CIA asset in Iraq that had caused his unseasonal departure from the SEAL Teams, he was not a fan of intelligence officers.

"Can we get you anything?" Jonathan, ever the host, inquired. "Beer, wine, liquor?"

"No, thank you, I'm fine. Is there a private place we can talk?" The question was clearly directed at Raife.

The father and son exchanged words in Afrikaans.

"Use my office upstairs," Jonathan offered. "I'm here, if I can be of service."

The pair ascended the stairs and took seats in an office off the master bedroom. The walls were adorned with pictures from the Bush War days, and the shelves were packed with books from and about the old country. A monstrous Cape buffalo shoulder mount extended from one corner, and a full-body leopard mount was situated on the limb of a tree on the opposite wall.

"Mr. Hastings," Vic began.

"Call me Raife."

"Raife, as you know, we've cited national security concerns up to this point to keep a lid on this, but that won't hold up for long. I need to talk to Reece, and I need to talk to him now."

Raife looked the shorter man in the eye and nodded.

"Reece told me you were one of the good ones. He wants to talk to you, too."

Raife reached across the desk and handed Vic a phone number on scratch paper.

"Dial it from the landline here. It's to a sat phone."

"Where is he?"

"He's not far, but he needs a little time. He'll explain."

Vic took the paper.

"Are all members of your family accounted for?"

"Everyone but my sister Hanna. She's in Romania. If you could have someone from the embassy check in on her and bring her in, my family would be grateful."

"That will be my first call," Vic said, standing to switch places with Raife so he could use the phone. "You and your family did good work today."

"We've had some practice."

True to his word, Vic called Langley. The desk officer immediately contacted the chief of station in Romania. Within the hour, two embassy vehicles were on their way to the town of Moldavia.

He then dialed the number Raife had given him.

"Vic?"

"Well, Reece, looks like your days of peace and quiet have come to a screeching halt."

"Someone had other plans. Your phone call saved our lives."

"I can't lose you before I even officially bring you on board."

"Yeah, I guess I'll have a harder time saying no next time you ask me to do something."

"I'm going to do that now. Where are you?"

"Close. There was something I had to do before law enforcement arrived."

"Please tell me you don't have a live suspect in custody."

"If I did have someone, they wouldn't be a suspect, they'd be an enemy combatant. I'll share what I can, when I can. In the meantime, I need you to hold off the FBI until I figure this out."

"A dead Russian hit team on one of the most respected ranching outfits in the state won't stay secret for long."

"What have you found out on your end?"

"I can only share that with cleared Ground Branch staff."

"If I don't get thrown in prison for what I'm about to do, I might be just that. What do you know?" Reece pressed.

"This morning I received a call from a retired spook from the old days. He was Moscow station chief near the end of the Cold War. Knew your dad. He told me he got a personal call from a Russian intelligence officer named Aleksandr Zharkov, who warned him of an attack in Montana targeting James Reece and Raife Hastings."

"What? Why would an SVR official want to save my life?"

"That's the million-dollar question, Reece. I don't know. Zharkov's father is Ivan Zharkov, a Russian mob boss. He runs the Tambov Gang out of St. Petersburg."

"That fits. The EKIA look like Russian mafia. They're covered in prison ink."

"FBI made the same assessment. So, my first instinct is that this is directly related to the intelligence package I gave you last year on Colonel Andrenov."

Reece remembered firing the RPG-32 that turned Vasili Andrenov, a man responsible for manipulating markets with terrorist attacks across Europe and an attempted Russian coup that almost killed the president of the United States, into mulch.

"Vic, I'm going to have to get back to you. I have work to do."

CHAPTER 48

SVR Headquarters, Moscow

THE FULL INTELLIGENCE REPORT on the Hastings family was on Aleksandr's desk when he arrived that morning. It was more robust than even he would have imagined, with information going back to the 1970s. Soviet intelligence assets had aided insurgencies throughout the world and the Rhodesian Bush War was no exception. Detailed records of these operations were kept, and many duplicate reports from satellite nations were provided to the Soviets. The result was a treasure trove of information in the SVR's records that spanned nearly a century.

The GRU had identified two brothers, Jonathan and Richard Hastings, as members of the elite Selous Scouts and further identified the family's ranch in the nation's *lowveld* as a possible target in years and wars gone by. Jonathan Hastings's name came up again in Angola before he emigrated to the states and fell off the communist intelligence radar. Richard, it appeared, had never left the continent of his birth.

The remainder of the information had been gathered from open-source information and by hackers, including biographical, educational, and financial records on the entire family. They had significant landholdings in Montana as well as sizable sums in various investment vehicles. Jonathan Hastings had done very well for himself.

He examined the reports for Raife and Victoria Hastings and found nothing actionable. The final report was for Hanna Hastings. According to her social media profile, she was working in Romania on some type of agricultural project.

Aleksandr's thumb and forefinger sensuously rubbed the human hair bracelet on his desk. Feeling a spark of arousal, he picked up the phone and placed a call.

CHAPTER 49

Saint Petersburg, Russia

GREY WALKED INTO THE office. His steps were slow and heavy and the gleam in his eyes had been replaced by a dull stare. He had aged over the last forty-eight hours. Svetlana felt a flicker of empathy for the man, as not all of her affection for Grey was false. Over the years, she had learned to find some attractive quality in each of her subjects so that she could make the illusion of her attraction to *them* real. In Grey, she had found intelligence and an almost boyish innocence that brought out her own maternal instincts. Still, his seduction was a job, a way to survive. Her mother had taught her that if she did not look out for herself, no one would. Her mother had been right.

The look on her face was one of genuine sympathy when she took his coat and bid him good morning. Grey acted as if she were invisible as he walked into his office and stared blankly at the monitor before him.

His plan had failed. Reece was alive, and a dozen of Zharkov's men were presumed dead. His operation had been a complete disaster. If this had happened back at the Agency, he would have been ruined, banished to sort mail the remainder of his career. Here, however, he was afraid that he would meet a different end, one that might involve a bullet and a ditch.

There was nowhere else for him to run. He would march down to Ivan's office, give him a full report, and throw himself on the mercy of the *Pakhan*. He asked Svetlana to set the meeting and occupied his time by arranging the documents for the brief. Forty-five minutes later he looked at the Rolex on his wrist. It was time. He rose from his desk and marched dutifully toward his judgment.

One of the double doors to Ivan's office was partially open and Grey rapped lightly to announce his presence. The patriarch looked up from a stack of papers on his desk and beckoned the former CIA man inside. To Grey's relief, there was no plastic on the floor and no thugs waiting in the corner to drag him away. The office, half-encapsulated in the mirrored glass that made up the building's exterior, was tastefully decorated with relics of Zharkov's travels: a basket of tribal spears in the corner, a Cossack's saber hanging on the wall. The most striking element, though, was the lion. A snarling black-maned cat stood mounted behind Ivan like a guardian in contrast to the Russian's measured demeanor. It stood for the power of the brotherhood that he led. Ivan could speak softly because there was an army of lions behind him, waiting to pounce.

He motioned for Grey to sit and offered him tea. Grey politely declined.

"*Pakhan*, I will get right to the point. I have some very bad news to deliver."

"Go on."

"The operation in the U.S. appears to have met with unexpected resistance. Someone must have warned James Reece of the attack; he stopped just shy of the ambush, turned around, and sped off. Vitya's team pursued him to the Hastingses' ranch but that was the last we heard from them. I cannot reach Dimitry. I fear the worst."

Ivan paused as if deep in thought. He already knew about the disaster in Montana but feigned ignorance.

"What do you think went wrong, Oliver?"

"I don't know, sir. It's possible that U.S. intelligence caught wind of it somehow, but I used every method available to avoid their detection. I know how they work. The only plausible explanation is that we were betrayed."

"You're saying we have a traitor in our midst?"

"I don't know. Maybe if we can figure out the 'why' we will figure out the 'who'? Why would someone in your organization, our organization, want to help Reece?"

"What do you know about lions, Oliver?"

"Lions?" Grey asked, slightly confused.

"Yes, lions. *Panthera leo*. African lions."

"I'm not much of an outdoor person."

"Well, I know them, Oliver. I hunted for twenty-one days before I took this brute behind me in Mozambique. We shot bait animals and chained them up in trees. We waited and waited until his hunger overcame his sense of danger. He was an old male who had been kicked out of the pride to die alone. One day he was the most powerful animal on the block and the next he had lost all respect. Do you know who did this to him, Oliver?"

"No, sir."

"His son. When a lion's son gets to maturity, he challenges his father for the right to lead the pride. Eventually this comes to a head, and they fight, sometimes to the death. If the father is lucky, he survives, and he limps away to live in solitude for the rest of his days. It's the natural order of things, Oliver."

"I don't understand what this has to do with James Reece, sir."

"That's because—forgive me for being blunt—you didn't have a father, and you don't have a son. It's a struggle as old as mankind itself."

Oliver took a moment to consider the situation and everything the old man had just relayed.

"Your son, Aleksandr, is an intelligence officer. He wants to take over the *bratva* and would have his own assets imbedded in your organization?" Grey asked, thinking of Svetlana and finally comprehending the significance of the lions. *Could she have betrayed him?*

Ivan nodded slowly.

"But why? Why would he want James Reece alive?"

"So that he can hunt him, Oliver."

CHAPTER 50

Boundary County, Idaho
United States/Canadian Border

THE ALBATROSS CIRCLED THE lake, its iridescent waters a colder version of Caribbean blue. Officially known as an "inholding," Senator Thornton's wilderness retreat was located in a remote section of the Kaniksu National Forest, on the border between Idaho and Canada. Privately held from a time before the area was designated a national forest in 1908, Thorn used it as an escape during his years in Congress so his staff could truthfully answer that he was "out of the state" when he needed a reset.

Reece remained in the back of the plane with their prisoner, curiously studying the man he would soon kill. The Russian's head was bagged, his eyes underneath taped over with riggers' tape. They'd given him four oral disk fentanyl wafers for the pain, and to knock him out for the flight to a more remote location. Reece's memory flashed back to the chaotic days at the height of the war when enhanced interrogation techniques were the order of the day, and a time when Iraqi units who did not abide by such rules did what came naturally. War brought out the best and worst in one's fellow man.

Reece saw the Russian leveling his AK at those he cared about, those who had provided him sanctuary: Katie, Raife, Annika, Jonathan, Caroline, Thorn. It was his fault. He had been targeted on U.S. soil and even with all the security precautions in place, they had found him. Reece was going to find out who they were. As the plane began its final approach, he saw the prisoner level his rifle at Katie's head and pull the trigger, her frightened face turning into that of his beautiful wife before being riddled with bullets. Suppressing an urge to choke the life out of the man before him, Reece closed his eyes.

Patience, Reece. You need him.

As Liz put the plane down with expert precision and floated to a dock, Reece unbuckled his harness and stuck his head into the cockpit.

"How's Khrushchev doing back there?" Liz asked.

"He's still alive. Where's the cabin?"

"You'll be able to see it back in the woods momentarily."

"Beautiful spot," Reece offered.

"Yeah, Thorn usually flies in alone, but, every now and again, he'll have a guest and I'll ferry them to and from the airport. Make yourself useful and tie us up."

Reece jumped from the side door of the antique aircraft and secured the amphibious bird to the cleats spaced along the mooring. Liz cut the engine and joined her friend on the pier.

"I'll need your help getting him to the cabin, Liz. After that, I want you to come back to the plane and wait. I don't want you to see this."

"Are you forgetting what those savages almost did to me in Iraq? You think I'm squeamish about this? Whatever you are going to do, I can help. These Russian clowns almost killed me and the closest thing we both have to a family. Whoever sent them wanted you and Raife dead for a reason and they didn't care who they had to kill to get to you. Whatever you are going to do to this asshole, not only does he deserve it, but it's not you who's responsible; it's whoever sent him. Find out, Reece. And don't feel one ounce of pity."

"Did you see the prison tattoos? This is going to take a bit of work."

Reece and Liz secured the Russian to the plane's Israeli stretcher with wrap upon wrap of riggers' tape and maneuvered him through the hatch and up to Thorn's cabin. Steps offered access to a spacious yet rickety deck adorned with a basic black Weber grill showing its age next to a handmade picnic table. Liz opened the door, allowing Reece to take stock of his surroundings. It was a humble structure by necessity, quite literally cut from the wilderness. Each and every piece had been flown in or borrowed from the surrounding environment. The result looked more like a trapper's cabin than an escape for one of the wealthiest men in Montana, and that was just what Thorn was after. The main room hosted a small kitchen, one round table, and an old iron wood-burning stove. A loft with a narrow staircase overlooked the gathering area, and a short hallway led to two guest bedrooms. Tall trees surrounded the refuge, filtering the late afternoon sunlight and leaving the room in perpetual shadow. It was perfect.

"Let's get him in a chair. I'll take it from there."

CHAPTER 51

Community Agricultural Project, Moldavia, Romania

THE SUN WAS SETTING as Hanna Hastings leaned against the fender of her Renault pickup, making notes on her tablet. The harvest was going well, despite a lack of modern combines. The single machine they had dated back to the 1970s and had already broken down twice. What these farmers lacked in technology, they made up for in resilience. When the machinery malfunctioned, the most skilled mechanics of the group would go to work on it, despite a complete lack of replacement parts. While those repairs were taking place, the community came out and continued the harvest with hand tools just as they'd done for centuries. These were hard men and women from a harsh land; they reminded her of her family in Montana.

Windswept hills provided fertile soil but droughts threatened to ruin crops and crush wills. Hanna had received a grant to dig a well, build a basic irrigation system, and introduce the local farmers to modern seeds and chemical fertilizers. The results of their efforts were paying off. This year's yield appeared to be the best that anyone could remember, despite a relatively dry summer.

Hanna was a horticulturist and crop specialist with a master's degree from Utah State University. She had been born in the United States after her family had immigrated to Montana and, as the baby of the family, she had always rooted for the underdog.

She was only eight years old when she found her first cause. The ranch hands had moved some cattle to a fresh pasture and a newborn calf had been separated from the herd. They quickly discovered the oversight and reunited the calf with the herd, but her mother would not claim her. The calf was dehydrated and weak when Hanna first became aware of her plight. Caroline drove her to the feed store in Winfred, where she used her allowance to buy a nursing bottle and a large bag of milk replacer. She also made a deal with her father: if the calf survived, she would never be sent to auction. Jonathan reluctantly agreed; he'd never been good about saying no to his youngest daughter. She named the calf Patches and nursed her back to health in a hastily built pen. Patches regained her strength and was soon able to rejoin the herd, living a long life and having many calves of her own. Those calves earned thousands of dollars in revenue for the ranch, which Jonathan dutifully placed into Hanna's savings account. One of the family's favorite photos was a snapshot of Hanna sitting inside Patches's pen with her legs crossed, bottle-feeding her rescued calf.

It came as no surprise when Hanna turned down a potentially lucrative career with a seed company and chose to work for an NGO educating farmers in developing countries. She was currently helping modernize the farming practices of one of the poorest countries in the European Union. She stayed in touch with her family through email and Skype and planned to return to Montana for Christmas.

Her father always joked that Hanna was the bleeding heart of the family, but that wasn't exactly true. Though she was incredibly compassionate, she was very much of the "teach them to fish" mind-set. Her father was right about one thing, though: she couldn't save the entire world by herself. She looked forward to going home in a few short months. She'd been away too long.

• • •

An hour later Hanna picked at her dinner at the small table that served as a dining room, her laptop next to her. The living conditions of the small farmstead apartment should have been uncomfortable for a wealthy American, but she had a genuine appreciation for the simplicity of it all. She tried to email her parents, but the farm's satellite internet signal was down, as usual.

Headlights flashed across the ceiling as a vehicle turned onto her lane, the beams casting eerie shadows as they filtered through the high window frames. She heard footfalls on the stone walkway as a figure approached. Visitors after nightfall were not a normal occurrence. Listening to her sixth sense, Hanna looked around for something to use as a weapon and picked up a battered kitchen knife. The knock at the door sent a shiver down her spine, but a woman's voice put her at ease.

"Excuse me," the woman said in Romanian.

Hanna peeked through the window shade and saw a young, well-dressed female.

"Can I help you?"

"My husband and I are lost. Is this the road to the bed-and-breakfast?"

She could see that the woman was holding a smartphone, presumably trying to find a location on the map that would not come up due to that lack of coverage in the area. Still suspicious, Hanna unlocked the door and stepped out to help, holding the knife in her right hand, the blade pressed upward against her forearm to conceal it. The woman smiled and held out the phone so that Hanna could see the map. She leaned in to see where she was pointing.

"Thank you so much."

Hanna opened her mouth to respond but was grabbed in a powerful bear hug from behind. She slashed backward with the knife and felt the resistance of clothing, flesh, and bone. The vise grip loosened as her attacker grunted in pain. Twisting away, she turned and ran back through the doorway, sprinting through her home for the back door that led into the night. If she could get out of the house, she would have a two-hundred-yard dash to the forest. She heard footsteps behind her and threw a chair into the doorway to slow her pursuer.

Almost there. The back door. A chance to escape.

Slamming her shoulder into the back door, she catapulted herself toward the tree line and was knocked to the ground with a two-by-four to the face. She fell backward, crashing back into the door frame, the knife slipping from her grasp. Bloodied and barely conscious against the side of the house, she had no defense when the man she had stabbed appeared and struck the left side of her head. Before the others pulled him off, he landed another blow where her jawline met her ear, sending her spiraling into darkness.

CHAPTER 52

Boundary County, Idaho
United States/Canadian Border

HE'D SEEN THE TECHNIQUE once before, and it had stayed with him. Having been attached to the CIA in the days when IEDs became a tactical weapon of strategic importance, Reece had witnessed the unleashing of the most aggressive elements of the U.S. intelligence apparatus. Though Americans were strictly prohibited from practicing the darkest arts of tactical interrogation, they could teach host-nation forces some of the more refined elicitation methods and then leave the room when partner force interrogators applied their most recent knowledge on the enemy. Reece knew the importance of maintaining the moral high ground in war. Sometimes that's all that distinguished the good guys from the bad. If you abandoned the moral high ground, all was lost.

You've lost your way, Reece. Tell that to your wife and daughter.

Reece swung the med kit from his shoulder and looked at the man strapped naked to the leather chair in front of him. Reece and Liz had set the chair on a tarp to help contain the inevitable DNA. Riggers' tape secured the prisoner's legs, arms, and upper chest to the chair. A rope fixed in a noose was looped securely around his head and was tied to a beam running the length of the cabin. He wasn't going anywhere.

The man was covered in ink. Almost every inch of his body was overwritten by intricate tattoos; saints, angels, skulls, and coffins covered his chest and back, a giant cathedral with multiple domes dominated the scene. A hooded executioner branded each shoulder and roses stood out from his forearms, one twisting around a dagger, the other wrapped in barbed wire.

Reece didn't know much about Russian tattoos, but what he did know was that they signified the man before him had spent time in some of the toughest prisons on earth and survived.

While working for the CIA, Reece had learned techniques carefully designed to elicit responses from the most hardened Islamic terrorists. What he took away was that regardless of the technique, as an interrogator, you had to offer hope. Hope was the key. He wondered how it would work with a hardened *bratva* enforcer. He was about to find out.

Reece moved forward and felt the pulse at the man's neck, slow and weak. He needed the Russian alive for at least an hour. Returning to the med kit, Reece took out an IV and a length of 550 cord. He threw the cord over the exposed beam that held the noose and attached it to the IV bag dangling just to the side of the Russian's head. His veins stood out like pipes, probably due to the copious amounts of steroids that sustained his muscular physique. Reece stabbed the needle of the 18-gauge catheter into a vein running through the rose and dagger on his subject's right arm. He pulled the hub, withdrawing the needle and leaving the plastic sheath in the vein. He then attached the tube and opened the IV spin valve to flood the tubing with fluid after taping it to the arm. He ran the bag wide open to replace the fluids necessary to stabilize the Russian for questioning. When the first bag had drained, Reece attached a second, watching an air bubble move down the tube.

"Enjoy your rest, my friend," Reece whispered. "You'll need all your strength for what's coming."

And so will I, Reece thought.

The Scoville scale measures heat in Scoville Heat Units, in this case specifically the heat of peppers, a heat that comes from the neuropeptide-releasing agent capsaicin, which they contain. Reece put on rubber gloves and clear eyeglasses from the med kit and dumped Jonathan's red ghost peppers out on a cutting board in the small kitchen. Reece was after the capsaicin.

He had seen the process done in sterile conditions at the CIA over a series of days. Reece didn't have days. He had hours. He was going to do what SEALs did best: improvise.

Preheating the oven to 350 degrees, he moved back to the cutting board and sliced the ghost peppers down the middle, removing the seeds and separating the white pith that contained the capsaicin. Careful not to touch his face, he put the pith on a baking sheet and threw it in the oven to dry it out.

Opening and closing cupboards, Reece found what he was looking for: a coffee grinder, French press, and a bottle of Jack Daniel's.

Sinatra Select. Not bad, Reece thought.

Five minutes later, Reece returned to the oven and removed his baking sheet. He then slid the dried pith into the hand grinder, which he cranked over a bowl, turning it into a coarse powder.

He then added four shots of Jack Daniel's finest and began to stir. If time was not of the essence, he would have let it sit for a week or two in pure alcohol.

I hope this works.

When the consistency was that of slush, he poured it into the French press and pushed down on the strainer, leaving a hazy brownish solution of pure liquid.

Carefully, Reece filled a 60cc syringe with his concoction, remembering the CIA doctor who had taught him this technique all those years ago. When Reece had asked how hot it was the doctor had answered, "If you were eating a jalapeño pepper, it would measure about five thousand Scoville Heat Units. This solution has a Scoville Heat Unit measurement of over three million. It will burn them alive from the inside out, but without the fire."

The Russian's head was beginning to sway, signifying the fentanyl was wearing off.

Good.

Reece sealed his resolve and approached the man he hoped had answers.

Reece brought his leg up and slammed it down directly on the Russian's broken leg, eliciting an animalistic scream.

Reece stepped behind him and tore the riggers' tape from his eyes, then grabbed a chair from the small kitchen table and turned it around so that its back was facing his subject. He sat down, rubber gloves, eye protection, and syringe all clearly visible to the Russian, who blinked his eyes and slowly took in his surroundings.

"Hi," Reece said as pleasantly as possible. "I'm James Reece. You tried to kill me and Raife Hastings earlier today. I have some questions for you."

The Russian's breathing was slow and labored. His head was restrained by the noose, but his eyes moved to his leg, then back to Reece.

In heavily accented English he responded, "My leg. Something for my leg."

"Oh, don't worry about your leg. That's about to be the very least of your problems." One of the first rules of interrogation was to only ask questions to which you already knew the answers. Reece started with what he already knew from his phone call with Vic Rodriguez. "Let's start with an easy one: Who is Ivan Zharkov?"

"Schas po ebalu poluchish, suka, blyat!" the Russian spat, his muscles straining to break free of the tape that kept him securely in place.

Without a word, Reece stood and walked behind him and grabbed the noose, wrenching his head back and to the side, slamming his free hand onto his adversary's face and prying his right eye open. With the syringe, Reece administered a drop of the capsaicin solution and stepped back.

The effect was immediate. The Russian's eye turned an instantaneous red, and his mouth opened in a roar of agony from a level of pain he had never experienced, body thrashing as his hands desperately fought to break free of the tape that bound them to the chair. Had they been free he would have ripped his own eyeball from his head, the agony feeling like a blade pivoting through his eye from the deep recesses of his brain.

"That's one drop, comrade," Reece said. "I have this entire syringe and more where that came from. Let's try that again; who is Ivan Zharkov?"

The Russian blinked, blood tears running down his face, his body doing its best to clear itself of this foreign invader. Then, taking a moment, he took in his antagonizer. This was James Reece. His target. He knew Ivan should have used a team from Wagner Group. He was a *Bratok* in the *bratva*. He hadn't broken in

Black Dolphin Prison and he certainly wouldn't break for this American. Ivan Zharkov had gotten him out of that hellhole. The *Pakhan* would get him out of this one. He was almost a brigadier in the organization. He would not break.

"Cigarette?" the Russian asked.

"Nope. Those things will kill you."

The Russian looked at his tormentor. "*Suka, blyat!*" he said, attempting to spit at Reece.

"I was afraid you might say that. Don't go anywhere," Reece said, standing and returning to the med kit.

He's not giving you a choice, Reece.

Reece closed his eyes and took a breath, seeing a vision of the Russian standing above a gagged and bound Katie, terror in her eyes.

Reece selected another 60cc syringe and filled it with tap water.

He then ripped open a Foley catheter bag from the kit and emptied its contents on the table.

Do it, Reece.

Reece opened the 14-gauge catheter and lubed it with the provided K-Y jelly. He then turned and marched back to his subject. Ignoring the stream of threats in Russian, Reece grabbed his prisoner's penis with his gloved hand and threaded the catheter down his urethra. Unable to move, the Russian continued to thrash his head as much as the noose would allow. Reece applied pressure to his captive's broken femur with his elbow and only stepped back when he saw yellow urine appear in the drainage bag. Reece then attached a 10cc syringe preloaded with saline to a side port, which blew up a small balloon, anchoring the system inside the bladder. Reece gave it a yank to ensure it was in place.

"You think you can make me talk, American? I used to rape guys like you in prison. I used to rape wives in front of husbands, daughters in front of fathers, and then chop them up in little pieces. You think you are tough, American? I think I'll fuck that little blond bitch of yours right in front of you. How would you like that, you weak piece of *shit*."

Reece kept his composure, unhooked the catheter bag, and attached the syringe filled with the capsaicin solution. He took another look at the bloodied mafia hit man in front of him and pushed in 5cc's of pain.

Eight seconds later the Russian's body contorted in agony as his bladder erupted in an uncontrollable spasm coupled with the most intense cramping imaginable. His body naturally attempted to curl up and vomit, but the noose and tape held him in place, vomit spewing from his nose and mouth, eyes bulging from his head.

Reece waited thirty seconds and then attached the syringe with water, flushing the capsaicin from the Russian's system.

Reece stepped back, waiting for his breathing to return to normal.

"Maybe that first question was too difficult," Reece said, disconnecting the clean syringe and reattaching the one with capsaicin. "Let's try something easier. What's your name?"

What harm could that do? Dimitry thought. Instead, all that came out between labored breaths, chunks of vomit still falling from his mouth, was *"Fuck you."*

Reece didn't hesitate. Depressing the plunger, he sent 15cc of his homemade mixture, three times the original dose, into the Russian's bladder. Then he stepped back.

The results were horrific; the man's neck strained against the noose as he began to foam at the mouth, choking, cramping, vomiting, emitting a visceral cry reserved for those in the throes of death.

Reece counted the seconds ticking by on his watch, giving a full minute this time before flushing the system again.

Then he waited as the animal became human, trying desperately to breathe.

Who was this American?

"I already know that Ivan Zharkov ordered the hit. I know he is the head of the Tambov Gang. I know you work for him. You won't be betraying him. I'm already going to hunt him down and kill him. Nothing you say will change that. And, as you've probably figured out, you are not leaving here alive. What I need to know is *why*. If you can tell me that, I can offer you a quick death."

His detainee paused in thought.

"James Reece. I studied you. I *knew* we needed a professional team, yet we almost killed you with a group of thugs. In the *bratva* we learn, too. They will come again. And this time they won't just be after you and your friend. The next time they come, it will be professionals. You've insulted their honor now. That is something that *bratva* will not let, how do you say? Lie? They will kill you all, wives, children, especially children. The *bratva* doesn't want to fight another generation. They might even fuck a few of your women to death and make you watch. They will come for you and they will kill every last one of you."

Reece knew it was true. In his head he saw visions of the dead. There was only one way this ended, and it was up to Reece to finish it.

Reece slowly picked through the med kit until he found a connector from the IV kit and attached it to the syringe, which he then connected to the "Y" port on the IV drip.

"Last chance," Reece said.

"*Fuck you,*" the Russian said without much enthusiasm.

He's close.

Reece slightly depressed the plunger, releasing what he hoped was about 1cc of capsaicin into the IV drip and directly into the Russian's bloodstream.

A bloodcurdling scream filled the cabin as every single pain receptor in the Russian's body ignited at once. Like a bolt of lightning hitting brain, muscles, and organs, a pain worse than the previous two capsaicin exposures threatened to boil the Russian from the inside out. Intestinal fluids began to spew from his lungs while brain secretions worked their way into his nasal cavity and labyrinth of his inner ear. His heart felt like it was about to explode.

Via the bloodstream was the most painful delivery method for the solution, but it was also the most short-lived. A person would metabolize the 1cc solution in about thirty seconds to a minute depending on weight, composition, and body type.

Reece kept slowly injecting the serum as he sensed it was beginning to subside.

"What? I can't hear you," Reece said over the screams. "Only you can stop this. Ivan is as good as dead. Just tell me why he sent you, and I'll end your pain."

Sensing that the Russian's body and brain were about to give out completely, Reece gave the man a moment of reprieve.

"Dimitry," the man said, coming down from what felt like a blowtorch working every portion of his body and brain. "My name is Dimitry Mashkov."

"See, that wasn't so hard. Keep talking or I keep pushing this shit into your system."

"Please, please . . ."

"It's all up to you. Remember, Ivan Zharkov put you here."

The Russian attempted to catch his breath. He wanted to die.

"I was a prisoner in penal colony number six for seven years. Do you know this place?"

"I can't say I'm familiar."

"It is the oldest prison in all of Russia. They call the prisoners, 'the maniacs'—a fitting term, no? Terrorists, child molesters, serial killers, even cannibals. Life sentences only. No one gets out."

"No one but you?"

"*Da*. Ivan Zharkov got me out and brought me back to the brotherhood. Promoted me. *Phakan* did not put me here. The one who betrayed us did. The only reason I am talking to you is so you can find the man who betrayed this mission."

"How do you know someone betrayed it?"

"How do you Americans put it? This was not my first, uh, cattle drive? You avoided the ambush and now you are asking me about Ivan Zharkov a few hours later."

"Tell me about him."

"He worked his way up. He was a foot soldier, like me. In 1991, Russia became like your cowboy West, I think you say? He saw opportunity and is now one of the most powerful men in Russia."

"Why would he want to kill me?"

Dimitry hesitated.

"*Why!*" Reece demanded, shaking the capsaicin syringe attached to the IV line.

"I think it has to do with the American."

"The American?"

"A CIA man defected to Russia and now works for Zharkov."

"What CIA man?" Reece asked with renewed interest.

"One I escorted from Argentina to Russia. He was an old Soviet mole, involved with the President Zubarev assassination."

Son of a bitch, Reece thought. *Oliver Grey.*

"And who do you think betrayed you?" Reece asked.

"Someone I should have killed long ago. Ivan's son."

"Son?"

"He has many, but the one who is most valuable to the organization is Aleksandr."

"Why?"

"He's a director in the SVR."

"The SVR has ties to the mafia?" Reece asked, pretending he didn't already have the information.

"This is Russia. The *'bratva,* intelligence, political triad' is strong."

"I want you to think long and hard about this one. Why would Aleksandr Zharkov call a contact at the CIA to sell you out moments before the attack?"

Reece watched as his detainee's eyes flashed with recognition.

"Tell me."

"It is said that Aleksandr is sick."

"He's dying?"

"No, sick, like how do you say, 'crazy'?"

"I don't understand."

"Aleksandr is what I hear called 'not right in head.' He hunts humans."

"What? Where?"

"He leases an island in the Russian Far East from the government. Medny Island. It is said he imports people from Africa, but this is only how do you say? Guess? But if Aleksandr called your CIA to warn you of the attack, then I want you to kill that *suka.* I know you can't let me live. In exchange for this information I want you to kill Aleksandr Zharkov. Send him to me in the afterlife."

"You have my word."

Reece would have preferred to put a bullet in Dimitry's head but that would have left DNA all over the former senator's cabin. This was going to be hard enough to clean up as it was.

Depressing the syringe's plunger, Reece pushed the remaining 30cc's of solution into Dimitry's veins, flooding his system with an overdose of capsaicin. The right side of his brain stroked immediately, the left side of his face dropping into paralysis as blood filled his retinas and brain, the red fluid attempting to escape from its dying host through his nose, mouth, and ears. Almost simultaneously, his bladder and bowels released a mess of bloody excrement. Seconds later his heart went into fibrillation, and Dimitry went to hell to wait for Aleksandr Zharkov.

Reece stepped outside and grabbed the railing of the deck for balance, taking deep breaths of mountain air while suppressing an urge to vomit.

Oliver Grey was in Russia working for the mafia, working for a man whose son was a senior intelligence official with a penchant for hunting humans. That same son had called a contact at the CIA to betray his father's, and Grey's, plan to kill him. *Why?*

Reece waved to a worried-looking Liz on the dock, then picked up the sat phone to call Raife via the landline at the main ranch house.

"Hanna?" Caroline Hastings picked up on the first ring, a hint of panic in her usually steady voice.

"No, I'm sorry, Caroline, it's Reece. Is Raife there?"

"He couldn't wait. He's in the air on his way to Romania to look for Hanna. She hasn't answered her phone or any of our emails. Vic has the embassy trying to track her down but Raife doesn't trust them. He just couldn't sit around and wait."

He could tell she had been crying.

Reece paused. "I would have done the same."

"I know."

"Is Vic still there?"

"Yes, but he's about to return to D.C.," the Hastings matriarch answered after composing herself.

"Good. Please tell him I'll meet him at Langley. I don't want to cause another commotion by flying back to the ranch with LE still combing the place. How's Katie?"

"She's a strong woman, Reece. I think it's all still sinking in, but she's fine."

"Please give her a hug for me and tell her I'll meet her at her place in Alexandria tomorrow. Can you get her home for me?"

"We can certainly handle that."

"Thank you. I'm so sorry I brought this on you, Caroline."

"Where is all this leading, Reece?"

"Russia."

CHAPTER 53

THE FLIGHT FROM DULLES was well within the eight-thousand-mile range of the G550, but it was still almost 5:00 a.m. when they finally landed. The combined flights had exceeded the crew rest requirements for the two pilots, but, given the emergency nature of the trip, they were willing to push it. Despite the creature comforts of Thorn's Gulfstream, for Raife, rest was an impossibility.

Raife rented a car as rapidly as was possible in Romania from a man speaking passable English and headed directly for the farm where his sister lived, driving the small Opel sedan as fast as he dared.

His parents had tried to contact Hanna several times during the past twenty-four hours without success and the embassy personnel had predictably been unable to track her down. A sense of dread permeated Raife's very being; his instincts were usually correct.

The navigation app he was using was next to worthless in this area, so Raife had to rely on a paper map that he kept in his lap as he drove. Just like the old days. The sun was beginning to rise, illuminating the small farmhouses and villages that dotted the rolling hills, the local residents already moving into the planted fields to bring in the harvest. It was a simple, meaningful existence, and Raife quickly realized why his baby sister had fallen in love with it.

He pulled the sedan off the road and compared the small brick building and nearby barn to a photo on his iPhone. This was the place. Not wanting to disturb anything or anyone, Raife left the car near the road and walked toward his sister's temporary home on foot. He walked around the barn and saw that a small pickup truck, presumably belonging to Hanna, was parked outside.

Maybe she was home, and her internet was just down?

As he walked farther, he saw that the door to the small home was open. A burst of adrenaline surged through his body as his mind put the pieces together.

He was unarmed, a requirement to clear Romanian customs. The old wooden door creaked as Raife pushed it open. A chair was on its side, and blood was visible on the tile floor. Raife pushed the horror of the moment from his mind and put his tracking skills to work. The fact that her body wasn't here meant she was probably still alive. He pulled the small pack from his back and retrieved a pair of nitrile gloves from the first aid kit inside.

At first glance, it appeared the droplets of blood on the tile floor led outside but, upon close inspection, the pattern indicated it was leading inside the home. The bleeding had begun outside. Raife went down to his hands and knees and used a small but powerful LED light to search for evidence. A kitchen knife had slid underneath a table and appeared to be covered in blood. Hanna had fought, and for a slight moment a sense of brotherly pride broke through the pain. The beam from his light found a strand of hair that appeared to belong to his sister on the floor, an arm's reach away from the knife.

Raife backtracked outside and searched the soft dry ground. He paced the area with his eyes on the ground, stopping, kneeling, then going prone, just as Melusi had taught him back in Africa.

The tracks will tell the story. Let them speak.

After twenty minutes of study, those tracks had given their testimony. A vehicle, a van by the looks of it, had stopped by the road and two large males wearing work boots had stepped out. One set of boot tracks led to the back of the home, where he'd knelt next to the door. The other set of tracks led to the front door. It swung outward and he'd positioned himself on the hinge side so that he would be hidden when it opened.

A woman wearing high-heeled boots had traded places with the driver and driven the van up the driveway toward the home. The tracks led to the door, where she'd likely lured Hanna outside. The man had probably pounced on his sister from behind in the darkness, and, based on the greenish hue of the blood trail, had taken a knife to the guts for his trouble. Hanna had been subdued just outside the back door. The drag marks left by her feet led to the van, which indicated that she'd been unconscious, either knocked out, drugged, or both.

Where would they take her? That was the psychology of tracking; learn from the spoor and anticipate your prey's next move.

Raife needed to get inside the head of whoever had taken her. The tracks were only a few hours old, but Raife didn't have any leads as to where they might be headed. He was in an unfamiliar land, didn't speak the language, and had no local network on which to rely.

Raife walked back inside the farmhouse, and this time his eyes were up, looking for anything he'd missed on his first pass. He didn't have to look far.

A piece of paper was on the small kitchen table, torn from a notebook. On it was written a URL of seemingly nonsensical letters, numbers, and symbols followed by two additional sets of similarly random alphanumeric combinations without the URL designation.

A user name and password. The Dark Web.

Feeling a vibration, Raife reached in his pocket and answered the phone.

"Tell me," he said.

"It's not good. Did you find Hanna?"

"I'm at her place now. She's been taken."

Raife heard his friend pause on the other end of the line.

"I know who did it and where she is," Reece said.

When Reece was finished relaying the information he'd learned from the interrogation of Dimitry Mashkov, Raife's eyes moved back to the paper in his hand.

"He's hunting her," he said.

"Or, he's using her as bait. Come back, and I'll talk to Vic about mounting an operation to get her out."

"There's no time for that. He wants me, or he wants you, probably both. See what you can do about it through official channels. In the meantime, I'm going to book a hunt."

CHAPTER 54

Medny Island, Russia

ALEKSANDR SAT AT HIS desk in his fortress on Medny. The island was first sighted in 1741 by Vitus Jonassen Bering, a Danish cartographer employed by the Russian Navy. It wasn't until a few years later that Yemelyan Basov explored and hunted the island, bringing back a host of valuable furs to Kamchatka and on to trading posts throughout Russia.

Aleksandr looked at a seal pelt on the wall.

Fitting, he thought.

Native Aleuts had moved to the island in the late 1800s and set up a whaling station. Relying on harpoons, they hunted whales and seals until the government moved the settlement to neighboring Bering Island. It was a frontier post with Cold War military significance up until 2001, when it was abandoned.

The Zharkov family dacha on the Black Sea would not do for what Aleksandr had in mind so, when the opportunity presented itself, the entrepreneurial young intelligence officer had leased the island from the government. He needed a remote outpost to partake in his most dangerous of games. Siberia was remote. An island in the Bering Sea was even more so.

Hunting the woman from Montana had ended in a most unsatisfying manner. He hadn't been able to feel the pleasure of releasing his arrow into his quarry. She'd also managed to kill two of his best dogs. No matter, Sergei had others to take their place. Luckily for him a plane was about to land at a remote strip in Kamchatka. There, six new prisoners from the Central African Republic would be transferred to an Mi-8 transport helicopter for the flight to Medny Island. They would provide ample opportunity to sharpen his skills before the ultimate chess match.

Americans were so easy to manipulate. Hanna Hastings had served her purpose.

Aleksandr had received word that an American had arrived in Romania and traveled to her farmhouse. It wouldn't be long before he put the pieces together and connected via the Dark Web using the note left on his sister's table. The trap was baited. Now it was time to wait. His prey would come, and Aleksandr would finally put himself to the test against the most worthy of adversaries.

He felt like more tea. "*Sergei!*" he called out.

Where was that mongrel half-breed? Probably out training the dogs or practicing with that old bow of his. Sergei and all those who carried the blood of his people remained stuck in the past, aboriginals fretting out a meager existence much as they had for centuries. They had not adapted to the changing environment. They had even attempted to defend themselves against Russian colonization with bows and spears. The result had been catastrophic. Where disease and war failed, alcoholism and forced migration picked up the slack. Sergei, whose Koryak blood had been diluted through breeding and the ravages of a war the world knew little about, still favored the ancient bow of his people over the modern crossbow that Aleksandr carried on their hunts. Aleksandr scoffed at the thought. The Siberian native had been conscripted into the Russian Army. There he'd excelled in the ranks of the *spetsnaz*, serving with distinction in the Second Chechen War, putting down the insurgency using the tactics and techniques that had earned them the respect of the mujahideen in the Soviet-Afghan campaign. Sergei's unit had been responsible for the targeted assassinations of Chechen separatist leadership. *By any means necessary.* In the Russian Army, he'd learned an appreciation for the Russian martial art of Sambo, to which he continued to devote himself with zeal. Aleksandr couldn't fathom why the huge Koryak dedicated so much time to unarmed combat. After all, his size seemed sufficient to deal with anyone reckless enough to fight him hand-to-hand. It seemed to be the one vestige of his time spent with the *spetsnaz* that he carried forward into his work for Aleksandr. He'd spent months building a *baidarka*, a kayak made of driftwood with a deck covered in seal and sea lion skins. The fool even hunted from it in the tradition of his people. He knew the dogs, though, and, much like the canines whose company he kept, he was loyal to the man who fed him. For that, Aleksandr would allow him his little bow and kayak.

A light on a computer used for only one purpose roused him from his musings.

Aleksandr hovered over a Tor network icon and depressed his keypad before entering a twenty-eight-character password and entering the world of the Dark Web.

The platforms that hosted illicit activity on the Dark Web changed as international consortiums of law enforcement built cases on a virtual battlefield. Silk Road, AlphaBay, and Hansa were but a few of the cyber auction houses whose specialties catered to the dark side of man. Weapons, child pornography, human trafficking, and illicit drugs were the mainstays of the realm, traded for with bitcoin cryptocurrency, moving people and destroying lives at 50 megabits a second. The Dark Web was where Aleksandr offered a specific service to a discerning and niche customer. It was where Aleksandr offered the hunt of a lifetime.

To those who had adorned their walls with most every species the planet had to offer, a few longed for one more trophy, one they wouldn't be able to brag about at cocktail parties in polite society. They yearned to experience the hunting of man.

Marketed via the Dark Web, the prey were described as prisoners destined for execution. These hunters would be fulfilling a civic duty. For $500,000 USD in bitcoin, rich Russians, Europeans, and Americans had traveled to Medny for the experience that had thus far eluded them in life.

Aleksandr ran his tongue along his bottom lip as he read the email.

"It is so nice to make your acquaintance, Mr. Rainsford."

PART 3

THE KILL

"I am still a beast at bay..."

—Sanger Rainsford,
The Most Dangerous Game by Richard Connell

CHAPTER 55

Boundary County, Idaho
United States/Canadian Border

REECE WOULD HAVE PREFERRED to somehow bring Dimitry's body back to the Hastingses' property and leave it where a bear could dispose of it. Dimitry dying in the firefight at the ranch made a lot more sense than him sustaining life-threatening wounds there, then wandering a hundred miles to a property coincidentally owned by Tim Thornton. But, with law enforcement still combing the crime scenes, Reece and Liz had no choice but to dispose of the body in the deepest part of the lake.

"I think the chair's a goner, buddy," Liz said as they contemplated how to clean up the cabin.

"I'm afraid you're right."

Donning surgical masks from the med bag, and using bleach from under the sink, they cleaned off the leather chair as best they could. The tarp and towels went into a trash bag along with the coffee grinder, French press, and baking tray. Reece dismantled the chair with an ax and wrapped it in trash bags as well. When they were done sanitizing the crime scene, they loaded it all into the plane.

With Thorn's G550 somewhere in Eastern Europe, and wanting to get things moving as quickly as possible, Reece had Liz drop him in Billings. Liz borrowed a van from the Corporate Jet Center and took her "trash" to a landfill. Reece was able to catch a commercial Delta flight to Minneapolis that connected into Washington–Reagan National.

After spending several months of solitude in a rural and isolated environment, it took Reece some time to adjust to the sights and sounds of the modern world. His mind had adapted to the natural order of the wilderness and rebelled against his reentry into society. By 10:00 p.m., he was relieved to be stepping through the doorway of Katie's condo in Old Town, Alexandria.

"I told you it wouldn't be long," he said.

Katie had beaten him to Virginia by thirty minutes and, despite the late hour, she made coffee while Reece caught her up on the developments of the past forty-eight hours.

"How are you feeling?" Reece asked.

"Like I'm grateful that I wasn't kidnaped by a psycho assassin who likes to wrap women's heads in det cord."

"Thank goodness for small favors."

"I'm okay, Reece. I just keep thinking about how lucky we were that Caroline Hastings is such a great shot, and that you showed up when you did. And . . ."

"And, what?"

"I'd be lying if I said I didn't wonder if life with you is always going to be this way."

Reece nodded.

"I've wondered the same thing myself. Before we delve into that, though, I have an important question to ask: Do you have any honey?"

"Ha! Oh yeah, I forgot you take your coffee like most of my old sorority sisters."

Returning to the table with honey and a small carton of half-and-half, she watched as Reece doctored his brew.

"I have something to tell you, Katie, and I need your help to think it through."

"What is it?"

"Raife's little sister, Hanna, is missing. She was working in Romania and, not long after we were attacked, someone took her."

"*What?*" Katie whispered in disbelief. "The same people who were after you?"

Forcing the rational side of her brain to restrain her emotions, she closed her eyes and processed the news.

"How can I help?"

"Well . . ."

"Hold on," Katie interrupted.

She picked up her iPad and phone, depositing them in her bedroom before closing the door. She then unplugged the LCD television hanging on the wall of her living room. Satisfied, she picked up a legal pad and sat back down.

"You're as paranoid as I am."

"It's not paranoia if someone's really after you," she said.

I've heard that somewhere before, Reece thought.

"Here's what we know. Oliver Grey was a CIA analyst who went off the grid several months ago. It turns out he was working for Vasili Andrenov, a former colonel in the GRU. He recruited Grey near the end of the Cold War and kept him on retainer even after the fall of the Soviet Union and Andrenov's ouster from the new Russian government."

"He's the Russian billionaire who was blown up in Switzerland last year?"

"That's him. Grey helped plan the operation that killed the Russian president and attempted to kill ours. After the follow-on chemical attack in Odessa, he went underground and ended up in Argentina."

"I thought they only hid Nazis."

"They're branching out. Anyway, after that, he makes his way to Saint Petersburg, Russia, and started working for someone named Ivan Zharkov, who runs one of the big crime families in the *bratva*, the Russian mafia."

"Why would Grey want to kill you? Why wouldn't he just lie low in Russia?"

"I can think of a couple reasons. First is that he knows I'm going to track him down. He's right about that. He's one of two people left who had a hand in killing Freddy. He wanted to put me down before I got the chance."

Katie frowned at the casual way Reece referred to killing like it was a normal everyday occurrence and she had to remind herself that for him, it was.

"And the second?"

Reece thought of the stainless steel Submariner that used to adorn his father's wrist. He'd purchased it in a PX in Vietnam, and worn it every day Reece could remember.

"I think Grey had my father killed, Katie. I can't prove it, but I've been doing some reading while I was in the mountains. I asked Vic for some files after the Odessa incident."

"When you save the life of the president it probably opens a few file cabinets."

"It doesn't hurt. I had Vic put together a list of my father's postings at the CIA from just before 9/11 until his death. Oliver Grey was in Buenos Aires the night my father was killed."

"I thought you told me he was an analyst, a desk guy."

"He was. I think he used the recruitment skills that Andrenov taught him to recruit a contract agent named Jules Landry to do the actual killing."

"But why, Reece? Why would a former Soviet spy want to kill your father? Because of something that happened in the Cold War? I thought a lot of the warriors on opposite sides of the Iron Curtain were actually friends now?"

"I wondered the same thing. It goes back farther than that. It turns out that Grey signed out a file in 1993. That file was an after-action report from a MACV-SOG operation in Vietnam that resulted in the death of a Russian advisor. Can you guess the advisor's last name?"

"Andrenov."

"That's right. And can you guess who led the mission?"

"Tom Reece."

"Right again. I think Andrenov recruited Grey to find out who killed his father and then all those years later finally got his revenge."

"I think we need to switch to something stronger than Black Rifle coffee. I need a drink," Katie said, standing up to retrieve two glasses from the cabinet.

"I don't have any Semper yet, but I do have a nice bottle of Sea Smoke."

"That'll do."

"It's a 2013 TEN. My dad gets a case on his birthday every year from his golfing buddy, Nick Coussoulis. He and his wife, Tina, own a golf course out in California and get it at cost for the restaurant there. My dad always saves me a bottle," Katie said as Reece organized his thoughts.

"That's nice of him."

"That reminds me. There's no good time to tell you. He sent me three boxes to give to you. My parents were listed as next of kin when your mom passed away. You were presumed dead, so the nursing home shipped the last of her things to my parents. I have them in the back closet when you want them."

"Thanks, Katie. I'll go through them when this is all over. Now, where were we?"

"You were just getting to the part where Grey almost kills us."

"Right. I think Grey saw an opportunity to use both the protection and resources of the Russian mob to launch a hit on me on U.S. soil."

"Why Raife as well?"

"That's a question I'm going to put to Vic tomorrow."

"And who tipped off the CIA about the attack in Montana?"

"That's where this gets a little strange. A former Agency case officer who spent a lot of time in Russia got a call from a Russian intelligence official named Aleksandr Zharkov, warning him of the attack. He called Vic, who contacted us just in time."

"Any relation to Ivan Zharkov?"

"It's his son."

"So, let me get this straight." Katie's analytical mind was going to work. "A Russian mob boss hires a former CIA mole who then plans your murder but gets sold out by the mafia don's son?"

"As best as I can figure it."

"Anywhere else but Russia, that would be crazy."

"Fair point," Reece conceded.

"Maybe they went after Hanna when the attack in Montana failed to draw you and Raife out so they can try again?"

"It's possible."

"There's something you're not telling me, isn't there?"

Reece nodded.

"During my interrogation of the Russian who survived the attack he told me that Aleksandr Zharkov imports humans to his own private hunting ground on an island off the Kamchatka Peninsula."

"To do what?" Katie asked, already dreading the answer.

"He hunts them. Raife is on his way there now. I'm going to see if I can talk Vic into mounting a rescue operation but the odds of that happening are slim. What I really need from him is information."

"Why, may I ask?"

"This is the part you might not want to hear."

Katie took off her small pair of black-rimmed glasses and set them on the legal pad covered with her hastily scribbled notes and looked at him, her blue eyes clouded with sadness.

"Even if the CIA says no, you're leaving again, aren't you?"

"It's my fault, Katie; the attack in Montana, Hanna's disappearance, now Raife. I need to find her. One way or another, after I get what I can from the Agency, I'll have to go."

"Where?"

"Medny Island."

CHAPTER 56

Central Intelligence Agency, Langley, Virginia

IT WAS EARLY AND they'd beaten rush hour, so traffic on the George Washington Parkway was relatively light. It was already hot and oppressively humid, the aging 4Runner's air-conditioning struggling to cool the SUV's interior. As they made the scenic drive along the Potomac River, Reece couldn't help but think about the last time they'd been on this road together, going to say good-bye to his parents at Arlington. It looked different now, the deep snow having transformed into lush green grass. They drove by the airport on the right and then the Pentagon on the left and eventually passed Arlington National Cemetery. Sweat-soaked joggers and cyclists were out in force on the sidewalks that flanked the river, many of them crossing the Memorial Bridge into D.C. proper.

Katie took the exit that led directly to the north security gate and rolled down her window as they approached a team of guards wearing body armor and BDU-style uniforms. Reece leaned over the console and held out his green contractor badge for the officer to inspect.

"She's just dropping me off. I've got a meeting at six thirty."

"No problem, sir, but you're going to have to get out here. We can give you a ride up to the building."

"Thanks." He turned to Katie. "I'll text you when I'm done."

"You be safe, James Reece."

"Semper," he said with a wink.

The security officer directed Katie to where she could make a U-turn and another waved Reece toward a Chevy Equinox with a light bar on the roof for the short drive to the headquarters building. Reece had been to CIA headquarters on a few occasions in the past but had never asked about a large black aircraft that towered above the road on a pedestal.

"Is that an SR-71?"

"Everyone thinks that but it's actually an A-12 Oxcart, the Agency's version. It was a tad faster than the Blackbird and it only had one crew member."

"Guess you've answered that question before."

"Every day, man, every damn day. Here we are," the officer said as he pulled the small SUV to the curb outside the "new" and "old" headquarters buildings.

"Thanks for the ride."

He had scrounged up a collared shirt but even if he'd worn a suit, there was nothing about James Reece that blended in at Langley.

He entered the hallowed ground of the old building, stepping across the mosaic Central Intelligence Agency seal. As was his custom, he walked to the Wall of Honor on the north side of the lobby, where black stars representing the fallen were chiseled into the white marble. Flanked by the flag of the nation and the flag of the Agency, the stars were a daily reminder to those who crossed the threshold that they were the country's first line of defense. Above the 133 stars were the words:

IN HONOR OF THOSE MEMBERS OF THE CENTRAL
INTELLIGENCE AGENCY WHO GAVE THEIR LIVES IN THE
SERVICE OF THE COUNTRY

Reece looked down at the glass case protruding from the wall that held the Book of Honor under lock and key. A black Moroccan goatskin logbook lay in wait for its inch-thick glass to be opened yet again; for another date to be inscribed and sometimes a name to correspond with a new star on the wall above. Reece slowly scanned the names visible through the glass in silent respect, hovering over those he knew. He was in the company of warriors. The page had already been turned on the seventy-ninth star representing Johnny "Mike" Spann from one of the first battles in the War on Terror. It had also been turned on the page with Chris Mueller and "Chief," whose actions under fire in Afghanistan defined heroism. The current pages displayed under protective glass were almost at capacity and soon the page would be turned yet again. Reece's eyes hovered over the names of ████████, Glen Doherty, Ty Woods, and ███████. Nineteen other stars stood out on the page, names withheld. Reece knew more than a few, their names and the circumstances of their deaths locked away on secure hard drives and in the memories of those who were there.

Reece ran his fingers over the newest star, the one that represented his friend Freddy Strain. Reece had been there for the ceremony, as had the president. Memories of his old teammate flashed through his mind: sniper school, their first post-9/11 deployment, Mozambique, Odessa, the funeral, Freddy's family. Reece closed his eyes, Freddy's face coming to him from beyond the grave.

"I'm sorry, brother," Reece whispered, knowing that if it were not for him, Freddy's kids would still have a father. He closed his eyes tighter. *I'd trade places with you if I could. I should be the one in the ground.* Freddy smiled, his face blurring in Reece's memory, morphing into another face. This one was hazy, and Reece couldn't quite make it out. But the blur had a name; Nizar Kattan, the Syrian sniper who had pressed the trigger that took Freddy as he rendered aid to a wounded Secret Service agent on a rooftop half a world away. Reece had anonymously set up a trust to take care of Freddy's special needs child. The money he'd used had been a reward from the British Crown for taking out the terrorist some had come to call Europe's Osama bin Laden.

Reece knew that Freddy's was one of the names not written next to his star; classified, just like the star that represented Thomas Reece. A bureaucrat somewhere in the building had decided omitting the names was necessary so as not to expose certain sources and methods.

Reece stepped back and took a breath, composing himself as CIA staff came and went behind him, wearing suits and carrying briefcases. Glancing at the opposite wall, Reece read the unofficial motto of the Central Intelligence Agency from Scripture, John 8:32: "*And ye shall know the truth, and the truth shall make you free.*"

We'll see, he thought.

Reece badged through the turnstile and headed for the elevators. He felt the eyes of staffers, agents, executives, and security officers burning through him. As he navigated the maze of the world's premier intelligence service, he remembered that it wasn't that long ago they'd been part of the manhunt to capture and kill him.

Vic's administrative assistant waved him through the open door into a spacious office. They didn't bother sitting; instead they walked directly into the adjoining SCIF, Secure Compartmented Information Facility, which was a fancy name for a secure conference room. Reece placed his iPhone into what looked like a small post office box, locking it inside and pocketing the key. Once inside the soundproof room he took a seat across from the director of Clandestine Services.

"It's good to see you, Reece. Thanks for coming in."

"Good to see you, too, sir."

"If you came on board full-time, we could do this on a regular basis. You might even get a parking spot one day."

"We'll see how it goes. What do you have for me?"

Reece had briefed Vic on the phone from Billings, speaking in riddles in case unwanted ears were listening.

Vic tapped a key on a secure laptop that was connected to a large LCD screen on the wall.

"The Bureau folks have been surprisingly generous with sharing information on this one. Frankly, I think an attack on U.S. soil against a former senator, whether he was the target or not, scared the shit out of them."

Reece nodded.

"As you know, there were two teams: the one that attempted to ambush you on the highway and the second that moved on your friend Raife at the ranch."

A group of pictures, along with an aerial photo of the ambush site, appeared on the screen.

"After you drive out of the ambush, the first team moves to the ranch, where Caroline Hastings puts a world of hurt on them until you arrive. We believe that everyone on that team has been accounted for."

Vic advanced the slides and a close-up of six dead bodies were displayed.

"Except for the female they used as bait," Reece said.

"Correct," Vic continued, tapping the arrow key again.

A photo of an attractive young woman filled the screen.

"We've determined that she was working in Whitefish as a bartender. She's a Russian national on a valid green card. Our guess is that she reconned this entire operation. She has not been back to work since this went down but we'll find her."

"She looks familiar. I've seen her around town."

"On that second group, the initial forensics report says that one of them is missing; there was blood on the scene with no body to match. You know anything about that?"

Reece shook his head.

"Didn't think you would. They're still running full profiles, but it looks like they were all ethnic Russians."

"The tattoos made that clear. Anything on the weapons?"

"ATF is working on it but they were all Russian-made AKMs, so they didn't come through legal channels. Millions of those guns were made so that probably won't give us much to go on."

"What about Hanna Hastings; anything on who might have grabbed her?" Reece asked, wanting to confirm his findings from the interrogation.

"Nothing yet. We pulled in some local assets to investigate and our station chief in Bucharest is working with their national police force, but honestly, I'm not optimistic."

"Do you have any theories?"

"Smart money says they grabbed her as a consolation prize when the attack on you and Raife failed, but there's something else, something darker."

"What?" Reece asked.

"After the accusations and evidence of Russian intelligence meddling in our elections, infiltrating social media platforms to influence our political process, the director is not in the mood to play games with them. The power vacuum left by the assassination of their president has their intelligence agencies running wild without adult supervision. Financial crimes, the election meddling, it's like we're back in the Cold War but without the rules. We've done a deep dive on their leadership, particularly Aleksandr Zharkov. Our cyber capabilities are impressive, thanks to some help from Silicon Valley. We all know that there is human trafficking that's being facilitated through the Dark Web, and we've found evidence tying Zharkov to brokering humans as prey for trophy hunting. For a half a million dollars, you get to hunt what they call 'criminals destined for the gallows.'"

"'The Most Dangerous Game.'"

"Exactly. Our records show that Zharkov is a big hunter type, shot animals all over the world while posted overseas for the SVR. At some point, his tastes crossed over from four-legged to two-legged game. You know what Hemingway said, 'Once you've hunted man . . .'"

"That all squares with what I found out on my end."

"Oh, really?" Vic asked with renewed interest.

"Do you think that Aleksandr blows his father's op so that he can have a crack at me and Raife?"

"That's my own pet theory, yes."

"And he's using Hanna for the bait."

Vic nodded.

"That confirms what I learned in a conversation with a recently deceased Russian mobster."

"I am going to pretend I believe it was just a conversation," Vic said.

"Now your intel is confirmed via my HUMINT. What are our next steps?"

"The director is preparing a presidential finding that would authorize a hostage rescue mission. She thinks the connection to you and Freddy, and the attempted assassination, will help sway the president. He's not running for re-election and if we can convince him that this won't start World War III, I think we have a chance. You did save his life after all."

"Even so, he's not going to green-light a hostage rescue on Russian soil."

"Don't be so sure. The operators will all use AKs to make it look like it's a Russian criminal syndicate hit on the son of *bratva* leadership, just enough plausible deniability and confusion to make this a nonattributable action. Believe me, if you knew half the classified history of this place, you'd know this is one of the most *sane* paramilitary operations the CIA has ever proposed. If denied, we'll have no choice but to pass it to Alpha Group via diplomatic channels."

"Alpha Group? Vic, we do that and she's dead."

"I know."

"Who's got it from our side? ████████?"

"The ████ commander has two COAs," Vic continued, using the acronym for courses of action. "The first is SEALs from ████ jumping into the Pacific just south of the Bering Sea to link up with an amphib. From there they head south to rendezvous with a submarine carrying a platoon from SDV1 on a ████████████. They'll come from the sea, hit the lodge, and extract back out to sea just like we've done with ████ ██████ ██████████ in the past. It's a proven COA."

"Even with the AK ploy, if someone goes down and gets left behind, facial recognition technology will confirm it was us."

"That will be fully explained to the president."

"What's COA 2?"

"The ████ commander is an Army general so he wants ████ in on the action as well," Vic said, using one of the nicknames for the Army's ████████████ ████████████████████████, better known to the public as ████ ████. "Second COA is to launch ████ in MH-X Black Hawks from an amphib. In and out."

"Riskier COA," Reece observed, remembering the Army helicopter that went down on his last Afghanistan deployment.

"True. We are pushing for COA 1 but it will take a couple days longer to get that one in motion. We are lucky that SDV was deployed for a ████████████. Part of their work-up is the ████████████████████████ ████████████████. National Command Authority will advise the president."

"Vic, you know if the president tries to go through diplomatic channels, he's signing Hanna's death warrant."

"I promise I'll do everything I can to ensure that doesn't happen."

Reece leaned back in his chair, his mind racing to analyze the possible contingencies.

"I need to be there."

"Negative, Reece. You've never trained for SDV ops," Vic countered, having anticipated the request.

"All I'd do is get in the back and breathe whatever concoction they breathe. It's not like I'd be driving the thing."

"First off, they don't 'drive' it, they 'pilot' it. The answer is no."

"Well, at least put me on the ███ op."

"No."

"They don't know this guy."

"Neither do you."

"I know him better than you think," Reece snapped.

Vic interlaced his hands and brought his index fingers to his lips.

"There's something else," Reece said.

"I'm not going to like this, am I?" Vic asked.

"Raife is headed for Medny Island. He signed up for a hunt on the Dark Web. They left a URL with a log-in and password in Hanna's kitchen in Romania. He's going to get her."

"*Shit!* You didn't try to talk him out of it?"

"I can see you don't know Raife very well."

"Did you get the URL and password?"

"Sure did," Reece said, passing the CIA executive a piece of paper from his pocket.

"*Shit*," Vic said again. "Just what we need: a former SEAL in the hands of Russian intelligence."

"I can help, Vic. Get me on this op."

"Again, *no.*"

"What if I go full-time?"

Vic had been trying to convince Reece to come work as a Ground Branch officer in the Special Activities Division of the CIA since they first met.

"You put me on this mission, and I come in for at least four years."

Vic tapped his index fingers together in front of his face, contemplating the offer.

"You're on."

"You knew I was going to offer that up, didn't you?" Reece asked.

"Let's just say I was prepared for your offer. The assaulters are already down at ▇▇ ▇▇ training on a mock-up of the lodge on Medny Island."

"You move fast."

"We're the CIA," Vic said, rising to shake hands with his newest recruit. "Nicole Phan and Andy Danreb are already down there. Remember them?"

"I remember," Reece said, thinking back to Andy's role in exposing the assassination and chemical weapon threat to Odessa the previous year.

"As gruff and cynical as he is, with the Russia connection, Andy is our foremost expert. Nicole will be the connection back to Langley and the Counterterrorism Center. She plays much better with others than your friend Andy." Vic looked at his watch. "If you leave now, you can make it in time for tonight's brief and FTX."

Reece wondered if Vic knew about Oliver Grey's connection to his father's death, or his obsession with taking out the sniper who had killed Freddy. He knew Vic would think those emotions would cloud his judgment and he didn't want to discuss anything that would threaten his involvement in the mission. If Vic didn't know that the real reason Reece was coming on board was to settle a personal score, Reece certainly wasn't going to tell him.

Reece left the executive level and made his way back to the lobby. This time he didn't stop at the Wall of Honor, though he did pause ever so slightly as he walked across the eagle and compass rose of the Agency seal. Visions of Freddy Strain and Thomas Reece had been replaced with the file photos of Nizar and Grey; the Syrian and the traitor were clearly focused in his crosshairs.

CHAPTER 57

IT TOOK JUST OVER ███████ to drive the Agency Suburban down to the CIA training facility. Situated on a peninsula ███████████████████████ ███████████████████████████ is a secluded ███████ training site that had gained notoriety as the rehearsal site for the raid that killed Osama bin Laden. A full mock-up of the compound in Abbottabad, Pakistan, had been built so the assault force could memorize the layout of the world's most wanted terrorist's home. The SEALs tasked with completing the mission had been successfully assaulting compounds of every shape and size, year after year, on virtually a nightly basis since 9/11, but the Abbottabad mission would have worldwide geopolitical repercussions, so nothing was spared to stack the deck in their favor.

The special operations community is a small one and, though he was older than many of them, Reece recognized a few of the Army commandos from various training schools and deployments. Navy Seabees were hard at work building a mock-up of the lodge on Medny Island for full mission profile rehearsals. Nothing was known about the inside layout, as all they had to go on was satellite imagery, which would ensure the outside was almost an exact replica of the target. Forty assaulters from ███████████ had arrived a day earlier and had been preparing for what they had been told was a hostage rescue mission. They had assumed it was for a target in Somalia or Syria and had not yet been told mission specifics. That was about to change.

When Reece drove in, most of the assaulters were in the chow hall waiting for an upcoming intelligence briefing.

"The Unit," as it is known by the skilled operators in its ranks, drew heavily from the Army's 75th Ranger Regiment. An entire Ranger element had been killed alongside Reece's troop in Afghanistan two years earlier. As Reece sat down with his tray of food, a handful of ▮▮▮▮ assaulters, including their troop sergeant major, approached.

"Mr. Reece," the large bearded man began in an accent that betrayed a southern upbringing, "I'm Christian Holloway, troop sergeant major. I just wanted to thank you. We all knew the boys killed with your troop in Afghanistan; the Rangers on those birds. You did right by them."

One by one, the ▮▮▮▮ operators shook Reece's hand.

"Also, heard about what you did in Odessa. Sorry to hear about Freddy. I worked with him in '09 in Iraq. Solid as they come. See you in the briefing," Holloway said with a respectful nod.

· · · ·

Reece stood at the back of the stadium-style briefing room and wondered if this was the same room where his friends had first received word that the UBL mission was a go. The assaulters and a few support personnel filled the first four rows of seats, talking and joking among themselves. It was not that long ago that Reece had been in a similar room receiving the mission that would lead to the deaths of his SEAL troop, Army Rangers, and aircrews on a dark Afghan mountain.

The door at the front of the briefing room opened and Reece immediately recognized the looming figure of Andy Danreb. The Chicago native missed nothing and nodded to Reece without breaking stride. His customary blue oxford shirt was rolled up at the sleeves. He was ready to work. Nicole Phan was almost the polar opposite of the older, disgruntled Cold War relic. She was young, spry, and always chipper. Reece couldn't remember ever seeing her without a smile. Anyone who mistook her kindness for weakness, though, would soon find themselves on the losing end of an intellectual battle of wits. Born in America to a family who escaped Vietnam in 1975, she was one of the CIA's most talented targeters. After the fall of Saigon, her grandfather had blended in with the boat people as a refugee to escape the wrath of the NVA. She was not the first in her family with ties to U.S. intelligence. She caught Reece's eye and waved.

Some might find it intimidating to stand up in a room surrounded by hardened special operators whose lives depend on the information presented. If Nicole felt that way, her demeanor did not betray it.

"Good evening, everyone," she began. "I'm Nicole Phan. I'm an SSO targeting officer from the CTC. This is Andy Danreb, from the Russian Desk at the Directorate of Analysis, formerly DI for those of you who remember."

Andy nodded, his haircut and stern look giving the impression that he may once have worn the uniform even if it was thirty years and forty pounds ago.

At the mention of Russia, more than a few operators began to send questioning looks toward the front of the room.

"This operation will be recognized as a Special Access Program, so thank you for signing the NDAs earlier," Nicole continued. "I know you all have a lot of practice."

She hit a button on the remote in her hand and a picture of a young woman filled the center screen.

"This is Hanna Hastings. American citizen. She was kidnapped in Romania by what is suspected to be a rogue element of Russian intelligence. We believe she was moved overland through Moldova and into Ukraine, where her captors crossed into Russian-held territory. An unscheduled flight of an An-26 transport departed Zavodska airfield in Crimea less than twenty-four hours later. The flight made two brief stops for fuel and terminated at Sharomy Naval Air Station, a remote base in Kamchatka, Russia."

A map detailing the flight appeared on the screen along with satellite imagery of the isolated but paved three-thousand-meter runway.

"This is Aleksandr Zharkov," Nicole continued, advancing the slide to a file photo of the alleged perpetrator. "He is the deputy director of Directorate S in Russia's Foreign Intelligence Service. In layman's terms, he manages their illegals program, running agents without cover status; sometimes deep penetration programs and other times simply sleeper agents. His father is this man, Ivan Zharkov." A black-and-white photo of the mafia boss replaced that of his son.

Andy nodded curtly and pointed to the screen. "Ivan Zharkov. He's the *Pakhan*, or head, of the Tambov Gang in the *bratva*, also known as the Russian mafia. When the Iron Curtain fell in 1991 it was chaos, but a select few saw opportunity, hence the rise of Russian organized crime. Ivan was more adept than most. He thought ahead and pushed one of his sons, Aleksandr, into the Foreign Intelligence Service. He wanted his own mole. We believe it was information from Aleksandr that allowed Ivan to crush his competition and consolidate power under the St. Petersburg Tambov Gang. He used his son to orchestrate the arrest of rival gangs through INTERPOL. You may remember, the arrests made headlines in Spain back in 2008. Dismantling a criminal network made Russia look strong in the eyes of the international community. They elevated Ivan Zharkov to the undisputed position of *Vor v Zakon*, a top authority for the *bratva*, eliminating his rivals, and making him the second-richest man in Russia behind their president. Point being, Ivan is a long-term thinker and not someone to be trifled with. There are uncorroborated reports of a rift growing between Ivan and his son. Aleksandr was recalled from a posting in Belarus after he was tied to the murder of a prostitute. It was covered up, presumably through hush money from the elder, possibly by intimidation of the investigators by *bratva* thugs. With newly acquired intelligence"—Andy's eyes moved to Reece—"I correlated the information we have on Aleksandr's postings with unsolved murders and, although the information is incomplete, the timing certainly suggests that Aleksandr Zharkov may be responsible for a series of murders around the globe."

A series of crime scene photos moved across the screen, each one showing a young female.

"Why not just turn all this over to INTERPOL?" an operator built like a tank asked through a thick southern drawl.

"INTERPOL has a surprisingly strong presence in Russia but all that would do is tip Aleksandr off. If, and I say *if*, this mission gets the green light, you are her only chance."

"Thank you, Andy," Nicole said. "Aleksandr Zharkov left Moscow thirty-six hours ago on an An-26 and landed at Sharomy air station earlier today. An hour later, an Mi-8 took off for Medny Island, just east of the Kamchatka Peninsula. Medny is the smaller of two islands known as the Commander Islands and was all but abandoned in 2001. It's small, only about seventy-one square miles, but over the past two years we have seen increased signs of military activity there."

Satellite imagery was projected of the island.

"There is a bunkerlike structure in addition to a larger metal building that houses vehicles. This summer, an array of structures was erected on various points of the island. Our theory, based on its proximity to Alaska, is that it is some type of radar or early warning site, but we can't be sure. We believe that Ms. Hastings was taken to the island and that she's still there. For how long, we don't know. We also believe that Aleksandr Zharkov is on the island with her."

A three-dimensional terrain model image of the island showed up on the screens.

"To the best of our knowledge, this is the target structure. The Seabees are almost finished with a mock-up for rehearsals but remember, we have no intel on the interior layout."

"Any other locations they may have taken her?" asked a man with the physique of a triathlete.

"Ivan Zharkov has a dacha on the Black Sea where he doesn't spend much time. He also has a compound in central Siberia," she said, bringing up a map of Russia and zooming in on an area in the middle. "It's located at the epicenter of the Tunguska Event, of all places. He frequents it in the spring and fall but we do not have any reports of Aleksandr accompanying his father there in quite some time."

"Enemy situation?" asked a laid-back looking operator chewing gum in the second row.

"Aleksandr is an odd one," Andy chimed in. "He doesn't trust his own military or intelligence services and instead has contracted security from the Wagner Group."

Heads nodded in recognition.

"As a refresher," Andy continued, "Wagner is a private military company; think the Russian version of Blackwater."

"Didn't they get tied to the killing of those journalists in the Central African Republic last year?" the same operator asked.

"Yes, along with disappearances and 'suicides' of more than a few in opposition to Putin's policies. They've been very active in Africa, specifically in CAR, Madagascar, Sudan, and Libya. They continue to grow in power and influence, propping up Russian-backed dictatorships in Venezuela, Syria, and elsewhere. We estimate that Aleksandr has eight to ten Wagner contractors on the island and possibly a personal bodyguard, but we can't be sure."

"How well trained are they?"

"The Wagner rank and file are mostly filled with regular Russian Army personnel who are trained up at a Wagner compound in the North Caucasus region of southern Russia. They do have a small special operations component for special activities who handle operations like targeting those journalists in Africa."

The inquisitive assaulter nodded like these were normal everyday occurrences in the life of being a commando, which, in fact, they were.

"The big question here is, why?" asked Sergeant Major Holloway, verbalizing what they were all thinking.

"I'll take that one," interjected Reece from the back of the room, making his way to the front. Nicole and Andy stepped to the side to give him the floor.

"I'm James Reece. I met most of you tonight. I'm a former SEAL currently working for Ground Branch, though I think we are supposed to call it something else these days."

The comment elicited a chuckle from a room full of people accustomed to senior ranking officers renaming programs as a way to fill evaluations, insinuating that a highly successful established entity was entirely their idea before moving up the ladder in the chain of command.

"Some of you may know Raife Hastings," the former frogman continued.

Heads nodded again.

"Hanna is his sister. She was abducted in retaliation for events last year in which Raife and I were involved. Raife has gone dark. Our last communication was from his sister's residence in Romania. I think he's on his way to Medny alone."

"*Shit,*" Holloway said, leaning forward in his chair. "So, what you are telling us is that we have two potential hostages in Russian territory?"

"And that's not all." Reece hesitated. "Recent intel suggests that Aleksandr has moved on from his serial killing of prostitutes and is hunting humans on Medny Island. He's going to hunt Hanna, but her real purpose is bait. What he really wants is to hunt me and Raife."

"*What?*" Holloway asked in disbelief. "How reliable is this intel?"

Reece thought of Dimitry in Thorn's cabin, the capsaicin flowing through his veins cooking him from the inside out.

"Very," concluded Reece, not bothering to use the military terminology associated with source verification.

Holloway shook his head. "This is a new one. Though it's not usually my place to ask, how will this be handled diplomatically?"

Nicole stepped forward to take the question.

"If approved, President Grimes would call the Russian president *only* if things went south. Insert and extract via MH-X Black Hawks," she said, referring to the "stealth" helicopters made famous by the raid in Abbottabad. "We have AKs and Russian ammo sourced in Russia to make the actions on the objective look like a rival gang hit. This needs to be nonattributable to U.S. forces. Fallout could be a house cleaning inside the *bratva*. Off the record, I think the president will do little to downplay any rumors of U.S. involvement. He will be eager to show the world that he is not a puppet of Russia after all the accusations of Russian meddling in the last elections, when he was the ticket VP."

Holloway stood up and looked at his watch before turning to address his men.

"WARNO in thirty minutes. Time is of the essence on this one. It's going to be a long night. The next time you sleep we might be on our way to Russia."

CHAPTER 58

Washington, D.C.

REGINALD PYNE RELISHED HIS role as gatekeeper to the president. One could say that the president of the United States was the world's most powerful figure but, in Pyne's mind, the man who controlled access to the president held the real power. A soldier for most of his life, President Grimes was acutely susceptible to Pyne's influence and manipulation, not having been raised in the literal and figurative swamp that was Washington, D.C.

Roger Grimes had spent a career as an army officer and was selected as vice president to provide ideological balance to a ticket that would have otherwise leaned too far left for many of the nation's crucial swing states. With a decorated hero of the War on Terror by his side, the previous president cruised to an Electoral College victory.

After Grimes was sworn in as vice president, he found that he was soon relegated to the background, rarely meeting with the president or his senior staff. It became clear that he had been mere arm candy during the campaign and that the close advisory role that had been promised to the American people had been a façade. Grimes handled it like a professional and took it upon himself to focus on veterans' issues, appointing a commission to assess the VA health care system and then overseeing the implementation of its recommendations.

Pyne, a longtime Washington insider and former lobbyist, helped guide then–vice president Grimes through the morass of the federal government as he tried, mostly in vain, to advance the causes of those who had served their nation in uniform. The VP learned to trust Pyne's political judgment and took his advice as he would that of an executive officer in the Army. For his part, Pyne played the loyal soldier, biding his time for an opportunity to gain even greater influence. He couldn't care less about the VA. Those soldiers were stupid enough to volunteer knowing the risks. They were lucky to get free medical care for life. *So what if they had to stand in line for a few hours?*

Pyne found that the techniques from a book he'd read at Harvard on how to manipulate women into bed worked equally as well outside the realm of sexual coercion. Its methods helped him to influence and control both male and female politicians on policy issues. Sometimes he couldn't believe how easy it was.

He'd started his professional lobbying career during a time when the tobacco industry was under attack. He'd learned that the old ways of throwing money at politicians and then threatening to support their opponents in the next election if they didn't stay on board didn't work the way they had in the fifties, sixties, and seventies. The opposition had organized and adapted. One had to play the game differently.

There was no law against stupidity. If these idiots wanted to smoke and make the tobacco industry even more profitable, who was the government to stop them? *Volenti non fit injuria.* To a willing person, no injury is done. Besides, the U.S. government needed those tax dollars. How else were they to pay for a cradle-to-grave welfare state?

He'd successfully delayed a 2006 court order mandating that tobacco companies advertise the ill effects of smoking. The government was forcing private companies of a legally available product to spend their hard-earned profits to undermine their own business. He had tied them up for ten years in appeal after appeal. That the product he defended killed more than 480,000 of his fellow citizens annually didn't bother Pyne in the least. It was a free country. And imagine the health care costs if those half a million people a year lived. The country would have to care for them for even longer. One of his main takeaways from a philosophy class while in college in Boston were the words of French biologist

Jean Rostand: *Kill one man, and you are a murderer. Kill millions of men, and you are a conqueror. Kill them all, and you are a god.*

Pyne thought about how lucky they were that the media was so focused on the so-called opioid epidemic. With multiple states' attorney generals and their plaintiff lawyers distracted by the mere seventy thousand opioid deaths a year, tobacco could recover from the hits they'd taken in the nineties. That his company was killing Americans at the equivalent rate of a 9/11 attack every three days didn't faze Pyne in the least. While Vice President Grimes was fighting for his country, Pyne fought to keep tobacco addictive and profitable.

His success in dealing with unconstitutional decrees from the government caught the attention of the budding vaping industry and Pyne was offered lucrative stock incentives to draft the strategy to deal with emerging federal regulations from the Food and Drug Administration and backlash from do-gooder groups like the American Academy of Pediatrics, the Campaign for Tobacco-Free Kids, and the American Cancer Society. Big Tobacco acquired controlling stakes in the leading vape companies early on, infusing them with capital for growth. They recognized the small electronic devices with candy flavored liquid smoke were a gateway to their tobacco products and an opportunity to co-opt the next generation of customers.

Pyne managed to hold off regulation and a government-mandated review of vaping's health impact as long as he could among an avalanche of increasingly devastating evidence. He'd been involved in D.C. lobbying long enough to know when it was time to abandon ship. The writing was on the wall. The multibillion-dollar e-cigarette industry was about to be regulated into submission. Pyne took his money and ran for an even more distasteful occupation: political operative.

Although his salary peddling cigarettes and the windfall of exercising his e-cigarette stock options in the vaping industry put him into what was increasingly referred to as the "one percent," Pyne was still an outsider. The families that controlled the tobacco and vaping companies had the homes, the cars, the jets, the multiple ex-wives, and the art collections. They had their names plastered over everything from university chairs to the wings of world-renowned museums. In both instances, Pyne once again felt left behind, a hired gun to be kept content with leftovers from the plates of royalty. Where would they be without him slogging through painful media training, reading depositions, being deposed, and sitting through state and federal congressional testimony?

He'd thought the newer and hipper e-cigarette company would welcome him into the clubs and parties he'd yearned for since his youth. It turned out that the gates to the kingdom were guarded by the same old boys' network that had plagued him all his life. They just wanted him to work the same magic on vaping that he had on tobacco and then go home. After discovering that money alone was not enough to open the coveted door, Pyne had given notice and exercised his stock options. On the way out, he leaked an internal memo on the company's advertising practices and an independent medical study on what was intended to show the benefits of vaping as an alternative to combustible smoking. The marketing memo clearly outlined the promotion of candy flavorings via social media marketing campaigns targeting children. The medical study warned that because the vape liquid contained lipoid components and toxins, when heated they caused an acute chemical inhalation injury to the lungs, or as a federal lawmaker whose daughter had died at a college party after vaping with friends stated, "It poisons and kills our kids from the inside out. This is murder."

Pyne had gotten out just in time, leaving those at the company to rearrange the deck chairs on the *Titanic* as it headed for the inevitable. His memo and medical study, leaked to New York regulators and a producer at *60 Minutes*, along with a *New England Journal of Medicine* study on vaping-induced lung injuries, ensured the opioid epidemic was quickly replaced by outrage levelled against the beleaguered vaping companies. Say what you would about opioids, at least they'd never concocted a branding strategy around addicting children to their products. They specifically aimed their deadly prescription drugs at adults.

Reginald Pyne had grown up one of the worst kind of impoverished, a working-class kid in a sea of wealth. Even as a child he insisted on being called Reginald. When his classmates found out how particular he was, they tormented him by bestowing him with the nickname "Reggie-boy," a name he detested. His father had been a firefighter until a devastating injury almost killed him. After the accident, the Pynes continued to live in what had turned into an exclusive enclave of New York, although across the border in neighboring Connecticut. His mother combined her meager salary working at the front desk of the very prep school Reginald attended with her husband's disability checks to make ends meet. Her position at the school discounted the tuition enough to allow Reginald to enroll with the children of means; the Pynes wanted the best for their only son.

Reginald would watch his friend's mothers zip off to play tennis after dropping their kids at school, the fathers having left in chauffeured vehicles for the commute into Manhattan well before dawn. There they managed the hedge funds and banks of Wall Street, which provided the money that gave them the power to look down their noses at the likes of the Pynes. Reginald's family didn't belong to the exclusive clubs reserved for the top echelon of society, nor did they summer in the Hamptons or on the Cape. None of this went unnoticed by young Reginald. Years later, his success would certainly surprise the kids from his old Greenwich prep school, half of whom were probably addicted to Xanax and whose kids were almost certainly destroying their lungs with watermelon-flavored toxic smoke. They'd be asking him for favors soon enough. All he needed to do was bide his time. His patience had finally paid off when the previous sitting president was forced to resign over what became known as the Capstone Scandal, the testing of an experimental PTSD drug on active-duty SEALs without their knowledge.

Overnight, Roger Grimes was president and Reginald Pyne was his most trusted advisor. Thrust into the most overwhelming job in government, Grimes relied heavily on those around him. As chief of staff, Pyne wielded a tremendous amount of power. It was the opportunity he'd waited for his entire life. This morning, he was meeting with the CIA director and her senior staff for a highly classified briefing in the secure White House Situation Room. Ordinarily, such a meeting would be attended by members of the Joint Chiefs of Staff, the director of national intelligence, as well as representatives of the various agencies that made up the U.S. intelligence community. That was the "old way," as the staff called it. "Pyne's way" was different.

Under the new regime, the only people in the room would be Pyne, the CIA director, Janice Motley, and Victor Rodriguez, her head of Paramilitary Operations. Even with all of the security clearances involved, the White House and cabinet leaked like sieves. The chief of staff could not risk word getting to the president over, under, or around him. If you wanted the president, you had to go through Reginald Pyne. All the clubs he wasn't invited to growing up now held the door open for him. He'd finally found the elusive power he sought. He was somebody.

The CIA executives were ushered into the secure White House Situation Room, a low-ceilinged conference room dominated by a large table that ran its length. Identical black leather chairs surrounded the table and Motley and Rodriguez chose two near the head while they waited for the chief of staff to enter. The number of empty seats made the room seem bigger than it was, the inner sanctum of the world's last remaining superpower.

Janice Motley was a deadly combination of intelligence and toughness. An African-American woman in her mid-fifties, she was a relative newcomer to the Agency but had a long background as a staff attorney for the Senate Intelligence Committee. She had been appointed by the previous president to rein in what he saw as a cowboy culture among the clandestine service but her initial decisions surprised her former colleagues. One of those was to approve bringing James Reece back into the fold as an asset, which was an enormous political risk given his status as a domestic terrorist. Subsequently she'd approved the operation that resulted in Reece and Freddy Strain saving the life of the U.S. president by foiling a sniper and chemical weapons attack in Odessa, Ukraine. Those events had propelled her to the directorship. She hadn't forgotten that it was the bold actions of Reece and Freddy who had made that happen.

Pyne let them simmer for a good twenty minutes, the oldest power play in the book. He then entered in a flourish, with his trademark blow-dried salt-and-pepper hair and capped-tooth smile. Despite a job that required long days indoors, his skin was tanned a deep copper. It didn't seem like the job was keeping him too far away from the golf course. He offered both a decent handshake and took a seat at the head of the table, in the chair embroidered with the presidential seal. The signal was an obvious one; in this room, I am the president.

Pyne glanced at his watch. He wore an Ironman digital to work to appear folksy, a subtle but important manipulation. His Patek Philippe was at home. As was his custom, he started the briefing without small talk, indicating with a twirl of his index finger that the director of the Central Intelligence Agency was on the clock.

Director Motley cleared her throat.

"Thank you for meeting with us, Mr. Pyne. As you know from the President's Daily Brief, an American citizen named Hanna Hastings was abducted in Romania. Evidence suggests that her captivity was at the direction of a senior Russian intelligence official named Aleksandr Zharkov and that she has been transported to Medny Island, a remote island in the Bering Sea off the Kamchatka Peninsula."

Rodriguez was handling the visual elements of the presentation, using a laptop to advance the PowerPoint slides on the large LCD screens that lined the walls.

"How confident are you that this individual is on the island?"

"Based on IMINT and HUMINT, our confidence is high," Motley replied, not giving up anything that would lead to further questions about the source of the HUMINT, a source Vic had been reluctant to reveal.

"But no SIGINT corroboration?"

Vic winced in his seat, but Motley remained unfazed.

"Correct, sir."

"Go on."

"We believe that Aleksandr Zharkov, deputy director of Directorate S in Russia's Foreign Intelligence Service, is also currently on the island. He is the son of a well-known member of Russian organized crime in Saint Petersburg. I know that you are aware of the recent attack on a Montana ranch owned by the Hastings family. That was an attempt to kill one of our personnel and was carried out by members of Ivan Zharkov's crime syndicate."

"Who is that?" Pyne interrupted.

"James Reece, sir," the director answered.

"*Great.* That guy should be in prison. Only reason he's not on death row is because of that stunt in Odessa. Go on."

"After the hit in Montana failed, Director Zharkov kidnapped Hanna Hastings in Romania in an attempt to lure her brother and possibly James Reece to Russia to look for her."

"Why would he do that?"

"Here is a psychological profile on Zharkov," Director Motley said, pushing a file to Pyne.

"CliffsNotes version, please. I have a country to run."

"He's a serial killer. He kills to fulfill an abnormal sadistic psychological gratification; thrill seeking and sexual. In Zharkov's case it was brought on by finding his mother after her suicide."

"This is giving me a headache. What's his endgame?"

Rodriguez advanced the slide to a screen shot from the Dark Web.

"What the *hell* is this?" Pyne asked.

"This," Motley continued, "is from a site on the Dark Web. For five hundred thousand dollars U.S., one can apply to hunt a person on Zharkov's island."

"What?"

"He imports prisoners from Africa. They become the prey. The website describes them as the worst type of criminals. Zharkov has taken care of the judge and jury parts. For half a million dollars, you get to be the executioner."

"And you are telling me he wants to bring in some bigger game?" Pyne asked.

"That is correct, sir. He was using Hanna Hastings as bait and it worked. Two days ago, Ms. Hastings's brother, a former Navy SEAL, contacted Aleksandr Zharkov via the Dark Web. His last communication indicated he was booking a human hunt in Kamchatka. Apparently he does not trust us to get his sister out. He has not been heard from since. He had a TS/SCI clearance and there are a few things in his head we would prefer the Russians not access."

"*Fucking* SEALs," Pyne said, rolling his eyes. "If they are not writing books, they're causing international incidents."

Director Motley ignored his sophomoric comment and continued: "In coordination with ▆▆▆ and the Joint Staff we've developed two courses of action for your consideration and would like to brief the president as soon as possible."

"What are our options?"

"Mr. Rodriguez will walk you through plans, sir."

"Thank you, Director."

The acoustics of the room were unusual, and Vic felt like his voice sounded louder than the situation dictated.

"Mr. Pyne, we briefed the Joint Staff this morning and they have moved assets into place to facilitate multiple COAs if the president decides to move forward with a hostage rescue mission to return Ms. Hastings and her brother to the United States. As you know, we have successfully extracted ███████ ███████ ████████████ with SDV assets."

"The nuclear physicist last year. I remember approving the mission."

Vic bit his tongue, knowing the president approved the mission, not his chief of staff.

"Yes, sir. This mission would use that same profile but instead of a rendez-vous and extraction, the SDV would carry assaulters from ████████████ █████████████████. They would infil to the target, and conduct actions on the objective using non-U.S.-attributable weapons."

"What does that mean?"

"They'd use AKMs with 7.62x39 sourced rounds from Russia to make it look like a mafia hit on the son of a rival."

"And the second option?"

"CAG, aviators from the 160th, Agency and FBI HRT operators have been rehearsing at a secure location. The plan is to stage out of Alaska, fueling low-signature aircraft on the Aleutian Islands, and inserting teams via HAHO—that's high altitude, high opening—onto Medny under the cover of darkness."

"I'm familiar with HAHO," Pyne lied. "They'd use those same Russian guns?"

"Correct, sir."

"Continue."

"After insertion, the teams would move overland, breach the target building, and secure the hostages. The helos, the same kind used in the bin Laden mission, would then move in from an amphib in international waters and extract all U.S. personnel."

Pyne leaned back in his chair and made a production of closing his eyes and heaving an audible sigh. He then leaded forward.

"You want to invade Russia?"

"No, sir, our plan is to briefly visit Russia to return an American citizen held against her will."

"Interesting semantics. In both of these COAs, how long would your people be on the ground?"

"Four hours for the SDV option. One, possibly two hours for the airborne option."

"Could this be some sort of sanctioned rendition of a former SEAL for something he did in service against Russia?"

"We do not believe that it is condoned by the Russian government. We also believe that if we go through official channels, Director Zharkov will be tipped off, which will cost Hanna Hastings her life."

"Is that COA 3?" Pyne asked.

"Sir, if we go the diplomatic route it is imperative that the president understand that he is signing the death warrant of a kidnapped U.S. citizen."

"You don't know that," Pyne cautioned.

"That is the official analysis of the Central Intelligence Agency."

"Like weapons of mass destruction in Iraq?"

Director Motley held his condescending stare.

"That was before my time, Mr. Pyne," she responded without a hint of the fury she felt boiling inside.

"Enemy order of battle?" Pyne asked, bringing the briefing back on course and using a term he'd heard the president use on occasion. He'd made a note of it.

"Aleksandr Zharkov doesn't rely on official Russian protection. He uses private security contractors from the Wagner Group. Ten are currently with him on the island. We do not believe that they expect a rescue attempt."

"Don't bullshit me," the chief of staff said, directing his question back to Director Motley. "What is Zharkov's beef with the Hastings family and this Reece character?"

"It is possible it is retaliation for what they suspect was James Reece's involvement in thwarting the assassination of President Grimes last year in Odessa and the subsequent assassination of Colonel Vasili Andrenov and the poisoning of General Qusim Yedid," Director Motley said, quite intentionally bringing Reece's involvement in saving the president's life into the conversation.

"Yes, most curious," Pyne said, leaning back in his chair. "I've heard rumors that Mr. Reece is responsible for both of those assassinations. What do you know about that?"

Rodriguez visibly bristled in his chair while Motley met the president's chief of staff's stare without flinching.

"We confirmed that those were just rumors, sir. Both of those men had lists of enemies a mile long."

"I see. And why would we risk an international incident, even war with Russia to *kidnap* a girl and her brother who the Russians will say were there of their own free will?"

"If we don't," Director Motley answered, "an American citizen kidnapped *against* her will is dead, and a TS/SCI-cleared operator will be exploited for intelligence by the same country that manipulated the very technology *we* developed to influence our last election. This is a chance to hit back."

Pyne tapped his finger on the closed cover of his iPad case.

"How soon could you go?"

"All assets are standing by, sir," Rodriguez said. "We could have the teams on C-17s within forty-five minutes of the president's signature for either COA."

Pyne continued tapping his iPad, thinking through options and worst-case scenarios.

"I want you to thank the men and women who have been preparing for this possibility." Pyne paused for effect. "But, there's no way in *hell* that we are invading a nuclear-armed Russia to get back one girl and her brother who are probably already dead. Do you have any idea what kind of international incident this would cause? Relations with Russia are already in the *shitter*. This could start another Cold War, or worse, World War III!"

"Sir . . ." Motley attempted to interject.

"You had your chance to speak, young lady; now it is mine. There will be no presidential finding. There will be no mission. Send your men back to Bragg, or Coronado, or wherever they came from. I want NDAs signed by everyone who is in the know on this. I don't need any of these assholes whining to their congressman about it."

"Sir, shouldn't the president weigh ..." Rodriguez interjected.

"As far as you're concerned, *I* am the president. He will not be briefed on this and any attempt to go around me and get to him will be career ending for everyone involved. Do I make myself clear?"

The two spies remained quiet but nodded in recognition.

"Good." Pyne's tone switched from enraged to almost effeminate on a dime. "This room is secure. Leave your OpPlan for the executive files. Now, I'm sure the CIA has other threats to our national security on which to focus. Thank you for coming and please enjoy the rest of your evening."

He rose and strode out the door without shaking hands. He had just been passed a valuable piece of information. If he could relay it in time, it could pay dividends for him once the president was out of office. He needed to visit an old friend.

Information truly was power.

CHAPTER 59

REECE PEERED THROUGH THE thermal optic on his SR-25 E2, scanning the scene around the bunker structure for any sign of human activity. The Light Weapon Thermal Sight was mounted forward of his Nightforce day optic and made any living thing in his scope stand out like coal on snow. Reece was at the closest of three overwatch positions, just over six hundred yards from the target building. The only movement he spotted was from the assault elements approaching the structure from two directions. Operators moving swiftly and silently with the experience of hundreds of missions in hostile territory, they swarmed the building, masters in a deadly ballet.

Reece shifted his weapon and, using the optic, scanned behind his position to ensure that no one had moved in behind them. All clear. His overwatch function, devoid of the responsibilities and chaos of command, reminded him of the good old days as an enlisted SEAL sniper. He turned his attention back to the objective in time to see the assaulters set their breaching charges on the concrete building. Instinctively, he averted his eyes.

A violent explosion rocked the building, the lead element stormed through the openings created by the carefully prepared shaped charges. The distance and the suppressors masked the sound of gunfire but Reece knew that the engagements were swift and violent. After ten seconds that seemed like as many minutes, Reece heard Sergeant Major Holloway over the radio, "Objective clear. I pass Touchdown Dugga Boy. Touchdown Lioness."

The operators were maintaining a perimeter around the target site, their precious cargo well protected at its center inside a phalanx of armor-clad operators. A quick glance at the screen of his chest-mounted ATAK device, essentially a smartphone with detailed mapping software configured for military use, confirmed the position of friendly forces and the location of the LZ. The lines between war and video games had officially blurred.

Reece and the rest of his sniper element were two hundred yards out when they heard the odd-sounding whine of the stealth helicopters approach. He watched as the assaulters loaded the hostage into the first Black Hawk, which lifted off immediately, spiriting her to safety. He picked up the pace to a jog, turning every few seconds to check their six. He instinctively ducked as he passed through the rotor wash and climbed inside the helo alongside his sniper team and part of the assault element. His stomach sank as the pilot cranked the throttle and the powerful bird jolted skyward. Reece's legs dangled out the open cargo door of the Black Hawk, his rifle ready to support the crew's 7.62mm miniguns if necessary. They were soon off the objective, skimming low over the terrain at high speed. Barring a mechanical failure or an interception threat from a Russian fighter jet, they were in the clear.

"All elements, this is ARGO SIX. Endex, I say again, Endex." Reece heard the command element's call over the Peltor headset that he wore under his ballistic helmet. That was the signal ending the exercise. From Reece's perspective, it had gone exceptionally well.

Now they just had to do it for real, against an armed enemy defending home soil.

. . . .

Even seasoned professional commandos felt the euphoria of a job well done and the mood during the debriefing was light but serious. Every pilot, operator, and support soldier involved in the operation was in the room. Men in sweat-stained combat uniforms sipped coffee, Kill Cliff, Gatorade, or Red Bull, each fighting their body's circadian rhythm, which told them it was long past time to go to sleep. The clock on the wall indicated it was just after 0400 and, despite having trained every night and slept during the day for the past five days, everyone was exhausted.

The special operations culture is unique in its willingness to ignore rank when it comes to providing brutally honest assessments of an action. Though the mission went well, there was always room for improvement and the men in the room made no bones about what could have gone better. Drone footage of the assault was played back on the oversize screens and paused at various intervals to allow for discussion. The movements of each individual operator could be tracked using the ATAK software and were displayed and scrutinized the way that game films were in a football locker room. The technology left no doubt as to who did what, when.

Reece's role was that of a Ground Branch liaison, there to support the highly capable operators who would perform the rescue. He had a reputation as a solid combat leader and because his postwar exploits had given him near-legendary status in this community, Sergeant Major Holloway asked if he had anything to add.

"Just that if it was me on Medny, there is no other group of killers I'd want kicking in the door to do the job. Thank you all for . . ." Reece's phone buzzed. "Excuse me," he said, seeing Vic's number come up in the caller ID.

Walking a few steps from the Army commandos he accepted the call. "Talk to me, Vic."

"It's a no-go, Reece."

"Shit!"

"President's chief of staff shut us down."

"You didn't even talk to the president? Get me his number. You're the C-I-A. Get me his private line. I'll call him directly and cash in those chips from Odessa."

"I know you're pissed, Reece. Director Motley and I have been talking all night about how best to handle this, but right now our hands are tied."

Reece was about to continue but instead switched gears. It was time to think, not fly off the handle.

"Sorry, Vic. Understood. I'll let the crew here know."

"Pass on the director's sincere thank-you to everyone on site. Get some rest and take your time getting back. We will figure this out. Like you said, we're the CIA."

Reece ended the call and turned to see the room of sweaty operators looking at him, already knowing what he was going to say. They'd been spun up only to be turned off more times over the years than they could recall.

"Mission is canked," Reece said. "Director Motley thanks you all for your efforts, but it's a no-go."

A few heads hung in silent resignation before they started to shuffle to the door.

Sergeant Major Holloway approached Reece.

"Sorry, friend."

"Yeah. You guys got a bar around here?"

"How'd you guess? Follow me."

• • •

Most of the seats and bar stools were already taken when Reece and Christian Holloway entered the makeshift bar.

"What a find!" Reece remarked, looking around the cavernous interior.

"Well, we've been down here so much over the years we figured we needed a place to call home. Your Seabees built it for us. Built one for Blue, too."

Plaques adorned the walls, red party lights were strewn from the ceiling, and speakers linked to one of the operator's playlists filled the small structure with the songs of Johnny Cash.

"Join us for a beer?" Holloway asked.

"Give me a few minutes," Reece said. "I'm going to grab a whiskey and do a little thinking."

"Dangerous stuff, that thinking business," Holloway remarked with a smile.

"That's what they tell me," Reece replied, making his way behind the self-serve bar, nodding to the ██████ operators, who raised their glasses as he passed.

After picking through a seemingly unending supply of whiskey bottles, Reece selected a Woodford Reserve on ice and settled into a bar stool at the far end of the bar, swirling his whiskey and ice with a plastic stirrer.

The sun was coming up as the last operators left the bar. Reece's ice had long since melted and he still hadn't taken a sip, his thoughts lost on Hanna, Raife, Ivan Zharkov, Aleksandr, Oliver Grey, and Medny Island. He didn't even look up when the looming figure of Andy Danreb took the seat next to him.

"How's the whiskey?" Andy asked. "Looks a little watery."

Reece picked his head up and looked around. "Are we the last ones here?"

"Brilliant observation. You should come to work for the CIA."

"Guess I lost track of time."

"Bars will do that."

"That water?" Reece asked motioning to Andy's drink.

"Vodka. It's like water, only better. I *am* from the Russian Desk."

"Makes sense."

"What are you doing, Reece?"

"Just thinking."

"Ah," Andy said, taking a swig of his vodka. "In the Cold War days, we used to do a lot of that."

"What?"

"Figuring out how to get the job done when senior intelligence officials or politicians told us we couldn't."

"How did you handle it?"

"We out-thought them," Andy said, tapping his temple with his finger. "We used to call it *plausible deniability*. Sexy term for giving your superiors the ability to say they had no idea what you were up to and 'yes, sir, I'll rein those cowboys in right away and this will never happen again, sir.'" Andy chuckled. "Your old man did it more than once."

"You knew my old man? Why didn't you tell me?"

"Everyone knew your old man, Reece. If not in person, then by reputation. And I didn't tell you because it wasn't pertinent the last time we met."

"And it is now?"

"It is," Andy said taking another sip of his drink.

"How?"

"Once, your dad was ordered to stand down and hang a certain doctor he was running in Czechoslovakia out to dry. Do you know what happened next?"

Reece nodded.

"Good. What do you need to pull it off?"

"Take a breath, look around, make a call," Reece muttered.

"What was that?" Andy asked. "I'm a bit hard of hearing these days."

"It's something an old troop commander of mine used to say. 'Take a breath, look around, make a call.'"

"Well, you've taken your breath. Now look around."

Reece picked his head up, his eyes slowly taking in the plaques and mementos that adorned the walls commemorating the exploits of one of the best special operations units the world had ever known. He smiled.

"Thanks, Andy," Reece said, moving off his stool, leaving his Woodford untouched on the bar.

CHAPTER 60

REECE STEPPED INTO THE early morning light, stopping briefly to shield his eyes from the sun as he fished out his Gatorz sunglasses and slid them into place.

Running toward one of the hangars used as a staging area for gear, he could see the ▮▮▮▮ operators already inventorying gear and packing up for the journey back to Bragg.

"Christian," Reece called, seeing Sergeant Major Holloway checking on his troops.

"Hey, buddy, hope you don't mind us sliding out on you this morning. You looked like you didn't need anyone disturbing you."

"No worries. Listen, I just got a call from Vic at the Agency. He's working some other options on this Russia mission. He wanted me to see if we could 1149 some equipment?" Reece said, mentioning the form that serves as a requisition and invoice document anytime something of value trades hands in the military.

"Really?" Christian said.

"Yeah, just want to make sure it's all official. I'll sign the 1149s and take custody of the gear. Should get it back to you in a couple weeks."

"Reece, has anyone ever told you that you are the worst liar on the planet?"

Reece shrugged and raised his eyebrows.

"What, exactly, do you have in mind?"

"Just some parachutes, NODs, radios, and 416s?" Reece asked. "Oh, and to go with the chutes we'd need CPS thermal suits, heated Wilcox nav-boards, oxygen kits, basically anything necessary for a high-altitude parachute insertion in arctic conditions."

Sergeant Major Holloway folded his arms and dropped his head in thought.

"Well, I guess that's more reasonable than trying to 1149 one of the helos. How many?"

"Five should do."

Holloway rubbed a hand through his heavily stubbled face as if calculating the possibilities.

"I think I can probably part with five kits like that in the name of inter-agency cooperation. Post-9/11 we are all supposed to share our information *and* our toys. As you know, we always travel with extra gear, especially when we are not sure of the mission ahead of time."

Reece took a sigh of relief. "Thank you."

"Don't mention it. I'll get Marcus to put together the 1149s for you to sign and the boys will help load everything up."

"And, Christian, just curious, how long would we have before these would come up in the system?"

"They will come up at next inventory in . . ." Holloway looked at the date on his G-Shock. "Twenty days. But even then, they will come up as 1149'd to you. Until we need them back, which we won't, those are officially the property of the Central Intelligence Agency."

• • •

The airfield was jointly operated, half Coast Guard and half civilian, with ▮▮▮▮ ▮▮▮▮▮▮▮▮▮▮▮▮▮▮▮▮▮ aircraft sitting opposite a collection of civil aviation aircraft, mostly single-engine propeller-driven planes. Though ▮▮▮ didn't ordinarily see much Gulfstream traffic, its ▮▮▮▮▮▮▮ runway offered plenty of room for the business jet to land. It touched down gently, tufts of blue smoke swirling off the tires.

The pilot steered the jet toward the black Chevy 2500 Suburban parked outside of one of the civilian hangars near the FBO on the south side of the airfield. James Reece was leaning against the hood. The engines were still whining when the door folded downward and Liz Riley descended the steps.

"You're flying this thing now?" Reece asked.

"I'm just the copilot. I'm working on my pilot rating. It won't be long with you and Raife jetting all over the world! Thanks for helping me with my hours."

"Liz, I have some gear to load. It's not much but I'm guessing it should go in cargo. Do you have a laptop on board? I need to do some planning on the way back to Montana. Does this thing have Wi-Fi?"

Liz nodded. "Of course it has Wi-Fi. It's a G550. What do you think we are, Spirit Airlines?"

The two friends wasted little time opening the rear of the SUV and loading the Pelican cases and kit bags into the Gulfstream. Liz assessed the approximate weight of the gear and made some notes on an iPad.

Twenty minutes after the G550 had touched down, the fuel had been topped off, the cockpit crew had filed their flight plan, and they were airborne again, on their way to Kalispell.

CHAPTER 61

SVETLANA REALLY DID FEEL sorry for him. He'd morphed over the last month, gained confidence as he put his plan in place, only to have retreated into his shell as that plan had deteriorated into abject failure. She couldn't help but wonder if the thumb drive she'd provided to the SVR had anything to do with it. Maybe she'd even take him home one night and help him find pleasure in a true sexual experience instead of the manufactured embarrassments she'd employed to gain access to his computer. *Who knows?* She might even enjoy it herself.

"I've made you some tea."

"Thank you, Svetlana," he said, continuing to stare into his computer. "Are you taking the metro home tonight?"

"Oh, Oliver, you work too hard. The metro only runs until midnight. It's already half-past."

"I am so sorry. I lost track of time. Let me get you a cab," Oliver offered, reaching for his desk phone.

"You are too kind, but don't trouble yourself. The city is full of them, even at this hour. I can manage. Don't stay up too late."

She lingered for a moment, resting her hand on his shoulder and giving it a sensuous squeeze. She did not see movement in his pants.

"I won't," Oliver lied. "Until tomorrow."

"Until tomorrow," she repeated.

"Good night, Svetlana."

As soon as she was gone Oliver picked up his cell phone and sent a text. He then reached for his pipe and stood, moving to the large glass window that dominated the wall of his office.

Four men took their positions on the deserted street below. One walked past the building and took up station at the far end of the street. Another loitered at the opposite end of the block while two others stepped into an alley.

Oliver would have known they were *bratva* thugs even if he hadn't just texted them to let them know their target was about to leave the building. In their dark jackets, jeans, and watch caps they looked the part.

Svetlana looked up and down the street for a cab and then began walking north to a corner where hailing one would be easier.

She'd never make it.

The two enforcers stepped out of the shadows into her path. Oliver's heart beat faster as he saw her stop and take a step back, then hold out her purse to them.

She stole a glance up at his office window and when she did, Oliver lit his pipe. As the fire from the wooden match illuminated his silhouette through the glass, the knives came out. They were upon her. Oliver could see the three bodies mix together in a violent clash for survival and caught the glint of a blade reflect off a streetlight.

His breathing rate increased with the excitement of his voyeuristic encounter. He might not be able to lead men into battle, but he'd proven adroit at hiring low-level criminals to ambush the unsuspecting. He'd done it long ago in Buenos Aires.

Observing the primal dance taking place on the gloomy street, he felt a now-familiar rise against the fabric of his trousers.

His hand found its way past his belt and into his pants. One stroke and his knees shuddered as he leaned into the wall for support, almost dropping his pipe as his body spasmed.

Regaining his composure, he watched as a black Mercedes sedan pulled up to the curb. The lookouts had joined the knife men and all four squeezed into the German import before it sped away.

Oliver thought of the life slipping out of his matronly assistant, her blood running into the gutters of the old city. Straightening himself up, he set his pipe on his desk and went to the bathroom to clean up.

CHAPTER 62

Glacier Park International Airport, Kalispell, Montana

REECE GAZED OUT THE window as the jet rolled to a stop. There, waiting on the tarmac and leaning against a two-tone early-nineties F-250, was Elias Malick. Jonathan had emailed Reece in flight to let him know the team was assembled and would be waiting on him.

Liz opened the door from the cockpit.

"We have to do some post-flight and get ready for tomorrow. Eli is out there waiting to take you and the gear to the ranch. I'll be about an hour behind you."

Reece descended the steps and approached his longtime friend.

"What's up, *Kahuna*?" the larger man asked. People often assumed Eli was from Hawaii due to his dark skin, affinity for all activities water related, and fondness for inserting words from the ancient Polynesian language into everyday speech. He had an aptitude for language and picked up a few words during his time attached to SDV-1 on Ford Island. Few knew his patriotism and devotion to country really stemmed from his family's escape from their native Lebanon in 1981 to his mother's home country of Sweden and eventually on to the United States.

Eli's early years were spent just northeast of Beirut. He remembered the pine and cedar trees, eating pine nuts while watching the deer, squirrels, and rabbits, and even his introduction to skiing not far from his home. As Maronite Christians, those memories faded to recollections of his father and uncles picking up rifles and leaving to defend their enclave while the Lebanese Civil War destroyed what had been called the "Switzerland of the East." With the dawn of the 1980s, the writing was on the wall; the old Lebanon was gone. It was time to leave. As they made their way to the airport, passing roadblocks in the uncertainty of a new decade, he remembered his mother telling him, "be strong, my *'lilla kri gare.'*" *My little warrior.* Fluent in Arabic, Lebanese Arabic, Swedish, French, and English, and with the features of a Swedish mother and Lebanese father, Eli could pass as a "local" almost anywhere on earth, a trait that would make him a valuable asset to the U.S. military following 9/11.

The two embraced in a hug Reece thought might squeeze the life out of him.

"Thanks for being here, brother. How's the family?"

"Jules and the kids are a little unsure what to do this far from the water, but they're adapting. I want them to live the mountain life for a few years while I help Raife stand up his Warrior/Guardian program. Then we'll probably head back to Cali or the islands. There are a couple business opportunities in the CBD space that I think can really help some of the guys struggling back at the command."

Eli had dropped out of college to serve his country at a time when the Navy needed corpsmen. With the recruiter's promise of a slot at BUD/S "just as soon as you finish corps school," Eli dove headfirst into the world of combat medicine. First assigned to the 1st Marine Division at Camp Pendleton, California, Eli found that getting to BUD/S once you were in the system was a difficult proposition. He also found he had a propensity for taking care of those in need. Dive Med Tech and 1st Class Dive schools followed with eventual orders to SEAL Delivery Vehicle Team One in Hawaii. It was there that Eli's eyes were opened to the world of special operations. Following the events of September 11, the call went out to those with language skills and Eli raised his hand. He soon found himself on the front lines of the War on Terror as a combat medic for the ███████ ████████████████████████████████. He never made it to BUD/S, but he'd seen more combat than most who'd passed the crucible in Coronado, and he'd more than earned the respect of those who wore the Trident.

"I have some gear in cargo," Reece said, nodding back to the plane behind him.

"Well, let's load it up, *Kahuna.* The rest of the team is waiting at the ranch."

CHAPTER 63

Columbia Country Club, Chevy Chase, Maryland

IF THERE WAS A downside to Reginald Pyne's job, it was the hours. After a highly lucrative career, he'd played golf five days a week working on the relationships necessary to move up the political ladder. Now he played once a week, if he was lucky.

He had joined his usual Saturday foursome early that morning, monitoring the events of the day on his iPhone as he moved across the fairway in his signature pastel pink polo with popped collar. Though the use of cell phones was prohibited on the exclusive club's property and calls were usually restricted to members inside their cars, Pyne's position meant that he could bend the rules for official business related to national security.

Pyne shot well that day, scoring only two over par according to his scorecard. He'd picked his ball up once and kicked it out of the rough a few times, but didn't everybody? After a kale salad lunch in the grill overlooking the eighteenth green, he headed for the indoor pool, glancing at his watch as he walked through the sliding glass doors to confirm that he was on time. A lone figure was rhythmically swimming laps, his body gliding through the water in long, powerful freestyle strokes.

Pyne took a seat on one of the padded wicker chaise lounges and waited patiently for the man to finish his workout.

The swimmer emerged from the pool, paying Pyne no notice as he ascended the steps and pulled off his goggles. He wrapped one towel over his Speedo and picked up a second before taking a seat on the chair across from his visitor.

Grant Larue was tall and relatively fit for a man in his sixties, the result of his daily pool workouts. Still, a paunch of belly fat he couldn't quite defeat dangled over the towel as he turned his attention to the president's chief of staff.

Larue was a D.C. lobbyist whose primary clients were overseas companies, mainly Russian. Larue played by the rules and was paid handsome retainers by businesses based in the largest country in the world. This also gave him plenty of reasons to meet with Russian businessmen on a regular basis.

Pyne had first met Larue through a tobacco industry campaign to counter anti-smoking efforts in Russia. The two Washington power players had formed a long and mutually beneficial relationship over the years. In exchange for information from the executive branch, Pyne would have a soft spot to land as a partner in Grant's lobbying firm after the next election. *Quid pro quo.*

"How was your swim, Grant?"

"Refreshing as always," the older man responded, toweling off his short gray hair. "What is it that brings you off the greens?"

"Just a quick chat. I have some information that might be of use to you."

"Shoot."

"It seems that one of your Russian friends has a problem with a Montana family, last name of Hastings. There was a big shoot-out at their ranch, and someone grabbed their youngest daughter in Romania. Word is they've taken her to some island in the Bering Sea and that her brother, a Navy SEAL of all things, has somehow joined her. Sounds like one of your friends is there with them both."

Larue stopped drying himself. "I'm listening."

"You should also know that the CIA wanted to launch a hostage rescue mission and I put the kibosh on it."

"My business associates will appreciate that."

"That's not all. Given the personalities involved, I wouldn't be surprised if these deplorables try to go it alone. Your people should be ready."

"How credible?"

"They're former spec ops types, SEALs and whatnot. They have money behind them so they may actually have the resources to pull off an attack, a rescue, or whatever you call it."

Grant rubbed his angular chin, his eyes drifting toward the ceiling.

"Understood."

"Do you, Grant? I want to make sure we are absolutely clear here. Your *associates*, they need to get rid of these Hastings people and make sure the bodies are never found. I don't need the president getting all patriotic on me. No evidence."

"That's a bit harsh, Pyne, even for you."

"I just want to avert World War III."

"If they are still alive, I can assure you they will not be for long. It will be as if they never set foot in Russia."

"Good."

"My friends will not forget your discretion when your man is out of office."

"I'm counting on that," Pyne responded as he rose to leave. "Let's do lunch one of these days."

"Let's do that."

Absolute power.

CHAPTER 64

Kumba Ranch, Flathead Valley, Montana

AS REECE AND ELI approached the main house, the door swung open and Jonathan stepped onto the porch. A motley crew emerged and walked down to the circular gravel driveway. Reece almost choked up, seeing the men who had once been as close to him as brothers answer yet another call. This time it wasn't for the country, it was for a man who had fought with them and offered them a way to transition from military service to the private sector while reconnecting with their families as part of the Warrior/Guardian program.

"Farkus," Reece said, approaching a redhead who bore an unfortunate resemblance to the bully character in *A Christmas Story*. In special operations and aviation circles it was best to just accept your nickname and learn to live with it. The fact that he, like his Hollywood namesake, wore a permanent scowl only added to the legend. A native of Boston, Sean Fleming had been a RECCE team member at his last command. He'd specialized in Advanced Force Operations, inserting into denied or nonpermissive areas, performing reconnaissance missions to identify targets, threats, HLZs, DZs, potential avenues of approach, and escape and evasion corridors. As part of this specialized role, Farkus was a subject matter expert on free-fall parachuting. With thousands of jumps under his belt, he was a tremendous asset when it came to putting men onto a target from the air. Upon his retirement the previous summer, he had come to work for Raife's outfitting business without hesitation to get some fresh air and figure out his next move.

Wearing Carhartts and a T-shirt from Tucson's Trident Bar and Grill, Farkus spit into an empty beer bottle and smiled. "Looks like we'll be jumping out of a perfectly good airplane tomorrow. As I recall, jumping is not your favorite activity."

"Good memory," Reece responded. If Reece never exited an aircraft with a parachute again it would be too soon. He preferred his feet remain firmly planted on the ground.

"Just follow me out the back as usual. Nothing to worry about."

"Just gravity." Reece smiled and moved on to the next man in line, slapping hands and embracing in a half man-hug.

"What's up, Devan?" Reece asked, as he greeted the golden-haired, board-shorts-, flip-flop-, and tank-top-clad SEAL. Reece couldn't remember ever having seen Devan without a smile. "How's Edo doing?"

Edo sat obediently at his handler's side awaiting a command. The Belgian Malinois had been Devan Blanding's last multipurpose canine as part of the Naval Special Warfare canine program. When Devan was sidelined by an IED that almost killed him in Yemen, Edo never left his side. Knowing that, had he been killed, Edo would have been put down by a system ill equipped and not funded to run a retirement home for aging attack dogs, Devan found his purpose.

After consulting with Raife, Devan had packed up his 1976 Volkswagen Bus pop-top camper and headed to Whitefish. There he found a beautiful piece of property about twenty minutes outside of town that would allow him to build his dream, Devine K9s. He built a canine facility where he could train personal protection dogs, many for the high-net-worth clients of Raife's program, as well as service dogs for citizens with impairments and disabilities. With Raife's help he started a foundation called Rescue 22, named for the twenty-two veterans who took their own lives each day in the United States. He trained service and emotional support dogs for veterans dealing with PTSD, traumatic brain injury, and the physical and emotional trauma of combat. A separate section of the property was reserved for retired or transitioning military and police working dogs, animals who would otherwise be quietly put to sleep. He set up an entity called the Warrior Dog Foundation to give them a beautiful place to live out their lives in dignity. Though he still had it, the VW Bus had been retired in favor of a new Mercedes 4x4 Sprinter Van, custom built for moving dogs to and from the airport in Kalispell.

"Edo's doing great, buddy. I think he knows something's up and it's time to come out of retirement."

"Can I pet him? Does he remember me?"

"Go ahead. He won't kill you unless I tell him to," the dog-man said only half in jest.

Reece knelt and ran his hands down the back of Edo's head, remembering just how many dogs had saved his life over the years. Without multipurpose canines and dog handlers like Devan, more than a few operators would never have made it home.

Standing, Reece turned to the last man in line. Barefoot, he wore dirty jeans and a gray T-shirt depicting half the face of a Sioux warrior, eagle feathers dangling from his braids. Reece knew the meaning of the feathers, as did the man who wore the shirt. Lawrence Chiaverini was one of Reece's favorite people. No one called him Lawrence, or even Larry. Even fewer knew he was actually Italian, most guessing by the dark hair that fell to his waist and the name of his custom knife company that he was Native American. Despite the fact that he had no Native American ancestry, he'd been called Chavez y Chavez after the *Young Guns* character since first crossing the quarterdeck at Team Five ten years before.

He had grown up in the Black Hills of South Dakota, where his father had the interesting distinction of being the go-to attorney for the bars lining Main Street and the pop-up clubs that appeared out of necessity to handle the overflow drinking traffic just outside of town. He had the respect of the community because he wasn't just some white-collar lawyer there to make a buck; he also ran a motorcycle restoration and mechanic shop specializing in bikes from the 1960s, '70s, and '80s. The law firm paid the bills, but his heart was in the bikes. Young Chavez learned engines and the art of motorcycle restoration and maintenance at the hands of a true master.

His dad never talked about the war, but every year when thousands of leather-bound bikers descended on the small town in August, a group of aging special forces veterans would make a pilgrimage to the shop. Chavez recognized the SF crest with its motto De Oppresso Liber, *free the oppressed*, on many of the men who passed by to share a drink with his dad. He heard "Project Delta" mentioned more than once but the war was something not discussed in the Chiaverini house, perched on the hill overlooking the Black Hills National Cemetery.

The machines in his father's shop led to an early interest in knife making. Working on bikes provided young Chavez enough money to slowly acquire the equipment that would one day define him as one of the country's most sought-after knife makers: grinder, files, drill press, sander, forge, and anvil. Though he worked long hours on bikes, and pursued his passion for the traditional skills still being kept alive through a select few Native Americans in the Badlands, his mother still managed to ensure that he would be able to survive in polite society. She taught him to cook, about the subtleties of fine wine, and instilled in him a knowledge and love of Renaissance and Baroque art, all skills and areas of knowledge that would cause more than a few to scratch their heads in wonder.

On his fifth deployment in as many years, he was shot multiple times during a room entry that turned out to be an ambush. Before being airlifted to Balad and on to Landstuhl, Chavez escaped from the FOB medical facility and was found naked, knife in hand, on his way to the Iraqi side of the base, threatening to scalp the Iraqi commander he suspected had set them up. The culture of senior-level leaders in the SEAL Teams was shifting. What was acceptable, and even normal, at one time was now grounds for "medical retirement."

After the medical board cut short his time in uniform, Chavez returned to the Black Hills, adrift. By this time the reality show frenzy had long since hit but cameras still followed more than a few "stars" into the adventure that was the Sturgis Motorcycle Rally. A producer who knew his father asked the recently unemployed Chavez if he'd ever done any stunt work in Hollywood. He was about to produce a movie on Benghazi and needed someone who knew special operations to take a few falls.

Now, between movies as a fall guy in LA and creating custom Half Face Blades in his shop in Kalispell, many for Raife's clients, Chavez had found a semblance of peace, though he still wanted to scalp that Iraqi commander.

"Been too long, Reece," Chavez said.

"That it has."

The two comrades-in-arms shared a hug. Then Chavez reached into his back pocket and pulled out a blade in a leather sheath. "It's a Hunter-Skinner. I made it when I heard you were headed back here."

The passing of a blade between warriors who have spilt blood together carried a unique significance.

"Thank you, brother."

"Okay, now that you lovebirds have become reacquainted, what's the plan?" Jonathan said, looking down from the steps.

Glancing at the road behind him, Reece turned back to the Hastings family patriarch.

"While we are waiting on the pilots, we have some weapons to sight in."

CHAPTER 65

Medny Island, Russia

ALEKSANDR ZHARKOV SAT IN a high-backed leather chair, his feet resting on an ottoman in front of the fire. The outside of the bunkerlike building disguised its luxurious interior, which had the look and feel of a cozy wilderness hunting lodge. Despite the Victorian-era feel of the room, the bunker was equipped with state-of-the-art satellite communications gear, which was appropriate given its joint ownership by the military and Russia's primary foreign intelligence agency. He scanned the sender and subject lines of his email inbox on the laptop computer balanced on his thigh, a steaming cup of tea cooling on the side table.

One name caught his attention and he double-clicked to open it, waiting impatiently as the message was decrypted by the software. It was from his station chief in Washington, who was running an illegal named Grant Larue. It was marked "Urgent." He read it carefully and a smile came to his lips. His intended target had taken the bait and intelligence from Larue confirmed that there would be no official rescue. That meant a small force of private citizens were likely on their way without a quick reaction force to back them up. His men would tear them apart and if any survived, he would hunt what was left, the prey of a lifetime. His last chase had left him unsatisfied after his quarry had chosen to take her own life rather than die at his hand. Like a lover who pulled away at the very moment before climax, her act had planted a hunger inside him, one he needed to satiate.

He called to Karyavin Vasilievich, the top Wagner contractor tasked with protecting the island. Wagner was a private military contracting firm with close ties to Russia's intelligence agencies and was used as a surrogate army in both Ukraine and Syria. Many of the men were veterans of the 2nd Spetsnaz Brigade of the GRU and all had combat experience. Vasilievich, who had worn the rank of captain while in the *spetsnaz*, appeared in his winter combat uniform with a handgun in a drop leg holster on his right thigh. He stood rigidly, not quite at attention, maintaining the bearing of his military days.

"Captain Vasilievich, we can expect the Americans any day now."

"I will increase patrols immediately. Do we know their method of insertion?"

"I suspect that they will come from the sea but there's no way of knowing. We must be ready for anything."

"Yes, sir."

"Keep all of your equipment shielded inside the bunkers unless directed otherwise. That is all."

Aleksandr swore he'd heard the man's heels click before he departed, despite the rubber soles of his winter boots.

CHAPTER 66

Kumba Ranch, Flathead Valley, Montana

AFTER CONFIRMING DOPE ON the rifles 1149'd from the Army, Jonathan led the men into his gun vault.

The former Selous Scout was a serious collector of firearms and his gun room was a sight to behold. The one-thousand-square foot rectangular room was constructed of thick concrete, reinforced within by a web of steel rebar. A vault door sealed the room off from the rest of the house, protecting the valuable collection from fire and theft. The interior was finished with rich walnut paneling, giving the room the warmth and glow of a London club. Rack after rack of rifles, shotguns, and handguns lined the walls, ranging in vintage from centuries-old flintlocks to sporting rifles used in the safari heyday of Jonathan's beloved Africa. Alongside them was a selection of modern assault rifles that would rival anything at Fort Bragg ▮▮▮▮▮▮. The guns were arranged from left to right in chronological order, with everything from highly engraved Purdey percussion-era fowling pieces to the coveted Heckler & Koch 416D. As the holder of a Type 7 FFL as well as a Special Occupational Tax from the Bureau of Alcohol, Tobacco, Firearms and Explosives, Hastings was able to buy dealer samples of the latest military-grade firearms, including machine guns and suppressors.

The team wasn't in the room to admire the collection. They were there because it was the closest thing to a secure conference room. It was highly unlikely that anyone was attempting to listen in on their planning session, but in this business, it was best not to take chances. A large LCD screen had been positioned on a table at the front of the room and folding chairs were arranged facing it. Caroline had prepared a feast at the rear of the room and a silver urn of coffee would provide everyone with a steady stream of caffeine as they completed the mission planning process.

Thorn had scarcely left Jonathan's side since this ordeal had begun and he soon joined the growing group of participants. He introduced himself and his two pilots, Liz Riley and Navy veteran Chip King, before Reece took over.

"I want to start by thanking all of you for being here. You didn't have to be. The government has decided to opt for a diplomatic solution to bringing Raife and Hanna home. From what I've learned about our enemy in the past few days, my assessment is that we are working with days, not weeks, to resolve this. My estimate is that as soon as the politicians start talking about this, Raife and Hanna will be killed and dumped in the sea. I want everyone to consider what's at stake. This is an invasion of a sovereign foreign country. All of us could be executed or rot in a Russian or U.S. jail for this."

"You have to survive the jump first, Reece," Farkus interjected.

"Good point," Reece conceded.

"And that's if you can get out the door before we're shot down by a Russian MiG," Chavez reminded everyone.

"There is that." Reece smiled, knowing the dark humor was part of the deal. "If you have any doubt, now is the time to say something. Trust me when I tell you that all of us will understand."

Reece paused and looked each individual in the eye for signs of hesitation. As expected, they were all in.

"All right then."

Reece clicked a remote and began the intelligence briefing he'd borrowed from Andy Danreb at the CIA.

"The Agency was kind enough to put this target package together for us," Reece continued, working through the same briefing he'd received at ███████ ██████ before moving into the tactical portion of the plan.

"The initial idea was to stage out of the Aleutians and HAHO in from low-signature aircraft onto the remote side of the island. The rescue force would have then patrolled to the objective, located Hanna and Raife, then exfiled via the special helicopters the government insists don't exist. The rotary-wing assets would stage off an amphibious ship in international waters. Since we don't have those resources, the plan is to use Thorn's G550 to perform a HAHO jump from international airspace, using the winds to get us into Russian territory and onto Medny Island. From there we will patrol to the target, though with far fewer ground assets."

"Without the stealth helos, how do we get the package home?" Farkus asked.

"Good question. Thorn will land his Albatross on the east side of the island, here," Reece said, pointing to a cove on the map. "We make our way to him and skim the wave tops until we are back in international airspace. Then it's on to Alaska."

"Why not use the Grumman for the insertion? A lot less risk than a jump," Devan asked, thinking of jumping Edo in arctic conditions.

"It's likely the island's radar would pick us up coming in. With the reduced signature of coming in via HAHO, we can hit the ground and maintain the element of surprise. For extract we don't have much choice. If the Albatross pings on their radar, we will be turning it around and getting back into international airspace before the Russians can positively ID us. If we inserted on it, we'd be sitting ducks."

"Check."

"What about coming in by boat?" Eli asked, wanting to cover all the options.

"Finding a boat of sufficient capability and moving it into position could take days; we just don't have that kind of time."

"Roger that. I sure miss being able to drop high-speed boats out of a C-17 on a few hours' notice."

"There is something else," Reece said. "Three of us are going to jump Russian-sourced AKMs. With such a small force we are going to need every technical and tactical advantage we can get so our primary weapons are the

416s on loan from ████. If the only brass left on sight is Black Hills 77 grain made in the U.S.A. we could raise U.S.-Russian tensions to a level not seen since the Cuban Missile Crisis. Wherever we put bodies in the dirt we are going to have to fill them with 7.62x39 and leave Russian brass all over the scene. It won't hold up to scrutiny by the SVR, but it will be enough to give the U.S. plausible deniability and avert a war. The Agency was planning to bombard their systems with enough disinformation to sow the seeds of mistrust amongst the rival gangs. The official stance will be that this looks to be an organized crime hit on the son of *bratva* leadership."

"What could go wrong?" Chavez asked. "That was rhetorical in case anyone was wondering."

"Chip, Liz," Reece said, nodding to the pilots.

"Hey, guys, I'm Captain Chip King. You can just call me Chip. By the looks of it I think I've been doing this since before most of you were born and I've been working for Senator Thornton since he left Congress. I'm going to put you where you need to be so don't worry about that. I'm afraid I have the easy part."

Chip outlined the G550's flight plan, which would move the team from Kalispell to the west coast of Washington and then skirt British Columbia on its way to Anchorage. They would land in Anchorage, refuel, and check the weather. The projected winds between the Aleutians and the Russian Commander Islands would determine their exact path toward the target.

"Liz will cover the drop," Chip said, deferring to the former Army aviator, who was much more in tune with the language of special operations. Dressed in the Alexo Athletica workout gear and University of Alabama ball cap she wore whenever she wasn't in her pilot's uniform, Liz wasn't a known quantity to anyone in the room other than Reece, Chip, and Thorn, but it quickly became clear that this was not her first mission brief as she projected a schematic of the G550 and explained exactly how the plane would be configured for the jump. Reece noticed that her trademark south Alabama accent abated slightly as she began her portion of the briefing. She could crank it up at will when she needed to lay on the charm and virtually turn it off when she thought it weakened her position. She wasn't in charm mode today.

Farkus followed Liz with a briefing on the pre-jump and exit procedures, sounding like he did it every day, which for many years he had.

"What's the medevac plan?" Eli asked.

"After the drop, we divert to Adak, refuel, and wait for the call," Liz piped in. "There's an old Air Force field with a ten-thousand-foot runway at Eareckson Air Station on Shemya in the Aleutian chain. It's used as a civilian diversion field now so we can land there if necessary. If Hanna, or anyone else, needs immediate medical attention, we can land at Shemya and transfer the patient from the Grumman onto the jet. We can have them on the ground in Anchorage within two hours, far faster than the Grumman. If there are no casualties, we will fly back to Anchorage and rendezvous there for the trip home."

"What happens if there's a mechanical failure and the Grumman doesn't make it in?"

"Then y'all better be good swimmers or we'll have to land the senator's expensive jet in Russia." Her comment, in her thickest southern drawl, lightened the mood and evoked a few laughs. Thorn grimaced.

"When do we launch?" Devan asked.

"Tomorrow morning, 0600," Reece said. "That gives everyone time to prep gear and Thorn and Jonathan can get a head start in the Grumman. They are leaving as soon as this briefing is over. They have a long, noisy trip ahead of them. Anything else?" Reece asked, scanning the room.

"Yes," Tim Thornton spoke up. "A lot of you know John Barklow down at Sitka."

Heads nodded around the room at the mention of a man who had put most of them through their cold weather warfare survival training on Kodiak Island in the SEAL Teams. He now used that expertise as the big-game manager for Sitka Gear in Bozeman.

"I called down and had him send up survival kits for each of you. I know you've gotten used to having an AC-130 overhead and QRF just minutes away. This is not Iraq or Afghanistan. This is Russia. I also have a flare gun up there for each of you. If we can't establish comms and you get to the coast but can't locate me, put up a flare and I'll come to you. Jonathan will be with me and we will be looking. By that time, there shouldn't be anyone left alive on the island to see it."

Heads nodded again as the gravity of what they were about to undertake sank in.

"Jonathan?" Thorn said, indicating he was finished.

"Just one thing, lads," the old warrior began. "That you are doing this for our son and daughter means more than my family can ever express. There isn't enough money in the world to compensate you for taking this risk but as a small expression of my thanks you will each receive two hundred thousand dollars for your work. It's the very least I can do. If you don't come back, your family will be taken care of. That, I assure you."

Reece looked around the room, not knowing what to say next.

"Sir." Chavez stood and addressed the man before him. "I certainly can't speak for everyone but please give my money to Freddy Strain's kid, the one with the special needs."

Reece swallowed hard as a chorus of voices followed suit.

"I'm not one for this kind of emotion, as Caroline can attest," Jonathan said, "but, thank you, lads. The deposit will be made. In whose name?"

Reece looked around the room, "From the Warrior Guardians."

CHAPTER 67

Medny Island, Russia

ALEKSANDR DESCENDED THE SPIRAL stone staircase into what most would call a dungeon. The intelligence officer thought of it as his *hypogeum*, the intricate final staging area for man and beast before they were raised into the floor of the ancient Roman Colosseum to meet their fate. In this case, the cages were jail cells with two entrances and exits. One opened to the inside, the area into which Aleksandr now ventured, and one on the opposite side opened to a ramp leading outside, into Aleksandr's coliseum: Medny Island. Sergei followed close behind, carrying a large leather satchel.

Most people thought of the gladiatorial games as pitting the fiercest fighters in Rome against one another in barbaric battles for the joy of the crowd, but Aleksandr preferred the *venation*. It was a spectacle in which the beasts of the republic were set loose against *venatores*, the most respected hunters in Rome. Though Aleksandr hunted humans, he thought of them as game. They were his *dentatae*.

The level had room for eight single cells. Six held the Africans from the Central African Republic who had arrived on the latest flight, criminals from the mines who would be executed in Africa or hunted in Russia. Better they have a fighting chance against Aleksandr and his clients than die on their knees as slaves in the red dirt of their homeland.

Aleksandr and Sergei passed the seventh cage, now empty after its occupant had given Aleksandr a good warm-up two days prior. He was ready; his skills were sharp. He was hungry. They stopped at the last cage and Aleksandr came face-to-face with the adversary he'd been seeking.

"S. Rainsford, a clever pen name. I am Aleksandr Zharkov."

Raife remained silent, studying his foe with an intensity that sent a chill down Aleksandr's spine.

A worthy opponent.

"My sister," Raife said.

"Your sister is dead. But just like the deer that comes to the feeder, or the leopard who climbs the tree after rotting zebra meat placed there by those who hunt him, you are here."

"You are a sick *fuck*," Raife spat.

"Oh, come now, S. Rainsford, your writing on our sport is so eloquent. Do not stoop to such a level. Leave that to the Africans. Tomorrow we hunt, or I should say, I hunt. You will be fed well tonight and just before dawn the cell doors behind you will open. A ramp will lead you up to ground level, where another door will be open. Sergei will have you in the sights of my very capable Dragunov. It's the only time he uses a modern weapon and rest assured, he will not miss if you force him to take a shot. Some have chosen this option, but I know that you will not. You *want* to kill me. I had to ensure you would come and that you would play. It's a pity that your friend James Reece isn't here with you. How I would have loved to hunt you both."

"If I don't kill you tomorrow, he'll finish the job."

"Unfortunately for us both, that will not be the case. Your friend Reece is on his way here now with a makeshift band of misfits. In all likelihood they will be slaughtered by my security forces as they make landfall. You look surprised, S. Rainsford. Do you think our intelligence apparatus died at the end of the Cold War? I can assure you, it is still very much in place, stronger now than it ever was."

"And, if I don't play?"

"Ah, you will play, S. Rainsford. You will play because that is your only chance to kill me. I hunted your sister out of this very cage," Aleksandr said, looking around as if recounting a fond memory. "Don't worry, she was treated well. She was not violated. I needed her in top condition. She was strong, that one. Strong and smart."

Raife and Aleksandr's attention was drawn to a scraping sound as Sergei pushed a table across the cold cement floor, positioning it in front of Raife's cage.

"I want you motivated tomorrow, S. Rainsford. I know you will be, but just in case, this should help."

Sergei handed his master the leather satchel, which Aleksandr placed on the table, unclasping the two brass buckles that held it closed. With great respect and ceremony, Aleksandr reached inside and pulled out a large glass container. Looking admiringly at its contents, he placed it on the table in front of Raife's cell.

"Good luck tomorrow, Rainsford," he said, before walking to the stairs that led to the main level. Already thinking of the thick moose steaks Sergei would grill for their supper.

He left Raife alone in his cell, staring into the lifeless upturned eyes of his dead sister.

CHAPTER 68

Glacier Park International Airport, Kalispell, Montana

A GULFSTREAM G550, ALSO known as a GV-SP, is one of the most versatile and luxurious business jets that money can buy. With a $45 million price tag, it was built for comfort and speed over extended distances. Despite its spacious interior, which can accommodate up to nineteen passengers, it was not designed to accommodate five HAHO jumpers, a dog, and all the weapons and gear necessary to perform a clandestine night insertion into a foreign nation via parachute.

The aircraft's interior was divided into three main sections: a forward club section with four leather seats facing one another over a small table, a four-place divan configured sideways with two seats across the aisle, and an aft sleeping compartment. This arrangement allowed every member of the rescue team a seat, leaving their gear distributed around the cabin and in the aft baggage area. For operators accustomed to making transcontinental flights on the nylon-strapped seats of military transport aircraft, it was a crowded but welcome change.

The team inspected, checked, and double-checked their gear before loading it into the plane. As jumpmaster, Farkus carefully inspected each parachute rig before they were loaded, since conditions before the jump would not be as ideal for doing so. If one didn't know any better, it looked like a professional soccer or rugby team was boarding the aircraft for an away match.

"Farkus, can you rig this up for me?" Reece asked, extending the Echols Legend his father had given him.

"I knew you were going to grab a sniper rifle." Farkus smiled. "Yeah, I'll rig it up."

"Just in case," Reece said.

"Just in case," Farkus acknowledged.

In the absence of a flight attendant, Liz performed the FAA-mandated safety briefing and indicated the location of the emergency exits. "The forward cabin door is the primary means of exiting the aircraft but additional exits over the wing can be accessed in an emergency," she said, doing her best flight attendant hand sweep toward the window exits. "In the event of a high-altitude jump over a hostile nation, the aft baggage door is the preferred method of egress," she said, evoking a laugh from the team.

The plane accelerated down the runway and surged skyward thanks to its powerful Rolls-Royce engines. Within minutes, they were at their cruising altitude of 40,000 feet, moving at a steady speed of Mach 0.83. What always surprised Reece was how quiet this aircraft was, its engineers obviously spending far more time and effort on passenger comfort than those who designed airliners. As soon as the plane took off, every operator went into their own world; listening to music, reading, or sleeping. Eli went into the crew rest compartment and began laying out medical gear in case the Gulfstream became an air ambulance. IV drips were prepared, bandages arranged, and various medications were lined up on the nightstand. Satisfied that things were as ready for an emergency as they could be, he returned to his seat and opened a Russian-language app on his iPhone. Reece couldn't sleep. He spent his time deep in thought, going over the jump, the contingencies at every phase of the operation. With no backup, there were only two words to describe what they were about to attempt: suicide mission.

• • • •

Those who were sleeping were jolted awake as the plane touched down in Anchorage and slowed to turn off runway 7-Right. The operators peered out the windows at the unique array of aircraft; everything from balloon-tired Super

Cubs to various floatplanes were visible in what seemed like every direction. Due to Alaska's size and the remote location of many of its cities, towns, and wilderness areas, it has the highest per capita rate of aircraft ownership in the nation.

The Gulfstream taxied to Signature Flight Support, one of the field's fixed-base operators, where the engines were shut down. The window shades were lowered, and Liz opened the cabin door to coordinate refueling. All five of the rescuers stayed on board and out of sight; no sense arousing any suspicions about the nature of their journey or cargo. The cold air blowing through the open door was a warning of the temperatures they'd be facing when they eventually exited the aircraft. Eli made a comment under his breath about these being "sub-Hawaiian" temperatures as he pulled a stocking cap over his head.

Once the plane was fueled, the pilots used an iPad application called Fore-Flight to file their flight plan electronically. According to that plan, they would travel from Anchorage to Haneda Airport in Tokyo, Japan, via Bethel, Alaska, and onto route R220, which passed almost directly over the Commander Islands, though they had no intentions of following that route all the way to Tokyo. They also filed an eAPIS report with the Department of Homeland Security, a requirement when filing an international flight plan. Only the pilots' names were listed on the report since the five commandos in the back would not be aboard when the plane made its next stop.

Since they had so recently landed, the pilots performed a "rotor-bow," motoring the engines for thirty seconds to thermally stabilize them before the start sequence was initialized. All systems read normal as the engines idled and the takeoff procedures began. They were wheels-up within the hour and, once airborne, Liz announced they were three hours and twenty-six minutes out from the drop.

Reece leaned back in his seat. Next stop, Russia.

CHAPTER 69

AS THEY FLEW OVER the Alaskan Peninsula, Reece warmed up dinner: piping-hot bowls of venison chili and freshly baked corn bread, all prepared by Caroline Hastings in advance of their departure. They devoured what they knew could be their last meal.

Reece pressed his head against the window and looked down at the lights of sparsely populated villages. He wondered how many Americans remembered that the only land battle of World War II fought on American soil took place on the barren volcanic islands 30,000 feet below. The Battle of Attu was all but forgotten these days. Five hundred forty-nine U.S. troops lost their lives defending home soil from Japanese invaders in May 1945; 1,148 were wounded, and 1,814 were taken out of the fight for cold injuries and disease. The battle marked one of the largest banzai charges of the war. Of the 2,379 Japanese troops that began the battle, only twenty-eight survived to be captured. The battle also drove the military to improve cold weather warfare gear, innovations that continued to evolve into what Reece and his men would use on Medny Island.

One by one, they hit the lavatory and began dressing for the mission. When exiting an aircraft at this altitude, temperatures could be -50 centigrade. Without protection from the cold, they would freeze to death in minutes. These extreme temperatures required them to wear several layers of synthetic clothing specially designed for arctic warfare. The clothing system, known as the Protective Combat Uniform (PCU), was developed by the Army's Natick Soldier Systems Center with input from alpine climbing legend and Gym Jones founder Mark Twight, and manufactured by Patagonia. White and gray splotched Multi-Cam Alpine combat overwhites completed the ensemble, topped off with body armor before donning specially designed HAHO gray synthetic thermal suits that would be discarded once they hit the ground.

Farkus received a weather update from the cockpit that he used to make his final navigational calculations. The Gulfstream was indicating winds from 250 degrees at 40 mph, which matched the earlier forecast and gave him confidence that the report was accurate. They would be at the absolute limits in terms of their gliding distance to the target. If the winds shifted or, worse, reversed, they would find themselves in the icy Bering Sea, dead within minutes. Farkus reinspected each man's gear, physically running his hands across every strap, every buckle, every seam; there would be no second chances.

Route R220 ran parallel to Russia's Air Defense Identification Zone, or ADIZ. It was important to stick to established commercial airline routes when making a covert insertion into denied territory. If they deviated too far from the official route, Russian radar operators monitoring the Petropavlovsk/Kamchatsky airspace would take note of their location and alert interceptor aircraft based in Magadan. A MiG-31 could shoot down the Gulfstream from two hundred miles away. To avoid that disaster, the pilots only allowed their course to divert slightly from the center of the route, putting them at the absolute edge of the ADIZ, 48.5 miles from the tip of Medny Island.

Devan let Edo walk among the operators, sniffing and saying hello. The dog handler wanted Edo to know the difference between friend and foe if he was given the command to bite.

Using the buddy system, the band of mercenaries donned parachutes with ATAK, or Android Tactical Assault Kits, in a chest-mounted Juggernaut Navigation Board MFF-T2 with backup Garmin Foretrex GPS and Oceanic compass in case the primary system failed. The ATAK was a military-specific smartphone app that provided users with real-time geospatial situational awareness, communication, navigation, and targeting information. Their weapons had been fitted with tape to hold down anything they didn't want flying off in the violence of exiting an aircraft moving at 500 miles per hour. The muzzle, ejector port, hand guard, optics, laser, and magazine all had riggers' tape adhering them to the rifles, which were mounted horizontally across their waists. Reece had the added benefit of having the Echols Legend strapped vertically to his right side in a padded case with foam taped around the scope. *Just in case.*

Weapons were strapped to jump harnesses, and with a final check of NODs, helmets were secured in place, oxygen masks dangling to the sides. The G550 was flying at 35,000 feet but the cabin was pressurized for 8,000. An hour out from the drop, the cabin pressure was adjusted to 10,000 feet. The commandos took their seats and plugged into a supplemental O_2 unit on the floor of the aircraft. Resembling a large Pelican case with dials and knobs that looked foreign to Reece, it allowed the jumpers to breathe 100 percent oxygen without depleting the small green tanks strapped to their chests. Edo had a nasal cannula rigged inside his muzzle. Reece always wondered how much O_2 the dogs were actually getting.

Decompression sickness, otherwise known as "the bends," is an ailment usually associated with scuba diving, but the risks of such a physiological event are equally as great during high-altitude parachute jumps. Residual nitrogen in the bloodstream can, upon descent, turn into bubbles that can migrate throughout the body and cause pain, paralysis, and death. To prevent the onset of decompression sickness, they pre-breathed for an hour. Any nitrogen remaining in their bodies, even any ingested while switching oxygen tanks, could be deadly.

The exercise of breathing pure oxygen prior to exiting the aircraft allowed them to get into the zone, running through the contingencies of the complex mission. Reece reviewed METT-TC: Mission, Enemy, Terrain, Troops Available, Time, and Civilian Considerations. The mission was clear: find Raife and rescue Hanna. Enemy: the target package from the Agency briefing ▇▇▇▇▇▇▇▇ estimated that Aleksandr had a security detail of no more than ten private contractors. Terrain: mountainous, harsh, and cold. Troops Available: Reece looked around the plane at his assault force. Five plus a dog. Time: if they made it in without detection, they would have four hours to complete the mission and make it to meet Thorn and Jonathan in the Albatross at extract. Civilian Considerations: non-applicable. All civilians had been force-relocated fifteen years ago. Reece found himself wondering, why? Aleksandr didn't have the island then. The Russian government had moved them.

Never mind that now, Reece. Focus.

At twenty minutes out, the silence was broken by Liz's voice over the intercom system. Farkus switched to his portable bailout O_2, moved to the rear of the cabin, and pushed open the polished door that led to the aft baggage compartment. The jumpers all wore clear goggles so the team medic could check for signs of decompression sickness: the bends, the chokes, neurological hits, and skin manifestations. Eli looked for pupil dilation or constriction, which could signify a nitrogen bubble expanding in the brain, and checked for signs that anyone was hyperventilating or scratching at their suits. The team looked ready.

At ten minutes out, the interior cabin lights were extinguished and everything went completely dark. Reece flipped down the L3Harris GPNVG-18 nightvision goggles attached to his helmet. The 97-degree panoramic view provided by the four images intensifiers helped eliminate the "tunnel vision" effect of the earlier NODs he'd used in the SEAL Teams. It wasn't quite daylight with the goggles in place, but it gave them an advantage over those without them.

At the two-minute mark, oxygen lines were disconnected, leaving the men to breathe from their bailout bottles attached to their kit. Each jumper checked their buddy's O_2 system: pressure, regulator, indicator, connections, and emergency equipment. Reece considered the possibility that his oxygen system would freeze in the extreme air temperatures. If that happened, hypoxia would set in quickly and he would die a euphoric death, no doubt unaware of his fate. He shifted his thoughts to the jump sequence, suppressing the notion of when he'd last worn a parachute.

The pilots donned their emergency oxygen masks, took a few deep breaths to ensure a good seal, and checked the internal microphones. Then, with a concerned glance at one another, they depressurized the cabin to a cacophony of master caution warnings and audio alerts. Both pilots had added layers of clothing to protect them from the frigid air. The men in the rear stood in single file, the first two inside the baggage area and the rest lined up behind them in the aft lavatory and into the cabin. Farkus reached up and activated the infrared strobe mounted on his helmet and each man followed suit. Soon all eight strobes flashed inside the cabin, which was disorienting to say the least. The flashing lights, invisible to anyone not wearing night-vision equipment, would help the jumpers keep track of one another in the darkness until they could stack up and turn them off; bad guys sometimes had night-vision devices as well.

One minute out, the whine of the twin turbofans abated significantly, slowing the jet's airspeed to one that wouldn't rip the jumpers and their gear to pieces when they exited the aircraft. With the aircraft trimmed to just above stall speed, the cabin differential pressure was equalized to allow Farkus to turn the handle and open the aft baggage door, which slid up along internal tracks. He attempted to open it slowly, but the hurricane-force winds snatched the latch from his hands and slammed it open so hard that he thought it would be ripped from its hinges; the engineers in Savannah had done their jobs well and it stayed attached to the plane. The cargo door on the G550 lies just below the left engine nacelle at the rear of the aircraft, which meant that the risk of impacting the fuselage or any other part of the aircraft upon exit is minimal.

The quiet ride suddenly became deafeningly loud. The combination of the howling winds and the jet engine just above the hatch drowned out any chance of verbal communication. The cold air was equally shocking to the senses, even with all the layers of specialized clothing. Farkus studied the open hatch as well as his ATAK screen in sequence, the NODs exaggerating his head movements as he did so. He pantomimed a countdown from five seconds. Then, without hesitation, he exited through the open hatch into the darkness, each jumper following as closely behind him as the cramped space allowed.

The sound of the jet engine was overwhelming as Reece passed underneath but it faded away almost instantly as the aircraft sped into the night. He found a stable body position and deployed his primary parachute. The small pilot chute unfurled the nylon canopy and violently arrested Reece's free fall. After confirming that his canopy had deployed as designed, he scanned for the flashing strobes that indicated the position of his teammates. One by one he counted them until he'd confirmed that the other jumpers' chutes had opened. They didn't bunch up, to avoid creating a radar signature. Instead they switched off their IR strobes and flew in a loose formation behind Farkus's lead, twenty-five yards apart. After the exhilaration of free fall and the dread of ensuring everyone was accounted for, Reece concentrated on maintaining his position behind Devan. He could see Edo's head and tail. The dog was strapped into Devan's harness, and Reece couldn't help but wonder what the canine was thinking as he descended from the heavens.

As they glided toward the objective, Reece made tiny course corrections by reaching up and pulling on the parachute's toggles, their forward momentum carrying them deeper into Russian territory and toward their target. Despite the cold, it was quite peaceful, the only sound the wind howling at their backs. Reece looked down and, below his boots, saw only darkness.

According to the ATAK screen, they were on course and maintaining sufficient speed and altitude to make it to Medny Island with a bit of air to spare. His oxygen appeared to be flowing normally and his mind was clear and alert. All Reece had to do for now was follow the leader. So far, despite the long odds, everything had gone according to plan, but as Reece knew all too well, no plan survives first contact with the enemy.

CHAPTER 70

40,000 feet above the Bering Sea

IT TOOK ALL OF Liz Riley's significant body strength to wrench the aft baggage door into the closed position. Thankfully, when she wasn't flying airplanes, she was moving large stacks of iron in the weight room. She knelt in the baggage area in silent prayer, asking God to watch over the avenging angels who had just leapt into the darkness. After a few moments of quiet reflection, she unhooked the safety line she'd rigged to prevent her falling into the abyss and made her way back to the cockpit. The captain immediately began the repressurization of the cabin and cranked the onboard climate control to its highest heat setting. Fifteen minutes later, both pilots were able to take off their oxygen masks and lose a couple of layers.

Making a hard turn off their flight plan was bound to raise a few eyebrows, so they carefully drifted back toward the center of their course and resumed their airspeed and altitude. They'd continue a full forty minutes past the drop, at which point Liz would call Anchorage Oceanic Control and report cabin pressurization issues. She would request a rerouting to Adak, where they could land and have the system inspected by maintenance crews. That would put them as close as possible to their emergency rendezvous location without arousing too much suspicion.

As the jet roared through the night sky, Liz couldn't help but return to her faith. She whispered a quiet prayer to the patron saint of paratroopers: "Saint Michael the Archangel, defend them in battle, be their protection against the enemy..."

· · ·

Medny Island, Russia

Aleksandr Zharkov was in the bunker's command center, where the weapon was controlled. Three uniformed operators manned the computer stations, each of them wearing headsets with lip microphones. One of them was in contact with the nation's air defense network, which operated early warning systems that dated back to the Soviet era. A jet traveling nearby had strayed a few miles from its course, putting it at the limit of the Air Defense Identification Zone. It was time. Grant Larue, his SVR-placed illegal, never failed to provide the highest-quality intelligence. He was running his own source inside the White House, the American president's own chief of staff, who believed he was passing information to a trusted friend who had a high-paying job waiting for him when he left politics. *A useful idiot...*

The weapon system on this island was the largest of its kind in the world and, so far, the tests had been extremely successful. The underground generators, capacitors, and dish emitters formed the basis of a directional EMP, designed to render the technological advantages of modern armies useless in an instant. An EMP is an electromagnetic pulse, a short burst of invisible energy. EMPs can be caused by coronal mass ejections from the sun, lightning, or nuclear detonations, varying significantly in size and scope. Though EMPs are harmless to humans, they can cause permanent damage to electronic components.

The system in place on Medny Island was a proof of concept, one that would activate an invisible dome-like shield above the area. It was Russia's experimental answer to the U.S. missile defense system. Guided missiles, aircraft, and even drones could be knocked out of the sky instantly. Mobile systems could send an entire battle space back into the nineteenth century while larger fixed weapons such as this one could potentially shield entire installations or cities from nuclear attack. Their only challenge at this point was projecting the pulse far enough into the atmosphere to interrupt nuclear-armed reentry vehicles. This system effectively protected the entire island up to an altitude of one thousand meters.

Zharkov glanced at the watch on his wrist before speaking. "Move the men inside the bunkers. In twenty minutes, begin pulses every sixty seconds."

"It will be done."

The contractors, their radios, and night-vision devices would be shielded inside the hardened bunkers while the weapon was in use. Once they had confirmation that the invaders were on the ground, Aleksandr would let slip his hired dogs of war.

CHAPTER 71

Medny Island, Russia

REECE COULD SEE THE island now, a long white blur against the dark sea below. He trusted their equipment and his belief in Farkus's abilities was near absolute, but it was still a tremendous relief to see dry land. He thought about the four SEAL operators who had drowned during Operation Urgent Fury in Grenada. No matter how hard you train, Mother Nature and the enemy still get a vote.

With the island in sight, Reece began to use his toggles to fly the chute toward the LZ, following the stack of jumpers before him. He glanced down at the ATAK screen and double-checked the oversize altimeter strapped to his wrist. Then Reece's entire world went black. He assumed that the cold had sapped the batteries in his NODs but, to be sure, he tried his go-to solution for all problems electronic: turn them off and then back on. Nothing. He flipped the NODs up and out of the way, seeing only a ghost of the illuminated image the night optics had provided seconds earlier.

The ATAK screen on his chest was as black as his NODs. Even though the device was set to the very dim night-vision mode, he should have seen at least a faint glow. He pressed the button on the side of the device. *What the hell?* Reece unbuckled the oxygen mask from his face, let it fall to one side, and pulled the boom mic on the Peltor headset toward his mouth. His other hand found the "talk" button through the fabric of his thermal suit.

"Spartan Two-One, this is Spartan Zero-One, over."

Nothing.

"Any Spartan this is Zero-One, over."

No response.

Straining, he heard a faint sound ahead, just above the howling of the wind, a human voice. The men were improvising, calling out to one another as beacons to guide them to the target. Reece pushed his earmuff headset ajar to better hear his teammates in the darkness; they risked detection by making noise but missing the target and landing in the icy waters meant certain death. Reece steered his chute by sound, following the voices in the wind.

As his eyes grew accustomed to the dark, he began to make out something in the distance; the faint white of the snow-covered island stood out in contrast to the blackness around it. Reece had spent enough time studying satellite imagery of the island to know where they were supposed to land. He was a product of an earlier era in which computers, GPS devices, and even NODs could not be depended upon. He'd been trained and mentored by Vietnam-era SEALs and had learned to navigate by terrain association. As a young frogman, Reece had lived by the map, compass, and iron sights. Those skills, ancient by the standards of today's generation of special operators, were about to save his life.

The analog altimeter strapped to his wrist still worked, the tritium-impregnated hands sweeping slowly as he descended. Reece confirmed that he had sufficient altitude to allow him to glide into the target; he would rather come in high and turn into the wind than risk being too low. He could hear the roaring waves crashing against the island's sheer cliff walls, which was yet another indicator that he was getting close. The wind picked up speed, pushing Reece more rapidly toward the unknown DZ. The combination of frigid air and the pounding surf made it difficult to discern the voices of his fellow team members. His course was a bit farther to the right than he intended so he tugged the toggle with his left hand. A drastic correction could be disastrous, so he was careful to make slight movements.

The island was long and narrow, resembling the far smaller but similarly configured profile of Long Island, New York. A series of high peaks ran across the center spine of the landscape, providing few, if any, suitable landing zones. Reece's target was a saddle between two mountaintops, roughly at the island's longitudinal center. He could make out two snow-covered mountaintops below and, as he steered toward them, he desperately hoped that they were the correct ones. His mind wasn't on the mission now; it wasn't on saving Hanna, finding Raife, or getting back to Katie. All of his focus was on landing his chute.

The terrain grew closer, rushing toward him as his perspective changed. Reece looked down over his boots and saw that he was officially "feet dry," meaning he had crossed from the ocean and was over land. His mind went through a checklist, consulting the altimeter, studying the terrain, making slight course corrections, and scanning the horizon for any sign of another jumper.

He glided toward the mountains, dropping rapidly. He needed to slow down, or risk overshooting his target. He had expected the wind to die off as he approached land, but the valley created the opposite effect. It effectively formed a wind tunnel that threatened to blow him into the sea. His airspeed provided him plenty of stability but not the angle of approach that he needed. He was still fifty feet off the ground and the saddle was beginning to fall away below him as the slope plunged toward the water.

Reece pulled hard on his left toggle, which put him into a steep turn that robbed his canopy of air. He turned 180 degrees and was now landing into the wind, which should have slowed his forward progress. Instead the wind gusted harder as it raced through the saddle, threatening to blow him backward over the cliff.

He pulled as hard as he could with one arm, effectively stalling the chute so that he would crash into the side of the mountain rather than into the water. The move sent him into a steep left turn from which there was no recovery. His feet touched the mountainside and his body went flipping across the snowy face like a downhill skier crashing out of control. He felt his NODs rip from his helmet and felt the receiver of his AR burst apart despite the tape intended to hold it together. After what seemed like an eternity of tumbling through snow rock and ice, his canopy again filled with a gust of wind, dragging him over the rough ground. Reaching up, he frantically searched for the release to arrest his momentum.

Got it!

The world was suddenly still and quiet.

Shit, that hurt.

Reece lay still, looking up at the sky, feeling the cold snow on his back. He started with his toes; he could feel them, which was a good sign. He then bent his knees and arched his back. Cautiously, he twisted his spine. Then he wiggled his fingers, moved his elbows, and slowly turned his head from side to side before pushing himself up into a sitting position and reaching for the Echols rifle, which had survived the fall.

Frogman luck.

Reece stood up stiffly and slid the Echols from its padded case, observing his immediate surroundings. His NODs were gone but his helmet was still attached to his head and had probably helped save his life. His first-line gear was still attached to his body, which meant he had his pistol and blades. Without a working light to check his sniper rifle he used his fingers to explore the familiar weapon system: barrel, scope, stock, sling. Everything was in place. Whether it retained its zero remained to be seen.

Gazing up at the mountains, he pulled out a small compass to get his bearings. He was alone, in enemy territory, without a working radio, and needed to rendezvous with his team. Their loss-of-comms link-up point was just a mile to the southeast. There was no sign of any other human life.

He was alive and had a mission to complete.

Alone, in a foreign land, he moved off into the night.

I am never out of the fight.

CHAPTER 72

Medny Island, Russia

CAPTAIN KARYAVIN VASILIEVICH JOINED his men on the high ground and checked their position, arranged overlooking a choke point along the most likely avenue of approach to Deputy Director Aleksandr Zharkov's lodge. He'd shut down the tactical EMP and patrolled to the ambush site with his seven-man team, all combat veterans of Russia's forays into its former territories over the past decade. It would take twenty minutes for the EMP to rejuvenate and store enough power for another shot but by that time the Americans would be on the ground wondering why their high-tech gear was fried. They needed that deadly advantage over the Americans, whose technological superiority would now be reduced to useless pieces of wires and metal.

The United States had outpaced their old adversary in technological advances since the fall of the Soviet Union. The new Russian Federation could stamp out machine parts and build the ever-reliable AK, but when it came to the weapons of the Information Age, computers and microchips, Russia was not even in the running. That meant they had to focus on how to eliminate the technological advantages of their enemies.

Though export restricted, the NODs and lasers that adorned the team's M4s were purchased in the United States legally by Aleksandr Zharkov's illegals. They were then dismantled and smuggled into Russia using the deputy director's *bratva* network to supply his private security detail with the best weapons and optics available. Night-vision tubes were disguised inside binoculars and M4s were disassembled and disguised as machine parts, then reassembled once safely inside the borders of Mother Russia.

The one sniper in the group cradled a Chukavin rifle chambered in 7.62x54R in his arms. A recent replacement for the revered Cold War–era Dragunov, he knew the Schmidt & Bender optic that graced its top rail was not what soldiers in the Russian military would be using. The expensive scopes were for demonstrations and show purposes. True to form, the bureaucrats would ensure that the ground pounders would be given suboptimal glass so that more of them could be fielded. *What was it Stalin had said about quantity?* No matter, he had his rifle, scope, and a U.S.-made forward-mounted night optic along with an IR laser. He would have preferred the Orsis T-5000 Tochnost in .338 Lapua but that could not be helped. He'd sent more than a few insurgents to their graves in Chechnya and Dagestan from behind the iconic-looking Dragunov, though having spent so much time with it, he knew the effective range only extended that of the AK by three hundred meters. This new Kalashnikov Concern Chukavin was different. With it, he'd kill his first American.

Vasilievich's men had emplaced MON-50 anti-personnel devices just minutes earlier on what amounted to the choke point at the most likely avenue of approach to the lodge. Though the men had no personal experience with the American Claymore mine, they knew the MON-50 was their country's equivalent and had seen their devastating effectiveness in combat in Chechnya and the North Caucasus.

His former soldiers knew their trade. Most important, they possessed the element of surprise and had taken away the technological advantages of their opposition.

Anyone the explosives didn't eviscerate would be systematically gunned down by his team.

Now it was time to watch and wait.

. . .

Aleksandr was awake at 3:00 a.m., admiring the falling snow. The Buran snowmobile was gassed up and was idling next to the KAMAZ 6x6 in the detached garage. Sergei's new dogs were not yet at the level of the two the Hastings woman had killed, though they were showing promising attributes. He'd shunned alcohol at dinner, as was his custom the night before a hunt, but still hadn't slept well. The anticipation overpowered his need for sleep. That worried him some. He wanted to be at his best.

The team coming to kill him would be slaughtered on their approach, thanks to the intelligence from Grant Larue and his lackey in the executive branch. The lobbyist lived and operated in plain sight, right under the noses of the Americans. The lobbying industry had been ripe for exploitation by the SVR.

What to do with the bodies? As the national deputy director of clandestine services, he could turn this into a major international incident and push the United States and Russia to the brink of war, but what good would that do? There was a smarter back-channel move to make.

Later; focus on the hunt.

He'd hoped to somehow capture Commander Reece alive but the odds of capturing any of the American force alive were slim. He might make an even more formidable adversary than his friend who waited one floor below, nourished but cold and, more important, inspired. His sister's head in a formaldehyde jar to keep him company all night should have given him all the incentive needed to make this Aleksandr's most challenging and pleasurable adventure to date.

It was time to hunt.

CHAPTER 73

Medny Island, Russia

EVERYONE ELSE ON THE team felt like they were back in the dark ages. Everyone but Reece. He was in his element. He'd grown up in the mountains with his father, who passed along the importance of map and compass work, terrain association, taking bearings, and triangulation. Their GPS devices, lasers, and NODs might be down, but that didn't mean that these warriors were out of the fight. They reconsolidated at the link-up point. Reece was the last to arrive, the others having managed to land in the same general vicinity.

Being most familiar with the routes and objective, Reece took dual point with Devan and Edo. The Belgian Malinois was off leash and alert, back doing what he'd been trained for. Much like the men he accompanied, Edo had been out of the fight too long and was ready for action. Eli and Farkus followed, with Chavez taking rear security. The lack of NODs meant they had to patrol closer together than they were accustomed to; they all knew the threat of being too close if a rocket, mortar, or IED hit.

They hadn't jumped snowshoes. Intel suggested the snow covering was light, but reality on the ground was different than it looked from satellites a hundred miles up. Even enveloped by darkness, over the snow-covered ground, the team moved with purpose toward their objective.

Their plan was to hit the lodge, grab Hanna and Raife, make it to extract, and kill anyone who got in their way.

Reece knew it was a bit harebrained; if he were still a SEAL there was no way he would green-light five assaulters and a dog hitting a lodge on an island off the coast of Siberia. He also knew that if the situation were reversed, Raife would move heaven and earth to get him out.

They were committed. They were going in.

Devan froze. He raised his left hand in a fist at head level.

He gave Edo the command to halt. "*Blif,*" he hissed in Dutch, following it with an immediate "here."

Edo returned to Devan's left side, going prone on the snow, waiting for the next command.

Devan had noticed the dog's body language change. It was something only those in tune with their partner would sense; his ears moved forward, his gait became more aggressive, and his tail changed its rhythmic wag ever so slightly. His next move would have been to "finish," or find the IED. Edo had not forgotten the ways of war. Neither had Devan. He did not want his dog to "finish," which meant sitting right at the IED; certain death.

The team sank to their knees.

"Explosives ahead," Devan said under his breath.

"Are you sure?" Reece asked, already knowing the answer.

"Positive. Edo alerted on it. Lucky we were coming in from downwind or we might have walked right past it."

"How far?"

"Hard to tell exactly, but in these conditions? Fifty to a hundred yards."

Edo's head snapped up again, ears erect, body stiff and ready to launch, looking ahead at an angle.

"Ambush," Devan declared.

Reece was squinting into the darkness when the first round took him square in the chest.

CHAPTER 74

DEVAN HIT THE GROUND and sent ten rounds in the direction of the ambush before yelling, "CONTACT FRONT!"

"*Plotz!*" he yelled at Edo over the sound of his rifle, ensuring Edo would stay down and by his side.

"ON LINE!"

Eli low-crawled toward Reece, Devan, and Edo, elbows sinking into the snow, digging in with his knees and feet to propel himself forward. In the darkness they didn't have targets and he'd only caught the slightest hint of a muzzle flash as he hit the deck moments earlier. *Suppressors.*

Firing from their aggressors ceased.

They had been on a slight incline and the fact that they weren't all dead meant that Edo had kept them out of the kill zone. If they stayed down, they were below the enemy's line of sight, meaning they were *en defilade.*

Win the fight, Eli thought. *Hard to do with nothing to shoot at.*

Farkus was by his side in an instant. They grabbed Reece by his pant leg and began dragging him back toward a rock formation protruding from the snow behind. Devan pushed himself back close behind, Edo low-crawling right along with him toward their rear security.

"I have an out," he whispered, guiding the rest of the team to the rock behind him.

Devan and Farkus helped form a perimeter around their wounded leader as Eli went to work assessing his patient, running his hands up and down Reece's body feeling for severe bleeding and massive injuries. As he went to check for breathing, Reece's eyes opened wide.

"I'm okay. I'm okay," he said coughing.

"Quiet, brother," Eli responded. "You just took a round to the chest. Must have hit your head when you fell."

Reece's hand went to his chest and felt the pieces of ceramic plate that had split into fragments, absorbing the bullet's impact just as it was designed.

"Well, this thing is useless now," Reece observed, struggling out of his plate carrier and tossing his magazines to Eli. "Where's my rifle?"

"Here you go, boss," Devan said. He'd grabbed the Echols Legend on his crawl back to the rock.

"Thanks. Okay, what do we have?"

"Shooting stopped right after you were hit. Looks like they were set up with IEDs, mines, or an antipersonnel explosive device of some sort. We must be out of their line of sight here, but I'd wager they are maneuvering on us right now. That shot that took you was accurate. I'd guess they have NODs and suppressors, possibly IR lasers."

Shit.

Devan turned in toward the former SEAL commander. "Edo will let us know when they're coming."

Raife and Hanna were to the west. Extract was a few hours out to the east. They were pinned down on an enemy island where their adversary held the technical and tactical advantages.

Think, Reece!

Take a breath. Look around. Make a call.

He looked at the men around him. They were all there to help Raife and Hanna, but they wouldn't have put their lives on the line unless Reece had asked. He looked back at the rifle in his hands, wood stock, NightForce optic, similar to what his father had used in Vietnam, only more accurate. That was it: *Vietnam.*

"Bring it in!" Reece whispered, the others scooting in closer so they could hear the combat-tested leader.

"Do you still have your flare guns? The ones we were to use in a loss of comms emergency extract to signal the bird?"

Heads nodded around the circle.

"Okay then, we are going to take their advantage and even things up. The Vietnam guys who taught me had to fight at night without night vision. They had to turn night into day. We're going to do the same thing, but we have to do it fast."

Hands were already going into kits and removing the small nautical flare guns Thorn had given them before they departed.

"It's not like the 40MM flares we had in the Teams but it's all we have. I'm going to move to high ground just north; that hill we passed a couple hundred yards back. If my map study is correct, it should put me in a position slightly above theirs. If they flank us or start coming in, let the dog go and start putting up those flares and engaging. If I can get to high ground, I'll fire my flare and start putting them down. Time it right; we only have about five seconds per flare, so this is going to happen fast. How many flares per gun?"

"Two," Eli answered.

"Okay, I'll initiate with one of mine. As one flare goes out, put up another. Do not put two up at the same time; it's going to be close as it is. If they are moving in on us, we will have them in an L ambush."

"Let me come with you," Eli pleaded.

"Negative. You stay here. I need three of you on the guns and one of you putting up those flares. Besides, I work better alone these days."

Reece looked around the circle, and though they couldn't see it, he smiled. He was a sniper. And he was going to high ground.

CHAPTER 75

REECE PUSHED HIMSELF FORWARD at a full sprint, no small feat over snow-covered ground in the dark. He hadn't been shot in the back yet, which meant the enemy couldn't see him.

An even darker shape appeared out of the darkness; the hill was just to his left. Reece veered toward it and began to climb. It was steep enough that the snow only held to the more horizontal ledges. His feet slid out from under him as he worked his way up the scree, thin pieces of rock causing him to slide back a step with every two he took forward.

Slinging his rifle across his back he grabbed at anything that would give him purchase, his hot breath visible in the cold early morning air.

Keep moving forward, he heard his dad's voice urging him on. *Always improve your fighting position, son.*

His legs burned and he felt the rocks and ice tearing at his hands.

Up he went, continuing his scramble.

Almost.

There it was. His sniper's perch beckoned.

Sliding into an elevated position above those moving in to kill his team, Reece unslung his rifle and flipped up the scope covers before going prone and setting the flare gun to his right. He was about to find out what they faced.

Stock to shoulder, cheek to its rest, body nestled in among the rocks and ice, safety off.

Reece reached for the flare gun, cocked it, pointed it skyward over what he estimated was the enemy position, and pulled the trigger.

. . .

Vasilievich watched his flanking element approach the enemy's suspected position. They moved in slowly, weapons up, scanning the terrain before them. Even with the advantage of the NODs the ground was treacherous and the Americans were armed.

How had they identified the MON-50s right before they entered the kill zone? They must have a dog with them. Fucking dogs!

The flanking element would have them in sight any moment now.

A popping noise to his left took his attention from the scene below and a second later his NODs erupted in bright white.

. . .

Reece was on the gun and on the trigger when his first flare illuminated the ground below. He'd been slightly off on his estimation of where the opposing force's base element would be situated, but not by much.

Without a laser range finder, Reece estimated distance by one of the ways he'd been taught almost twenty years before. He used a map study. Actual distance to target, five hundred and fifty yards, altitude, temperature, velocity, bore height, ballistic coefficient of the .300 Win Mag Barnes TTSX, elevated at a thirty-five degree incline; 2 mil adjustment for a 39.5 inch drop. Wind approximately five miles an hour. Full value; 8.5-inch hold right.

Reece made the adjustments in his head and pressed the trigger sending 180 grains of Barnes triple shock through the spine of the far left shooter. Quickly throwing the bolt, Reece chambered his second round and let it fly.

He aimed at the upper torsos of his targets. The bullet's nose peeling back instantly on contact into a copper petal of death, tearing through the heart and lungs of his second target.

A third soldier was struggling to get into a kneeling position, suddenly aware that two of his teammates were no longer of the earth, when Reece's third bullet took him high in the chest. The bullet ripped through the breast plate and eviscerated both lungs before exiting out the back, removing an even larger chunk of flesh on the way out.

Reece had been so focused on eliminating the base element and had thrown the bolt so fast that he hadn't even noticed the flares start going up to his left. When his team's suppressed shots began penetrating the night air, Reece could tell the plan was working. They'd turned night into day. All they had to do was just not miss. If the Russians survived the initial onslaught, they would be back on top with their NODs and lasers. Reece's team would get only one chance.

He'd seen five figures in prone when his first flare had illuminated the landscape.

How many have my team sent up?

Don't worry about them right now. Do your job.

Reece reached for the flare gun, grabbed his second and last round from its rail, and broke the action only to find the spent shell didn't eject on its own. Grabbing it with his numb fingers he pulled it from the gun, fumbled, and dropped his last flare into the abyss.

CHAPTER 76

VASILIEVICH AND THE LAST living member of his base element rolled out of what they quickly recognized as a kill zone. Whoever was shooting at them was good. In three or four seconds he'd taken out more than half his force. Luckily the Wagner Group team leader still had his sniper.

How many flares did they have?

Recognizing that the tables had turned, Vasilievich focused his attention on the cliffs to the northeast from behind the boulder before him and motioned to his sniper.

"The cliffs. He's in the cliffs," he hissed.

The sniper had been set up to shoot down on the approaching force from the high ground and had moved from a prone to a sitting position that would allow him to find his new target in the cliffs above.

The night optic was good, but at a distance it was almost impossible to discern an unmoving camouflaged figure from the jagged mountainside.

There! Vasilievich saw a slight movement against a still backdrop.

"Five hundred meters. Halfway up the rocks!" he yelled at the sniper to make sure he knew where to shoot.

Vasilievich directed his M4 at his new target, lasers dancing in and around the location of the movement, and began to fire.

. . .

Reece's heart sank as his final flare dropped out of sight, bouncing off the rock face and falling into the darkness below.

Shit! My teammates are counting on me. Think, Reece. Adapt!

He saw the muzzle flashes. With suppressors, they were not as prominent as they would have been without them, but they were enough for Reece to make them out in the darkness. He thought back to the early days in Afghanistan, the automatic-weapons gunners shooting unsuppressed at an entrenched enemy position. He remembered the al-Qaeda guns turning toward the bright flashes of light at the breaks of the 5.56 and 7.62 machine guns. The man's head to his right exploding...

Reece knew he should change positions after his first shots, especially since he had now lost the element of surprise and the enemy had him zeroed, but he stayed where he was. What he suspected was that the enemy's IR lasers had been sighted in for a range of twenty-five yards to a point of aim, point of impact, a cardinal sin. In simple terms, it meant that the lasers would hit what they were aiming at if that target was at twenty-five yards. He also knew they had a sniper with them. The single round that had impacted him in the body armor had not come from a 5.56 weapon system. If the sniper already had him in his sights, he was a dead man.

Observe, orient, decide, act.

Settling back in behind his rifle, Reece took a breath and exhaled. He saw the full-auto muzzle flash from the suppressed M4 and noted its ineffective hits to his left. He was looking for the sniper.

Reece knew he had an advantage. He'd already put targets down and was perfectly dialed for the distance, angle, and elevation, and he knew the wind hold. His antagonist would be taking all those factors into consideration but had yet to confirm it with a shot. If the Russian sniper missed, he'd make the correction and would not miss again.

A single flash three meters to the full-auto gun's left registered in Reece's brain. He estimated back from that flash where the shooter's head would be on the stock of a long-range rifle and pressed the trigger.

. . .

Vasilievich heard the report of the large-caliber weapon reverberate off the canyon walls and saw the muzzle flash just as his sniper's head snapped back and away from his Chukavin, his body collapsing in an unnatural heap.

Without looking back up at the cliff, Vasilievich pushed himself to his feet and retreated into the darkness.

CHAPTER 77

THE SNOW CRUNCHED BENEATH his feet, his NODs fogging up from the exertion. He stumbled, fell, got back up, and pressed onward. If only he could make it to the lodge. Vasilievich's frantic radio calls went unanswered. Sergei never used radios; he despised all trappings of the modern world, and the director was on the hunt, focused on his newest acquisition—the American whose sister he'd killed days earlier.

What was that? The distinctive sound of Mikhail Kalashnikov's revolutionary invention echoed through the forest. It was too far away to be directed at him. *Was it possible one of his men had survived the encounter?* His contractors carried M4s. *Who on the island had an AK?* Then he heard it again. And again. Then it hit him. The Americans were putting AK rounds into the dead bodies of his men.

Now Vasilievich knew what it was to be hunted. His force had been defeated by the Americans. He'd become too comfortable with the night vision and lasers, knowing their adversary wouldn't have the advantage of technology after being hit with the EMP. He'd become overconfident, on home soil with the advantage of surprise and the technical superiority of owning the night.

The Americans had made them pay for their hubris.

He knew they had taken his force's helmets and night vision, probably their snowshoes and weapons with IR lasers as well.

If only he could get to the relative safety of Aleksandr's compound, he could contact the Russian military across the bay at Petropavlovsk-Kamchatsky or Avacha Bay and request reinforcements. With the weapons in the lodge, he, Aleksandr, and Sergei could hold off the invaders until help arrived.

Stopping to catch his breath, Vasilievich nervously scanned the path behind him. He'd be easy to track in the snow, and with early nautical twilight not far off, his pursuers would be able to pick up their pace. He closed his eyes, held his breath, and listened.

There, they were coming. Keep going. Get to the lodge!

* * *

Reece and his team charged through the snow, now outfitted in the snowshoes, helmets, rifles, and NODs of their enemy. Reece had warned them that the IR lasers were probably sighted in point of aim, point of impact at twenty-five yards, so anything past that distance would be dicey.

Devan had his eyes on Edo, who pushed forward on the track of their quarry. Reece took point and had his eyes up and out, looking for threats.

It was clear that the Russian was moving toward the lodge, probably to sound the alarm and warn Aleksandr of the approaching hit team. Reece was intent on him not making it.

Devan threw up his left hand, signaling the patrol to stop. He'd seen Edo change his behavior. They were close.

Not wanting to walk into another ambush, Reece gave the hand and arm signal for the two trail SEALs to punch out to the right. Farkus and Chavez would move out and ahead to flank their target, putting him in an L ambush and sealing his fate.

Reece and Devan waited, quiet and listening for any changes in the environment. Eli took rear security.

They'd give their flanking element a solid five minutes and then it would be time for Edo to go to work.

· · ·

They'd caught up quicker than Vasilievich had anticipated. *How many were there?* The Russian knew he would never make it to the lodge in time. He would have to outthink them.

His plan was a long shot, but one that just might pay off. With a dog on his track he'd double back, circling around and run parallel to them, closing the distance while moving in the opposite direction, essentially doing a large U-turn. The dog's nose would be on the track. If he could make the move before his pursuers noticed he was veering to his right, he just might have a chance. The tubes on these particular NODs were not the best for peripheral vision. It was like looking through two toilet paper tubes. Everything within those tubes was lit up in hues of green, white, and black. To see right or left, his head had to physically turn in those directions. He hoped that because they were exerting themselves to catch him before he got to the lodge, they would be too focused on making time through the snow rather than on the possibility their prey might be trying to outwit them with such a risky maneuver. By the time they figured out he was not going for the lodge, he'd have the drop on them.

· · ·

The two Americans and the lone Russian saw each other at the same time.

Farkus was in the lead. His weapon came up quickly, as he took the safety off, finger to trigger, but not fast enough for the Russian coming directly for him, who dove into his first available cover.

"Contact front!" Farkus yelled to Chavez, who immediately joined him online, both operators melting into the closest trees to evaluate the situation.

"He was doubling back on us," Farkus said, now in a hushed voice.

"You keep him pinned," Chavez said. "I'm going to punch right. Let's finish this guy."

"Roger," Farkus confirmed.

"Moving," Chavez said.

"Move!"

Before he could take a step, a Russian F1 hand grenade landed in the snow just shy of his cover.

Reece, Devan, and Eli heard the explosion.

"Shit, he was doubling back on us!" Reece exclaimed.

Oldest trick in the book, the former SEAL commander thought. *Should have anticipated that!*

"Send him!" Reece ordered.

Without a second thought Devan said, *"Fass"*—German for "bite"—and Edo charged toward the enemy.

Vasilievich angled his head out from behind the tree. He could see that both Americans were down but still moving. He'd finish them and then sprint toward the lodge. The snowshoes were a bit cumbersome but his remaining pursuers would have the same issue, and they just might proceed more cautiously now that he'd shown them he could exploit his tactical advantages just as well as they could. He was just getting to his feet when it felt like he was hit in the side with a sledgehammer.

Edo had been born and bred for this very task. While some dogs longed to chase tennis balls or retrieve ducks, Edo wanted nothing more than to kill terrorists. Though this one didn't smell or taste the way the ones had on his past trips to the warmer places with the one they called Devan, he knew this was his target. His job was to destroy the man before him, and Edo knew how to do just that.

Reece, Eli, and Devan were within twenty yards when they finally had a clear line of sight to the struggle between man and beast. They saw the Russian make a move to draw something from his waistline. Gun or knife, it didn't matter. Three lasers found his head, the warriors depressing their triggers in the same instant, each sending deadly projectiles into the brain stem of their target, who dropped straight into the snow.

"Here," Devan ordered, bringing Edo back to his master as Eli moved to the two downed SEALs.

Chavez was getting up, just a little dazed from the blast.

"You okay, buddy?" Reece asked, looking in his eyes and then doing a once-over of his body to ensure he still had all his fingers and toes.

"I'm good. Snow tamped the majority of the blast but Farkus was closer. I'll go take care of our *plausible deniability*," he said, unslinging the AK from his back and walking toward what was left of the dead Russian.

Eli was stuffing a wound on Farkus's upper leg with gauze below a tourniquet. Even through his NODs, Reece could tell it was a bad one.

Farkus was conscious and gritting his teeth to stay quiet.

"Farkus, you are going to make it. That shrapnel missed your artery, so it's not an arterial bleed. You have a bunch of small shards of shrapnel in there. It just hurts like hell. Take these," Eli said, handing the wounded SEAL a handful of pills. "They will ward off infection and we'll have you out of here and back to an ER in Alaska before they wear off."

While Eli practiced medicine, Reece reached into Farkus's pack and pulled out the small Kifaru Woobie, a twenty-first-century private sector version of the venerable military poncho liner. He extracted it from its small built-in stuff sack and wrapped it around the wounded Frogman. Next he pulled out the Sitka Gear Flash Shelter and wrapped that around the puffy poncho liner.

"This isn't perfect, but it will keep you from freezing to death out here. We'll be back. I need everybody for this assault. The lodge is just a klick east."

Reece thought of Hanna and Raife. Though he hated to do it, he was not going to be able to leave a member of the team behind to tend to Farkus. If they failed, Farkus was a dead man, if not from the Russian military assets that would descend on the island, then from the freezing temperatures of Medny and the infections that were bound to set in as soon as the antibiotics wore off.

"Crush them, sir. Don't worry about me. I have rear security," he said, holding up his rifle.

Reece nodded. The other members of the assault force were primed to execute, the familiar look of resolve on their faces.

Before storming on toward the target, Reece looked down at the smallest member of the team, the multipurpose canine who had saved his life yet again.

The dog was chewing on something.

It was a chunk of Captain Karyavin Vasilievich's triceps.

CHAPTER 78

RAIFE MOVED TOWARD HIGH ground, faster now that the sun was about to break the horizon.

Was Reece really on his way to Russia? Or was that just another one of Zharkov's sick mind games?

The image of his sister's dismembered head floating in formaldehyde burned in his mind, the hate keeping him warm. He squeezed himself into a rock outcropping and surveyed the terrain behind him. Weather was coming in off the Bering Sea. That might work to his advantage. He squinted back the way he had come and could just make out the monstrous 6x6 vehicle pushing through the tundra and snow, slowly gaining elevation in the early morning light. A snowmobile with a single skid in front followed a short distance behind. He knew he had been easy to follow. Now it was time to bait a trap of his own. He looked over the snow-strewn cliffs to the jagged rocks that met the sea at their base, and then carefully backtracked out the way he had come.

Aleksandr brought the KAMAZ troop transport to a stop, the tracks in front of him moving toward the very same cliffs where the sister had met her fate. Shaking his head, he grabbed his Ravin crossbow from the seat beside him. Sergei and the dogs would deal with anyone who survived his contractors well before they made it to this elevation. He wanted to test himself on this hunt. He'd only bring the dogs up as a last resort.

What tricks do you have up your sleeve?

Aleksandr swung down from the off-road vehicle's lowest step and attached his snowshoes, feeling excitement building inside him.

Finally, a worthy adversary!

Aleksandr ran his tongue along his upper lip, his eyes tracing the footsteps through the snow.

Don't make this easy on me, Rainsford.

He cocked his crossbow and inserted a bolt into the flight groove of his weapon before stepping off into the snow in search of his prey.

CHAPTER 79

WITH FARKUS OUT OF the fight, the assault team now consisted of four sea-soned operators and a dog. They would usually hit a compound like this with forty assaulters, air assets, a blocking force, and a QRF on standby. On the plus side, Reece didn't have some REMF squawking questions in his ear from back at the Tactical Operations Center.

Eli had maneuvered to the back of the building to catch any "squirters" who might head for the hills during the assault. As the most valuable member of the team with medical skills rivaling any ER doctor, keeping him out of the initial entry was the smart call.

Reece noted the surprising lack of security as they approached the entrance under cover of darkness. *Was it possible the intel was correct and the security ele-ment they'd eliminated were the only ones on the island?* The ten dead contractors would fit with the numbers from the Agency target package. Still, Reece had grown skeptical of all intel that was not generated at the tactical level.

They stacked on the door and Chavez took point, finger on the trigger, off safe, with Devan and Edo just behind him. Reece took rear security, giving him the best situational awareness. Had this been a sanctioned mission with the support apparatus that accompanies a Special Mission Unit operation, Edo would have had a small camera attached to his harness allowing Devan to see what was going on inside without committing assaulters. In this case, they didn't know how many people were in the target building and they needed to get to Hanna and Raife before the alert went out that might get them killed. This was an in-extremis hostage rescue operation. Unlike a capture/kill, they would bypass potential threats to get to the hostages. A dog in this situation could end up being a liability but with only four operators they needed Edo to lead them directly to the hostages.

Reece squeezed the back of Devan's left leg, indicating it was time to put Edo to work. Devan reached into his cargo pocket and pulled out a small Ziploc bag. Opening it up he removed a piece of a dirty T-shirt belonging to Raife he'd asked Annika for before they'd left Montana. He would have preferred to have one of Hanna's, but this was the best they could do.

Putting the scent-infused clothing to Edo's nose, Devan whispered in German, "*Revere*," and opened the door.

The entry was not even locked, once again raising the hair on the back of Reece's neck. *Could this be an ambush?* Too late for that. They were committed.

Edo broke the threshold, Chavez entering immediately left, weapon up ready to work. Devan went right, taking his corner and sweeping his rifle back just past the center of the room. Chavez was doing the same. Reece was right behind them, moving left to Chavez's side and taking the center of the room first.

Clear.

They didn't need to speak. Motions and instincts instilled from hundreds of raids and thousands of training exercises made the flow of clearing rooms second nature.

Moving.

Follow the dog.

They moved past the foyer into the great room that was part dining area and part trophy room. Light was beginning to crack the horizon, but the NODs were still the most effective way to penetrate the darkness. The remnants of a fire smoldered in an imposing stone fireplace.

Edo tore through the game room. He'd alerted. Raife was close.

The assaulters followed Edo across the room, their movements smooth, natural; man-hunters in their natural environment.

Focused on the door at the far corner of the room, Reece subconsciously noted the animals that adorned the walls. He shot past a tiger rug in front of the fireplace, moving between a South American jaguar looking down from its perch across from a snow leopard on the opposite wall doing the same. A full-body polar bear guarded the doorway through which Edo led the team. A walrus was mounted just across from the majestic white artic beast.

Does this guy hunt anything that's not endangered? Reece thought. *What an asshole.*

They followed Edo through the door and into a narrow stone staircase leading into darkness.

Reece gave the squeeze and the foursome started to descend, Chavez leading the way, Edo right behind. Reece was last in line, keeping his rifle pointed up toward the door behind them.

The stairs terminated in a locked steel door. Edo had clearly alerted on it and Reece prayed that Hanna was with her brother on the other side.

Reece gave Chavez the signal to breach. Ordinarily they would explosively breach it from the top of the stairs, using the thick walls as protection from the overpressure. In this case, breaching charges were conspicuously missing from the load-out. Chavez slung his weapon and reached behind him for the hooligan tool. Studying the inward-opening door, he cursed to himself, wishing he'd brought along the sledge, but when a small band of operators invade a country from thirty-five thousand feet, you can only bring so much.

Reece, Edo, and Devan backed up a couple of steps to give Chavez room. Whoever was on the other side would know well in advance that they were coming. In a hostage scenario, that was the last thing you wanted. They were giving up the advantage of surprise. Once the door was ajar, they'd double down on violence of action.

Chavez inserted the "hoolie" into the jam and, using its claw, started to pry. The door was solid. The rock wall into which it was built was not. Identifying the weakness, Chavez attacked the area where the locking mechanism met the wall. The stone began to crumble. After a minute, the entrance began to give way. Chavez seized the opportunity and turned the tool around, slamming the duckbill, designed to ram, into the lock again and again. The noise reverberated up the stairway, steel meeting steel, Chavez grunting with exertion as he gave the effort everything he had.

One final swing, and the door flew open on its hinges. Chavez flattened himself against the wall, making room for Devan, Reece, and Edo to make entry. Devan went left and Reece hooked around to the right, clearing his corner and sweeping back past the center of the room.

Silence.

"Clear, right," Reece whispered.

"Clear, left," Devan confirmed.

"Wait, what the . . . ?" Reece said aloud. "Belay that."

Edo had sprinted to the end of the room and was barking at the wall. Only it wasn't. What had at first appeared to be a wall under the alien illumination of the NODs was, in fact, a series of bars, and not just bars: prison cells.

The three operators read the room as a professor of literature would a classic novel. They pushed down the left wall, covering the cells with their weapons, sweeping back and forth across the uncleared area.

Movement.

"Hold fire," Reece commanded. "I'm hitting the light; stand by. Moving."

"Move," Chavez said.

Reece took a few steps into the center of the room, flipped up his NODs, and pulled down on a string attached to a single lightbulb.

The room was sparse, rock floor and walls, solid wood beams across the ceiling.

Eight prison cells were built against the opposite side of the room. The three commandos kept their weapons trained on the unknown, quickly processing the scene. Eight cells. Six occupied. Two unoccupied. No Raife. No Hanna.

The prisoners all huddled in the back corners of their cells, trying to determine if the new intruders were friends or foes.

"Chavez, Devan, clear the rest of the house with Edo. I think it's empty but make sure. Then, Devan, you switch out with Eli. I need him in here ASAP. Take up security with Edo. I'm going to see what intel I can get from these guys. Eli and I will prep them to move. We can't leave them here. We have to assume reinforcements are inbound. This time it's not going to be a few contractors, it's going to be a full-on Russian military response. Take these prisoners to extract. They might be the only witnesses to what's happened here and if this goes public, we will need them to keep us off the noose."

"Hey, boss," Chavez said from the far end of the room. The change in his tone was chilling.

He was standing by a table that had been moved in front of the last cell, a cell that was now empty. A large glass jar almost the size of a water cooler jug was on top.

Reece walked toward it, a sense of dread building the closer he got. Knowing what it was even before he stopped, he knelt down and came face-to-face with Hanna Hastings.

"What are you going to do?" Chavez asked.

Reece felt the hate welling up from the deepest recesses of his soul. He looked from Hanna's upturned eyes to those of his friend and teammate.

"I'm going hunting."

CHAPTER 80

REECE RAN IN SNOWSHOES, finding his rhythm, the Echols Legend rifle cradled in his grasp. He had reloaded with four rounds in its magazine and a fifth in the chamber. Five additional rounds on its cheek pad gave Reece quick access to more ammunition and put his eye at the optimal height behind the scope.

He'd traded his battlefield pickup for his bolt-action Echols because he wanted a tool he was comfortable with if he had to make a long shot. According to the African prisoners in Zharkov's dungeon, the Russian hunter and his accomplice had started tracking Raife when it was still dark, which meant he had at least a two-hour head start. In all likelihood, Reece would have to even up that distance with a bullet.

He'd thought the team might mutiny when he told them he was forging ahead without them. He'd convinced them that with his sniper rifle and with only two targets still in play, he was best equipped to handle them. Reece stressed that they needed to get back to Farkus and it would take the three of them to move him to extract. Two would carry the wounded SEAL and one would be on security while also accounting for the Africans. They'd have to rotate positions as they maneuvered overland to the Albatross and freedom. While all that was true, Reece also knew that anyone who stayed was probably not leaving the island. Going after Raife and Aleksandr meant they would surely miss the extract window. He couldn't live with the deaths of more of his friends and teammates on his conscience. He would continue alone.

Reece had dropped most of his gear for added mobility. He needed to move. His Half Face Hunter-Skinner and Winkler Sayok RnD 'Hawk were on his belt. A SIG P320 Compact was in a Blackpoint Tactical wing holster at his side.

The path was easy to follow. The tracks were from a four-wheel drive built to crawl over the snow- and rock-strewn landscape. The snowshoes kept him from potholing into the deeper patches of snow as he gained elevation. His labored breathing and the howling wind all but eliminated his sense of hearing.

Dawn had broken to an overcast sky. It would be snowing soon. He had to catch up with Raife and Aleksandr before the weather closed in, concealing their tracks.

The jar containing Hanna's head was seared into Reece's memory. The man responsible was at the end of the trail. It was time for him to die.

Reece's peripheral vision caught a blur of white to his right. On instinct born of a warrior's DNA, he pivoted and threw up his left arm to block his face, the dog's teeth sinking into the fabric of his jacket and piercing the skin beneath.

Dog!

Losing his balance on the snowshoes that had just turned from an asset into a liability, he dropped his rifle and spun the massive canine around into the snow. The primal growls of the beast so close to his face flipped a switch in the former commando; his "five-meter target" had just become this animal intent on killing him. Forcing the dog down in the powder, Reece took the mount position, and fired a palm strike against his own arm, slamming his radial bone deep into the dog's mouth to take away the jaw's mechanical advantage and prevent it from shredding his arm to pieces. Having been taught to defend against dogs bred and trained to kill, Reece shot a second palm strike into its sensitive nose before going for his pistol. With his arm blocking the dog's face, Reece raised the SIG toward its brain. The thrashing animal was not accustomed to being on its back, which made an accurate shot difficult even at contact distance. To prevent a pistol stoppage from the mess that the animal's hair, skin, and bones were about to cause, Reece braced his thumb on the back plate and fired one round into its head. Ignoring the instantaneous ringing in his ears from the close shot, Reece pushed clear and struggled to get the awkward snowshoes back under him while attempting to clear his self-induced malfunction from the contact shot.

Before he could rack the slide, the second dog hit him in the ribs, sending the SIG into the snow.

Fuck! How many dogs do these guys have?

As Reece reoriented toward his newest threat, he had another chilling thought: *Where is his handler?*

Reece adjusted to the new, larger dog and tried to rip the snowshoes off his feet. The dog lunged, its sharp teeth finding purchase near Reece's collar bone, ripping with its head but coming away with only bits of jacket.

With one snowshoe now free, Reece swung it at his new aggressor, the terrain and the animal's power keeping the SEAL on his knees as it charged in again. Grabbing for anything he could, Reece pushed one arm into the dog's muscular chest and wrapped his hand around its left leg. Feeling the teeth sink into his shoulder, Reece remembered the weakest part of a multipurpose canine. He grabbed the animal's front legs and snapped them apart like a wish bone, breaking the dog's base. Its primal bark instantaneously became a painful whimper.

Rolling around as he would a human on the jiu-jitsu mats, Reece clinched its head and wrapped his arm around its neck, putting it in an anaconda choke. The dog thrashed and pawed in desperation before depleting the last measure of its strength and going limp in Reece's arms.

Falling to his back, Reece sucked in precious oxygen. He took stock of his injuries while noting how much longer it took to choke out a dog than a human.

The handler! I need to find my SIG.

Reece scrambled to his feet, the one snowshoe still attached to his foot making standing a tougher proposition than usual. Scanning the immediate area, Reece froze. A sound he knew all too well permeated the ringing in his ears: the sound of an action cycling on a bolt gun. He turned toward it and found himself looking at a huge man in skins and furs. He was holding a .300 Winchester Magnum. It was at his hip, pointing directly at Reece.

CHAPTER 81

REECE WATCHED AS THE bear of a man ran the bolt, sending a cartridge into the snow. His face remained expressionless as he cycled the action once more, ejecting another round. He then moved the rifle to his shoulder.

Click.

Reece inadvertently flinched at what had just become the loudest sound in the world: a firing pin going forward on an empty chamber.

The beast smiled as he turned the rifle around and, holding it by its barrel, swung it like a bat, letting it fly off into the snowy tundra.

Reece dropped back to a knee, fumbling with the clasp on the snowshoe in a desperate attempt to free his foot, the monster slowing his approach as if to give Reece time.

The snowshoe free, Reece went for the blade at his belt but was stopped by a spinning back kick, which sent him careening into the ground, hitting his lower back on a rock hidden just beneath the fresh coat of snow.

Who is this guy? A spinning back kick coming with such speed from a man of that size was not a good sign.

He's comfortable here, Reece thought, getting back to his feet and shooting in for a double leg takedown.

His opponent sprawled, then spun to take Reece's back, lifting him up until his hips were over his head, slamming him down like a rag doll.

Reece's face met the snow, which luckily softened the impact.

Sambo, Reece thought. *Russian military.*

His opponent backed off, allowing Reece to start to stand.

He's toying with me.

The Russian then moved in with an agility Reece had not seen in years, taking Reece back down with a scissor sweep, then recovering in the mount position.

Reece covered his face in a vain attempt to block the blows that rained down from above. He heard the Russian laugh, saying something in his native tongue that Reece couldn't understand.

An image of Raife's head in a glass container next to his sister's appeared in Reece's mind.

Reece thrust his hips up, surprising the gigantic Russian and moving him forward. That move gave Reece the space he needed to draw his blade. Twisting up on his left side and scooting right, Reece plunged the sharp steel into the Russian's hip, then slammed his free hand into the back of the hilt to drive it in as far as possible.

Writhing in pain, the Koryak warrior pushed Reece away, giving them both time to stand. A mutual respect for the fighting prowess of the other caused a slight tactical pause. His smile and laughter gone, the Russian drew a large skinning blade from his belt and watched as Reece's right hand moved behind his back, returning with his Winkler RnD 'Hawk in a hammer grip, his left hand still holding Chavez's gift. Both men knew only one of them was leaving this desolate patch of terrain alive.

The sharp weapons felt at home in Reece's hands, the grips designed to offer a hold even when awash in the blood of enemies.

The two fighters moved toward each other, the Russian using his reach to his advantage, attempting to slash at Reece's stomach. The American anticipated the move. Reece's short blade connected with the larger man's arm, drawing a superficial wound. Reece used his momentum to swing the tomahawk at the Russian's head. Sergei evaded by swaying left, ready to press the attack. Recovering from his missed swing, Reece bent his knees to change levels and hooked his ax behind his target's ankle. He yanked back, sweeping the Russian off his feet. Capitalizing on his dominant position, Reece rushed in to destroy his opponent but the Russian threw up his feet and used them along with Reece's momentum to throw the smaller man over his head.

This is why you train, Reece. Push the offensive, capitalize on his first mistake, and kill him.

The native Siberian closed the distance and reentered with a massive downward slash. Reece blocked it by striking his attacker's forearm with the shaft of the tomahawk and, in a move he'd learned studying the Filipino martial arts, hooked his opponent's arm with the beard of the weapon, swinging it down and away. The violent motion ripped his tomahawk down his opponent's arm and through his knife hand in a move known as "disarming the snake."

Sensing the Russian was both surprised and off balance, Reece swung his left hand around and planted his blade squarely in the large man's clavicle. Reece moved off centerline and swept the Russian off his feet, which also inadvertently ripped the knife, still stuck in the Russian's collarbone, from Reece's hand

Finish it.

Leading with the ax, Reece moved to end the fight but was blasted back with a powerful kick from the Russian.

Don't get careless, Reece.

Close the distance, get inside his range. Take that advantage from him.

Pushing the ax head down in his hand into a punch grip, the bottom of the ax head resting on the top of Reece's fist, he squared off again. Sergei entered with a jab.

Mistake.

Reece used his left elbow to guide the punch directly into the spike of the hawk, splitting the Russian's hand in two. Howling in pain, a look of madness in his eyes, Sergei fired a reverse punch at Reece's head with his uninjured hand. Reece covered and crashed in, punching the head of his ax into the Siberian's face, taking off the bottom of his nose and leaving part of his cheek dangling and exposed. The Siberian attempted another futile rage-filled swing, but Reece passed his opponent's arm with the shaft of his ax and darted in to clutch his enemy's head, digging the back spike of the 'Hawk into his neck. Taking his other hand, Reece clinched him close, bumped his hips, and took the huge Russian to the ground, landing with his right knee on his chest.

In full survival mode, Sergei wrapped the ax with his one massive working hand, gripping it for dear life. Unable to use his most formidable weapon, Reece reverted to a palm strike to the side of the Russian's head and followed it with an elbow. Seeing his blade still protruding from his enemy's collarbone, Reece grabbed the exposed hilt and ratcheted it back and forth like a joystick. Primordial screams of pain erupted from the large man as the vicious blade cut deeper. Reece pushed it downward toward the subclavian artery, pleural sack, and the top of the lungs, trying to force a tension pneumothorax.

Sensing what Reece was trying to do, the Russian moved his enormous fist to the SEAL's left hand, which was working the blade into his body. *Another target.* Reece sliced through the Russian's last functional hand. He turned the blade over and pressure-cut across his neck and throat before planting the blade into the left eye socket.

Slippery with blood, Reece drew back the ax and used his hip to bump the ax to a hammer grip. He then raised it and chopped it directly into his adversary's skull. Quickly ripping it free, he continued to cycle full-power blows to the head and neck, driven by a vision of Hanna's upturned eyes, her hair floating around her severed head. In one last attempt at salvation, the giant rolled over, wrapping up Reece's ankle. This exposed his side and back, giving Reece new targets, which he attacked with a vengeance. The SEAL continued his onslaught until the ax severed his antagonist's spinal cord with a strike to the base of the neck.

Exhausted, and steaming from the fluids evaporating into the cold air, Reece sank back on his heels, enveloped in a fog of death.

He closed his eyes and steadied his breathing before kneeling on the Russian's face and ripping the blade from his eye.

There was still work to be done.

CHAPTER 82

ALEKSANDR DELIBERATELY FOLLOWED THE tracks, aware that he was not pursuing a sub-Saharan savage, but a highly trained hunter and man of war. He wouldn't find Rainsford cowering in fear at the end of the trail like he did so many of those imported from the African continent, half frozen to death in a foreign land. No, Rainsford would be thoughtful, he'd be tricky.

Put yourself in his shoes, Aleksandr mused. *Where would you go? What would you do?*

Rainsford was a military man. What did military men the world over do when pressed? They went to the high ground and they flanked, two of the basic tenets of warfare, confirmed time and time again throughout history.

Or, would Rainsford know I know this and do something only an amateur would do because I won't expect it?

Will he be waiting for me in my bedroom when I return tonight?

Look, he's going to the same point where his stupid sister thought she could hide, no doubt hoping the weather would cover her tracks. She hadn't counted on the dogs. Maybe he isn't, either?

Soon enough, I'll put this bolt through your heart, S. Rainsford, and I'll mount your head in a jar right next to your sister's in my sleeping quarters.

. . .

Raife watched his tormenter from the rocks fifty feet above. He'd gone as far he could in the snow, stopping at a place where he could rock climb toward a cave in the side of the cliff. His ruse was intended to make the Russian think he had found refuge there. Instead he had backtracked out until he made his way to a section of the snow- and rock-strewn mountainside that allowed him to leave his trail. He had carefully picked his way up the slope, using rocks, ice, and the occasional exposed root to hide his tracks.

Hope is not a course of action. I know. But sometimes it's all we have.

He watched as the man who hunted him edged closer to the cliff's edge. He could sense the calculations going through his mind, attempting to anticipate Raife's moves.

Raife had seen the contractors, heard the dogs. Without a weapon or proper clothing, his odds of surviving the night were slim. The man below had hunted his sister on this very patch of earth. Raife imagined her terror in those last moments of life, pursued by this madman, his native tracker, and hunting dogs. If he was to avenge her, he might not get another shot.

. . .

Aleksandr's eyes followed the tracks until they left the snow for the rock of the cliff face. He imagined the route Rainsford and his sister had taken to the cave, inching their way across to what they believed was sanctuary.

Was he going to spend the night in there? Was he just getting out of the elements, preparing for the coming storm?

The Russian's eyes slowly moved back from the cave, along the cliff face, to the tracks just to the right of his feet, then back in the direction of his vehicle.

His quick step to the rear probably saved his life. A football-sized rock connected with his shoulder instead of his head, and sent him crashing into the snow.

Rainsford!

My weapon!

Aleksandr scrambled to his knees. Crawling to his crossbow, he brought it to his shoulder, his eye finding the scope as Raife Hastings descended from above in a controlled fall.

• • •

Raife flew down the rock face, his feet finding just enough purchase to direct his movement as he hurled himself toward his sister's killer.

He felt the arrow take him in the right shoulder. Its broad head pierced tissue and penetrated bone, his right arm immediately incapacitated. His target struggled to get to his feet, fumbling with a second bolt from his quiver. Raife's left foot found a solid stone, planted firmly, and launched him into his antagonist, sending both of them over the edge of the precipice.

CHAPTER 83

FIFTEEN FEET TO THE right and they would have both been killed on the jagged rocks. Instead, they went over the edge onto a scree slope just shy of vertical. Raife felt Aleksandr take the brunt of the first hit as his body connected with a protruding rock, sending them careening toward the sea. Raife's face made contact with the earth and he momentarily lost consciousness, his frame briefly becoming a rag doll. He came to as his already-disabled arm shattered against a rock just before he splashed into the knee-deep surf, his leg twisting into an unnatural position with an audible snap.

Before the frigid water could completely take his breath away, Raife pushed himself to a sitting position. Gasping for air and attempting to take stock of his injuries, he wondered what happened to Aleksandr.

"Looks like a compound fracture," a voice in heavily accented Russian said above the cacophony of the surf. "You of all people know that injuries like that almost certainly lead to death in this country. Look around you. No hospital for thousands of miles."

The waves surged in across the rocky beach, and Raife used the one arm that worked to keep his head above the icy froth.

"You were indeed a worthy adversary. Very similar to your sister. She died right here, just up the beach on those rocks. The stupid whore jumped to her death. Killed one of my dogs, with a bone of all things, and then took the other one with her. I never even got a shot off. The pursuit was thrilling, though. So much better than the savages we import for sport. With you, S. Rainsford, I did get a shot off. How's the shoulder? I'm about to get another shot off and add you to my collection."

As he spoke, he used the crossbow's versa-draw system to retract the string and cock the weapon. He then loaded a short arrow from the quiver into the rail and clicked it into position on the bowstring.

"I have bested the *great* SEAL and tracker, S. Rainsford. I am the supreme hunter!"

"You're no hunter. You're nothing but a killer, a sick, demented killer," Raife spat.

Anger flashed in Zharkov's eyes.

"Your friends are all dead by now. No one is coming. Sit up, so I can kill you like a man."

Raife struggled to bring his broken leg under him and get in a sitting position. He was going to face his death head-on. He admired the beauty of the coastline, the rocks and gravel beneath him, the arctic water rushing past. The sounds, the birds, the cliff, reminded him of Kodiak, and he remembered that this was exactly the reason the SEAL training facility had been built there; to mimic these conditions.

"Just remember to watch your back."

"What?"

"Someone is coming for you. Someone who will not stop until he pulls your beating heart from your chest and shows it to you. You are about to find out what it's like to be hunted."

Aleksandr put the crossbow to his shoulder and took aim. In all likelihood the bolt would go right through Raife at this distance, taking out both lungs and the heart; he wanted to preserve the head for his collection. The imperialist Navy SEAL and world-renowned hunter would be his most prized trophy.

"You'll be with your sister in a few seconds. Be sure and tell that *bitch* I said 'fuck you' for killing my dogs. Her head does make an attractive trophy, though."

What was wrong? Aleksandr willed his finger to pull the trigger, but nothing was happening. He tried again, confused. His breathing was heavy, and his head felt like someone was slowing turning down the dimming switch of a lightbulb. He sank to his knees on the gravel beach in front of his quarry, his crossbow falling from his grasp. He looked down to see the wooden shaft of an arrow protruding from the left side of his chest. He admired its craftsmanship, trying to place where he'd seen it before as his body jolted forward, a second shaft appearing alongside the first. Aleksandr gazed at the native arrowheads in an odd mix of wonder and bewilderment, then fell forward into the crashing surf.

"Raife! Raife!"

Reece scrambled down the rocks toward the beach, sliding along with the scree in a semi-controlled descent. He had watched Raife fall to his side and disappear beneath the waves, the powerful undertow dragging him out to sea along with the man who, moments earlier, had him dead to rights.

Reece hit the beach at a dead sprint, the wet pebbles doing their best to impede his progress. He crashed into the surf, arms searching desperately for his friend.

A body.

Reece held tight and heaved it out of the water, turning it over and looking into the open death stare of Aleksandr Zakarov.

Fuck!

Reece pushed the body away, frantically feeling for a second one.

"Come on!"

There!

A shoulder rolling in the surf.

Reece surged toward it as the ocean gave him one last chance.

Got him!

Reece grabbed his friend as another wave surged over them, quickly rushing back out to sea underneath itself and working to bring the two warriors along with it. Reece wrestled through the icy water, looking back at the incoming waves, dragging Raife toward shore. He dug in to resist the undertow, then heaved forward in the brief respite between waves. In knee-deep water, then ankle-deep, Reece continued to hoist his comrade from the current that threatened to pull them into the depths.

Finally, above the relative safety of the low-water mark, Reece scanned the cliffs above for threats before turning his full attention to his friend.

Reece had no idea what had transpired before he sent the two arrows through Zakarov's heart, so he immediately assessed his patient, worried that the cold water could mask a massive arterial bleed. Even through his pant leg, Reece could tell there was something seriously wrong with Raife's leg. His right arm was bent in an unnatural position, the swelling increasing by the second, to say nothing of the arrow shaft that protruded from his shoulder. Reece felt for breathing and a pulse. Pulse was weak. No breathing.

Shit!

"Stay with me, buddy!"

A quick check of Raife's airway confirmed that it was clear, so Reece delivered two quick rescue breaths, watching his friend's chest rise and fall with the lifesaving respiratory assistance. Reece jerked back as Raife's body involuntarily lurched up, his eyes opening wide as his lungs drew in the much-needed oxygen.

Raife's eyes came to focus on the man who had just saved his life. As he returned from the dead, he was hardly able to form his first word: "Zharkov?"

Reece shook his head. "It's done, brother."

Raife closed his eyes and nodded.

"We need to get you off this beach," Reece said, assessing the routes up.

"Get this *fucking* arrow out of me!"

Reece knew he had to do something with the bolt. It had penetrated completely though Raife's shoulder. The razor-sharp broadhead was projecting out his back.

"Turn on your side and try to think of something pleasant."

Reece positioned his friend on his side and carefully unscrewed the arrowhead from the bolt. He then grabbed the shaft from just below the fletchings and, without warning, pulled the carbon intruder from Raife's body.

A heavy grunt was all that escaped the SEAL's lungs.

"That wasn't as bad as I thought," Reece said.

"Speak for yourself. I think my leg's broken. Arm, too."

"I believe you're right," Reece responded, checking Raife's distal and pedal pulses. "Don't go anywhere."

Reece charged up the rocky shore and grabbed two pieces of driftwood, snapping one over his thigh before running back to his patient.

"I'm going to splint these, buddy. No sense in dragging you out of here if the bones are going to grind through those arteries."

Reece attached the thicker makeshift splint to Raife's upper leg, lashing it in place with his tourniquet and belt. He then did the same for Raife's arm, using Zakarov's crossbow sling to secure the improvised splint in place.

"How did you get here? How are we getting out?" Raife asked.

"Your dad and Thorn are coming in with the Albatross. The boys are here, too; Farkus took some shrapnel to the leg. He's in bad shape but Eli, Devan, and Chavez are moving him to extract along with your cell mates. Even Edo made the trip."

"*What?* You invaded Russia?"

"Didn't have much choice. And if we don't make it to extract, we are getting left behind, so let's get you up and out of here."

Raife turned his head to look at the steep scree slope before them.

"I'm really glad you joined me for those workouts. Looks like I'm back to owing you one," Raife said.

"If I make it to the top of this hill, you will. Up you go," Reece said as he grabbed the larger man by the wrist and leg, rolling him up and into a fireman's carry.

One step at a time, Reece.

CHAPTER 84

REECE PUSHED THE SIX-WHEELED off-road vehicle through the falling sleet. Raife kept drifting in and out of consciousness in the second row of seats. Without a GPS to guide him, Reece drove toward the rising sun just visible as a lighter section of the horizon, hidden behind a gray wall of clouds. They were two hours late for extract and Reece knew the odds of getting off this island with his friend were minuscule.

They had launched with too little information and broke the cardinal rule of mission planning: they had no secondary or tertiary plan for extract. Everything hinged on making it to the Albatross, which Thorn would pilot as close to the wave tops as possible until hitting international airspace. Russian technology remained encapsulated in the late 1980s, which gave them a slim chance.

Never tell me the odds.

The weather was turning for the worse. If Thorn and Jonathan had delayed extract it was likely they were all trapped on the island with no means of escape.

Reece rounded a bend and turned the wheel right, leaving what passed for a road and going directly for the Bering Sea, a horseshoe-shaped cove visible through the windshield. It looked protected enough from the weather; it would be possible to get a plane in and out. The only thing missing was the plane.

Reece slammed on the brakes as a lone figure stepped into their path fifty yards ahead, a Belgian-made FAL rifle pointed directly at them.

Reece managed to find the door handle and pushed it open, showing his empty hands to the old gunfighter before exposing his head and identifying himself to Raife's father.

The old man lowered his rifle and charged toward the vehicle.

"What the *bloody* hell? Where's Raife?"

Reece paused and closed his eyes.

"Raife's in the back, sir. He's pretty banged up. I think a broken arm and a bad leg break. Probably a concussion. If we don't get him medical attention, he's not going to make it."

The old man's eyes bore straight through the younger commando in front of him, the same green eyes as his son, asking the question without saying the words. *What happened to my daughter?*

"Eli told me, Reece. He told me Hanna is dead."

Reece's eyes filled with emotion. "I'm sorry, sir. We were too late."

Jonathan was a man accustomed to the loss that comes from a lifetime of war in the African bush, but now the old man felt a new and awful emptiness move into his soul. He'd left the death, the executions, the genocide, and the torture behind on the Dark Continent and even so, the darkness had found him. Now his youngest was gone. Her wild spirit was free.

"Jonathan," Reece said in a measured tone. "We have to get out of here. How long ago did the plane leave?"

The usually stoic old warrior swallowed hard. He'd aged a decade since Montana.

"Jonathan!"

"They left an hour ago. Thorn, Farkus, Devan, Eli, and Chavez, along with the prisoners. Farkus wasn't doing well. Those crazy bastards all wanted to stay but I wouldn't hear of it. They'd done enough. If my son and daughter weren't leaving this island, then I wasn't, either. I couldn't go home without my children. They could go home to theirs."

"Attu Island is our only way out. It's directly east. Load up."

"What are you going to do, lad? Drive there?"

"There has got to be a way to communicate in that lodge. These Russians had working night vision, which means they had a secure area where whatever they hit us with to take out our electronics wouldn't penetrate. We need to find it and reach the naval base on Attu."

"No one is going to send the Coast Guard to invade Russia and rescue us. We're a band of mercenaries. Thorn and the team are probably getting locked up as we speak. I saw it in Africa, Reece. No one is coming but Russians. I plan on taking as many as I can with me before I go."

Reece nodded in understanding. He had wanted to die when his wife and daughter were taken from him, and he'd wanted to kill as many of those responsible before he went down. He opened his mouth to argue, but another voice broke through the sub-Siberian air, an American voice with no hint of a Russian accent.

"Drop your weapons or die."

CHAPTER 85

REECE AND JONATHAN INSTINCTIVELY went to a knee as three dark dry-suit-clad commandos holding M4 carbines converged on their position.

"Names!" the unknown voice commanded.

"Fuck you," Jonathan hissed.

Reece pushed his FAL toward the ground.

"It's okay," Reece said before directing his attention to the new threat. "I'm James Reece. I'm here with Raife and Jonathan Hastings."

"I'd ask you the word of the day, but I'm sure you don't know it," the man who was obviously in charge said as he moved in closer, lowering his rifle. "I'm Lieutenant Kevin O'Malley, SDV Team One. You guys must be pretty important to divert us from a ███████████████"

██

██

██

██

██

███

"We've got a man down in the back of the truck," Reece said, moving to his feet. "He can't walk and needs a medic. Multiple EKIA are down. I don't think there are any others, but Russian military is probably inbound."

"Oh, they're inbound all right," the SEAL leader confirmed.

"Charlie-zero-one to Nautilus, I pass TOUCHDOWN. I say again, TOUCH-DOWN," the platoon commander said into his OSK headset. Then, hitting a push-to-talk attached to what Reece recognized as an L3Harris AN/PRC-163 handheld radio, he said, "Charlie one-one, call in the z-birds, and send Spanky up; we've got a nonambulatory friendly here."

O'Malley put out his hand. "Nice to meet you, sir. I've heard a lot about you. Not sure what you're doing in Russia, but whatever it is, we are here to get you out."

The team's medic emerged out of the morning light and climbed into the odd-looking 6x6 to assess his patient.

"What happened?" he asked as his hands checked for a pulse and worked his way down Raife's body.

"He took a tumble off a cliff and nearly drowned," Reece replied. "That was after he was shot with a crossbow. Is he going to make it?"

"He's hypothermic. He's breathing and has strong distal pulses, but these displaced compound fractures have me worried. Starting IV. Need to get him to the IDC. We need to extract *now*," the medic directed at his platoon commander.

O'Malley turned back to Reece. "Sir, we have got to get you off this beach. We have a JMAU SRT standing by. He'll be in good hands. The extract platforms are on their way. They might be a little different than the ones you used. Sub is waiting for us four nautical miles out."

"What? How did you know where we were?"

"Above my pay grade," O'Malley said, clearly not sure what he was allowed to divulge. "All I know is that this is an Agency-directed op. We have a Maritime Branch liaison on the sub with us who helped coordinate."

A change in the tone of the surf caused Reece to pick his head up.

"That's our ride," O'Malley said in response to Reece's questioning look.

The two Zodiacs, or Combat Rubber Raiding Craft, that emerged out of the fog looked more akin to stealth fighters than the z-birds Reece had used in the Teams.

"Times change," O'Malley said before keying his mic. "Chief, we need a couple guys to help carry. Time to load up."

Two SEALs wearing dark green dry suits materialized from the perimeter and two more maneuvered up the beach from the black Zodiacs. One carried a SKEDCO Tactical SKED that he transformed into a stretcher in the center of the perimeter. They all assisted the medic in moving Raife's broken and unconscious body from the vehicle and strapped him into the green flexible plastic stretcher, IV bag on his chest.

Reece grabbed a handle and heard O'Malley say, "Moving," into his radio.

They patrolled toward the ocean, toward freedom, the naval commandos bracketing the stretcher in a tight diamond formation with weapons up looking for threats. As they reached the surf zone Reece could see that their extraction platforms were very similar to the Zodiacs he'd used in the Teams, but had what looked to be a radar-deflecting or absorbing shell over the top to eliminate or reduce radar signature. The engines were muffled or possibly even electric to reduce sound.

The naval commandos turned the boats so the bows were pointed back out to sea in a well-practiced maneuver. They loaded from the front as the helmsman timed the waves, waiting for everyone to climb aboard, judging his opportunity to race through the breakers.

As they loaded Raife into their extract platform, Reece turned to Jonathan and over the sound of the cascading surf pulled him close: "I'm not coming with you."

"What the *bloody* hell?"

"My mission's not over. You go. Get home to Caroline. Mourn your daughter. Take care of Raife. Also, I need you to talk with Thorn and have him get in touch with Vic Rodriguez at the CIA. It is imperative that he lets the Agency think I made it back with you through official channels. The Russians can't think I'm still here."

"Get in the boat, you *bloody* idiot!" Jonathan shot back.

"The man who killed my father is here, not on Medny, but he's close. And I know where."

Overhearing the conversation, Lieutenant O'Malley turned, the angry sea surging around his waist, the other operators looking impatiently at their senior officer.

"Sir, my orders are to bring you back. We can't have an American captured dead or alive on Russian soil!"

"Don't worry, Lieutenant, I have a history of doing things like this."

"You'll never leave here alive, son." Jonathan's demeanor changed as he unslung his FAL and handed it to the former frogman.

"If that's true, I want you to tell Katie something for me."

"What's that?"

"Semper."

With that, Reece turned and sprinted back up the beach.

CHAPTER 86

Siberia, Russian Far East
Winter

AS WINTER SETTLED UPON the harsh land, a rumor began to swirl among the villages of the Krasnoyarsk Krai. A ghost was moving across the tundra, sometimes taking the shape of the animals that inhabited the wilderness. Some of the stories described him as half man and half beast. Still others were sure one of the brown bears that inhabited the interior had killed a nomadic hunter, merging their souls. The stories were passed along in the way they had since the first peoples had moved into this land, following the herds that gave them sustenance.

The ghost would occasionally steal food and supplies from villages along his path, always a gift left in exchange. No one knew his destination, but it was rumored he was heading west, toward what or whom, was unknown.

Mothers maintained an attentive eye on their children, keeping them closer than usual. Fathers and hunters took an extra minute to pause and study the landscape before closing their doors at night.

Once a village heard a gunshot in the distance. Even specters had to eat.

A native kayak had been found by children playing on the peninsula. It had been dragged into the tree line. Its owner was nowhere to be found. A motorcycle had disappeared in Elita and the phantom had stolen a snowmobile in Tanzybey. When the men of the settlement caught up with it, it was abandoned and empty of gas. An offering of fresh meat was on the seat as payment, tracks of native snowshoes leading off into the snow. The men knew better than to track an apparition, wearing snowshoes or not. That would not end well. It was best not to meddle in the ways of the spirit world.

The wise old men of the villages believed the hunter was caught between this world and the next. He was on a journey and wouldn't rest until it was done.

Village to village the rumor spread, some leaving offerings to the spirit as he drifted across the land: flour, smoked fish, sugar.

On he went, passing villages and settlements; in his natural element, moving toward his target.

He had never felt so free.

There was only the hunt.

CHAPTER 87

Krasnoyarsk Krai, Russia
Six months later

REECE HAD SPENT DAYS watching from his hide-site in the hillside. The animal skins kept him warm and the marmot jerky he'd most recently dried nourished his body. He knew he'd lost weight and muscle mass moving over two thousand kilometers across Siberia, hunting for the man who had killed his father.

Hate kept him warm. Thoughts of Katie, his homeland, his future, were buried.

He had built fires when he was able, slept in snow caves or debris shelters, and kept moving. One step at a time. Always forward.

He used the FAL sparingly. The bow became his primary weapon for the procurement of food; he preferred it that way.

He traveled as the ancient hunter-gathers had moved; nomads following the migrating herds, foraging as they went in a constant struggle to survive. Reece had a different purpose that pushed him forward. A violent nomad, he had a mission: death.

He knew they'd come. The Mi-8 circled and landed on the gravel HLZ just outside the main house. An older man emerged from the helicopter first, the lead from the advance detail running to the chopper door to escort him and his guest to the relative warmth of the dacha.

Then came the little man. At this distance a positive identification was not possible, but Reece was not working within the confines of the law. Reece knew. The small man bundled up against the cold was his prey: the traitor Oliver Grey.

Reece would watch for another day and then make his move.

• • •

"Oliver, why do you keep looking out that window?" Ivan Zharkov asked, looking up from the stove. He preferred to cook for himself when he was at the dacha; it reminded him of his humble beginnings. His children had missed the struggle of the early days and that saddened him. While he had been forged through adversity, his children had grown up with the trappings of wealth, which bred a softness. All except Aleksandr, whose sickness had been his downfall.

"There's not even a fence out there, *Pakhan.*"

"That is because Siberia is our fence. Even the native people only infringe on the very edges, superstitious about the event that gave us this beautiful land."

Oliver had known about what the world termed the Tunguska Event and had heard Zharkov tell of his connection to the area many times. The old man was fascinated with it.

"The indigenous Evenks and Yakuts believe a deity sent a fireball as a warning. It was one they heeded. It destroyed two thousand square kilometers, Oliver. Those that didn't initially believe were convinced afterward when the sky glowed for days."

"Did they ever figure out what it was?" asked Oliver, knowing there had been numerous theories and speculation over the years.

"There was no crater. Some think it was a meteor that disintegrated before impact, the soft ground devouring its remains, absorbing its power. Others say it was an underground volcano. It may have been a comet, its ice becoming part of the land. I've even heard that it could have been a small black hole colliding with earth. No one really knows. Over a hundred and ten years later it remains the largest recorded impact event in recorded history and nobody knows what it was. Regardless, we are in the epicenter of that event. Everything for eight hundred miles in every direction was destroyed except for right here. Those trees are all that are left," he said gesturing out the large windows before him. "Like the Genbaku Dome at the epicenter of the Hiroshima bomb the Americans dropped on Japan, those trees are all that remain. We too shall remain, Oliver. With the changing tides of geopolitics, the *bravta* will remain."

"I think you should still have additional security measures in place, *Pakhan*. If James Reece comes, our guards won't stop him."

"Oliver, how many times must we discuss this? Our source in the United States confirms that James Reece is in Maryland. I have people watching the airports, train stations, shipyards. All ports of entry have his facial recognition data in their systems. He won't set foot inside Mother Russia without us knowing. He did take care of a rather nasty problem for me. Aleksandr is no longer a threat, planning to push the old lion out of the pride. My other children are enjoying their spoiled lives as the progenies of a Russian oligarch. There is nothing but tundra and wild animals in every direction."

"James Reece is not going to let me go, *Pakhan*."

Oliver diverted his attention back out the windows that overlooked the helipad. Lights from the generators illuminated all sides of the compound. Beyond that was darkness.

Stirring the borscht on the stovetop, Zharkov continued: "Do you know what would have happened had that impact event occurred just four hours later?"

Oliver turned back to his new mentor, his brain searching for an answer.

"Think about it, Oliver. The rotation of the earth would have centered the hit on my very home city of St. Petersburg. In 1908, the capital of the Empire would have been destroyed. I would have never existed. In all likelihood there would have been no Soviet Union. The German army would not have had an eastern front to contend with and would have been able to put all efforts into defeating the Allies in the West. No Cold War. It would be a different world."

As one of the most powerful men in Russia, Zharkov drew strength from what he considered a sacred place. Oliver was not so sure. He would have much rather been at one of the more opulent dachas on the Black Sea, where the other oligarchs chose to invest their considerable wealth, and where Zharkov's broods enjoyed the fruits of their father's labor. But Oliver was not in a position to dictate the schedule to the head of the Brotherhood.

The pleasant smell of the red beetroot soup calmed him. He turned his eyes outward from the epicenter of what had been a fifteen-megaton explosion, out from the heart of *bratva* power, toward the blackness, wondering what was beyond it.

· · ·

Reece had counted nine total: the three in the advance team who had been dropped off two days prior and the three that arrived with Zharkov and Grey. That plus the pilot made nine.

Reece didn't factor in the odds of one man against nine. He'd faced worse. He only knew he was going to kill them all.

· · ·

The explosion threw Oliver to the floor. In a panic he looked to his benefactor, who gripped the stove with a wild excitement in his eyes.

Had the gods returned to Krasnoyarsk Krai?

Two men from Zharkov's security element immediately entered the room. Ensuring their principal was alive, they took positions away from the windows, holding their AKMs at the two entrances to the room with the senior man shouting into his radio. They wouldn't dare push the leader of the *bratva* to the ground, though they all knew that is where he should be.

"*Pakhan*," the man who had just been on his radio said as he moved to the side of his boss, "there's been an explosion at the front of the dacha. It destroyed the truck and killed Grigori, Misha, and Viktor."

Nikolay Khristenko had been GRU before being lured into the world of organized crime. He had been to the dacha many times with Zharkov and though he did not believe in the superstitions surrounding the area, it had always made him feel uneasy.

"What was it?"

"We don't know, *Pakhan,* but we need to move you to a more secure location."

"*Da,*" the elder mafioso said, and nodded, though Nikolay suspected he would rather stay and find out if the fireball from the heavens really did come from a supernatural source.

"*Pakhan,* we have to leave," a terrified Oliver pleaded as he scampered toward the relative safety of the stove.

Zharkov looked at the former CIA man and to his head of security. He then decided their fate.

• • • •

Reece had waited until he had as many of Zharkov's security personnel in the kill zone as possible before detonating the explosives. He'd emplaced the MON-50 devices two weeks earlier after watching the empty dacha for three days to ensure it was unoccupied. Reece had taken a foreign weapons course years ago and was familiar with the antipersonnel device developed in the former Soviet Union and exported around the world. Its green body was easy to camouflage in the tundra turned soft by the melting snow. It had been set for use against him and his team on Medny Island, where Reece had collected it before beginning his journey westward into the interior. It worked precisely as designed, destroying the Laplander vehicle parked out front and ripping half of Zharkov's security detail to shreds.

• • •

If one was not going to walk, there was only one way out of Krasnoyarski Krai, and its rotors were already beginning to turn.

"*Idti! Idti!*" *Go! Go!* Nikolay shouted as the turbines of the Mi-8 spooled up, ushering his boss and his underling toward their extraction platform.

The youngest man on the detail knelt by the helo, weapon pointed out into the unknown.

. . .

Reece knew he had to work quickly. The FAL was not equipped with a suppressor, which meant that its muzzle flash would be visible to the security detail.

Prioritize the threats.

The fore end of the stock was nestled securely on the leather satchel he had carried first through Kamchatka and across the Sea of Okhotsk and then on to the mainland, and then by foot across Siberia. The fire from the still-burning Laplander off-road truck he'd destroyed moments earlier provided just enough illumination for him to use his iron sights. Covered in the mossy green tundra that had once absorbed the most powerful impact event in modern history, his position was located outside the ring of the light. Fire had once provided safety to those who stood within its sphere, warding off tigers, leopards, and bears. Now that light from the burning vehicle was the death knell for those it illuminated.

Six targets. Only five bullets remained.

As the group of four men arrived at the helicopter door, Reece's finger depressed the trigger.

His first bullet caught a man kneeling by the helo directly between the nose and mouth, showering the rear security in brain particles. Before his AKM could answer, two 7.62x51 rounds from Reece's rifle took him in the upper chest just above his body armor and sent him crashing into the front of the helo and onto the cold ground.

Seeing men falling around his helicopter, the pilot yanked up on the collective and increased pitch even before his passengers had boarded the aircraft.

Nikolay shouted over the chaos, beckoning the pilot to return the bird to the ground. He'd be executed later for his insolence and cowardice.

Nikolay then watched in horror as the pilot's body contorted violently, the helo just eight feet off the ground.

. . .

Reece's last two rounds had entered under the pilot's right arm, tearing through his body before exiting through the glass on the opposite side of the helicopter. The pilot lurched forward against the stick as a bloody froth erupted from his mouth and nostrils, inadvertently pushing down on the collective and sending the chopper in a violent left spin. The rotors tore up the gravel walkway, the sounds of metal thrashing against the earth permeating the taiga before the giant bird cartwheeled into the dacha.

Nikolay pushed his principal to the ground as the machine collided with the wood structure. He knelt and let loose with a fully automatic burst from the Russian rifle he knew so well.

• • •

Reece waited in the prone position, his rifle now a useless piece of metal without the ammunition to sustain it. He watched the Russian take Zharkov to the ground and fire in the general direction of where he perceived the threat to be. As he brought the AKM into his workspace to change magazines, Reece stood, drew the ancient weapon that had been his constant companion since leaving Medny Island, and sent an arrow into the left eye socket of Zharkov's head of security.

• • •

Oliver Grey gawked in horror at the wooden shaft protruding from Nikolay's head, visible in the dancing light that escaped from the burning helicopter and vehicle. Imagining a similar fate for himself, he turned to run, tripping and falling to the rocks.

"Stop, Oliver," his benefactor commanded, himself rising to his feet and brushing himself off. "Let us meet our tormentor face-to-face, shall we?"

Was this man mad? He couldn't believe this was a supernatural deity, could he? Those were gunshots, for Christ's sake. And the object sticking out of Nikolay's face was an arrow!

Oliver's attention shifted from the arrow to the darkness outside the ring of fire as one of the shadows began to shift.

• • •

James Reece took a step forward. He'd been covered by the peat moss of the tundra for close to three days, the skins he'd stolen from native villages and others he'd tanned with the brains of animals he'd killed en route, creating an insulated makeshift burrow. His muscles were stiff from the patient act of lying in wait for his prey. He left the FAL where it was. Out of ammunition, now just a vestige of his odyssey, a link to his past. He slipped the tomahawk from its sheath on his belt and felt its weight in his hand. It felt right. Slinging his bow into the skin sheath on his back, he walked into the light.

• • •

Oliver did as he was told and pushed himself to his feet, looking from Ivan to the shape-shifting shadow that emerged from the wilderness. At first Oliver wondered if perhaps Zharkov's conjecture was not as far off as it had first seemed. Perhaps deities really did roam the tundra guarding it from intruders?

What emerged looked half human, half beast and it wasn't until the flickering flame caught the creature just right that Oliver saw it was a man. He was covered in animal skins as if he'd taken on their very essence. When the light caught his eyes, Oliver recognized the look of resolve. His executioner had arrived.

"James Reece," the Russian mafia boss began, almost in disbelief. "I see my source in D.C. has been compromised."

Even though the specter of the former SEAL had been his constant companion for months, Oliver never imagined that his killer would take the form that appeared before him.

Reece took a moment before responding, his mouth and lungs not accus-

tomed to forming words after not having spoken in the six months since he'd
left Medny Island.

"I'd say that's a safe assumption," he said. The words were raspy, akin to
starting an old car left idle for too long.

Oliver remained silent, his eyes now focused on the evil-looking tomahawk
in Reece's hand.

The elder Russian's gaze recognized the pelt of the great Siberian brown
bear that now adorned the phantom before him.

"And you walked across Siberia to kill us?" he asked.

"Yes."

"Remarkable," the elder man, said shaking his head. "Before you do, allow
me to thank you for putting my son out of his misery. I should have done it myself years ago, but blood, you see. Difficult business."

"You just allowed Aleksandr to play his sick games on Medny?"

"He was a very highly placed asset in Russian intelligence, and he was family. More of an arrangement of necessity. If transporting a few prisoners to Kamchatka who would have otherwise been executed in the African dirt was the
price to pay for controlling a percentage of the diamond and uranium trade, and
keeping a source in the Foreign Intelligence Service, then so be it. Sadly, he did
have designs on my position, and I fear would have expedited my demise had
you not come along."

Reece shifted his eyes to his new target, the man who had killed his father.
The man who had one piece of information Reece needed.

How could this little, balding, frightened, potbellied man have killed
Thomas Reece? *Don't underestimate him.*

"You have something that belongs to me," Reece said.

The smaller man's shaking hand moved to his wrist and removed a stainless steel watch, holding it out toward his judge, jury, and executioner.

Reece stepped forward and took possession of his father's Rolex. He slid
his thumb across its worn face before dropping it into the sheath with his bow.

"Nizar the sniper. Nizar Kattan. The Syrian. Where is he?"

Oliver sensed an opportunity. He might just live through this night if he played his cards right.

"I don't know."

"Then you are of no use to me," Reece responded, raising the tomahawk.

"*Wait! Wait!* I didn't say I couldn't find him. He was part of Andrenov's network, through General Yedid, both of whom you killed, I believe?"

"Keep talking."

Oliver acted as though he were deep in thought.

"It will take some doing. He is a freelancer now, but I know his protocols and patterns. I can find him for you, but I can't do that if I'm dead."

Reece lowered the 'Hawk. The traitor before him had killed his father using a proxy, stabbing him to death on the streets of Buenos Aires. He'd betrayed his country and helped set up a chemical attack on Odessa, the assassination of the Russian president, and the attempted assassination of the president of the United States. This same traitor just might be the only link to the Syrian sniper who had put a bullet through Reece's friend as Freddy had thwarted the assassination attempt on the U.S. president. The only reason Freddy was in the path of the assassin's bullet was Reece. Reece was responsible. Reece needed to find Nizar and put him down. He owed that to Freddy and to Freddy's wife and children, perhaps even to himself.

His decision made, Reece turned back to Zharkov, a cold breeze picking up and fanning the flames still smoldering in the driveway.

"And what of us then?" Reece asked the elder Russian.

"Yes, what of us?" Zharkov responded. "He killed your father. You killed my son. Very Shakespearian."

"Only in that it is all a tragedy," Reece acknowledged.

"By killing my son, you saved my life, Mr. Reece. Allow me to repay the favor. Allow me to offer you safe passage out of Russia."

Reece looked at the old man quizzically.

"Come, Mr. Reece. How did you expect to get home? Walk back across Siberia and kayak across the strait?"

"The thought had crossed my mind."

"You can't be serious."

"It's been done before."

"That it has. As sick as my son was, he had friends in Russian intelligence. Friends who would not take kindly to an American invasion of the motherland, or the killing of one of their senior intelligence officers, *Bravta* connected or otherwise. If they suspect you are still in Russia, they will find you."

"So, in exchange for your life you get me out of Russia?"

"Yes. We will use the satellite phone inside to call in another helo. My network will get you to the Black Sea and from there you will board a flight to the Central African Republic. I'm afraid I can't do much more for you from there. You will have to make contact with the Americans at their embassy in Bangui. You will be on your own at that point, but you will be alive."

Reece took a moment to take stock of the situation and then slowly nodded.

"I want to discuss something with you privately," Reece said to the head of Russian organized crime.

"Oliver, go to the house to get the sat phone. Mr. Reece and I have additional business."

Happy to still be breathing, Oliver said, "Yes, *Phakan*," and limped toward the main home.

Reece remained quiet, watching Oliver Grey move up the gravel walkway. Memories of his father raced through his mind: road trips in their old Wagoneer, hikes in the Northern California redwoods, canoeing the boundary waters, fishing the Taylor, and learning to live in harmony with the land out of their trapper's cabin in Alaska. He thought of the three of them, mother, father, and son, holding hands around the dinner table, saying grace over a meal of wild game.

"What was it you wanted to discuss, Mr. Reece?" interrupted Zharkov.

• • •

Oliver was nearing the back door to the house. He would make a call on the sat phone before bringing it out to the old man, informing Zharkov's security forces that an American was holding them hostage and that he should be shot as soon as reinforcements arrived regardless of what Zharkov was about to tell them. The old man was under duress and was being threatened with death by the crazy American.

Yes, that would work. James Reece was just as stupid as his father.

"Grey!" Oliver heard the American call out.

The former CIA man turned and looked back down the slight hill toward the man who moments before had held his life in his hands.

Reece reached into his pocket and pulled out a small oblong box and held it above his head. A wire led from the box to the ground at his feet, angling up toward the dacha.

"I changed my mind."

Reece depressed the detonator on the last Russian Claymore, sending an electrical charge to the imbedded blasting cap, detonating 700 grams of RDX, which explosively propelled 485 short steel rods at 4,000 feet per second through what had less than a second before been Oliver Grey.

The explosion that sent Grey to the afterlife took the aging mafia boss by surprise. He recovered quickly and looked back to Reece.

"And then there were two," Zharkov quipped. "He had just outgrown his usefulness."

Reece chose his next words carefully: "Mr. Zharkov, I have a proposal for you."

"I am listening."

"Get me out of Russia. To CAR. I'll find my way home from there. In the meantime, I want you looking into everything you can find on Nizar Kattan, the Syrian sniper who helped take out President Zubarev last year. You must still have contacts at the SVR. Use them. Get me something actionable."

"Don't you have the CIA?"

"Nizar was employed by a Russian through a Syrian proxy. I think you might have better access."

"And what do I get out of this little agreement?" asked the Russian, ever the dealmaker.

Reece looked at the tomahawk in his hand.

"In the short term, I won't skin you alive. Longer term, you will have a back-channel connection to the CIA."

"Are you offering to spy for me, Mr. Reece?"

"No. I am offering you a way to contact me. I'll run any request you have up the chain but know that even that access could be extremely valuable to you and your organization."

"And if I don't agree?"

"Then there's my short-term fix," Reece said, giving the Winkler Sayoc a spin in his palm.

"You Americans are too trusting, Mr. Reece. How do you know I won't agree and just have you killed when my detail arrives or change my mind a month from now and send hit teams to kill you wherever you are?"

"Because you are a practical man. I killed your son for you, and this alliance will help us both. If you have your men kill me, I have a friend who is even better in the woods than I am. Your son killed his sister. Put her head in a bottle of formaldehyde. He'll finish you off and, trust me, he won't be as kind about it as I would be. And, if you betray me later, I found you once in the middle of Siberia. Don't think I can't or won't do it again. I kind of like it out here."

The elder Zharkov weighed his options.

"I accept your offer, Mr. Reece. My son was a killer. We are hunters. I give you my word that no harm will come to you. I will guarantee your safe passage as far as Africa. From there you are on your own."

"And, Ivan, if you fuck me, I'll track you down and kill you in your own kitchen. Not only that, I'll kill your sons. All of them. I will erase the Zharkov name from existence. Your legacy will be that an American wiped your bloodline from the earth."

EPILOGUE

"Deep in the forest a call was sounding . . ."

Jack London, *The Call of the Wild*

Baltimore, Maryland

REECE WAITED ON A darkened section of street, rain pelting his rented Chevy Tahoe half a block down from the long-term storage facility in Baltimore, Maryland. The engine was on to keep the defroster working but his lights were off. The facility was ringed in barbed wire and security cameras; signs advertised a guard. He observed the entrance for an hour. No one came or went. It was open 24/7 if you had the right keys and an ID. Reece had waited until well after midnight to cut down on the number of people he might encounter. In this part of the city that didn't necessarily make it safer, but Reece wanted to be alone.

He'd been back in the States for six weeks, debriefing at an off-site CIA annex in Northern Virginia. They needed him close by as they figured out what to do. A team of American mercenaries—well, technically not mercenaries as none of them had accepted payment—had invaded a sovereign country and killed the Russian deputy director of their Foreign Intelligence Service, who just happened to be the son of the head of one of the most powerful organized crime syndicates in Russia. One of these mercenaries had stayed behind and traveled deep into the interior, killing an American defector from the Central Intelligence Agency. Everything was being kept very low-key as the CIA and executive branch figured out how best to play it.

The Associated Press had picked up a story of the slaying of a Russian intelligence official that first appeared in the Moscow daily *Rossiyskaya Gazeta* and on television from the state-owned news agency Novosti. The mafia-related assassination received little mention from U.S.-based mainstream media, who were all much more concerned with the circus surrounding the upcoming presidential election.

Receiving even less attention was the admission of a red-haired male to a level 2 trauma center in Anchorage with a mysterious piece of shrapnel in his leg. Alaskans were notorious for serious injuries that came as a matter of course as a result of the inherently dangerous professions that drew people to America's forty-ninth state. The emergency surgery that saved his life was even covered under Tri-Care.

In a not-so-random visit, the White House log indicated that the day the mercenaries departed for Russia, the director of Central Intelligence made an unscheduled 3:00 a.m. visit to the president's residence. A meeting took place in the Situation Room, a meeting in which only two people were present. It lasted thirty minutes. The next hour, an *Ohio*-class special operations capable SSGN submarine was diverted from a national tasking off North Korea and positioned off the coast of Russia. Because of the sensitivities that enshroud the subsurface fleet, this move went unnoticed and unreported by military and intelligence watchdogs.

In the weeks since Reece's return, prominent D.C. lobbyist Grant Larue had mysteriously gone missing at the same time the president's chief of staff, Reginald Pyne, had resigned, citing personal reasons. Journalists and conspiracy theorists had yet to connect the two events.

True to his word, Ivan Zharkov had used his illicit network to deposit Reece on a dusty airstrip in the Central African Republic. The CIA chief of station in Bangui was more than a little surprised when an American who looked like a homeless mountain man appeared at the front gate. Calls were made, bona fides were confirmed, and Reece found himself on a secure video teleconference with Vic Rodriguez. To the director of Clandestine Services' agitated and probing inquisition, Reece simply answered, "Just get me home, Vic."

Police sirens stirred Reece from his reverie, the blue and red flashing lights screaming by on the way to yet another call. Reece turned on the lights and put his SUV in drive, approaching the front gate and waving to the guard who manned the facility from behind a horizontal sliding barrier.

The guard hit a button and the iron gate rolled out of the way, allowing Reece to inch forward.

"Can I help you?"

"I'm looking for container 1855. I haven't been here in years. Can you tell me where it is?"

"Name?"

"Thomas Reece."

The guard scrolled through a database, confirming that Thomas Reece had a container in the storage facility and that he was fully paid up. Finding everything in order, he asked for Reece's ID.

Reece pushed the ID through the open window of his vehicle, intentionally holding his finger over the first name.

The guard yawned, consulted a map, and drew a circle on it before handing it to Reece and pointing into the labyrinth. "Take your first right and then the next left. It'll be about halfway down."

"Thank you," Reece said.

The lone guard nodded and went back to a night of monitoring security cameras, drinking lukewarm coffee, and eating stale donuts left over from the day shift.

Reece drove slowly past row upon row of storage units until he found himself parked outside number 1855.

When his mother had passed away, the last of his family's belongings had been sent to Katie's father. The Buraneks were listed as the next of kin after Reece. Because Reece was believed to be dead, three boxes had eventually been shipped from his mother's nursing home closet to Dr. Buranek, who ultimately sent them to Katie to give to Reece.

Katie had been none too pleased when Reece turned up at the U.S. embassy in the Central African Republic six months after she had seen him off. When he had not returned, both Raife and Jonathan had paid her a visit. They had been smart enough to call ahead so Katie wouldn't think they were arriving to give her the news that Reece was dead. She'd lived that nightmare once before.

Reece thought he would be welcomed back with open arms but found, much to his dismay, that Katie was pissed. Though the making up had been worth it, they decided that Reece should have his own place as he was debriefed at Langley and figured out his next move. Rodriguez wanted him full-time at the Agency, but Reece needed time. Time to figure out this next chapter in life; his next mission. *Purpose*.

Reece had waited until he was alone to unpack the boxes of memories from the nursing home. As he worked his way through old family photos and mementos from happier times, he'd come across a cigar box containing some military photographs from Vietnam, his dad's DD214, the paperwork everyone who has served in uniform since 1950 has received upon discharge from active duty, and an envelope containing a key. An address was printed on the envelope, the address of the storage facility.

Reece stood in the pouring rain outside the storage container and rubbed the key in his hand. The journey that had started with the death of his father in a back alley of Buenos Aires was finally over. The miles logged and bodies stacked since that pivotal moment had chiseled Reece into the warrior he was today. Why, as he stood in the rain looking down at the key, did he not feel a sense of closure? The man behind his father's death and the killing of Freddy Strain was now in the ground, just fertilizer for the Siberian tundra. The traitor's death begot life.

Looking right and left for threats, Reece carefully inspected the corners of the roll-up door with a handheld light, then checked the area around the lock before kneeling down to work the brass key into the old Master lock. It took some maneuvering to get it in and twist it, the mechanism fouled with years of grime and dust. True to form, it clicked open and Reece slid it from its post.

What secrets are you hiding? Reece wondered.

He could have used his Agency contacts to look into who was paying the monthly fees, but Reece didn't want to alert the most powerful spy agency in the world that one of their former case officers who died under mysterious circumstances had a storage unit set up to outlive him. Reece wanted to see what was inside first.

He pocketed the lock and key and pulled up on the door. As with the lock, it took a bit of work to get it up to knee level, at which point Reece squatted down and pushed it up. *Darkness.*

Reece retrieved the light from his pocket. Out of habit he held it in his left hand, his right remaining free to go to the gun if need be. The light moved slowly from left to right, revealing an empty shelving unit on the left and a tarp over what appeared to be a vehicle.

He approached with caution, walking around the car and looking underneath it for anywhere the dust was more recently disturbed. It had been backed in; Tom Reece combat-parked just like his son. Seeing nothing that set off any alarms, he went to the front left corner and pulled back the cover.

Reece couldn't help but smile. There, looking none the worse for wear, was his father's 1985 Grand Wagoneer. The tires were low, and the left rear was clearly flat, leaving the old Jeep much like a football player past his prime sitting on the bench waiting for that one last play.

He wiped the driver's-side window with his sleeve and peered through with his light. Looking at the handle for anything that looked cleaner than the rest of the vehicle, he pressed the button and slowly cracked the door. Shining his light up and down the broken seal, he examined it for anything unusual, particularly wires; once again all clear. Pulling the door all the way open, Reece used his light to inspect the front and passenger rows.

Sliding into the driver's seat, Reece put his hands on the wheel, remembering. He then leaned over and opened the glove box, rustling through some oil change receipts and a tattered owner's manual. Craning his neck, he looked in the rear seats.

Nothing.

Maybe Dad just left me an old Wagoneer? No, there is something else.

Thomas Reece wouldn't take such pains to ensure a storage unit in Baltimore would receive monthly payments fifteen years past his death so that someone could one day discover an old Jeep rotting away.

Reece exited the vehicle in which he had so many wonderful memories and walked to the back of the classic truck. The window was down, and Reece suppressed a chuckle. He'd learned more than a few swear words listening to his old man curse the notoriously inoperable motorized back sliding window that had to be down before opening the tailgate.

Reece depressed the button on the back of his tac-light and looked into the storage area. An aluminum rifle case gleamed back.

Even all these years later, Reece remembered exactly how to drop the gate. He reached inside and pulled up on the handle, assisting the drop into position.

"What did you leave behind, Dad?" Reece whispered.

Positioning the case across the gate, Reece inspected the clasps. A small travel lock secured the contents. Reece hesitated briefly to take a look at every point where the rectangular case might have been tampered with. Again, clear. Putting his light in his mouth, he pulled his Winkler/Dynamis Combat Flathead from his back pocket, a tool that looked like the most aggressive screwdriver in existence. He inserted it between the shackle and body of the lock, aggressively pulling back on the tool, and snapped open the padlock. He then flipped its closures and opened the box.

There, lying in the foam cut out to keep it secure, was a duckbill-modified Ithaca 37 shotgun with a pistol grip and canvas sling. Reece pulled his father's weapon of choice as point man in the jungles of Vietnam from its resting place and examined it. With the extended tube, Reece knew it held eight rounds. Four boxes of number four shot were nestled into the foam.

That's it?

As much as Reece admired the tried and true Model 37, he had expected something more.

A truck and 12-gauge?

Something didn't fit. If his dad wanted to leave him a Jeep and shotgun, he would have just left them in his garage.

The top left corner of the box caught his trained eye, the foam just a bit out of place. Reece pinched it with his fingers and pulled the top layer out of the case and onto the rifle, a key and a letter falling out with it.

Intrigued, Reece went for the key. A safe-deposit box key. Reece rolled it in his fingers and inspected it in the light. Nothing to show where it came from.

The letter. Reece reached for it. Sealed, he turned it over in his hands. It was addressed to James Reece in his father's hand.

A message from the grave?

Reece broke the seal, pulled out the letter, swallowed hard, and began to read.

He read it quickly at first. Then he went back to the beginning and read it again, hearing his dad's voice breathe life into the words that leapt from the page.

When he was done, he slowly refolded it and placed it back into the envelope from which it came before putting it and the safe-deposit box key in his pocket.

Then, moving back to the front of the old truck, he took a seat behind the wheel. He watched the rain hitting his Tahoe and the ground around it, each drop an attempt from Mother Nature to cleanse and refresh the world below.

Reece stared out the window in a self-imposed trance, his car illuminated every few minutes by a crack of lightning, losing track of time as memories of his father, his mother, the old Wagoneer, BUD/S, his wife and daughter, Iraq, Afghanistan, Siberia, Freddy, Nizar, and Katie, the living and the dead, passed through his mind's eye.

Pulling a burner phone from his pocket, Reece pressed in a memorized ten-digit number, hit send, and brought it to his ear. The director of Clandestine Services answered on the first ring, and Reece gave Vic his answer.

GLOSSARY

160th Special Operations Aviation Regiment: The Army's premier helicopter unit that provides aviation support to special forces. Known as the "Night Stalkers," they are widely regarded as the best helicopter pilots and crews in the world.

.260: .260 Remington; .264"/6.5mm rifle cartridge that is essentially a .308 Winchester necked down to accept a smaller-diameter bullet. The .260 provides superior external ballistics to the .308 with less felt recoil and can often be fired from the same magazines.

.300 Norma: .300 Norma Magnum; a cartridge designed for long-range precision shooting that has been adopted by USSOCOM for sniper use.

.375 CheyTac: Long-range cartridge, adapted from the .408 CheyTac, that can fire a 350-grain bullet at 2,970 feet per second. A favorite of extreme long-range match competitors who use it on targets beyond 3,000 yards.

.375 H&H Magnum: An extremely common and versatile big-game rifle cartridge, found throughout Africa. The cartridge was developed by Holland & Holland in 1912 and traditionally fires a 300-grain bullet.

.404 Jeffery: A rifle cartridge, designed for large game animals, developed by W. J. Jeffery & Company in 1905.

.408 CheyTac: Long-range cartridge adapted from the .505 Gibbs capable of firing a 419-grain bullet at 2,850 feet per second.

.500 Nitro: A .510-caliber cartridge designed for use against heavy dangerous game, often chambered in double rifles. The cartridge fires a 570-grain bullet at 2,150 feet per second.

75th Ranger Regiment: A large-scale Army special operations unit that conducts direct-action missions including raids and airfield seizures. These elite troops often work in conjunction with other special operations units.

• • •

AC-130 Spectre: A ground-support aircraft used by the U.S. military, based on the ubiquitous C-130 cargo plane. AC-130s are armed with a 105mm howitzer, 40mm cannons, and 7.62mm miniguns, and are considered the premier close-air-support weapon of the U.S. arsenal.

Accuracy International: A British company producing high-quality precision rifles, often used for military sniper applications.

ACOG: Advanced Combat Optical Gunsight. A magnified optical sight designed for use on rifles and carbines made by Trijicon. The ACOG is popular among U.S. forces as it provides both magnification and an illuminated reticle that provides aiming points for various target ranges.

AFIS: Automated Fingerprint Identification System; electronic fingerprint database maintained by the FBI.

Aimpoint Micro: Aimpoint Micro T-2; high-quality unmagnified red-dot combat optic produced in Sweden that can be used on a variety of weapons platforms. This durable sight weighs only three ounces and has a five-year battery life.

AISI: The latest name for Italy's domestic intelligence agency. Their motto, "scientia rerum reipublicae salus," means "knowledge of issues is the salvation of the Republic."

AK-9: Russian 9x39mm assault rifle favored by Spetsnaz (special purpose) forces.

Al-Jaleel: Iraqi-made 82mm mortar that is a clone of the Yugoslavian-made M69A. This indirect-fire weapon has a maximum range of 6,000 meters.

Alpha Group: More accurately called Spetsgruppa "A," Alpha Group is the FSB's counterterrorist unit. You don't want them to "rescue" you. See Moscow Theater Hostage Crisis and the Beslan School Massacre.

Amphib: Shorthand for Amphibious Assault Ship. A gray ship holding helicopters, Harriers, and hovercraft. Usually home to a large number of pissed-off Marines.

AN/PAS-13G(v)L3/LWTS: Weapon-mounted thermal optic that can be used to identify warm-blooded targets day or night. Can be mounted in front of and used in conjunction with a traditional "day" scope mounted on a sniper weapons system.

AN/PRC-163: Falcon III communications system made by Harris Corporation that integrates voice, text, and video capabilities.

AQ: al-Qaeda. Meaning "the Base" in Arabic. A radical Islamic terrorist organization once led by the late Osama bin Laden.

AQI: al-Qaeda in Iraq. An al-Qaeda–affiliated Sunni insurgent group that was active against U.S. forces. Elements of AQI eventually evolved into ISIS.

AR-10: 7.62x51mm brainchild of Eugene Stoner that was later adapted to create the M16/M4/AR-15.

Asherman Chest Seal: A specialized emergency medical device used to treat open chest wounds. If you're wearing one, you are having a bad day.

AT-4: Tube-launched 84mm anti-armor rocket produced in Sweden and used by U.S. forces since the 1980s. The AT-4 is a throwaway weapon: after it is fired, the tube is discarded.

ATF/BATFE: Bureau of Alcohol, Tobacco, Firearms and Explosives. A federal law enforcement agency formally part of the U.S. Department of the Treasury, which doesn't seem overly concerned with alcohol or tobacco.

ATPIAL/PEQ-15: Advanced Target Pointer/Illuminator Aiming Laser. A weapon-mounted device that emits both visible and infrared target designators for use with or without night observation devices. Essentially, an advanced military-grade version of the "laser sights" seen in popular culture.

Avtoritet: The highest caste of the incarcerated criminal hierarchy. Today used in association with a new generation of crime bosses.

Azores: Atlantic archipelago consisting of nine major islands that is an independent autonomous region of the European nation of Portugal.

Barrett 250 Lightweight: A lightweight variant of the M240 7.62mm light machine gun, developed by Barrett Firearms.

Barrett M107: .50 BMG caliber semiautomatic rifle designed by Ronnie Barrett in the early 1980s. This thirty-pound rifle can be carried by a single individual and can be used to engage human or vehicular targets at extreme ranges.

BATS: Biometrics Automated Toolset System; a fingerprint database often used to identify insurgent forces.

Bay of Pigs: Site of a failed invasion of Cuba by paramilitary exiles trained and equipped by the CIA.

BDU: Battle-dress uniform; an oxymoron if there ever was one.

Beneteau Oceanis: A forty-eight-foot cruising sailboat, designed and built in France. An ideal craft for eluding international manhunts.

Black Hills Ammunition: High-quality ammunition made for military and civilian use by a family-owned and South Dakota–based company. Their MK 262 MOD 1 5.56mm load saw significant operational use in the GWOT.

Bratok: Member of the bratva.

Bratva: The Brotherhood. An umbrella term for Russian organized crime, more technically referring to members of the Russian mafia who have served time in prison.

Brigadir: Lieutenant of a bratva gang boss.

Browning Hi-Power: A single-action 9mm semiautomatic handgun that feeds from a thirteen-round box magazine. Also known as the P-35, this Belgian-designed handgun was the most widely issued military sidearm in the world for much of the twentieth century and was used by both Axis and Allied forces during World War II.

BUD/S: Basic Underwater Demolition/SEAL training. The six-month selection and training course required for entry into the SEAL Teams, held in Coronado, California. Widely considered one of the most brutal military selection courses in the world, with an average 80 percent attrition rate.

C-17: Large military cargo aircraft used to transport troops and supplies. Also used by the Secret Service to transport the president's motorcade vehicles.

C-4: Composition 4. A plastic-explosive compound known for its stability and malleability.

CAG: Combat Applications Group. See redacted portion of glossary in the "D" section.

CAT: Counter-Assault Team; heavily armed ground element of the Secret Service trained to respond to threats such as ambushes.

███

███████████████████████████

Cessna 208 Caravan: Single-engine turboprop aircraft that can ferry passengers and cargo, often to remote locations. These workhorses are staples in remote wilderness areas throughout the world.

CIA: Central Intelligence Agency

CIF/CRF: Commanders In-Extremis Force/Crisis Response Force; a United States Army Special Forces team specifically tasked with conducting direct-action missions. These are the guys who should have been sent to Benghazi.

CJSOTF: Combined Joint Special Operations Task Force. A regional command that controls special operations forces from various services and friendly nations.

CMC: Command Master Chief, a senior enlisted rating in the United States Navy.

CQC: Close-quarter combat

CrossFit: A fitness-centric worldwide cult that provides a steady stream of cases to orthopedic surgery clinics. No need to identify their members; they will tell you who they are.

CRRC: Combat Rubber Raiding Craft. Inflatable Zodiac-style boats used by SEALs and other maritime troops.

CTC: The CIA's Counterterrorism Center. Established out of the rise of international terrorism in the 1980s, it became the nucleus of the U.S. counterterrorism mission.

CZ-75: 9mm handgun designed in 1975 and produced in the Czech Republic.

DA: District attorney; local prosecutor in many jurisdictions.

Dam Neck: An annex to Naval Air Station Oceana near Virginia Beach, Virginia, where nothing interesting whatsoever happens.

DCIS: Defense Criminal Investigation Service

DEA: Drug Enforcement Administration

██████████████: A classic 1986 film starring Chuck Norris, title of the 1983 autobiography by the unit's first commanding officer and popular name for the Army's Special ████████████████████████.

Democratic Federation of Northern Syria: Aka Rojava, an autonomous, polyethnic, and secular region of northern Syria.

Det Cord: Flexible detonation cord used to initiate charges of high explosive. The cord's interior is filled with PETN explosive; you don't want it wrapped around your neck.

Directorate I: The division of the SVR responsible for electronic information and disinformation.

Directorate S: The division of the SVR responsible for their illegals program. When you read about a Russian dissident or former spy poisoned by Novichok nerve agent or a political rival of the Russian president murdered in a random act of violence, Directorate S is probably responsible.

DO: The CIA's Directorate of Operations, formerly known by the much more appropriate name: the Clandestine Service.

DOD: Department of Defense

DOJ: Department of Justice

DShkM: Russian-made 12.7x108mm heavy machine gun that has been used in virtually every armed conflict since and including World War II.

DST: General Directorate for Territorial Surveillance. Morocco's domestic intelligence and security agency. Probably not afraid to use "enhanced interrogation techniques." **DST was originally redacted by government censors for the hardcover edition of True Believer. After a five-month appeal process, that decision was withdrawn.**

EFP: Explosively Formed Penetrator/Projectile. A shaped explosive charge that forms a molten projectile used to penetrate armor. Such munitions were widely used by insurgents against coalition forces in Iraq.

EKIA: Enemy Killed In Aciton.

Eland: Africa's largest antelope. A mature male can weigh more than a ton.

EMS: Emergency medical services. Fire, paramedic, and other emergency personnel.

ENDEX: End Exercise. Those outside "the know" will say "INDEX" and have no idea what it means.

EOD: Explosive Ordnance Disposal. The military's explosives experts who are trained to, among other things, disarm or destroy improvised explosive devices or other munitions.

EOTECH: An unmagnified holographic gunsight for use on rifles and carbines, including the M4. The sight is designed for rapid target acquisition, which makes it an excellent choice for close-quarters battle. Can be fitted with a detachable 3x magnifier for use at extended ranges.

FAL: Fusil Automatique Léger: gas-operated, select-fire 7.62 x51mm battle rifle developed by FN in the late 1940s and used by the militaries of more than ninety nations. Sometimes referred to as "the right arm of the free world" due to its use against communist forces in various Cold War–era insurgencies.

FBI: Federal Bureau of Investigation; a federal law enforcement agency that is not known for its sense of humor.

FDA: Food and Drug Administration

FLIR: Forward-Looking InfraRed; an observation device that uses thermographic radiation, that is, heat, to develop an image.

Floppies: Derogatory term used to describe communist insurgents during the Rhodesian Bush War.

FOB: Forward Operating Base. A secured forward military position used to support tactical operations. Can vary from small and remote outposts to sprawling complexes.

Fobbit: A service member serving in a noncombat role who rarely, if ever, leaves the safety of the Forward Operating Base.

FSB: Russia's federal security service responsible for internal state security and headquartered in the same building in Lubyanka Square that once housed the KGB. Its convenient in-house prison is not a place one wants to spend an extended period.

FSO: Federal Protective Service; Russia's version of the Secret Service.

FTX: Field Training Exercise.

G550: A business jet manufactured by Gulfstream Aerospace. Prices for a new example start above $40 million but, as they say, it's better to rent.

Game Scout: A wildlife enforcement officer in Africa. These individuals are often paired with hunting outfitters to ensure that regulations are adhered to.

Glock: An Austrian-designed, polymer-framed handgun popular with police forces, militaries, and civilians throughout the world. Glocks are made in various sizes and chambered in several different cartridges.

GPNVG-18: Ground Panoramic Night Vision Goggles; $43,000 NODs used by the most highly funded special operations units due to their superior image quality and peripheral vision. See Rich Kid Shit.

GPS: Global Positioning System. Satellite-based navigation systems that provide a precise location anywhere on earth.

Great Patriotic War: The Soviets' name for World War II; communists love propaganda.

Green-badger: Central Intelligence Agency contractor

Ground Branch: Land-focused element of the CIA's Special Activities Division, according to Wikipedia.

GRS: Global Response Staff. Protective agents employed by the Central Intelligence Agency to provide security to overseas personnel. See *13 Hours*. GRS was originally redacted by government censors for the hardcover edition of *True Believer*. After a five-month appeal process, that decision was withdrawn.

GRU: Russia's Main Intelligence Directorate. The foreign military intelligence agency of the Russian armed forces. The guys who do all the real work while the KGB gets all the credit, or so I'm told. Established by Joseph Stalin in 1942, the GRU was tasked with running human intelligence operations outside the Soviet Union. Think of them as the DIA with balls.

GS: General Schedule; federal jobs that provide good benefits and lots of free time.

Gukurahundi Massacres: A series of killings carried out against Ndebele tribe members in Matabeleland, Zimbabwe, by the Mugabe government during the 1980s. As many as twenty thousand civilians were killed by the North Korean–trained Fifth Brigade of the Zimbabwean army.

GWOT: Global War on Terror; the seemingly endless pursuit of bad guys, kicked off by the 9/11 attacks.

Gym Jones: Utah-based fitness company founded by alpine climbing legend Mark Twight. Famous for turning soft Hollywood actors into hard bodies, Gym Jones once enjoyed a close relationship with a certain SEAL Team.

Hell Week: The crucible of BUD/S training. Five days of constant physical and mental stress with little or no sleep.

Hilux: Pickup truck manufactured by Toyota that is a staple in third-world nations due to its reliability.

HK416: M4 clone engineered by the German firm of Heckler & Koch to operate using a short-stroke gas pistol system instead of the M4's direct-impingement gas system. Used by select special operations units in the U.S. and abroad. May or may not have been the weapon used to kill ██████████.

HK417: Select-fire 7.62x51mm rifle built by Heckler & Koch as a big brother to the HK416. Often used as Designated Marksman Rifle with a magnified optic.

HUMINT: Human intelligence. Information gleaned through traditional human-to-human methods.

HVI/HVT: High-Value Individual/High-Value Target. An individual who is important to the enemy's capabilities and is therefore specifically sought out by a military force.

IDC: Independent Duty Corpsman. Essentially a doctor.

IED: Improvised Explosive Device. Homemade bombs, whether crude or complex, often used by insurgent forces overseas.

IR: Infrared. The part of the electromagnetic spectrum with a longer wavelength than light but a shorter wavelength than radio waves. Invisible to the naked eye but visible with night observation devices. Example: an IR laser aiming device.

Iron Curtain: The physical and ideological border that separated the opposing sides of the Cold War.

ISIS: Islamic State of Iraq and the Levant. Radical Sunni terrorist group based in parts of Iraq and Afghanistan. Also referred to as ISIL. The bad guys.

ISR: Intelligence, Surveillance, and Reconnaissance

ITAR: International Traffic in Arms Regulations; export control regulations designed to restrict the export of certain items, including weapons and optics. These regulations offer ample opportunity to inadvertently violate federal law.

JAG: Judge Advocate General. Decent television series and the military's legal department.

JMAU: Joint Medical Augmentation Unit. High-speed medicine.

JSOC: Joint Special Operations Command. A component command of SOCOM, ███

███████

Katyn Massacre: Soviet purge of Polish citizens that took place in 1940 subsequent to the Soviet invasion. Twenty-two thousand Poles were killed by members of the NKVD during this event; many of the bodies were discovered in mass graves in the Katyn Forest. Russia denied responsibility for the massacre until 1990.

KGB: The Soviet "Committee for State Security." Excelled at "suppressing internal dissent" during the Cold War. Most often referred to by kids of the eighties as "the bad guys."

KIA: Killed In Action.

Kudu: A spiral-horned antelope, roughly the size and build of an elk, that inhabits much of sub-Saharan Africa.

Langley: The Northern Virginia location where the Central Intelligence Agency is headquartered. Often used as shorthand for CIA.

LaRue OBR: Optimized Battle Rifle; precision variant of the AR-15/AR-10 designed for use as a Designated Marksman or Sniper Rifle. Available in both 5.56x45mm and 7.62x51mm.

Law of Armed Conflict: A segment of public international law that regulates the conduct of armed hostilities.

LAW Rocket: M-72 Light Anti-armor Weapon. A disposable, tube-launched 66mm unguided rocket in use with U.S. forces since before the Vietnam War.

Leica M4: Classic 35mm rangefinder camera produced from 1966 to 1975.

Long-Range Desert Group: A specialized British military unit that operated in the North African and Mediterranean theaters during World War II. The unit was made up of soldiers from Great Britain, New Zealand, and Southern Rhodesia.

M1911/1911A1: .45-caliber pistol used by U.S. forces since before World War I.

M3: World War II submachine gun chambered in .45 ACP. This simple but reliable weapon became a favorite of the frogmen of that time.

M4: The standard assault rifle of the majority of U.S. military forces, including the U.S. Navy SEALs. The M4 is a shortened carbine variant of the M16 rifle that fires a 5.56x45mm cartridge. The M4 is a modular design that can be adapted to numerous configurations, including different barrel lengths.

MACV-SOG: Military Assistance Command, Vietnam—Studies and Observations Group. Deceiving name for a group of brave warriors who conducted highly classified special operations missions during the Vietnam War. These operations were often conducted behind enemy lines in Laos, Cambodia, and North Vietnam.

Mahdi Militia: An insurgent Shia militia loyal to cleric Muqtada al-Sadr that opposed U.S. forces in Iraq during the height of that conflict.

MANPADS: Man-Portable Air-Defense System; small antiaircraft surface-to-air guided rockets such as the U.S. Stinger and the Russian SA-7.

Marine Raiders: U.S. Marine Corps special operations unit; formerly known as MAR-SOC.

Maritime Branch: It's best to just google it.

Mazrah Tora: A prison in Cairo, Egypt. You do not want to wake up here.

MBITR: AN/PRC-148 Multiband Inter/Intra Team Radio. A handheld multiband, tactical software–defined radio, commonly used by special operations forces to communicate during operations.

McMillan TAC-50: Bolt-action sniper rifle chambered in .50 BMG used for long-range sniping operations used by U.S. special operations forces as well as the Canadian army.

MDMA: A psychoactive drug whose clinical name is too long to place here. Known on the street as "ecstasy." Glow sticks not included.

MH-47: Special operations variant of the Army's Chinook helicopter, usually flown by members of the 160th SOAR. This twin-rotor aircraft is used frequently in Afghanistan due to its high service ceiling and large troop- and cargo-carrying capacity. Rumor has it that, if you're careful, you can squeeze a Land Rover Defender 90 inside one.

MH-60: Special operations variant of the Army's Black Hawk helicopter, usually flown by members of the 160th SOAR.

MI5: Military Intelligence, Section 5; Britain's domestic counterintelligence and security agency. Like the FBI but with nicer suits and better accents.

MIL DOT: A reticle-based system used for range estimation and long-range shooting, based on the milliradian unit of measurement.

MIL(s): One-thousandth of a radian; an angular measurement used in rifle scopes. 0.1 MIL equals 1 centimeter at 100 meters or 0.36" at 100 yards. If you find that confusing, don't become a sniper.

MIT: Turkey's national intelligence organization and a school in Boston for smart kids.

Mk 46 MOD 1: Belt-fed 5.56x45mm light machine gun built by FN Herstal. Often used by special operations forces due to its light weight, the Mk 46 is a scaled-down version of the Mk 48 MOD 1.

Mk 48 MOD 1: Belt-fed 7.62x51mm light machine gun designed for use by special operations forces. Weighing eighteen pounds unloaded, the Mk48 can fire 730 rounds per minute to an effective range of 800 meters and beyond.

MP7: Compact select-fire personal defense weapon built by Heckler & Koch and used by various special operations forces. Its 4.6x30mm cartridge is available in a subsonic load, making the weapon extremely quiet when suppressed. What the MP7 lacks in lethality it makes up for in coolness.

MQ-4C: An advanced unmanned surveillance drone developed by Northrop Grumman for use by the United States Navy.

MultiCam: A proprietary camouflage pattern developed by Crye Precision. Formerly reserved for special operators and airsofters, MultiCam is now standard issue to much of the U.S. and allied militaries.

NATO: North Atlantic Treaty Organization; an alliance created in 1949 to counter the Soviet threat to the Western Hemisphere. Headquartered in Brussels, Belgium, the alliance is commanded by a four-star U.S. military officer known as the Supreme Allied Commander Europe (SACEUR).

Naval Special Warfare Development Group (DEVGRU): A command that appears on the biographies of numerous admirals on the Navy's website. Vice President Joe Biden publicly referred to it by a different name.

NCIS: Naval Criminal Investigative Service. A federal law enforcement agency whose jurisdiction includes the U.S. Navy and Marine Corps. Also a popular television program with at least two spin-offs.

Niassa Game Reserve: Sixteen thousand square miles of relatively untouched wilderness in northern Mozambique. The reserve is home to a wide variety of wildlife as well as a fair number of poachers looking to commoditize them.

NODs: Night observation devices. Commonly referred to as "night-vision goggles," these devices amplify ambient light, allowing the user to see in low-light environments. Special operations forces often operate at night to take full advantage of such technology.

NSA: National Security Agency; U.S. intelligence agency tasked with gathering and analyzing signals intercepts and other communications data. Also known as No Such Agency. These are the government employees who listen to our phone calls and read our emails and texts for reasons of "national security." See *Permament Record* by Edward Snowden.

NSC: National Security Council; this body advises and assists the president of the United States on matters of national security.

NSW: Naval Special Warfare. The Navy's special operations force; includes SEAL Teams.

Officer Candidate School (OCS): Twelve-week course where civilians and enlisted sailors are taught to properly fold underwear. Upon completion, they are miraculously qualified to command men and women in combat.

OmniSTAR: Satellite-based augmentation system service provider. A really fancy GPS service that provides very precise location information.

Ops-Core ballistic helmet: Lightweight high-cut helmet used by special operations forces worldwide.

P226: 9mm handgun made by SIG Sauer, the standard-issue sidearm for SEALs.

P229: A compact handgun made by SIG Sauer, often used by federal law enforcement officers, chambered in 9mm as well as other cartridges.

P320: Striker-fired modular 9mm handgun that has recently been adopted by the U.S. armed forces as the M17/M18.

P365: Subcompact handgun made by SIG Sauer, designed for concealed carry. Despite its size, the P365 holds up to thirteen rounds of 9mm.

***Pakhan*:** The highest-ranked Blatnoy in prison. Now more synonymous with "senior criminal."

Pakistani Taliban: An Islamic terrorist group composed of various Sunni Islamist militant groups based in the northwestern Federally Administered Tribal Areas along the Afghan border in Pakistan.

Pamwe Chete: "All Together"; the motto of the Rhodesian Selous Scouts.

Panga: A machete-like utility blade common in Africa.

Peshmerga: Military forces of Kurdistan. Meaning "the one who faces death," they are regarded by Allied troops as some of the best fighters in the region.

PETN: Pentaerythritol TetraNitrate. An explosive compound used in blasting caps to initiate larger explosive charges.

PG-32V: High-explosive antitank rocket that can be fired from the Russian-designed RPG-32 rocket-propelled grenade launcher. Its tandem charge is effective against various types of armor, including reactive armor.

PID: Protective Intelligence and Threat Assessment Division; the division of the Secret Service that monitors potential threats to its protectees.

PKM: Soviet-designed, Russian-made light machine gun chambered in 7.62x54R that can be found in conflicts throughout the globe. This weapon feeds from a non-disintegrating belt and has a rate of fire of 650 rounds per minute. You don't want one shooting at you.

PLF: Parachute Landing Fall. A technique taught to military parachutists to prevent injury when making contact with the earth. Round canopy parachutes used by airborne forces fall at faster velocities than other parachutes, and require a specific landing sequence. More often than not ends up as feet-ass-head.

PMC: Private Military Company. Though the profession is as old as war itself, the modern term PMC was made infamous in the post-9/11 era by Blackwater, aka Xe Services, and now known as Academi.

POTUS: President of the United States; leader of the free world.

PPD: Presidential Protection Detail; the element of the Secret Service tasked with protecting POTUS.

President's Hundred: A badge awarded by the Civilian Marksmanship Program to the one hundred top-scoring military and civilian shooters in the President's Pistol and President's Rifle matches. Enlisted members of the U.S. military are authorized to wear the tab on their uniform.

Professional Hunter: A licensed hunting guide in Africa, often referred to as a "PH." Zimbabwe-licensed PHs are widely considered the most qualified and highly trained in Africa and make up the majority of the PH community operating in Mozambique.

Protocols of the Elders of Zion: An anti-Semitic conspiracy manifesto first published in the late 1800s by Russian sources. Though quickly established as a fraudulent text, Protocols has been widely circulated in numerous languages.

PSO-1: A Russian-made 4x24mm illuminated rifle optic developed for use on the SVD rifle.

PTSD: Post-traumatic stress disorder. A mental condition that develops in association with shocking or traumatic events. Commonly associated with combat veterans.

PVS-15: Binocular-style NODs used by U.S. and allied special operations forces.

QRF: Quick Reaction Force, a contingency ground force on standby to assist operations in progress.

Ranger Panties: Polyester PT shorts favored by members of the 75th Ranger Regiment that leave very little to the imagination, sometimes referred to as "silkies."

REMF: Rear-Echelon Motherfucker. Describes most officers taking credit for what the E-5 mafia and a few senior enlisted do on the ground if the mission goes right. These same "people" will be the first to hang you out to dry if things go south. Now that they are home safe and sound, they will let you believe that when they were "downrange" they actually left the wire.

RFID: Radio Frequency Identification; technology commonly used to tag objects that can be scanned electronically.

RHIB/RIB: Rigid Hull Inflatable Boat/Rigid Inflatable Boat. A lightweight but high-performance boat constructed with a solid fiberglass or composite hull and flexible tubes at the gunwale (sides).

Rhodesia: A former British colony that declared its independence in 1965. After a long and brutal civil war, the nation became Zimbabwe in 1979.

Rhodesian Bush War: An insurgency battle between the Rhodesian Security Forces and Soviet-, East German-, Cuban-, and Chinese-backed guerrillas that lasted from 1964 to 1979. The war ended when the December 1979 Lancaster House Agreement put an end to white minority rule.

Rhodesian SAS: A special operations unit, formed as part of the famed British Special Air Service in 1951. When Rhodesia sought independence, the unit ceased to exist as part of the British military but fought as part of the Rhodesian Security Forces until 1980. Many members of the Selous Scouts were recruited from the SAS.

Rich Kid Shit: Expensive equipment items reserved for use by the most highly funded special operations units, usually part of ▪▪▪▪▪.

RLI: Rhodesian Light Infantry; an airborne and airmobile unit used to conduct "fire-force" operations during the Bush War. These missions were often launched in response to intelligence provided by Selous Scouts on the ground.

Robert Mugabe: Chairman of ZANU who led the nation of Zimbabwe from 1980 to 2017 as both prime minister and president. Considered responsible for retaliatory attacks against his rival Ndebele tribe as well as a disastrous land redistribution scheme that was ruled illegal by Zimbabwe's High Court.

ROE: Rules of engagement. Rules or directives that determine what level of force can be applied against an enemy in a particular situation or area.

RPG-32: 105mm rocket-propelled grenade launcher that is made in both Russia and, under license, in Jordan.

SAD: The CIA's Special Activities Division. Though it is now called the Special Activities Center, it's still responsible for covert action, aka the really cool stuff.

SAP: Special Access Program. Security protocols that provide highly classified information with safeguards and access restrictions that exceed those for regular classified information. Really secret stuff.

SCAR-17: 7.62x51mm battle rifle produced by FN. Its gas mechanism can be traced to that of the FAL.

Schmidt & Bender: Privately held German optics manufacturer known for its precision rifle scopes.

SCI: Special Compartmentalized Information. Classified information concerning or derived from sensitive intelligence sources, methods, or analytical processes. Often found on private basement servers in upstate New York or bathroom closet servers in Denver.

SCIF: Sensitive Compartmented Information Facility; a secure and restricted room or structure where classified information is discussed or viewed.

SEAL: Acronym of SEa, Air, and Land. The three mediums in which SEALs operate. The U.S. Navy's special operations force.

Secret Service: The federal law enforcement agency responsible for protecting the POTUS.

Selous Scouts: An elite, if scantily clad, mixed-race unit of the Rhodesian army responsible for counterinsurgency operations. These "pseudoterrorists" led some of the most successful special operations missions in modern history.

SERE: Survival, Evasion, Resistance, Escape. A military training program that includes realistic role-playing as a prisoner of war. SERE students are subjected to highly stressful procedures, sometimes including waterboarding, as part of the course curriculum. More commonly referred to as "camp slappy."

Shishani: Arabic term for Chechen fighters in Syria, probably due to "Shishani" being a common Chechen surname.

SIGINT: Signals intelligence. Intelligence derived from electronic signals and systems used by foreign targets, such as communications systems, radars, and weapons systems.

SIPR: Secret Internet Protocol Router network; a secure version of the Internet used by DOD and the State Department to transmit classified information.

SISDE: Italy's Intelligence and Democratic Security Service. Their suits are probably even nicer than MI5's.

SOCOM: United States Special Operations Command. The Unified Combatant Command charged with overseeing the various Special Operations Component Commands of the Army, Marine Corps, Navy, and Air Force of the United States Armed Forces. Headquartered at MacDill Air Force Base in Tampa, Florida.

Special Boat Team-12: The West Coast unit that provides maritime mobility to SEALs using a variety of vessels. Fast boats with machine guns.

Special Reconnaissance (SR) Team: NSW Teams that conduct special activities, ISR, and provide intelligence support to the SEAL Teams.

SR-16: An AR-15 variant developed and manufactured by Knight Armament Corporation.

SRT: Surgical Resuscitation Team. You want these guys close by if you take a bullet.

StrongFirst: Kettle-bell-focused fitness program founded by Russian fitness guru Pavel Tsatsouline that is popular with special operations forces.

S-Vest: Suicide vest; an explosives-laden garment favored by suicide bombers. Traditionally worn only once.

SVR: The Foreign Intelligence Service of the Russian Federation, or as John le Carré describes them, "the KGB in drag."

Taliban: An Islamic fundamentalist political movement and terrorist group in Afghanistan. U.S. and coalition forces have been at war with members of the Taliban since late 2001.

Targeting Officer: The CIA's website reads that as a targeting officer you will "identify new opportunities for DO operational activity and enhance ongoing operations." Translation—they tell us whom to kill.

TDFD: Time-delay firing device. An explosive initiator that allows for detonation at a determined period of time. A fancy version of a really long fuse.

TIC: Troops in contact. A firefight involving U.S. or friendly forces.

TOC: Tactical Operations Center. A command post for military operations. A TOC usually includes a small group of personnel who guide members of an active tactical element during a mission from the safety of a secured area.

TOR Network: A computer network designed to conceal a user's identity and location. TOR allows for anonymous communication.

TQ: Politically correct term for the timely questioning of individuals on-site once a target is secure. May involve the raising of voices.

Troop Chief: Senior enlisted SEAL on a forty-man troop, usually a master chief petty officer. The guy who makes shit happen.

TS: Top Secret. Information, the unauthorized disclosure of which reasonably could be expected to cause exceptionally grave damage to national security, that the original classification authority is able to identify or describe. Can also describe an individual's level of security clearance.

TST: Time-sensitive target. A target requiring immediate response because it is highly lucrative, is a fleeting target of opportunity, or poses (or will soon pose) a danger to friendly forces.

UAV: Unmanned aerial vehicle; a drone.

UCMJ: Uniform Code of Military Justice. Disciplinary and criminal code that applies to members of the U.S. military.

UDI: Unilateral Declaration of Independence; the 1965 document that established Rhodesia as an independent sovereign state. The UDI resulted in an international embargo and made Rhodesia a pariah.

V-22: Tilt-rotor aircraft that can fly like a plane and take off/land like a helicopter. Numerous examples were crashed during its extremely expensive development.

VBIED: Vehicle-Borne Improvised Explosive Device; a rolling car bomb driven by a suicidal terrorist.

VC: National Liberation Front of South Vietnam, better known as the Viet Cong. A communist insurgent group that fought against the government of South Vietnam and its allies during the Vietnam War. In the movies, these are the guys wearing the black pajamas carrying AKs.

Vor v Zakone: An individual at the top of the incarcerated criminal underground. Think godfather. Top authority for the *bratva*. Today, each region of Russia has a *Vor v Zakone*.

Vory: A hierarchy within the bratva. Career criminals. More directly translated as "thief."

VPN: Virtual Private Network. A private network that enables users to send and receive data across shared or public networks as if their computing devices were directly connected to the private network. Considered more secure than a traditional Internet network.

VSK-94: Russian-made Sniper/Designated Marksman rifle chambered in the subsonic 9x39mm cartridge. This suppressed weapon is popular with Russian special operations and law enforcement units due to its minimal sound signature and muzzle flash.

Wagner Group: A Russian private military company with close ties to the Russian government.

War Vets: Loosely organized groups of Zimbabweans who carried out many of the land seizures during the 1990s. Often armed, these individuals used threats and intimidation to remove white farmers from their homes. Despite the name, most of these individuals were too young to have participated in the Bush War. Not to be confused with ZNLWVA, a group that represents ZANU-affiliated veterans of the Bush War.

WARCOM/NAVSPECWARCOM: United States Naval Special Warfare Command. The Navy's special operations force and the maritime component of United States Special Operations Command. Headquartered in Coronado, California, WARCOM is the administrative command for subordinate NSW Groups composed of eight SEAL Teams, one SEAL Delivery Vehicle (SDV) Team, three Special Boat Teams, and two Special Reconnaissance Teams.

Westley Richards Droplock: A rifle or shotgun built by the famed Birmingham, England, gunmakers that allows the user to remove the locking mechanisms for repair or replacement in the field. Widely considered one of the finest and most iconic actions of all time.

Whiskey Tango: Military speak for "white trash."

WIA: Wounded In Action.

Yazidis: An insular Kurdish-speaking ethnic and religious group that primarily resides in Iraq. Effectively a subminority among the Kurds, Yazidis were heavily persecuted by ISIS.

YPG: Kurdish militia forces operating in the Democratic Federation of Northern Syria. The Turks are not fans.

ZANLA: Zimbabwe African National Liberation Army. The armed wing of the Maoist Zimbabwe African National Union and one of the major combatants of the Rhodesian Bush War. ZANLA forces often staged out of training camps located in Mozambique and were led by Robert Mugabe.

Zimbabwe: Sub-Saharan African nation that formerly existed as Southern Rhodesia and later Rhodesia. Led for three decades by Robert Mugabe, Zimbabwe ranks as one of the world's most corrupt nations on Transparency International's Corruption Perceptions Index.

ZIRPA: Zimbabwe People's Revolutionary Army. The Soviet-equipped armed wing of ZAPU and one of the two major insurgency forces that fought in the Rhodesian Bush War. ZIRPA forces fell under the leadership of Josh Nkomo, who spent much of the war in Zambia. ZIRPA members were responsible for shooting down two civilian airliners using Soviet SA-7 surface-to-air missiles in the late 1970s.

Zodiac Mk 2 GR: 4.2-meter inflatable rubber boat capable of carrying up to six individuals. These craft are often used as dinghies for larger vessels.

ACKNOWLEDGMENTS

WE ARE NOTHING IF not the accumulation of our experience, tempered by the advantage of introspection. In my case, that experience includes a lot of reading. From an early age I naturally gravitated toward novels with protagonists who had backgrounds and skills that I wanted to have in real life one day. I'll always be indebted to those authors who provided the inspiration during my formative years to pursue the profession of arms and of writing. It was a privilege to escape into the pages of books by **Marc Olden, A. J. Quinnell, J. C. Pollock, Louis L'Amour, Tom Clancy, David Morrell, Nelson DeMille,** and **Stephen Hunter.** Their writing provided my early education in the art of storytelling. I stand on the shoulders of giants.

Savage Son has been in the works for more than three decades, drawing inspiration from **Richard Connell's** *The Most Dangerous Game,* **Geoffrey Household's** *Rogue Male,* **David Morrell's** *First Blood,* and **Louis L'Amour's** *Last of the Breed.* Fans of those classic thrillers will notice a few intentional word choices in the pages of *Savage Son* to pay tribute and respect to these seminal works.

I owe a great deal to those who helped me with the Russian mafia portions of the book. A complex and intricate organization with a fascinating history that mirrors Russia's violent transitions of the past century, an entire novel could investigate the relationships between Russia's criminal underworld and political elites. In fact, I will probably be exploring that association in future novels as my education in the Russian underworld continues. In studying the *bratva*, I am deeply indebted to **Mark Galeotti** and his fascinating book *The Vory*. I have a feeling I will be returning to it time and time again in the years ahead. One particular line from *The Vory* stuck with me as I developed the plot and characters for *Savage Son*: "The new godfathers may call themselves *avtoritety*, have business portfolios stretching from the essentially legitimate to the wholly criminal, get involved in politics and be seen at charitable galas. But they nonetheless are the inheritors of the drive, determination and ruthlessness of the *vory*, men of whom even a New York mafia boss said, 'We Italians will kill you. But the Russians are crazy—they'll kill your whole family.'"

Thank you to **Oleg Tolmachev** for always being available to answer even the most basic questions on all things Russia at all hours of the day and night. I sincerely appreciate all your valuable insights.

And, to the **MUR**, *Moskowsky Ugolovniy Rozysk*, the criminal intelligence division of the Moscow Police, my hat is off to you for all that you do. Working through an intermediary, tapped phones, and a background check, one can't be too careful. Thank you for your assistance and support.

Though much of the terminology has remained the same from the pre-Bolshevik revolution days, through the era of the Soviet Republics and into the current incarnation of the Russian Federation, the definitions have morphed. Terms and positions that were once strictly applied within the gulag and then prison walls is now applied to organized crime more broadly across society at large. I have tried to remain true to the more modern understanding of the criminal hierarchy. All errors in any and everything to do with the Russian *bratva* are mine and mine alone.

Thank you to **Victor** and **Svetlana** at **Utgard Tours** for such a memorable and informative time in Kamchatka, Russia, and for putting up with my incessant questions. I swear, I am not a spy.

And, to **Jeff Kimbell**, bounty hunter, for organizing an expedition I will not soon forget. In fact, I think I may still be recovering.

To **Stephen Hunter**, who has long been a literary hero of mine. It was a true honor, and extremely humbling to start our last book tours together. It was one of the highlights of my life. I'm looking forward to sending some rounds down-range with you soon.

To **David Morrell**, whose *The Brotherhood of the Rose* cemented my path into the SEAL Teams. A groundbreaking novel that incorporated the best tra-ditions of UK and US spy fiction, David transformed the genre in the start of a trilogy that continues to influence writers today. Never one content to chase the market, he leads by example, writing works that make him and his readers fuller, more significant people. For additional wisdom from this master of the craft, read *The Successful Novelist* and visit the writing section of his website at *davidmorrell.net*.

To **Vince Flynn**, whose work defines the modern political thriller and to **Kyle Mills**, who continues to exceed all expectations in keeping Vince's legacy alive. #MitchRappLives

To **Mark Greaney**, author of *The Gray Man* novels, thank you for your friendship and for writing such a kick-ass series! I can't wait for the next install-ment!

And to **Brad Thor**, to whom this novel is dedicated and whose kindness and generosity made this next chapter in life possible. Thank you, Brad. I remain humbly in your debt.

To **Ray Porter**, whose voice brings James Reece to life in the audiobooks. Thank you for being one of the coolest guys I know.

To **Barbara Peters** of **Poisoned Pen** for being so welcoming and for taking me under your wing.

To **Ryan Steck**, aka **The Real Book Spy**, for what you do for the thriller genre and for thriller writers everywhere.

To **K. J. Howe**, author of *The Freedom Broker* and *Skyjack*, and Executive Director of Thrillerfest. Thank you for all you do for authors old and new.

To **Mystery Mike** for your continued support and for always finding those hard to find signed pristine first editions.

To **Tuck Beckstoffer**, I hope I did your wine justice. I'm probably drinking some as you read this.

To **Chip King** and **Christopher Ellender** at **Gulfstream** for the jet-centric portions of the novel.

To **Tim Fallon, Doug Prichard, Dave Knesek,** and all the instructors at **FTW Ranch.** Thank you for another amazing week behind the glass.

To **D'Arcy Echols** for making one of the most beautiful and accurate rifles on the planet.

To **Nic de Kock** and "**Hubert**" for the practical lessons on man-tracking in South Africa. Thank you for what you are doing to defend some of the last rhino on earth.

To **Larry Vickers** for your time in uniform, for always taking the time to answer my texts and emails about the minutiae of firearms, and for the 1911. It is the jewel of my collection.

To **James Rupley** for your work on the *Vickers Guide* series of books and for your careful review of this manuscript. For those who do not have the collection of *Vickers Guides*, they are beautifully photographed coffee table books that are a treasure trove of information. Check them out at *vickersguide.com.*

To **Jason Morton** at **CZ** for the incredible history of the Brno .375. I could do an entire book on that single rifle.

To **Susan Hastings** for the two-year loan of your books on Rhodesia, for inspiring a character, and for the use of your last name.

To **John Devine** for answering all my dog questions and for what you are doing at **Rescue 22,** training service and support dogs to help stem the tide of veteran suicide.

To **John Dudley** at **Nock On Archery** for taking a look at the archery sections of this book, for your friendship, and for being such a solid ambassador for those who pick up the bow.

To **John Barklow** for your years in the Navy, your time on Kodiak passing on your lessons to the next generation of SEALs and for what you do now at **Sitka Gear.**

To **Jeff Rotherham** for always picking up for one of my technical questions about homemade explosives. For the NSA who *may* be listening—it's for *informational purposes only.*

To **Dylan Murphy** for your knife fighting expertise. Readers may not know how much work goes into the knife fighting chapters in these novels. Dylan gears up in the clothes and equipment the characters are using and choreographs the violence in a way that never fails to blow me away. An added benefit is that I get to add to my knife fighting skills. One day I hope to publish the videos.

To **Katie Pavlich** for always being there. If you have not read Katie's books *Fast and Furious* and *Assault & Flattery*, pick them up today!

To **Dan Gelston** at **L3Harris Technologies**, you may have missed your calling as an editor. Thank you for your detailed review.

To **Elias Kfoury** for the use of your back story and for all you have done on the battlefield to bring our warriors home.

To **SIG Sauer CEO Ron Cohen, CMO Tom Taylor, Jason Wright, Samantha Piatt, Teddy Novin, Dave Farrell, Olivia Gallivan, Aisling Meehan, Max Michel, Lena Miculek, Daniel Horner, Hana Bilodeau**, and **Mato**—my former Command Master Chief at SEAL Team TWO—and the entire team at **SIG**, you are crushing it! Thank you for your support.

To **Craig Flynn** for a lifetime of friendship. You finally made it into a novel.

To **Clint** and **Heidi Smith** at **Thunder Ranch**, thank you for adopting me and my family all those years ago.

To **Josh Waldron** for your friendship, creativity, and vision.

To **James Jarrett**, who inspires everything I do.

To **Mike Oberhelman**, CEO of **Blue Tide Marine**, for your service to the nation at the highest levels of special operations and for your disaster relief efforts in response to hurricane Dorian. It was an honor to start our journey in special operations together.

To **Evan Hafer, Mat Best, Jared Taylor, Logan Stark, Richard Ryan**, and **Tom Davin** at **Black Rifle Coffee** for the example you set for all veterans on how to transition to the private sector and crush it!

To **Jonathan Hart**, founder of **Sitka Gear**, for changing an industry.

To everyone who supported this effort through modern-day word-of-mouth, spreading the word via social channels, radio shows, TV programs, and having me on your podcasts; you are the reason people know about the book. Thank you to Jocko Willink, Andy Stumpf at Cleared Hot, Chad Prather of *The Chad Prather Show*, Mickey Schuch and Carry Trainer at Higher Line, Marcus Torgerson at IKMF Krav Maga, Fred Burton at Stratfor, Trevor Thompson, Cole Kramer, Jeff Reid—aka Frozen Trident, Amy Robbins at Alexo Athletica, Mike Ritland at Mike Drop, Ken Hackathorn, Rob Bianchin at Cabot Guns, Joe Hahn at Integrated Tactical Training, Pat McNamara at TMACS, Eric Frohardt, Mike Sauers and Samantha Bonilla at Forged, Jeff Houston at Tac 7, Sean Haberberger at BluCore, Sean Evangelista at 30 Seconds Out, Kurt Schlichter at Townhall, Keith Walawender at Tomahawk Strategic Solutions, Chip Beaman, John Nores—author of *Hidden War*, Brent Gleeson at Taking Point Leadership, Tim Clemit, Bill Rapier at Amtac Shooting, Monty LeClair at Centurion Arms, Joe Collins, Johnny Primo at Courses of Action, Ryan Michler at Order of Man, Clay Hergert at ATX Precision, Eddie Penny at Contingent Group, Jason Swarr and Ben Tirpak at Skillset, Herman Achterhuis at Achter Knives, Maddie Taylor, Ross Kaminsky at *The Ross Kaminsky Show*, Chris Osman at Rhuged, Gerber Gear Fan, Clint Emerson of *100 Deadly Skills*, Eva Shockey, Tim Brent, Sergio Lopez, Eli Crane at Bottle Breacher, Cory Zillig at ZF Technical, Christian Schauf at Uncharted Supply Company, Mark Bollman at Ball and Buck, Brian Call at the *Gritty Podcast*, Jared Ogden at Triumph Systems, Gavy Friedson at Israel Rescue, Rick Stewart at American Zealot Productions, Adam Janke at the *Journal of Mountain Hunting*, Joe and Charlotte Betar at the Houston Safari Club, and Jeff Crane and PJ Carleton at the Congressional Sportsman's Foundation.

To Hoby Darling, Erik Snyder, and Mike Augustine, and the early morning workout crew—I'll be back!

To authors Eric Bishop, Sean Cameron, Mike Houtz, and C. E. Albanese of *The Crew Reviews Podcast*, thank you for having me on as your inaugural guest.

To Lucky Ones Coffee for all you do for the community and for the example you set for the world.

To the entire cast and crew at SEAL Team CBS for taking such efforts to bring the human side of special operations to life. And, to Justin Wren and

A. J. Buckley, along with Justin's organization **Fight for the Forgotten**, for spearheading the effort to support **Rayden Overbay**. The outpouring of support for this young man with autism was nothing short of astounding. Thank you to **David Boreanaz, Max Thieriot, Neil Brown Jr, Toni Trucks, Jess Paré, Judd Lormand, Tyler Grey, Justin Melnick, Dita the Hair Missile, Garrett Golden, Scott Fox, Mark Semos**, and everyone involved with **SEAL Team** who stepped up to stand with Rayden. #StandWithRayden

To **Tom Flanagan** for all you've done in service to this great nation and for all you continue to do through *Eagles & Angels*.

To **Kyle Lamb** for your service at the tip of the spear and all you continue to do for freedom.

To **Ironclad Media** for creating three of what have to be the sweetest book trailer videos ever produced.

To **Damien and Jennifer Patton**, I am so excited for what's ahead at **Banjo**. You won't be able to remain in the shadows for much longer.

To **James Yeager** at **Tactical Response** for all you have done to make these novels such a success. I'll never forget it.

To **Biss** for everything we've been through and for an exciting road ahead. Thank you for your support, brother.

To **Dom Raso** at **Dynamis Alliance** for leading by example and crushing everything you do. Thank you for all you have done for my family.

To **Daniel Winkler and Karen Shook** of **Winkler Knives**, thank you for your friendship and for all you do for those who continue to go forward and answer the call.

To **Jon Dubin** for all you did at the FBI, for including me in **Pineapple Brothers Lanai**, and for our future adventures!

To **Lacey Biles**, for your friendship.

To **Michael Davidson, Adnan Kifayat, Natalie Alvarez, Ben Bosanac**, and everyone at **Gen Next** for everything you are doing for future generations.

To **Daysha McGrath** for addicting me to **Kill Cliff**, which supported the late-night editing sessions on this novel and for all you do at **Tomahawk Charitable Solutions**.

To **Sean Parnell**, Army veteran and author of *Outlaw Platoon*. Best of luck with your congressional run in Pennsylvania's district 17!

To all the authors who have been so welcoming and supportive: **Lee Child, Steve Berry, Brad Taylor, A. J. Tata, Marc Cameron, Simon Gervais, L. A. Chandler, Nick Petrie, Christine Carbo, Gregg Hurwitz, Mindy Mejia, Matt Coyle, Josh Hood, Matthew Betley, Desiree Holt, Tom Abrahams, Don Bentley, Rob Olive,** and **Kevin Maurer**. It is an honor to be part of such a talented and supportive group.

To **Kevin O'Malley, Frank LeCrone, Jimmy Klein,** and **Andrew Kline,** you guys are simply the best.

To **Brendan O'Malley** for my first bottle of **Leadslingers Whiskey**.

To **Andrew Arrabito** and **Kelsie Bieser** at **Half Face Blades** for always going all in. Thank you.

To **Johnny Sanchez** at the **Team Performance Institute**—without your being the amazing person you are I shudder to think where I'd be today. Thank you, my friend.

To **Chris Cox, David Lehman,** and **Phil Hoon** at **Capitol 6 Advisors**, I could not be more excited to see this all-star team together and can't wait to see what's ahead!

To **Graham Hill,** for always being there, even in the lingerie section of the Hill Air Force Base Exchange book signing.

To **Stacey Wenger** for showing up with the most amazing book cakes ever made!

To **Nick Seifert** at **Athlon Outdoors**, at some point we should meet up in Park City.

To the **Yale Club of New York City** for providing me with a quiet library in which to work on my more frequent forays into the Manhattan jungle.

To my friends who have supported me both in the military and out: **Billy and Meaghan Birdzell, Mike Camacho, Trig and Annette French, Christian Sommer, Jimmy Spithill, Terry Flynn, Scott Grimes, Jason Salata, Shahram Moosavi, Garry and Victoria Peters, Shane Reilly, Jim and Nancy Demetriades, Larry and Rhonda Sheakley, Martin and Kelly Katz, Razor and Sylvia**

Dobbs, Mike Atkinson, Mac Minard, Mike Port, Alec Wolf, George Kollitides, Bob Warden, Wally McLallen, and Nick Pontikes.

As always, to Rick and Esther Rosenfield for your love and support.

And to Nick and Tina Cousoulis for your wisdom and guidance.

To Chris Pratt and Jared Shaw for the exciting road ahead!

To Brock Bosson, Joel Kurtzberg, and the team at Cahill, Gordon & Reindell for the painful task of dealing with the Department of Defense during the review process. Thank you for running interference for me.

To Norm Brownstein, Steve Demby, and Mitch Langberg at Brownstein Hyatt Farber Schreck, thank you for your patience and expertise and for always having my back.

To Garrett Bray for your creative vision and for your patience with me on all things technical. You are truly the CMO of this venture and I feel so fortunate to be working with such a dear and trusted friend.

To Dr. Robert Bray at DISC Sports and Spine Center, for making my transition to the private sector possible, for the steady hand during my spine surgery, and for always being there for me and my family. We wouldn't be where we are today without you and Tracey by our side.

To my agent, Alexandra Machinist at ICM, thank you for your energy, honesty, and expertise.

To Josie Freedman at ICM on the Hollywood front. Thank you for navigating the territory you know so well.

To Carolyn Reidy, president and CEO of Simon & Schuster, thank you for your encouragement and vote of confidence. I am humbled to be part of such an amazing team.

To Jon Karp, president and publisher of Simon & Schuster, for your leadership and drive.

To Libby McGuire, senior vice president and publisher of Atria Books, thank you for your continued support.

None of this would be possible without the best in the business doing what they do behind the scenes each and every day. To the incredible Simon & Schuster marketing team of Liz Perl, Sue Fleming, Sienna Farris, Saimah Haque, Kristin Fassler,

Dana Trocker, and Milena Brown. To everyone in accounts and sales working tirelessly to get the books out into the wild: Gary Urda, Colin Shields, Chrissy Festa, Paula Amendolara, Janice Fryer, Lesley Collins, Gregory Hruska, and Lexi Dumas. I sincerely appreciate all your efforts. And to Chris Lynch, Tom Spain, and Sarah Lieberman at Simon & Schuster Audio. Not a day goes by where I don't hear how much someone loves the audiobook. Thank you for all the time, energy, and effort you take to ensure that listeners are blown away!

To Emily Bestler, the best publisher and editor in the industry, for your friendship, mentorship , guidance, and for taking a chance on a complete un-known. You made this dream a reality. And, thank you to the entire team at Emily Bestler Books for all the work it takes to transform an idea into the book that launches into the world.

To Lara Jones, for keeping us all in line and for keeping me on schedule.

To David Brown, publicist extraordinaire, the man behind the wheel of the Atria Mystery Bus, and my partner in crime on getting the word out about the James Reece series. Thank you for your friendship and for the excitement you bring to everything you do!

To production editor Al Madocs, for your patience and understanding. in dealing with a thirty-day government review that stretched past two hundred. As they told us at Airborne school, "this is two days of training crammed into three weeks."

To James Iacobelli, for the stunning cover. Thank you!

To Jen Long at Pocket Books for knocking it out of the park with the paperback editions of *The Terminal List* and *True Believer*. Can't wait to see what you do with *Savage Son*.

To all the booksellers who have stocked my novels on your shelves, talked with readers about a new author and protagonist, and welcomed me through your doors to discuss the art of storytelling, I humbly thank you. There are few places I feel more at home than "a clean, well-lighted place" for books.

To my mother for instilling in me a lifelong love of books and reading, and to my dad for taking me to all the action movies in the eighties when I was prob-ably too young for them.

And finally, to my beautiful wife, **Faith**, for your love and support, for keeping the coffee flowing through all the late nights and early mornings and for holding down the fort while I was locked away writing in the office or half a world away in the wilds of the Russian Far East or Sub-Saharan Africa, researching this novel. Your strength inspires me daily. Thank you for marrying me. And to our three kids who are growing up too fast, you are always in my thoughts.

CPSIA information can be obtained
at www.ICGtesting.com
Printed in the USA
BVHW081954261022
649718BV00002B/2